Spirits in the Oak

L. J. Hutton

ISBN: 13: 9781655959363

Published by Wylfheort Books 2020

Copyright

The moral right of L. J. Hutton to be identified as the author of this work has been asserted by her in accordance with the Copyright, Designs and Patents Act 1988.

All characters in this book are fictitious, and any resemblance to actual persons living or dead is purely coincidental.

All rights reserved. No part of this publication may be reproduced, stored in a retrieval system or transmitted in any form, or by any means, without the prior permission in writing of the author, nor to be otherwise circulated in any form or binding or cover other than in which it is published without a similar condition, including this condition, being imposed upon the subsequent purchaser.

Chapter 1

Jenna wrestled with the key to her flat and just about managed to turn it with her arms full. She dashed up the stairs, barging into the living room to the table, before the pile of essays escaped from the cardboard folder which was too big to go into her bag. Looking at them she grimaced. It was going to be a long few days while she ploughed through them and discovered just how little attention her students had been paying to her this term. Even without looking at them, she had a pretty good idea of who the high fliers and the no-hopers would be, and although the essays had been submitted with only student numbers attached, she had a fair idea of who was who. Having taught them for nearly two terms now, and having handed back two sets of essays already last term, it hardly required a genius to put a number to a name. She would still carefully avoid looking at any of her own records until she'd finished marking, but while the usual clump of middle ranging work remained anonymous more easily, the really awful ones usually leapt out at her within a few paragraphs. Oh well, hopefully there would be a couple of near-firsts in amongst them to compensate.

She turned back and trotted downstairs to close the front door, then slid the chain across it. This wasn't such a bad area taken in isolation, but it was right on a bus route and was easily accessible from some of the less salubrious estates only a mile or so down the road. Better safe than sorry. There were always those who saw people who live alone as easy prey.

Once upon a time this had been a row of 1950s council-owned houses, but as more and more people had wanted at least a space outside their house to park a car on, this handful set back at right-angles to the road on a walkway had been changed into flats, most going to the elderly. Going into her kitchen and putting the kettle on to make a much needed decaf coffee, Jenna could hear old Mrs Wilson's television blaring out the inevitable late afternoon quiz show in the flat below. All the ground floor flats were occupied by old people, but the flats made out of the houses' upper floors were often harder to fill, despite the housing shortage. They could only accommodate two people at the most – having only one rather small bedroom – and were far more comfortable for only one. Yet the steep stairs precluded most of the elderly, since each former house hardly warranted a lift, and taken alongside the lack of parking and no second bedroom, it meant that the number of potential tenants reduced considerably. Which was why, despite being a young, single woman without a child, she had been able to get this flat from the housing association who currently owned the cluster of buildings. For most homes she wouldn't have even been on the list, let alone in the running to get one.

She gratefully pulled off her boots and sank, coffee mug in hand, into her battered but comfortable armchair. The essays lurked in full view on the old dining table which served as Jenna's desk, which was pushed up to the front window to catch what usable daylight there was. Not tonight, though, she thought. No, the marking could start tomorrow. Instead she sank a little deeper into the chair and allowed herself to unwind as she sipped at her hot mug-full, and contemplated her agenda for the next few days. It was Monday, and at least she'd done all her part-time teaching for the week in one clump today. Several sessions going over the same ground had left her shattered, but it was better than the way the university had handed out the bought-in teaching in some previous years. At least this way she could get a run at the essays, and maybe have them out of the way, before she had to go into her regular three full days' work at the local supermarket on Friday, Saturday and Sunday. Staff discount was undoubtedly useful, and there was no way that she could survive without that steady income when the teaching was all short-term contract stuff and often sporadic, but she could never pretend that she enjoyed that side of her work.

Oh well, she thought, at least she had the compensation of a nice piece of fresh, breaded cod for her dinner tonight. She'd done quite well in snapping up the vegetable bargains at the end of the day yesterday, as well as finding some good fish and meat amongst the end of day reductions, some of which had restocked her tiny freezer, and she eased herself out of the chair and began pottering about in the kitchen. She was just about to put the vegetables on to steam on the little double ringed hob, and the cod into the tiny countertop oven, when the doorbell rang.

She froze, then gently edged herself closer to the kitchen window. The door to her flat was at the side of the house, and it was all too easy for people to step beyond her door into the back garden and look up to the kitchen. Who on earth was calling on her? It was hardly a sociable hour of the day. Moreover, she'd only just got in in time, because it was now bucketing down with rain, turning the March evening darker than normal for the hour. Hardly the night for canvassers to be out and about, and anyway, this kind of property didn't attract many double-glazing salesmen.

"Jenna? ...Jenna? ...Are you there?"

The voice was unmistakably Claire's, and Jenna groaned. She really didn't want to talk to Claire just at the moment. It was a shame considering how close they'd been once upon a time, but their friendship had been getting ever more strained, not helped by Claire's persistent thoughtlessness. It was typical that she would turn up tonight, having forgotten that Jenna had been working flat out for the last four days, and never for a moment considering that Jenna might not feel up to listening to Claire's catalogue of woes. Not that Jenna was an unsympathetic person by any means. But as Tiff, the closest of her friends, had observed, if in a drunken moment Claire decided to jump off a bridge over the M5, then there would inevitably be a truck full of feather beds passing underneath just at the right moment. That was Claire's kind of luck! Yet Claire never saw how extensive her good fortune was, nor did she take it into consideration when she chose to meddle in the lives of those she saw as needing her guiding hand.

Jenna peered gingerly over the work counter, and saw Claire appear on cue out on the scruffy patch of grass. Luckily she hadn't put the light on yet, either here in the kitchen or in the living room overlooking the front pavement – she'd actually been quite enjoying the half-light after a day under florescent light and had intended to just light a few candles later, so the flat was quite dark. If she kept very quiet then maybe Claire would think she wasn't in. Claire disappeared then the doorbell rang again and Jenna heard her name called again. She almost held her breath, keeping very still and willing the house to appear empty. Then to her horror she heard Mrs Wilson's quavering voice.

"She's in there, dearie. I heard her come home not so long ago," and then the murmur of voices as Mrs Wilson must have come to the adjoining front door to speak to Claire. Furious, Jenna crept to the bathroom, waited until she heard Mrs Wilson's door close, and then flushed the toilet before hurrying downstairs.

"Oh there you are!" Claire declared huffily, the moment Jenna opened the door, and taking no notice of Jenna's subterfuge for not coming to the door sooner. She dropped her dripping umbrella on Jenna's hall mat and pushed past her to flounce up the stairs to the living room. Gritting her teeth, Jenna closed the door reluctantly and followed her, only to have Claire turn on her the moment they were both on the same level.

"How could you, Jenna?"

Jenna was nonplussed. "How could I what? What are you talking about?" She'd hardly seen Claire in the last few weeks, so it was beyond her to fathom how she could have caused offence.

"Kyle!" Claire retorted. "You've been deliberately avoiding him! He's been very upset with the way you've been treating him, you know? He's been trying to talk to you all weekend and you've been playing hard to get! He's called here several times a day since Friday!"

Jenna could feel a slow rage building inside her. This was ridiculous! She'd broken up what little of a relationship she'd had with Claire's kid brother Kyle over six months ago, and it was hardly her fault if he was twisting his often childish fantasies into something Claire had misconstrued.

"I was out!" she shot back, but was cut off before she could say more.

"You? Out? Oh don't make me laugh! Or were you lying to me all those times when you've said you don't have the money to come out with me and the girls from the gym?"

Tired and provoked beyond caring, Jenna exploded. "Out I said and out I meant! At bloody *work*! Where else *would* I be? But do you remember that? No of course you don't! How long have I had that job, Claire? Ever since I went to university over six years ago! Nothing's changed! I'm stuck with it and you know damned well why. But you? *You* don't have to work! And clearly you've forgotten what that's like. *You* hardly have to think twice over doing *anything* you want. *You* can go out any day of the week you want to, providing you have some poor sap to look after the kids." Claire was notorious for strong-arming all and sundry into baby-sitting duties. "*I* have to live on what little I earn, *and* I have to cope with being on my feet for pretty much nine hours a day constantly every bloody weekend! Even if I had any spare cash, it's not a job I can do half-wrecked from rolling in in the small hours like you do! So don't you dare accuse me of lying to you, when it's you forgetting about everyone else that's caused the trouble."

Claire looked abashed for a moment, knowing full well that Jenna was right on all counts, then her head came back up with a twisted sneer of a smile on her lips.

"Well if you'd play your cards right you could get married and be a kept woman!"

"A kept woman? What? With your Kyle? Oh don't make me laugh!"

Claire's expression became even darker. "Our Kyle's a good bloke! He would've moved in with you if you'd given him a fair chance. And you're not such a catch yourself, Jenna Cornwell, that you can afford to be so picky! You're thirty now. If you wanted to pick and choose so much you should have started playing the field a lot earlier!" Then she seemed to realise just how badly she'd put her foot in it, but it was too late. She'd crossed a line. A line she should never have gone anywhere near – especially knowing Jenna's history as she did.

"How dare you!" Jenna snarled through gritted teeth. "You *know* what I went through! How hard I've had to work to even get this much of a life back! But you couldn't stop yourself, could you? You had to interfere. "He's been in the army," you told me…"

"…well he has!"

"…He was a bloody cook for the Territorials!…"

"…no he wasn't!"

"Yes he damned well was!" And with a flash of insight, understanding belatedly dawned for Jenna. "Oh… of course! You've not *listened* to him over the years any more than you have me, have you? You heard the word 'army' and put your own twist on it! Well let me enlighten you! The only sharp implement your Kyle's ever wielded is a vegetable knife! And do you know why? Because he's so bloody useless, nobody in their right mind would let him anywhere near anything more lethal!"

Claire began to splutter but Jenna was relentless. "And it's a damned miracle that he never poisoned them too, because he certainly can't cook a decent meal! He must have spent his entire time peeling spuds and sprouts! You and your mom and your sisters have spoiled him rotten, just as much as my mom has our Martin and William. The difference is that with Martin and William being so much younger than me, I never played a part in making them the irritating brats that they are now. I'd been booted out long before they were old enough to take any notice of anything I did. And I don't close my eyes to what they are, either. But you can't see what everyone else does. That Kyle isn't looking for a wife. He's looking for someone who'll pick up where your mom leaves off! He's shit scared that all of you are off and married, and your mom is getting older, and one day he might just have to pick his own underwear up and wash it…"

"…That's unfa…!"

"…It's the bloody truth! No, don't you dare pout at me, Claire! Not this time! You hear me out! I met Kyle with an open mind when he came to stay at your house, and you shoved us at one another. Or was that your Garry putting his foot down for once, and wanting him gone as soon as possible? He didn't last long living with you did he?" Claire's small flinch told Jenna that she'd hit the mark on that one. "Well maybe Garry sees him clearer than you do. Because the truth is that he isn't interested in having a wife whom he has to help support. Oh, he's all for the idea of having kids! But that's because he has some cockeyed vision of playing with a train set with the kids all day. He hasn't worked out that any woman with a grain of sense wouldn't set up home with him, because they can see that they'd be the ones going out to work every day, while he lounges on the sofa watching daytime TV and getting pissed!"

"But he's got a job!"

"No he *hasn't*! Not a proper job. Not something regular which he works at month in and month out, let alone for years! He takes on casual work in kitchens in the area. He picks up work here and there with companies who do events and odd occasions. He's got *nothing* permanent and hasn't had in the entire time I've known him!"

"Well you're a fine one to talk! You're hardly flying high after all that time as a student!" Claire's mouth shut with a snap. Another line crossed. Another nail in the coffin of their friendship.

"Is that what you think of me?" Jenna demanded in a

voice so cold it would have given a penguin frostbite. "A lay-about student who bums around?"

Claire blinked with the suspicion of tears lurking in her eyes but got no chance to say anything further.

"How fucking *dare* you!" Jenna snarled. "You, who've been cosseted all your life, and who moved from a loving family home to one with a husband who panders to your every whim! You have *no* idea! None!" She'd stepped closer to Claire and now was standing right in front of her, eyes flashing with fury and oblivious to how much Claire was suddenly frightened by what she'd dredged up and unleashed. "*You've* never had to be removed from your mother for your own safety because of the man in her life, to be passed around from foster family to foster family. *You've* never been attacked on your way home from work as a teenager, and beaten up just because you had the misfortune to look like someone else! Yes, I may not be earning the big money, but I *do* use both my first degree and my Masters. And if you think that's just messing about, then let me remind you, lady, that my job on the deli' is permanent – God help me – and that I stick it out come hail, rain or sunshine!

"Which is unlike that useless wastrel of a brother of yours! Move in with me? Not on your life! I can just about keep my head above water now, without him frittering away what little I have. And let me enlighten you on why I booted him out of my home, back in the autumn, and told him not to come back. It was because I was making lasagne in the kitchen, and came back in here unexpectedly to find him going through the few bits I have of my grandmother's. The cheeky bastard had the nerve to say that *we* could sell some of them! When I said that I would never sell them because of their sentimental value, and that they were of more value to me than any bit of money they might fetch, do you know the selfish shit said? That I should be thinking of him and his comforts now, not dwelling on the past!

"So then I demanded that he turn out his pockets before he left, and Gran's lovely little locket was in there! You *know* how much I treasure that! But thanks to bloody Kyle I very nearly lost it for good! The one and only thing I've got with a photo of Granddad in it! Your brother's a petty thief, Claire! I should check your jewellery box if I were you when you get back. You might find some of the bits you don't wear very often have already gone!

"*And* I know why the little shit is possibly creeping around me again at the moment, despite it being so long after I broke it off with him. It's got nothing to do with any other woman disappointing him, or him realising what he had with me, or any other cock-and-bull story he's spun you. It's because he's pissed off some serious people this time! And how do I know this? Because I had a *copper* on my doorstep last week warning me, that's why! They picked up some scumbag and found my address scrawled on a bit of paper.

"Luckily for me they got it out of the nasty rat why he'd got it and whom it concerned. And since my name came up on their computer because of the attack and the protection I had during the trial, *they* – thankfully! – saw me as a potential victim instead of being implicated, and thought to warn me. You ask Kyle the next time you see him! Ask him for the bloody truth! Oh he might be going out every morning from your mom's pretending he's off to work, but that's because he scared stiff that they'll be round and beat the shit out of him for sticking his hand in the till, or whatever he actually did to steal from them!

"He's got no job, no place to go outside of his family, and if he stays at your mom's, he knows damned well he's soon going to have to start telling you lot why he's around in the day, and not going out, because someone's going to spot him and say something." Claire's mom was notorious for knowing every scrap of gossip on the estate where they lived, as they both knew.

"Well you might be daft enough to put up with him bringing his trouble home with him, but I'm not! I will *not* have him holed up here. It isn't just that he isn't my problem and has no claim on me or my time – although that's true enough, and should be a good enough reason for anyone who thinks to call themselves my friend! No, it's about what he'll do to me in the process. This isn't my property and I *won't* have my position here jeopardised! *I* have nowhere to run to if this falls apart, and I won't go back to where I was at twenty, living at someone else's sufferance and scared of my own shadow!"

She stood back, calmer and cold now. "So you can get out," she said harshly, placing herself in such a position that Claire either had to go back down the stairs from the tiny landing or risk being pushed down them.

"I'm..." Claire began.

"Not another word!" Jenna snapped. "You get out, and you don't come back. Ever! We're through, Claire. You're no friend to me. You've proved that to me tonight. You're a user! It's all about you and how you can manipulate people. Well your fancy friends from that expensive gym you go to might be able to afford the fallout from your schemes, but I can't. Not financially and not emotionally. I've given out my time and attention to you, and all too often at the expense of other friends who I can now see treat me better.

"There's nothing else I could have given you, but it's never been enough, has it? All the times I've caught the bus to your house at the last minute so that you can gad off out, because Garry's rung to say he'll be working away, they count for nothing. Or that I've picked both your kids up from school at various times when they've been taken poorly, and you've been too far away – or stuck in some salon covered in gloop – to be able, or have cared, to go yourself. God, you'd have been stuck with some awkward questions to answer to Garry, and others, without me! And in return what have you done? You've saddled me with Kyle and all his troubles. The very sort of man I don't need! So that's it. Don't come back here again and don't bother ringing me. I'm not interested."

They'd reached the bottom of the stairs, and Jenna thrust the soggy umbrella into Claire's shaking hands before shutting the door rather more forcefully than she'd intended. Leaning back against the door she took in several deep breaths. She felt shaky from so much emotion – a toxic mixture of anger and fear. The fear came from the thought of Kyle lurking around here all weekend and dragging heaven knew what in his wake! What if one of the other tenants complained? Old ladies were pretty understandably bothered by men hanging about for no good reason. Jenna could well imagine one of them penning a letter to the housing association complaining of the kind of company the young woman upstairs had about the place.

Should she speak to Mrs Wilson? Not tonight. She was too fraught for that. But then if she asked Mrs Wilson not to encourage people who said they were her friends, would it make any difference? The old lady was getting increasingly muddled of late. Would she even remember what Jenna had said? She took another deep breath. Of course the up side of that was that Mrs Wilson might not actually remember how many times Kyle had called round. And if she'd already half forgotten, then was Jenna the fool for bringing it up, and giving the incidents an importance which might make them memorable should the association enquire later?

She shrugged her shoulders to relieve the tension and plodded back upstairs, drained. A bottle of wine was on the desk table, originally intended as her treat for the end of the days' marking tomorrow and the days after. She certainly didn't run to wine very often. Now, though, she felt she needed that drink!

Chapter 2

She put the dinner on and had just taken her first mouthful of the deep rich Rioja when the doorbell went again. Oh this was too much! Bloody Claire! Couldn't she even take 'piss off' in the way it was intended? Jenna had expected some sort of syrupy phone messages in a few days' time, but surely not yet? The anger flared up again and she went down the stairs like one of the Valkyrie, flinging the front door open as she snapped on the outside light.

Kyle stood dripping on the doorstep, blinking like an owl in the sudden beam of light.

"You!" Jenna snarled and, in a completely uncharacteristic fit of assertion, she grabbed the front of his jacket and spun him round, dragging him to the small lean-to drying area in her share of the garden, well away from the house. She was oblivious to the fact that she'd left the front door wide open. Oblivious to anything apart from her anger towards this albatross who'd somehow hung himself around her neck. All she cared about was getting him away from here before Mrs Wilson came out and got involved. Later she was to reflect that what she did would not have been possible if Kyle hadn't been a small man, not much bigger than herself. Later, that was – and when the shock set in. For now, though, she was preoccupied with other matters. Shoving him up against the wheelie bins, she let go of the front of his rain-drenched sweatshirt and gave him another shove for good measure.

"Don't you *ever* come here again!" she spat furiously in his face.

"I wanted to…"

"Tough! I don't bloody care what you *wanted*, or what you *thought* would happen! Do I make myself clear? I've had it with you and your bloody sister! Yes she's already been round here tonight trying to make me into the villain of this fiasco! God, you two are bloody unbelievable! Neither of you give a monkey's about me! If you'd used what little brains you have – if you cared even a *little* about me, the way you protest so much to Claire that you do – it would have percolated through that thick skull of yours that I was at *work* when you came round. All you then had to do was walk up the road. I was all of a mile away! All you had to do was employ a little thought and consideration, and you could have spoken to me in my lunchtime. On any one of the *three* days I was there! Instead, you play these stupid, *stupid*, little boy, cloak-and-dagger games, upsetting my neighbours and killing what little feelings I ever had left for you. But that's you all over isn't it? It's all about you! You can't see further than the end of your own nose!"

"But…"

"No buts! Now get away from here before I call the police!"

"You wouldn't!"

"Oh yes I would, Kyle! I would because I have to get in first before my neighbours do! You've always run back home to mommy the first time things go amiss. But me, I've got no such option. If I get kicked out of here I don't imagine your mom is going to take *me* in, is she?"

He stood scuffing his feet like nine year old caught out. An image which only irritated Jenna further. God damn it, could he not show at least a little backbone? But then if he had some spine, some ability to behave like the man just turned thirty that he was, then they wouldn't be having this conversation.

"Go on, piss off!" she snapped, and began shoo-ing him towards the road with her arms. Suddenly she just wanted him gone and was aware of how soaked she'd become in the few minutes she'd been outside. Her hair was already plastered to her head, she could feel a trickle of water which had percolated through her outer clothes now running down inside her bra, and her feet were soaked through, which probably meant that her slippers were ruined. Those thoughts so distracted her that when they got by her door she was unprepared for Kyle to turn and grab her by the arm. His "but Jenna!" was lost in the sudden wave of panic which hit her. 'Not again!' her brain screamed. Without thinking she spun and kneed him hard in the groin.

"Let go!" she screamed. "I'm calling the police!"

Doubled in pain, Kyle stumbled away from her, white-faced and clearly shocked. Jenna shot inside and shut the door firmly, then for the second time that night leaned against it and listened for Mrs Wilson. Thank God for *Coronation Street*! The old lady had it on louder than anything else as usual, not wanting to miss a word of the latest drama, and someone on there was having a right barney over something. With any luck all the other old folk would be equally glued to the screen too.

Suddenly desperately tired, Jenna stumbled up the stairs back to the living room. She went to the window and looked out to see if she could see Kyle. For a moment she couldn't see anything, and in a fit of panic she ran back to the kitchen to look out over the back. Luckily she'd left the outside light on, so she could easily see that there was nobody there. Hurrying through into her bathroom, she stood on the edge of the bath and peered out of the tiny upper window, which just about gave her a view of the main road beyond. Peering through the gap between the buildings she suddenly saw him come into view, still bent over and although she couldn't see much through the rain, she knew he was clutching his groin. He stepped forwards into the light of the street lamp and a moment later a bus pulled up.

When it moved on from the stop, he was gone. Or at least gone physically, but the emotional and mental effects of such an exhausting hour – because that was actually all it had been – had stripped Jenna of the last of any energy she had left. It was all she could do to peel off the sodden clothes, shrug into her fluffy dressing gown, and wrap a towel around her hair.

Mechanically she ate the overcooked meal and cleared away after it, then the moment she sat back in the armchair she fell asleep. Unfortunately she woke just after midnight, cramped and cold. The central heating had gone off long ago, for Jenna was very economical with the use she made of it, often blessing the fact that Mrs Wilson kept the flat beneath at near sauna temperatures, and whose rising heat saved on her fuel bills. Tonight, though, it was too late to start running the shower to warm up, because the light in the bathroom automatically brought on a fan which made an awful racket, bad enough to be heard in the two flats in the other half of the former semi-detached houses too, and so she crept into bed and tried to get warmer.

Yet warmth was not forthcoming, and she lay shivering into the small hours, despite putting a thick blanket on over her duvet. Somewhere around dawn she finally got off to sleep, then woke around midday, muzzy-headed and far from refreshed. Forcing herself into something like wakefulness, she finally sat down and tried to make a start on the marking, but it was uphill work. Part of her brain was telling her that last night she had gone into shock. It wasn't just the row with Claire and then Kyle turning up. It was the whole thing of being out in the rain in the dark and a man grabbing hold of her. Too many memories, too much pain both past and present.

A week later she wasn't feeling that much brighter. The shock had worn off, but she still felt as though she was wading through quicksand for most of the day. Mercifully this Monday was the end of term, and was spent in giving the students feedback on the essays, all done in tiny sound-bites where she tried to give advice for improvement and be encouraging. By the end of it, though, she had no idea of what she'd said to most of them and had a dry mouth and a sore throat, but she had no inclination to go over to Staff House and join the other university staff in celebrating the end of the long slog from Christmas to Easter. Instead she trudged wearily out along the line of tall poplar trees, and out onto the road to walk down towards where the new hospital was in the final phases of construction, and to the train station to get the next Birmingham-Worcester train home.

Back in Worcester, she half contemplated a taxi back to Malvern, then, gritting her teeth at the thought of the expense, caught the bus. This journey was a drain all by itself. While she'd been a student, the rail card had eased the cost, but these days she was starting to wonder if she could really justify the expense, given what she earned. While she was getting all her teaching in one day it was okay, but if next year she was offered sessions over three days, she was coming to the dreaded realisation that she might have to decline, and that would be the end of her teaching days, she feared. Finally ploughing up the last short rise towards home, she was so focused on putting one foot in front of the other, that she didn't notice Tiff's Smart sports cars parked at the kerb until Tiff spoke.

"Bloody hell, Jenna! Whatever's wrong? You look awful!"

Jenna lifted her head and smiled weakly at her taller friend. "Gee, you really know how to make a girl feel better!" she tried to joke, but without success, then felt herself being enveloped in one of Tiff's hugs.

"Oh hon', you are in a state!" Tiff remonstrated, taking the bag off her and wrapping an arm around Jenna's shoulders as they walked around to Jenna's door.

Once inside Tiff began fussing about, insisting that Jenna sit down while she made them both coffee, and produced two slices of very sticky gateau from a box she'd hidden in her capacious shoulder bag.

"I bought these thinking we would be celebrating," Tiff explained, "but I think it's more comfort food that's needed, looking at those dark circles under your eyes. Whatever's happened?"

Haltingly at first, and then with increasing relief and ease, Jenna poured her heart out to Tiff, who sat making encouraging noises but tactfully said nothing until Jenna had run out of steam.

"God, that Claire's a selfish cow!" Tiff sympathised. "And what on earth did Kyle think he was doing?"

Jenna sighed. "I know. I mean, knowing me, why would he do something like grab hold of me like that? And at night too! That's been the worst of it, Tiff. It's been the old nightmares coming back, because standing there in the dark and the rain it brought it all back to me. Kyle as Kyle I can dismiss. He hasn't got the guts or imagination to be really spiteful or mean – although I'm fully aware that if he could ever stir himself to think about it, somewhere deep in that addled head of his is the information he needs to make my life a living hell again.

But I don't think he will, because he's just too idle, and I know Kyle can't manage to stick at anything for longer than a couple of days.

"No, it's that every time I lie down to go to sleep, my brain insists on dredging up those horrid snapshots of that *other* night. The way the rain was hammering down so hard I didn't hear the footsteps behind me until it was too late. That awful shock of being grabbed and spun round, and not really seeing anything much of 'him', because the first punch landed only seconds after I got my first glimpse of him. And you know what still freaks me? It's that in my nightmares it's always a faceless man. He turns and his face is a blank white disc. No eyes, no features, nothing. It's so creepy!

"Oh, I know I saw the real man at the trial. But somehow I never connect that face I saw in court with the one I didn't get to see on that night. All I remember of that man is his gruesome tattoos. Those bloody death's-head skulls on his fists as they kept coming towards me! But not the face of the man in court – he could have been *anybody*. It's like they were two totally different people."

Tiff knew all this. She'd heard it many times in the years since she and Jenna had been friends. Unlike Claire, though, she could fully sympathise with why Jenna needed to speak of it again. She looked at Jenna while she was talking and thought that she couldn't have had more than a few hours sleep in the whole week since it happened. No wonder she looked frazzled and at her wits end, she must be exhausted. And none of that could have been helped by having to keep everything bottled up inside on such a pressured week work-wise. No, Jenna desperately needed to vent some of those emotions. In fact what she really needed was a holiday, and at that Tiff had a bright idea. What Jenna needed was to get right away, not just from the jobs and Kyle, but this flat – which was in danger of becoming a prison more than a refuge to Tiff's mind — even if it was only for a few days, and Tiff had just the solution!

Tiff looked at her exhausted friend, and felt the warm glow of satisfaction as she realised she held the key to helping her feel better in the short term if nothing else.

"Hey, didn't you say that you'd booked next weekend off from work?" she asked Jenna.

"Not this coming weekend. That's Easter and you know how little chance I've got of getting time off from the counters then! No, it's the weekend after that I'm off."

"Brilliant! Even better!"

Jenna was jolted out of her despondency by Tiff's enthusiasm. "Why?"

"Because I have to go over to Ludlow for two weeks after Easter!"

Tiff worked for a large, multi-office legal and estate agent company in the centre of Birmingham as an office manager, but normally she didn't move about.

"How come?"

"Oh the company's due an audit and apparently the Ludlow office is in a right state. The old boy who's been running it since 1900-and-frozen-to-death has been given a hurried pension, and the plea went out for help. So I'm going along with Suzy from the Hereford office to blitz the place before disaster strikes. The thing is, Suzy can drive home each night, but they're putting me up at the local Travelodge. If I ask for a twin not a double, you could come with me!"

"Won't the company object?"

"Why should they? The price is for the room regardless of how many of us are in there. It's room-only, and I get to claim my meals back, so I can help you out with buying breakfasts and stuff. Come on Jenna! It'll be like when we were back at uni and sharing a flat! It'll be fun!"

When Tiff was in such a buoyant mood it was beyond Jenna to remain gloomy, and a flicker of a smile began to spread across her lips.

"Come on!" Tiff chivvied. "Bloody hell, woman, you're knackered! You desperately need a break! You've been going flat out at the teaching for two terms. I know this month will be a bit thin because you've only got the shop wages coming in until the exam marking kicks in, but you can't go into uni exams as flattened as you are."

Jenna sighed, although half of it was in relief. "No, you're right. I desperately need some time off. And I've already signed up to do external A level marking for the local authority, so that'll be hard on the heels of the uni exams."

Tiff shook her head. "Hon', we've got to get you a decent job, you know! You work harder at these odds and sods of jobs than most people do at a full-time one. I'm going to ring this contact I've got. She works for an agency up in the city centre. I've worked with her to put some graduates into internships with our partnership, so it's about time she returned the favour."

She was expecting Jenna to object. In the past Jenna had been holding out her hopes for a permanent part-time tutoring place at the university, or at least some other job on campus. As a university employee she would then get a serious reduction in the fees to do the PhD Tiff knew she longed to do. However, no job had appeared, and Jenna was hardly any better off than when she'd been a student. All the worse, Tiff thought, because Jenna had come in as a mature student of twenty-four, already living alone in an awful bedsit compared to which the student halls had been luxury, and had had to continue with the menial shop job all through her degree and then post-grad courses.

But Jenna had bravely stuck it out, and to Tiff's surprise had managed to keep going through two years of a part-time Masters too. Over the last year, though, Tiff had been seeing the cracks appearing. Jenna couldn't keep going on like this, and Tiff suspected that in her heart of hearts Jenna knew it, but to date she'd been denying it out loud, so Tiff had been expecting a bit more resistance than this. As if reading her mind, Jenna gave another sigh and, having wiped her finger around the cake plate to get up the last of the gooey chocolate, forced herself to sit up straight and looked Tiff in the face.

"I reckon I'm going to need that job, I'm afraid. I heard last week that there's unlikely to be enough teaching to keep me going next year, even if I could afford to keep making that horrendous commute three times a week. I've been trying not to think about it these last few days, but hints have been dropped already."

"Ouch! Why?" Tiff knew that Jenna was a good teacher who regularly got better feedback from the students than some of the permanent staff, so it couldn't be that she was failing.

"Oh, government cuts in funding," Jenna grimaced. "All very impersonal. And it's not just me that's feeling the pinch. All of us who keep turning up year after year for this part-time masochism are probably going!"

Tiff was shocked. No wonder Jenna was looking so knocked sideways. She'd set such hopes on being able to use her history qualifications. To lose that *and* have that mess with Kyle crop up at the same time was just rotten. Any comment on her bad luck didn't seem anywhere near an adequate response. Definitely time to send that e-mail! Jenna had been such a good friend to her over the years she could hardly do less, and if she got the chance, it would be a good bit more than that too.

Tiff dug in her bag and pulled out the state of the art

laptop which went everywhere with her. In an instant she had logged on via Jenna's connection, and had brought up the Ludlow Travelodge on the screen.

"There you are!" she said triumphantly. "We can have a family room to share." She clicked on the hotels details and brought up the map on the screen. "See? It's only a short walk into Ludlow! I probably won't bother to take the car in to get to the office, so we can even walk into the town together. So you can go and mooch round the castle and the other interesting bits and play the tourist, and then you can meet me after work, and we'll go and try out these super restaurants they're supposed to have there. My treat! I got a good bonus this year, so don't argue over that!"

Jenna laughed weakly. "You're such a force of nature when you're like this. You know that, don't you?"

"Well someone has to be! And you're not arguing about going, are you?"

Jenna shook her head resignedly. "No, I suppose I'm not."

"Right! Then you're definitely coming with me!" Tiff declared. "I shall pick you up about seven on the Tuesday morning after the bank holiday. Pack enough to see you through to the following Thursday. I shall shoo you off onto the coach or train to come back to get to work, because I shall probably be there over that weekend too if it's as bad as I fear. But that's no reason why you shouldn't have some play for a week, and Ludlow's a lovely place to chill out in! And then we can even go and find some nice country pubs for our evening meals if you don't want to do Michelin stars." And with typical Tiff enthusiasm she chortled, "Oh I'm *so* glad you're coming now! Having you with me will be great!"

Jenna shook her head, smiling. So very Tiff! She wished she had her friend's endless optimism, although it wasn't because Tiff had had everything in life go her own way. She was in a very different social position to Claire. Tiff's father was a very successful business man, but his relationship with his three children was distant to say the least. All of them had been packed off to private schools as soon as possible, and most of the time the only point when they registered with Ewan Fairbourne was when he thought they might be useful in helping to cement some deal. Marcia Fairbourne was a different kind of nightmare. Shallow and not very bright, she blew hot and cold with Tiffany and her two brothers, alternately smothering them with misguided affection, and then the next berating them for things which were only important failings within the orbit of her appearance-driven world. In fact it had been that lack of any parental support, beyond the provision of a roof over her head and money flung her way in place of any actual engagement with their daughter, which had made Tiff so comprehending of Jenna's life, and vice versa. Sometimes it took someone who'd had a taste of the same horrors to be capable of true understanding and empathy.

Therefore Jenna knew that Tiff's enthusiasm for having her along for the ride was out of genuine concern, and how could she refuse such generosity?

They planned and schemed for a while longer, but every so often their talk would wander back to the events of that evening a week ago. The more she heard, the more Tiff was seething underneath. That barbed comment about Jenna playing her cards right and getting a husband had really cut deeply, unless she was very mistaken. That was pretty rich, Tiff thought, coming from a woman who had so repeatedly jeopardized her own marriage with unguarded flirtations and foolish actions. Jenna thought Claire hadn't actually gone as far as to have an affair, but Tiff thought otherwise and now she said so.

"Honestly, Jenna, the woman's a bloody hypocrite!

There's you, who would give your all for the chance of a nice family life, and she's not only blatantly pissing it away, she has the unforgivable nerve to rub it all in your face! 'Play your cards right?' *Phaa*! How dare she? It would serve her right if Garry woke up and divorced her and went after you! Lord knows the man has sufficient cause!"

Tiff's righteous indignation finally made Jenna laugh out loud about the incident. "Thanks for the vote of confidence, but I wouldn't want Garry, thank you very much! Oh he's a nice bloke, and he adores his kids. But sometimes, Tiff, I think legally he sails very close to the wind with his business deals. I suspect that it was through him that Kyle got to know these undesirables in the first place. I certainly can't imagine Kyle moving in such exalted circles on his own merit. So you see it really does all fall back on Claire and her family if Kyle's in a mess."

"Maybe," Tiff declared sternly, "but she's still got a bloody nerve telling you to get out and play the field!" She decided she must change the subject, and swiftly, before she said any more and made things worse instead of better. Inside, though, she was incandescently angry at Kyle and Claire, and mystified as to why men could never seem to see the virtues Jenna possessed. Understandably Jenna was lacking in self-confidence. That was hardly surprising given that the attack in her past had come out of the blue, and without any possible means of predicting it might happen. It would have completely broken a lesser woman than Jenna, and Tiff had nothing but admiration for Jenna's grim determination to not let one night blight her life.

Yet in a way it inevitably did, because Jenna never shone at interviews when she had to confront strangers. That had limited her job choices, and for very similar reasons it meant that people who had chance encounters with her, tended to walk away with the impression of someone who was something of a nonentity – hardly the kind of impression to attract the sort of man Jenna needed. Tiff and the others from their university days knew full well that she was nothing of the sort, and possessed a wicked sense of humour once she was amongst people she had learned to trust. But how to get others to see it?

She would have to apply more thought and energy to this problem, Tiff could see. Already the germ of a scheme was forming in her mind. The Ludlow office would need a new manager once the audit was done, but it was a tiny affair compared to the huge office Tiff ran in the centre of Birmingham. Certainly it wasn't big enough to attract one of the company's rising stars, and her own boss had already spoken of his dread of finding someone competent enough to run the place when the career options weren't brilliant. If it hadn't been for the fact that the company got quite a bit of work from acting as duty solicitors for the police in the wider area around Ludlow, and also accrued some very lucrative commissions from the select few houses they marketed, Tiff knew they would be thinking about closing the office altogether, but in this economic climate profit was profit and not to be turned down – especially when they owned the whole building and got lucrative rents for the parts they didn't use.

However for Jenna the office could be a lifeline. If Tiff could ease her into the place and show her what the job entailed, she might just be able to swing her getting the job. In fact, Tiff was already imagining Jenna giving up this care-home-like flat amongst the elderly, and moving into some nice place with a view of the countryside, or even near the castle, over in Ludlow. So much more 'Jenna', but she'd have to take it carefully or she'd scare Jenna off.

Chapter 3

On a cool but sunny day, Jenna and Tiff drove across to Ludlow. The Smart car's tiny boot hadn't begun to cope with two women's luggage and Jenna had a bag on her lap and another under her feet, but it didn't dent her pleasure a jot. Between them they had an assortment of music from their days at university, and they sang along with great enthusiasm if little musical ability to the car's stereo, which was turned up loud.

They found the hotel just off the A49, and once inside, the family room turned out to have plenty of room for both of them without feeling cramped. Not being used to hotels, Jenna had feared it would be a shoe-box despite Tiff's reassurances to the contrary.

"Oh Tiff, this is just lovely!" sighed Jenna as she threw herself back onto the single bed and felt herself sink in – she'd insisted that Tiff have the double since she was the one in whose name the room was booked, but this was still plenty comfortable enough for her. "Thank you so much!"

"My pleasure!" Tiff replied. "And to celebrate…!" she moved her hand from behind her back and flourished a bottle of prosecco. "*Ta-da*! …So, what are you going to do first?"

"Oh, the castle!" Jenna declared with certainty. To Jenna's delight, on inspecting the town map Tiff had handed her in the car, Foldgate Lane where the hotel was ran straight down to the River Teme. From there it would be only a short walk along the riverside to the castle, but Ludlow wasn't that big that she couldn't easily walk the loop back through the town.

"Why am I not surprised at that?" Tiff chuckled.

"Well come on! You should know me by now! If there's a nice bit of medieval lurking around, I'm going to want to find it!"

Tiff joined her laughter, but secretly wished now that she'd pushed to stay in one of the lovely half-timbered hotels in the centre of the town. If Jenna was this thrilled just to get into a Travelodge, she'd have been near ecstatic to stop in somewhere like that. On the other hand, Tiff knew there was only so far that she could push her luck with her boss, even if she did have him wound around her little finger, and Travelodges and Premier Inns were the norm' for company visits anywhere.

They both wanted an early night, but after the best night's sleep she'd had in ages, Jenna was very happy to get up early with Tiff and join her for breakfast downstairs. With a whole day ahead of her to herself, and with such a lovely place to explore, Jenna could hardly wait to get outside. The castle was as impressive as she'd remembered from a visit back in their university days, and having taken a sandwich from a local bakery plus a can of coke in with her, she enjoyed a glorious spring day soaking up the atmosphere, and having her makeshift picnic up on the walls enjoying the view. It had been so long since she'd had a day with nothing to do in it, that she consciously had to stop herself from hurrying off in search of tasks which weren't there. It did make her realise, though, that Tiff was right, she did work harder at her strange combination of part-time jobs than if she had a regular full-time one.

Her stroll back through the town was no less satisfying, as she drank in the stunning Georgian and earlier black-and-white buildings of the town itself. By the time she met Tiff for dinner that night, she was full of the wonderful variations of Georgian frontages upon timbered buildings, as well as the joys of the castle and the magnificent parish church. As she expounded at length on the different things she'd been fascinated by, Tiff felt a glow of satisfaction. It had been so very long since she'd seen Jenna like this, bubbling and very happy, and consequently playing fairy godmother had brought its own reward. It was such a shame that Jenna couldn't find a way into permanent teaching, because her enthusiasm was so infectious, but Tiff had high hopes of finding something better for her friend than the jobs she was doing, even if she couldn't give her quite what she really wanted.

That evening they walked back into the town to *Ye Olde Bull Ring Tavern* – a glorious half-timbered and sprawling, four-storey confection of fourteenth century architecture, which dominated one of the small streets – and indulged in a very sticky dessert after their main course. They had eaten at *The Feathers* on the first night, which was a stunningly ornate Jacobean inn, and Tiff couldn't help but smile at the way Jenna's smile got even broader as she announced happily,

"But the *Bull Ring* is properly medieval!"

"You're probably the only person here to whom the two centuries difference is that important," Tiff teased, clinking her glass of wine against Jenna's.

"Three centuries!" Jenna admonished. "*Tut*, Tiff! Do the maths. And you an office manager as well! The 1640s is a fair hike on from the 1360s," but Tiff had seen how in both places Jenna's eyes had never stopped drinking in the details. After all, with preservation orders on ancient buildings like these, there was only so much alteration any owner could make, and there were enough exposed beams, leaded windows, and carved staircases, to populate Jenna's dreams for months to come.

And Jenna had sufficiently revived in the course of the two days to want to catch up with Tiff's news now as well.

"Come on then tell me the goss'! Is Carl still in the picture?"

Tiff rolled her eyes. "*Hmph*! He wouldn't be if he wasn't working in the same building!"

"Oh dear, the same old story?"

Tiff nodded. "Oh yes. By the time we'd been going out for three months, he'd got the wedding planned and how many kids we were going to have! Honestly Jenna, what is it with these men?"

Jenna waved the long spoon she'd been digging the last of her sundae out with at her friend. "It's because they know every man around looks at you. They want to tie you down and mark you out as theirs before anyone else can steal you away."

Tiff snorted. "I'm not a bloody pedigree poodle to be kept on the end of a leash! But I suppose you're right."

Whatever the indefinable 'it' was that made women attractive to men, Tiff had it in spades. Jenna had never known anyone quite like her for it. She only had to walk into a room and some man would be practically drooling in her wake. Of course, being a willowy six foot didn't exactly detract from the image. Tiff could wear just about anything and make it look good, she had that sort of figure – not catwalk model-like, painfully thin, but not Junoesque either. That often soured her relationships with other women, though, and Jenna knew she was one of Tiff's few true female friends. It usually went alright until a man came into the picture, but once whoever it was introduced their boyfriend or husband to Tiff, things inevitably deteriorated. Not that Tiff was anything like a marriage breaker. It was desperately unfair that those other women blamed Tiff for the fact that their men couldn't stop talking about her even when she wasn't there.

As if breaking into Jenna's train of thought, Tiff said, "It's pretty much put the tin hat on me and Gail, though. She's never quite forgiven me for even getting that first date with Carl."

"So she still fancies him like mad?"

"Oh yes. Even though I told her he's a pain in the neck once you get to know him."

Jenna smiled at her normally worldly friend's naivety. "Yes, Tiff, but you have to remember that she really wanted to be the one finding that out for herself, not having *you* – who could get any man you want – *telling* her."

"I guess you're right – as usual!" Then Tiff grinned again, losing the pained expression. "God it's nice to be sitting here and just chatting to another woman again! I really miss the old crowd from uni. There's nobody at work like you lot."

"In that way I think I'm luckier than you," Jenna said thoughtfully. "There's something to be said for being stuck down in the mire with people – we all rub along pretty well. Not that there are many of the folks I work with who I'd class as full friends in any shape or form. But we do help one another out, and there isn't the backbiting that goes with people trying to climb over one another to get to the top of the promotion ladder, largely because none of us is going anywhere within the company and we know it. But you're right, the old crowd was special."

"We were such an odd mixture," Tiff reminisced. "All so totally different from one another."

"But I think that's why we all got on. We were never stepping on one another's toes. We weren't in competition with each other the way you are with the girls in your office."

Tiff frowned. "I never really think of us like that. They do the legal work and I organise things around them."

"Maybe, but you're the one with the boss' ear. You've said to me that he listens to you in a way he doesn't the others. Now that might be because they're challenging him on legal things, and he probably thinks that his years of extra experience mean that they should be taking his word for it. Whereas you're doing such a sterling job of running the other side of the office that he depends on you. But if you were them, wouldn't you be pissed off that the one person who *isn't* a lawyer, yet who has some kind of power in the company, gets listened to over you?"

Tiff wrinkled her nose in distaste but muttered an "I suppose so." She speared the strawberry decoration from her dessert which she'd left until last, and ordered them both a coffee before asking, "Have you heard from Mel of late?" It wasn't an idle question, although she was trying to make it seem so. Mel had been the spiritually inclined one of their group, very much the New Ager, but who had been the best at soothing Jenna when they'd first come to know her. Tiff was a solid agnostic, but recognised that in getting Jenna to meditate with her, Mel had provided something which Jenna had subconsciously needed. Soon Tiff was going to have to break the news that she was going to be working abroad in the new year for several months, and she would feel a lot better about abandoning Jenna if she knew that Mel was at least close by once again. However the reply was not encouraging.

"The last letter I had from her was posted from India," Jenna answered, "but that was over two months ago."

"She's still with that hippy group?"

Jenna rolled her eyes. "They're not hippies, Tiff! I know you don't get what they do, but they're sincere." Mel was working with a group dedicated to helping third world communities make progress, and improve their standards of living without following the west into environmental chaos. "I've half thought of joining her, you know."

"Oh God, no! No, Jenna! You need stability and ...and ...well, ...not traipsing around the globe on a whim and a prayer!"

"I'm not that fragile!"

"No you're not fragile ...but you don't cope with stress very well. I don't mean to sound like the voice of doom, but you were freaked out enough by Kyle just grabbing your arm when he was blundering about. What would you do if one of the natives in ...in ...oh, wherever, decided that he wanted a 'nice English lady'? You know as well as I do that women's rights in many of these places are non-existent. Saying 'no' might not get you very far, and neither might yelling! You'd have to keep a cool head in that sort of situation, and think your way out of it. But you have so much baggage rattling around inside you that, with the best will in the world, you might not be able to stay calm."

"I guess you're right," Jenna said wistfully, "but you know sometimes, Tiff, I wish that I could just step outside of my life for a bit. Go somewhere where there are no memories to keep creeping up on me. It wasn't *just* Kyle grabbing me that did it. It was being outside, on an English city street – I was fine until we got back to the front door and near to the street and the traffic – in the dark, feeling cold, and with the English spring rain bucketing down all around me. That combination of noises. Of tyres on the wet road with people going past but not seeing me. It was that same smell of tarmac after a dry spell, when the rain washes all the dust out of the air, and when even the exhaust fumes are more pungent. Don't you see? It's the whole thing that triggered the memories. Even if I was grabbed at out in India during the monsoon, the smells would be different.

"Mel and I used to talk about that a lot, you know. Our sense of smell is very underrated these days – by everyone. We drown ourselves in synthetic perfumes, but ignore the primal smells which trigger instinctive reactions. Do you remember that trick that Mel taught us? To wear a particular scent when revising a difficult subject, and then wear it again during the exam, because it would help trigger memory? We all got through that second-year Byzantine module exam that way. Even you! Well Mel used some different scents with me when we were relaxing and meditating. She said that if I ever got stressed again that I should burn some of that incense she got for me and candles, because it would take me back to when we'd worked together and help me break the cycle."

"So why didn't you this time?" It wasn't said as a criticism, just trying to gain further understanding.

"Because the shops I can get to locally don't sell them, I'd run out, and I haven't had chance to go up into Birmingham city centre and hunt for more!"

Jenna suddenly started to sound a touch stressed again.

"Okay, point taken," Tiff said, not wanting to wind Jenna up when she'd just started to relax.

However Jenna hadn't finished, letting some of her often too controlled feelings out. "I always find the winter hard going because not only am I more tired with the extra teaching work, but then because of that, I find it almost impossible to switch my brain off enough to do the meditations Mel worked out for me. She's got even better at that as she's got older, you know. The last time she came to stay – when I bought that folding camp bed I have to keep hidden from the likes of Kyle – she was telling me all about the exciting stuff she'd learned in India. You know Mel, she'd make friends in a graveyard! In the villages they worked in, she made a point of finding the old wise men and women and talking to them. She's building this enormous body of spiritual knowledge. That's why she went back out to India – so that she could continue learning from them. Now I'm not saying that I'm ready to convert to being a Hindu or a Buddhist, but I feel a real pull towards the idea of living a life where there's time to think about something beyond the physical."

Tiff refrained from further comment, and swiftly moved on to talking about Kerry and Amanda, the other members of their five-some, who were mercifully living far less complicated lives. However, she couldn't help thinking that Jenna would be far less inclined towards thinking about a life which, to Tiff's eyes, seemed not so far removed from that of a nun, if there was a man in her life. Tiff, never having been without a boyfriend, or at least several casual male acquaintances, in all of her adult years, couldn't imagine why any woman would willingly live as celibately as Jenna did.

Privately she thought that Jenna would feel very differently about life if she could ever have a proper relationship again. She knew that Jenna had had boyfriends in her teens, and that at least one of them had been pleasantly physical. But the assault which had happened when Jenna was nineteen – and on the verge of going to university for the first time had the attack not happened – had spelled the end of the last one. The young lad had been completely unable to deal with the turmoil of emotions generated by having his girlfriend put into intensive care by a random beating.

These days, Jenna was completely understanding of why he'd been unable to face her after he'd seen her lying wired up to machines. For the first week it had been a bit touch and go whether she would make it at all, for there had been a real fear of blood clots going undetected, and causing one or more strokes as Jenna lay unconscious, unable to move or tell anyone if she was in pain or was suddenly feeling any strange discomfort. By the time she had surfaced, she was a patchwork of violently coloured bruises, her face swollen and virtually unrecognisable. Utterly unprepared for a world where he might suddenly have a disabled girlfriend, and yet at the same time feeling immense guilt at not having been there to protect her, the lad had fled the hospital and had not returned. There had been no tearful scenes, no formal breaking up, and by the time Jenna was able to go back to her crappy bedsit, she was already resigned to the fact that she wouldn't be seeing him again.

Since then Jenna had understandably found it difficult to trust men on short acquaintance. She was never going to be comfortable with going to nightclubs, or to bars alone with a man until she'd had chance to get to know him – a point Tiff had sadly proven when she'd taken Jenna out on the town with her on a couple of occasions. Both times Jenna had had to be taken home in tears. Nor had it helped that, having finally summoned up the courage to enrol at university in an effort to start her life over anew, Jenna had been at least five years older than all the males on their course, rather than their contemporary as Tiff and Mel were. There had been other mature students, and many of them a good deal older than Jenna, but they'd all been women. So while the other girls had dated often, if not consistently, Jenna had remained unattached.

Tiff had even half hoped that someone might emerge at the supermarket who would see Jenna for the great person she was and ask her out. Yet if anyone had, Jenna had never mentioned them, and Tiff prided herself on being able to get most things out of Jenna eventually. And on that score she had found herself, in theory, in agreement with the dreaded Claire – Jenna would be more likely to meet someone through the agency of a mutual friend where an element of trust was already established. And that was why just at the moment Tiff could cheerfully have throttled Claire for her stupidity. This episode with Kyle had only served to make Jenna wary even of the men her friends introduced to her.

For her own part, Jenna had been nursing her own quiet convictions, and prime amongst these was the opinion that few men would want her once they found out that she could no longer have children. It was one thing to go into a marriage thinking that you could have children and then be confronted with the discovery that they wouldn't happen. It was something else entirely, Jenna thought, to know even before you started, that children weren't even an option. And while she'd not met that many men through work whom she'd have called deeply paternal, there always seemed to be a certain expectation that a family would happen sooner or later amongst even the youngsters, albeit delayed for many years most of them hoped.

That beating had done a lot of internal damage as well as external, for once he'd pounded her down to the ground, Jenna's assailant had then used his heavy boots on her. So much so that a couple of years later Jenna had been back in hospital, the specialists reluctantly agreeing that although they were loath to perform such an operation on someone so young, that in this case a hysterectomy was the only solution to the dreadful pain Jenna was experiencing. The repair work which had been done immediately after the attack simply hadn't worked. And for once Tiff's wheedling hadn't extracted that secret from Jenna, not least because, since Tiff had no desire to ever have any children of her own, Jenna doubted whether she would understand just how devastating this was for her. The one person who did know was Mel, and at times like this, it was that deeper understanding which had made Mel such a sympathetic listener.

However Jenna was not so churlish as to make Tiff feel that she wished someone else with them when she'd done so much already. And so when Friday morning dawned wet and windy, Tiff suggested that if Jenna was done with looking round the town, that she bring her laptop down to the office and work on one of the stories she wrote as a pastime, while Tiff and Suzy continued with blitzing the accounts, and Jenna was quite happy to go along with the suggestion. She was oblivious to Tiff's scheming to get her into the office, but was already aware that sitting in the hotel foyer wasn't going to be comfortable, and that there were only so many coffees she could afford in order to secure her a place at a table elsewhere in the town. Tiff had promised days out in the car over the next two weekend days, but with Friday so inclement, the office sounded a good option.

Chapter 4

The office turned out to be in one of the gorgeous Georgian fronted, half-timbered buildings, up on the first floor above a ground floor shop, and Jenna was already gasping in delight as they made their way up the massive carved oak staircase.

"Oh Tiff, isn't this lovely!" she exclaimed as they reached one of the quarter-turns, and found a symbolic rose carved into the newel post.

Tiff played the cynic, theatrically rolling her eyes and drawling, "Yes, a Tudor rose. Very nice, I'm sure, but there must be thousands of those carved in houses across the country." Secretly, though, she was thrilled that Jenna was so taken with what could be her new work place. So much more her thing than a bland, modern, warehouse-style supermarket.

Jenna playfully slapped her arm. "Shame on you, Tiff! Surely you haven't forgotten the significance of Ludlow?" Then seeing the sudden worried flicker in Tiff's eyes, found her own chance to tease a little. "You have, haven't you! What would Dr Probert say! Come on, Tiff, you haven't become that much of the fluffy office girl, think back to that module on the Wars of the Roses. Who had one of their great seats of power here?"

Tiff's brow had creased into a frown of concentration, but now pulled a rueful face of confession. "Nope, sorry, Jenna, that one's fallen down a black hole."

Jenna, by now two steps further up than Tiff, and therefore able to look down on her taller friend for once, wagged a mocking finger of disapproval under her nose. "Shocking! You don't even remember reducing Dr Brookfield to a blushing tizzy on the field trip over here, when you wore that tiny denim skirt and went up the stairs of the castle ahead of him!"

Tiff stopped in her tracks. "Bloody hell!" and she collapsed in hoots of laughter. "God, I'd forgotten that! We did come here, didn't we? To the castle, and then we went on and looked at some of those old houses too."

"And why did we do that?" Jenna demanded, doing her best to come the stern teacher. "Who was so important?"

With a squeak of shock, memory suddenly came back to Tiff. "York! Oooh …*oooh*, I remember now! This was where Edward the whatever-he-was won that important battle, wasn't it?"

Jenna was the one who now rolled her eyes in mock despair. "That was at Mortimer's Cross, you muffin! Here was where the children of the House of York stayed, supposedly because it was safer than some of their other manors over on the eastern side of England. Everyone forgets that's why Ludlow was so important for so long; why it's got that huge Palmers' guild church too. Yes, it's got a castle, but the castle stayed important when others crumbled precisely because it belonged to the York family. So both Edward IV and Richard III spent a lot of time here as children. And thinking of that, Miss Smarty-pants, whose rose do you think it *might* be in that newel post, then, eh? Not a Tudor one, for pity's sake! It's a white rose of York! Only one layer of petals – or did you not notice? Tudor ones have two because they combine York and Lancaster."

They had reached the door to the office which was standing open, and another female voice said, "Wow! I never knew that!"

The owner of the voice turned out to be a rather plump woman of middle years, with a ready smile and a mop of brown curly hair which defied styling.

"Jenna, meet Suzy," Tiff said with a grin, then as an aside to Suzy, "Don't ask her about anything medieval or we'll be here all day!"

Suzy just laughed and held out her hand. "Lovely to meet you, Jenna," and for once Jenna wasn't daunted and gave a genuine smile as she took Suzy's hand.

Internally, Tiff gave herself a high-five. Marvellous! Suzy's first impression of Jenna had been a positive one, and that meant with a bit of luck, she would probably back Tiff's covert plan to instate Jenna here as the office manager. She'd seen the bright, intelligent academic, not the crushed and permanently scared woman whom Tiff had seen in previous weeks.

Then a man was getting up from his desk and coming round to meet them. Not much taller than Jenna, and definitely shorter than Tiff, he had a pleasant face that was already smiling and a hand extended to Jenna.

"I'm Mike, Mike Campbell, junior partner."

"And always likely to be if go around covered in damned dog hairs!" a much more upper-class voice said with haughty sarcasm. "For God's sake, Michael, smarten yourself up! What if a client walked in? You've got half the dog on your trousers."

Mike immediately blushed, but fixing the newcomer with a look of absolute hatred, riposted, "Well Silas and Marnie are moulting! And if you'd actually come in as you said you would this morning to open up for Suzy, instead of ringing me at the last moment to say you'd be late, then

I'd have had time to change from my dog-walking trousers."

The other man had come up the stairs behind them, and now that he was close to them, Jenna could smell the old cologne on him. He must have damned near bathed in it the night before, because he still absolutely stank of the stuff. Without realising she was doing it quite so obviously, she looked him up and down, taking in the rumpled shirt – still with several buttons undone to expose the medallion on his burst-sofa of a chest – the tie draped nonchalantly around the collar, and the fact that he hadn't shaved. Instinctively she recoiled as he swaggered towards her, clearly intending to hover over her, and in an uncharacteristic moment of bravery she said firmly,

"Well you wouldn't impress any client looking like that, either. I think I'd rather have a dog-lover than some who looks like a scruffy playboy."

The man stiffened, pulled himself up to his considerable height, glared at Jenna, then at the others in the room, then shoved past Suzy and strode across the outer office towards the window, and turned left into what had to be another office beyond, slamming the door shut behind him.

"Wow!" Tiff gasped, looking at Jenna in admiration, while Suzy had developed a case of the giggles the moment the door slammed. Even Mike was looking at her with in a cross between awe and delight.

Wiping her eyes, Suzy said with laughter still in her voice, "And that, ladies and gentlemen, is the rising star of this office – not! The man who thinks he can charm any woman into dropping her knickers in thirty seconds flat. Fell flat on his chops today, then, didn't he!"

Giving Jenna a little hug, Tiff explained, "That's Zachary Carlton Smith. Upper-class twit, supreme know-it-all, and all round pain in the arse."

Jenna managed to clear her throat, having had a moment of blind panic after she'd spoken. She'd been expecting them all to disapprove, not congratulate her. "I thought you said that the leading man here had retired, Tiff?"

Tiff waved an airy hand, "Oh yes, he did. That was old Mr Hornby, the senior partner and whose dad set up this office. Zach the Twat is only the second partner here, and then Mike's here to primarily do the duty solicitor stuff and some of the conveyance work. The thing is, Zach the Twat went to school – a very posh, private school – with Mr Hornby's son, which is how he got in here. Mr Hornby had hired him before telling anyone at head office, which didn't go down well, because they'd had someone else in mind when the previous second partner retired. But Mr H. didn't like their suggestion. Said that he wasn't 'the right sort' to be dealing with the clientele they have here."

"Which basically," Suzy interjected, "meant that having someone called Darius Rouhani – and who was not Persil white – in this office, was offensive to him, never mind his collection of heavily cultivated rich clients. Darius is a really good solicitor, sharp as a knife, and actually from a wealthy Iranian family who fled with the Shah – so he's not exactly an asylum-seeking street kid! In our office we thought that Hornby didn't want Darius here because he'd catch on too fast that Hornby was doing things his own way. Not exactly illegal, you understand, but we have codes of practice within the company, and he certainly wasn't complying with all of them. I won, though, because Darius is at Hereford with us now – which is a far busier office than here – and he's an absolute gem."

Mike agreed. "I started at Hereford," he explained to Jenna, "and I worked with Darius when he was new there.

Really nice guy. I wish it was him I was working with here now," and he cast a baleful glance at Zachary's closed door.

Jenna didn't need any further elaboration to guess that Zachary made Mike's life a misery, and so she ventured to ask, "But surely there'll be a new senior partner? Someone who comes in above Zachary?"

However Tiff was already shaking her head. "No, there won't. The only reason things have been allowed to run on this long has been because Hornby didn't have long to go before retirement, and it would have cost too much to get shot of him. But this office doesn't need another senior partner when Mike's doing all the lesser work. That's why Zach the Twat is being such an officious arsehole. He's already earmarked the other, bigger office for himself. He's just presumed that he'll get promotion and another underling. He hasn't grasped yet that he'll be expected to pull his socks up and run the place on the same salary that he has now."

"And that won't go down well," Mike sighed. "Sorry, Jenna, that's not a great introduction to the place, is it? Don't worry, his lordship in there won't be here for long. He'll check his emails, then bugger off home to change, and then he'll be out on the golf course schmoozing clients."

The phone on Mike's desk rang and he hurried to answer it. "Hornby, Wilkes and Jenkins, Mike Campbell speaking. ...Oh hello, Paul. ...Oh no, not again. Okay, hang on and I'll come over." He put the phone down and got up to grab his jacket. "Phil Wallace is in again for domestic violence. Never can afford a solicitor, so it looks like I'm dealing with him again." He shrugged the jacket on and hauled a battered briefcase out from under the desk. "At least Phil won't care about the dog hairs," and clattered off down the stairs.

Sure enough, only moments later, Zachary appeared out of the inner office. "Michael, I'm going …Oh! Where's he gone to now?"

"Doing his job," Tiff said with acid sweetness. "Duty solicitor call from the police station. You know, that bread and butter stuff that keeps this office open."

Zachary snorted and looked down his patrician nose at her. "Well I'm out to a meeting with an investment banker and his son." He looked around the office, then back at the three women. "I suppose it's alright to leave you three here?"

Suzy glared at him. "We're not going to nick the silverware, if that's what you mean! Go on, piss off!"

As Zachary's more leisurely footsteps receded down the wooden staircase, Tiff shut the door with a sigh of relief. "God that man's a pain! I don't know how Mike stands him."

Suzy pulled a face. "He's asked several times for a transfer back to Hereford, you know. It's only because his mum lives not far away, and she's not in the best of health, is why he stays in the area. He'd be snapped up by a big city firm with his track record, but his sisters have moved far away with their husbands, and he feels someone has to stay close to their mum. But if we don't do something about this office, and soon, it's only a matter of time before one of the other solicitors in the area have a vacancy, and then there's a real chance we'll lose Mike."

"And if we lose Mike, this office will close," Tiff told Jenna. "Nobody else would work with Zach the Twat, and he doesn't bring in enough work on his own. Head office knows this. They're just waiting to get this audit over and done with and then there'll be a big shake up here, mark my words."

Suzy agreed. "They've never had an office manager here. Just a typist who comes in four afternoons a week, and she's bloody useless! Look at this lot!" And she brandished the sheaf of files in her hand. "Filing going back five years still sitting in heaps! Poor Mike's tearing his hair out every time he wants to look back over something. That's why there're those heaps behind his desk. They're his current files that he's got in order so that he can find stuff. He's said it won't take long to file them away once we've got the rest sorted, and I believe him, but I can totally understand why he reached the point of not letting them out of his sight. Hornby's office looks like an ink-jet printer's had a seizure in it – several times over!"

There was a buzzer for visitors outside of the main office door, and so they locked that one and then all three of them went through to what had been the senior partner's office.

"When we got here," Tiff explained, "we had to fight our way through the mounds of papers on the typist's desk opposite Mike's. We sent the silly woman home, because all she kept doing was wringing her hands and saying, "Mr Hornby won't like it!" – like the doddering old fool is ever going to come back!"

"Gosh! How old was he?" Jenna asked, imagining someone at least in their seventies.

Suzy obviously realised what she was thinking because with a grin and a wink towards Tiff, explained, "Oh he was only fifty-nine, but he was the sort who thinks they're living in a past generation. We've got a few like that who come into our office. Still firmly wedged in the era of Miss Marple and Hercule Poirot! All upper-crust, of course. They're the ones with enough money to be insulated against the realities of modern life. But at least in our case they're just the clients, and we have to ease them into some of the harsher truths of what the law will allow – *droit de seigneur* doesn't hold much water in court these days."

Jenna blinked in shock. "Good grief, do people really think they can do that still?"

Tiff gave her a nudge with her elbow. "She didn't mean *droit de seigneur* literally, hon'."

"Thank God for that!"

Suzy was looking at the two of them with a bemused expression, and so Tiff explained, "*Droit de seigneur* originally meant that the lord of the manor thought he had the right to shag a bride on their wedding night – any bride! If you were on his lordship's land, he could turf the bridegroom out and have first dibs at the bride."

"God Almighty!" Suzy gasped. "I never knew that! ...Lord, no, Jenna! ...*Euw*! No I can't imagine old Sir Humphrey's got it up in years, much less goes around rogering his tenants!" And all three of them laughed.

It completely broke the ice between Jenna and Suzy, though, and Tiff was delighted that Jenna piled in and helped them with sorting out the heaps and heaps of paperwork. Tiff and Suzy gave her the wills to get into order, partly because although these formed a hefty percentage of the randomly piled files, they were also straightforward. Other documents required a bit more knowledge of where they ought to go, but the wills simply needed sorting into alphabetical order, and then into some sort of date order, with the ones relating to the same family all collected together.

"We'll sort out which ones can be archived once we can see what we've got," Tiff told her as they broke off for a coffee. Mike had returned from the station muttering darkly about his client, his unsavoury personal habits, and expressed his opinion that this time there was little he'd be able to do to avoid a custodial sentence.

"Have a chocolate Hobnob," Suzy said consolingly, offering Mike the biscuit packet she'd had hidden away from Zachary.

He looked so dejected that Jenna decided to ask him, "What sort of dogs have you got? It sounds like you have fun walking them."

Mike's face immediately broke into a smile. "Silas and Marnie? Oh, they're lurchers. Big deerhound lurchers. I had to go into the station one night because a bunch of travellers had been poaching on one of the estates, and the gamekeepers had caught them. Silas and Marnie got brought in with them, but the pound was already full." He sighed. "It's a terrible shame, but sometimes the dogs that come in like that have to be put down – especially if they've been used for fighting. Some of them are just too mentally scarred to ever cope with normal life again. They'd need someone very special to take them on, and you can understand people with kids not wanting a fighter on their hands. But Silas and Marnie were simply out and out terrified. They were cowering in the corner of the station, and I just knew I had to take them.

"I know a couple of the local vets, so I took them straight over there – not least because the poor souls were riddled with fleas, and I was pretty sure they had mange too. Charlie checked them over and kept them in for the night, and that was when it got a whole heap clearer as to how much they'd been abused. So I brought a private prosecution for cruelty and won, and between that and the poaching charges, the travellers got banged up for ten years."

"Good for you!" Jenna applauded, and Mike turned a pretty shade of pink.

Looking bashful, Mike fished his phone out of his pocket and said, "Would you like to see a photo of them?"

"Oh yes!"

She found herself looking at two grey, shaggy faces, with tongues lolling out in big daft grins. Another photo showed them hurtling into a brook after a stick, and several more of them lazing on a big old sofa in the sunshine. "Gosh, it's a dog's life, alright," she laughed. "They've got a bigger sofa than I have."

"I sometimes bring them in," Mike confessed. "Especially when he's not around," and he gave a glare towards Zachary's office. "They're really good if I have to interview a rape victim who I'm representing as duty solicitor. Somehow they feel a lot safer with the dogs." A twinkle came into his eyes as he added. "Marnie and Silas don't like Zachary. They growl at him …but then the vulnerable women don't like him either, so that always helps."

"And I can understand that," Jenna said vehemently. "There's something very creepy about that man. I don't know if Tiff's said anything, but I was badly assaulted – although not raped, thank God – and there's something about Zachary that really sends shivers down my spine. I wouldn't want to be alone with him …ever!" She gave herself a small shake and put a smile on. "But I think your dogs are gorgeous, and they have very good taste."

Tiff had turned away so that Jenna wouldn't see her worried frown. That could complicate matters if Jenna felt like that about Zachary. She'd obviously taken to Mike, which was a huge plus, but it was still not confirmed that Zachary would immediately leave the office. Of course he would have to accept the appointment of someone as an office manager, and Tiff was halfway sure that he wouldn't. The chances were that Zach the Twat wouldn't want someone who answered directly to head office keeping tracks of his comings and goings, and keeping his work-related diary for him. That would cramp his style way too much. But how long would it take to shift the bastard, Tiff wondered? If he hung on and argued the toss, then it would take a tougher manager than Jenna to stand up to him, especially while he was throwing tantrums, because Tiff knew Zachary could be a spiteful sod from some of the things Mike had told her. And once in place, another person would hardly be making way for Jenna after only a few months. Damn Zachary! Why couldn't he have cleared off when Hornby left?

She heard Jenna asking Mike, "When will he be back?" and Mike answering,

"Oh he won't. Not on a Friday. I've never known him work beyond about three o'clock. He'll want to be on the three-thirty train to Crewe, and then on from there on the London train. Ludlow doesn't have enough of a 'scene' at the weekend for the likes of him. He wants to bag himself a rich heiress so that he can live the life he's yet to become accustomed to."

"Is there such a woman?" Jenna asked, to which Mike just laughed, but Tiff had caught on to something else.

"What do you mean, 'doesn't work' after three on a Friday? We work until the job is done, surely?"

Mike gave a thin smile. "I do. Well you have to when you're the only partner who ever does duty solicitor. But Zachary? No, I've never know him to, not in the three years I've worked here. He started off with that arrangement with the old man and it's never changed. I don't know if Mr Hornby realised that it meant *every* week when he agreed to it, but he surely didn't put a stop to it when it worked out that way."

"And what about the rest of the week?" Tiff asked in disbelief. "How late does he work then? Some of our team regularly don't go home until seven during the week if there's a big job on. Okay, court appearances don't run on that late, but that doesn't mean you can't do the preparation."

Mike shrugged. "He doesn't get many court appearances. All of his stuff is the wills and commercial contracts. He's always out of here at five on the dot, if not a bit earlier — and you have to understand that he often opts to go and meet clients at their convenience, rather than them coming here, so I don't know half the time where he is. Mr Hornby was letting him do more and more of that running around at the wealthy clients' beck and call."

Suzy's jaw had begun to drop at this and now she spluttered, "But that's not where this firm earns its money! God Almighty, no wonder this branch is close to running at a loss! We're paying premium council tax here! We'd be better off with a tenant in here than the way things have been of late."

"Richard's going to have a fit when I tell him this," Tiff said sourly, Richard being her boss and a very senior partner within the wider company. Jenna had her suspicions that he had enjoyed what might be called a 'friendship with benefits' with Tiff for some time, although Tiff never mentioned actually going out anywhere with him. Wherever they met up, they were being very discreet about it, but it meant that Tiff had the kind of relationship with him where she could tell him such things without fear of it rebounding back on her — office managers were supposed to show a certain loyalty to the others they worked with, although this was an exceptional instance.

As if reading Jenna's mind, Mike said to her, "I'm not a tell-tale, you know. I've tried to be loyal to old Mr Hornby, but it's bloody hard when you get treated like the office tea boy, yet a lazy, useless sod like Zachary gets to lord it over you."

"I don't think it's telling tales," Jenna said firmly, "it's being honest. I can't stand people who creep around the boss just to get ahead. I know the world doesn't work that way, I'm not that naive, but I wish people got promoted because they're good at their jobs, not just because they're the ones with their noses wedged the furthest up the boss' bum!" and she and Mike exchanged grins of solidarity.

Oh please let this work out, Tiff silently prayed. Mike and Jenna – now they would make a lovely couple!

Chapter 5

"You were getting on very well with Mike yesterday," Tiff said, as she and Jenna helped themselves to the breakfast buffet the next morning. With great effort she had refrained from saying anything until now. As they'd packed up the previous day, Suzy had left to make the journey back to Hereford, but Mike had offered to treat Tiff and Jenna to a meal at one of the gourmet restaurants that Ludlow was famous for.

"I'd offer tonight," he had said apologetically, "but Silas and Marnie have been on their own all day. I really should get back and take them for a walk. Tomorrow, though, they'll be fine for the evening. We've got all sorts here – French, Italian, vegan, classic pub-grub, Indian – take your pick."

To Tiff's amazement, Jenna had said, "Surprise us – we're not picky," at which point Mike had suddenly given a secret smile and said okay. They had arranged to meet him at six-thirty, but until then they had the whole day to themselves.

"I think he's been very put upon," Jenna told Tiff, as she speared another piece of fresh pineapple with relish. "What a horrible position to be put in. If he said anything to your head office he'd only have been called a liar by the old man, and you have to think that his boss knew at least some of what was going on behind his back."

Tiff's fingers hovered in indecision between an almond croissant and a chocolate Danish, the Danish winning. "You're right there. It's a very difficult position to be in. I think it's fair to say that head office knew that this office was lagging behind in a lot of its practices, but they didn't know it was this bad."

"Mike won't get into trouble, will he?" Jenna asked worriedly, recalling Tiff's long and vigorous phone conversation with her own boss on the previous evening in their room.

Tiff shook her head, vanished off from their table to get more coffee, then came back and elaborated, "Richard's actually bloody impressed that he's managed to keep the place afloat, now that he knows who's been doing all the work. He was actually talking last night about maybe upping Mike's status within the partnership. It's a shame this office has got into such a state, so they can't make him up too far yet, but Richard's talking about definitely making him up to equal status to Zach the Twat."

"Ooh, that won't go down well."

"No it won't, but it will mean that Zach the Twat won't be able to boss Mike around once they're on an equal footing."

"Good!"

"Wow, you really like Mike, don't you?"

Jenna rolled her eyes at Tiff. "Stop match-making, will you? Yes, I do like him, but it's because of the way he was talking about how he handles vulnerable women clients. That bit about bringing the dogs in really resonated with me. I'd have felt so much better all those times when I sat in the offices of my legal team, trying to get them to see how I felt, if it had been someone like Mike sitting across the desk from me. I know they did their best for me, Tiff, but even so they made me feel like they'd only taken the case on once they knew that I was a random victim – not some girl who was 'asking for it'. That and the fact that the attack was so brutal that they knew it would be a newsworthy case once it came to court. If I'd known my attacker, I think their reactions would have been a lot cooler, if you know what I mean. I'd have given just about anything to have a genuinely sympathetic solicitor like Mike on my team. Someone who saw me as a human being, not just as a means of making their reputations."

Tiff nodded sagely, already guessing the other side of this. "And that's why you loathe Zach the Twat so much, isn't it? He only thinks of his own reputation."

Jenna brandished another piece of pineapple on her fork. "Exactly! Loathsome toad, that's what he is! …Why do you always call him Zach the Twat, though?"

Tiff giggled. "It's what he's known as in our office. There's another Zachary in an office we have a lot to do with – a lovely chap who's just a delight to work with. But we have to have some way of distinguishing which one we're talking about – you know, who we've had a phone-call off. Easy enough when you see them face to face, of course, but not so much when it's a call or an email. Well this Zach always makes some dreadful social gaff. Chats up the wrong person, offers some favour that's plain icky coming from someone like him, or gives his opinion when it's not warranted or wanted. You can imagine that can't you?"

Jenna grimaced. "God, yes! He's so in love with himself he can't imagine that anyone else wouldn't be."

Tiff hooted with laughter. "That's the best assessment of Zach the Twat that I've ever heard. I shall have to tell Richard that one." Yes, she thought, and I shall tell him how you spotted what a rodent Zachary is too! Come hell or high water, I shall get you this manager's job, my friend.

Oblivious to her friend's scheming, Jenna now moved on to what they were going to do for the day.

"Let's go out to Richard's Castle," she suggested. "There's a lovely old church I'd love to see out there, and then we could do one of the National Trust places, if you like. Croft Castle or Berrington Hall?"

Tiff looked them up on her phone and decided on Berrington, which wasn't a surprise to Jenna – a pretty mansion house was always going to win over a ruined castle and Iron Age fort for Tiff. And so the day was spent happily rummaging through the past, with them coming back to the hotel nicely in time to shower and relax before going to meet Mike. As they walked up the hill they could see him standing outside the office waiting for them.

"Blimey, he scrubs up well!" Tiff said approvingly. "Not sure about the tweed jacket with the elbow patches, mind you – that's either aging professor, geography teacher, or one of the hunting and shooting crowd in my book, and I don't see Mike as any of those."

"Oh, I don't know…"Jenna said softly as they got nearer. "To my eyes it looks more as though he buys good quality that he knows will last and last. He probably pays no less than nasty Zack does for his fancy rags, but Mike's will never go out of fashion or fall apart after twelve months."

Tiff sneaked a glance at Jenna and said, "So you approve?"

"About being sensible and practical? God, yes! …Where do you think we're going tonight?"

"*Ooooh*, I don't know." Tiff gave her a wink. "Ludlow's known for its Michelin-starred restaurants, you know – maybe he wants to impress us?"

Jenna stopped dead in her tracks, and when Tiff looked back at her she wished she could have sucked her words back in and swallowed them. All the light had gone out of Jenna as fast as a switch being flicked.

"I think I'd better go back to the hotel then, Tiff. I can't afford that kind of meal."

Tiff felt her own panic rising. Mike had already waved and was strolling towards them, this mustn't go wrong. "No, no, silly! I meant he might want to impress us!"

"But I couldn't ...I mean, I don't know him ...I don't work with him! I couldn't accept something expensive like that!"

Then Mike's cheerful voice came from behind her, "Something wrong?"

"No," Tiff said firmly, linking her arm through Jenna's so that she couldn't escape. "Just me putting my big foot in my mouth again as usual!" She swung into step with Mike, almost towing Jenna along with her. "So where are we going?"

Mike gave a beaming smile. "Somewhere I think you'll approve of," he said with a pointed look to Jenna.

He'd turned left at the top of the hill, taking them into the heart of the old town. Roads here were one-way out of necessity, because there was no way two vehicles could pass when the ancient buildings were so close together, but he then turned off again into an even narrower alleyway. Going under a brick archway, they were now into truly medieval Ludlow, where jettied upper storeys projected out over the narrow pavement, and though the buildings on the side adjoining the more main street running parallel to them were Georgian, on the other side they were definitely the older buildings.

"Oh *wow*!" Jenna gasped. "Oh look! You can tell these must have been the original merchants' houses facing onto an older, bigger, market place; and then later they built more houses within the market place, so these lovely old places effectively became shunted off down a side street."

Mike looked both impressed and pleased. "Well then I was right, you're going to love this place," and he pointed to a pub sign just up ahead which said *Rose & Crown*. As they came level with it, and before they turned in through the old gateway, he threw up a hand with a flourish to the sign on the wall.

Jenna read it then gave a squeak of delight. "1102! Oh my God, *1102*! Oh Mike, this is amazing, *oh wow*!"

Mike turned pink again, as Jenna walked into the courtyard with all the wonder of a child who had just been allowed through into Narnia.

"Gosh, this must be of a similar age as *The Trip to Jerusalem* in Nottingham," she breathed. "I wonder if this was originally the brew-house for the castle, too?"

Mike shrugged but pointed off to their left, saying, "Well the castle's only the other side of the little market square. I guess it's not impossible."

The food turned out to be lovely, but Tiff knew that for Jenna they could have been served a cardboard pizza with sawdust topping as long as she could have it here. It was a bustling place, and Mike had reserved them a table in the restaurant where they spent a happy couple of hours, Jenna opening up again and losing all of her wariness. To free up the table they moved down to the bar area, but even then Tiff was amazed to see that Jenna coped with the general noise of locals out on a Saturday night.

By the time they finally left Mike, who had gallantly walked them back to their hotel, and they got up to their room, Tiff was beginning to wonder whether Jenna wasn't right about her nervousness – maybe it was being in a big city at night and in the rain that dragged Jenna's nightmares back to the surface time and again?

"You were remarkably chilled out in the pub," she ventured to say, as Jenna flopped onto her bed and kicked off her shoes with a happy sigh.

"Was I?"

Tiff chose her next words carefully, not wanting a repeat of earlier in the evening. "Getting you stay even an hour in the pubs by the uni was always a struggle."

"Pubs? More like clubs," Jenna protested. "Full of people out to get off their heads. I never did like that kind of thing, even before you-know-what."

"And tonight was different for you?"

Jenna sat upright and fixed Tiff with a puzzled stare. "Well of course it was. For a start off there were a lot more older people in there, more families and proper couples. It all makes a difference, Tiff."

It also dawned on Tiff that there'd been no noise of traffic there – in no small measure because on-road parking was not easy to find, and everyone who came in from beyond walking distance used the public car parks on the fringes of the town centre. Was that another of Jenna's problems, that people had just driven by and not stopped to help her back on that dreadful night? If so then that was something else that was unlikely to happen in a tiny place like Ludlow. Presumably round here there'd always be some burly farmer's son who'd pull up in his truck and wade in to help?

Yet that only strengthened her resolve to get Jenna out of that horrid little flat. Moving away from Birmingham and the big city life had clearly helped a lot, but with Jenna still commuting up and down to the city it was as though she brought some of the anxiety back home with her each time. No, Tiff resolved, what Jenna needed was to move right away. To leave once and for all, and not go back.

Jenna interrupted her thoughts by saying, "I like the sound of Mike's house," around a stifled yawn, "and I can't wait to meet the dogs tomorrow."

As the evening had drawn to an end, Mike had invited them both around for Sunday lunch. His excuse of it being a thank you to Tiff for finally instilling some order into the office didn't fool her. It was Jenna he kept looking at to see if she was enjoying herself, and it had been her enthusiasm for meeting the dogs which had put a smile on his face.

Sunday morning dawned fair but chilly, and both of them donned thick sweaters, especially as Jenna declared her hope for being able to go for a walk with the dogs – this wasn't an occasion for Jimi Choos, Tiff decided with a sigh, rummaging to find the one pair of flat shoes she had with her. Mike had given clear directions on how to get to his house, and so having had only a light breakfast, again on Mike's instruction since he was doing a full roast, they set off.

"I wonder what sort of house Mike has?" Tiff said with a conspiratorial grin to Jenna.

"Well it won't be some flash place, thank God. Not like Nasty Zach, who probably has wall to wall chrome and mirrors to watch himself go by!"

Tiff inwardly sighed. Jenna's aspirations were so damned low, and there was nothing wrong in aiming a bit higher.

"I know he's only a junior member of our team, hon', but he is at the top of his pay increment level, you know. We don't pay our teams peanuts! He'll be on a heck of a lot more than the folks you work with, even your managers." Privately she was hoping that he would turn out to have one of the pretty black-and-white cottages so prevalent in the area. That would suit Jenna to a 'T', and he had seemed to be fairly knowledgeable about such old buildings, as if he might have more than just a nodding business acquaintance with them.

Yet when they turned into the tiny hamlet and Tiff's

sat-nav beeped to say they'd arrived, her heart sank. Oh no, this wasn't what she'd expected at all!

Jenna's exclamations of, "Oh what a sweet little place!" was hardly Tiff's reaction to the end one of a row of terraced brick cottages, and she had to really bite her tongue not to make some caustic remark. Okay, there was something which looked like a recent single storey extension on the side, but it was a far cry from her expectations. What was Mike thinking to be living in a place like this? He'd never be able to do any corporate entertaining here. But then Mike himself had opened the door and was beaming a smile of welcome at them, so she pasted her best professional smile on herself and got out of the car to join Jenna, who was already saying,

"Oh how lovely! A honeysuckle around the door!"

"An offspring of one from Mum's garden," Mike said enthusiastically. "Heaven knows what variety it is – definitely an old one – but the scent from it knocks spots off some of the ones you find in garden centres. Come on in."

Immediately they were greeted by the two lurchers coming and thrusting shaggy heads into their hands to be made a fuss of, and that Tiff didn't mind. She loved dogs, just didn't want the responsibility of one. Jenna, though, was crouching down so that she got affectionate licks on her cheeks as they both began leaning on her and nuzzling her.

"The long-dog lean," Mike said with a laugh as he managed to haul Silas off her before he pushed her over. "I'm afraid they all do it – greyhounds, wolfhounds, whippets. It's amazing they don't fall over more often, 'cause they seem to spend a fair bit of their lives leaning at a sixty degree angle on people, sofas, and anything else that appeals."

They'd managed to get beyond the tiny hall and into the lounge now, and if Tiff wasn't exactly echoing Jenna's coos of delight, at least she was rethinking her assessment of the place. What had once no doubt been a rather dark and gloomy living room had been opened out through to the kitchen, and was flooded with light from the ceiling-to-floor bi-fold glass doors that opened out from the kitchen onto what looked to be a small patio.

"Oh, Mike, this is lovely!" Jenna exclaimed.

He was doing that faint blush again as he explained, "Dad was a master carpenter, so I still have a few contacts in the trade. I knew I might need a place that I could mess around with, you see. Mum and Dad's house is a lovely half-timbered cottage, but because of the listing, you can't do much with it. That was okay while Dad was still alive, but once Mum was on her own I began to see that I might need to have her with me, and there's no way we could have installed things like bed-lifts into their place."

"There are such things as nursing home, you know," Tiff said, rather appalled that Mike should even have thought of nursing his mother while pursuing such a demanding career.

As Jenna glared at her for her tactlessness, Mike just shrugged and said, "I know, but the good ones don't come cheap – not when you might be looking at a decade of paying for them. Anyway, there's no way I could have put Mum into one until it became unavoidable. She'd have lost the will to live within a week. She's always been a country girl, through and through. Her dad was a gamekeeper on one of the big estates out on the Shropshire/Powys border, you see, and she met Dad back when he was apprenticed to a craftsman who specialising in restorations, and who came to do work on the big house. So when I moved back around here, I bought this place primarily for the garden and the view. I wanted her to be able to get outside at least on the nice days, not be cooped up in some over-heated modern rabbit-hutch where you can't even open the windows."

"Oh I so agree!" Jenna immediately empathised. "Normally on a Sunday I'm stuck in the back of a supermarket on the counters, never seeing daylight. You start to feel like a mole after a bit. And all that air conditioning isn't healthy. You get a bug come into our place and it rips through the workers like wildfire. Heaven knows what something like that would do in a place full of old folk. No, I totally get why you wouldn't want your mum in somewhere like that."

"A supermarket?" Mike gulped. "Good grief, aren't you wildly over-qualified for that?"

Jenna shrugged. "Yes, but some of us have to make do with the job we can get, not the job we want. ...Oh hell, that sound so 'poor me'. I didn't mean it like that. But the thing is, Mike, I've been having to stand on my own two feet without any back-up since I was sixteen. As soon as you turn sixteen that's you done and dusted with as far as the foster services are concerned, you see. Tough luck if you don't have anywhere to go – that's another department's problem, not theirs. So right from when I was that age, I've had jobs in shops of one description or another, because they're the people who want the cheap labour. Unfortunately, despite my master's degree, that tag of 'shop girl' seems to dog me at every turn when it comes to interviews."

Behind Jenna's back Tiff was making frantic 'stop' signals to Mike and mouthing, 'I'll explain later', and so he just smiled wanly and said,

"Would you like to see the rest of the place? ...Crap, I don't mean dragging you up to my bedroom ...bloody hell, that didn't come out right either! I meant the lounge and the garden!"

To his great relief, Jenna just laughed and said, "I'd love to see the garden," and so he took them through to the new extension, where there was a lovely lounge, again with the bi-fold doors opening to the patio.

"What I always thought would be mum's room is behind this, through that door, with an en-suite wet-room with wheelchair access," he said with a wave of his hand towards what was clearly the other half of the new extension as he opened one of the doors, and let the dogs go bounding through ahead of them.

"Thought?" Jenna picked up on. "Has something changed, then?"

Mike gave a sad little shrug. "Bowel cancer. She's in a hospice now."

Tiff gasped. "Oh God, Mike, I'm so sorry! We shouldn't be piling stress on you at work now if you're handling that!"

However, Mike just shrugged again. "She's already beaten the odds, Tiff. They gave her six months a year ago, and she hasn't gone yet. I love her dearly, but there's only so long you can go on putting your life on hold. It'll happen one day, but there's nothing to be gained by moping about waiting for it to happen. I call in to see her every other day, and that's all I can really do. For the rest it's down to the doctors and nurses. The only thing that gets to me these days is the unfairness of it. Mum never smoked a single day in her life, and she thought she was pushing the boat out to have a sherry with her Sunday roast. She used to walk for miles with the dogs we had when I was a kid, and even when she got older she was always out in the garden doing something. She was as fit as anyone of her age could be. Always ate good food – for God's sake, half of it came from her own garden! She's just been unlucky."

Desperately trying to change the subject without being too obvious, Tiff said, "So will you move into your parent's home at some point, then? It sounds as though you love the place."

Mike's face broke into a smile. "Oh yes, I do love it! But at the moment I've got a tenant in there. It seemed the sensible thing to do. I can get far more a month for that place than I would for here, and that all goes on Mum's care, so I feel it's worth it." He paused and then said, "Actually that's reminded me of something – I'll tell you over lunch."

Chapter 6

After a less mournful hour in the garden, first with Jenna admiring the plants – which she amazed Tiff by knowing far more of the names of than she would have believed – and then both Jenna and Tiff being prevailed upon to throw toys for the dogs, Mike declared that he'd better put the vegetables on. It was then that Tiff got chance to sneak inside while Jenna was still playing tugs with Silas and Marnie, and to rapidly fill Mike in on Jenna's situation.

"So I'm bloody desperate to get her out of there," she concluded. "Will you back me up to try and get her appointed as your office manager?"

"Absolutely!" Mike declared vehemently, then gave her a wink. "And I'm glad you told me this. That thing I was telling you about? Well it might serve as a bridge until we can get the office running properly."

He didn't say more because at the chink of cutlery, the two dogs came trotting in, noses twitching and clearly knowing that food was about to be served, and Jenna followed them. She and Tiff sipped their wine, sitting on the extremely comfortable squashy sofas, while Mike chatted to them while bustling about in the kitchen area.

When lunch came it turned out to be a joint of local Hereford beef that almost fell apart without the need for the knife, vegetables from his garden, and Yorkshire puddings that had even Tiff rolling her eyes in pleasure.

"Good grief, Mike, you could have a second career as a chef!" she said, raising her glass in a silent toast to him, after he'd produced an amazing lemon pudding from the Aga for dessert, which they devoured with relish. "So come on then, what is it that you were mysteriously alluding to in the garden?"

Mike looked faintly sheepish. "Well it's not exactly a mystery. But having had no trouble in getting a tenant for Mum's place, I've been astonished at how hard it's been to get a house sitter for one of our clients."

"Why a sitter?" Tiff queried. "Why not a tenant or a sale?"

"Ah," Mike said pointedly, "thereby hangs a tale!"

"A tale?" gasped Jenna. "Oh do tell! I love a good mystery!"

Mike laughed. "Well I don't know about a mystery, but here goes: we have quite a lot of wealthy clients from around here, but for once this one wasn't one that either Zachary or Mr Hornby wanted to deal with. For a start off he was a builder and a pretty coarse sort of bloke, but he was also damned shrewd, and he saw through those two from the word go. For reasons I've never fully understood, he made it a condition of bringing his work to us that I'd be the one to deal with it. My best guess is that it wasn't because he particularly liked me, but he watched me tearing around like a demented bumblebee the first time he visited the office, and I think he thought that I was far too busy with other stuff to run his bills up just sitting around doing nothing." He pulled a face. "I suppose I'm saying that he was just plain tight with his money.

"Well I did several conveyancing jobs for him in the first couple of years I was here. He specialised in doing small developments of expensive houses. So mostly no more than half a dozen at a time, always in really prime locations, and selling at premium prices."

"Very much the kind of client we need," Tiff agreed approvingly. "And I presume he brought this work in pretty regularly?"

"Oh yes. He usually had a couple of developments on the go at any one time. So one lot would be at the initial stage, getting the footings and ground work in, while the other would have the basic external work finished and be on to things like the wiring and plumbing. For the last two projects he did, I even dealt with the planning applications for him, and that's kind of significant because it means I know a fair bit about where these last three houses are.

"You see Brian Willetts got lung cancer. No big surprise there. Of course he couldn't smoke in our office, but you'd see him standing outside, chain-smoking a couple or three to get him through the time he was in here, and he always lit up again as soon as he was out of the door. His lungs must have had more tar in them than half the drives he put in."

"*Yuk!*" Jenna said with a wrinkle of her nose. "I bet he stank of it, didn't he?"

Mike smiled. "Even in the depths of winter, as soon as I heard him coming up the stairs I used to open the office window, and Delia used to find some excuse to work in Mr Hornby's office – not just because of the cold but the smell. Then we'd go round with the air-freshener after he'd gone, especially the seat he'd used, because his own clothes must have been so impregnated they used to leave the smell clinging to our stuff. ...So anyway, you can see why nobody was exactly astonished when he was diagnosed and only given six months. And like so many men of his sort, it was only then that he thought about making a will.

"Well I tried to advise him. Told him that what he wanted to do was bound to cause problems, but he wouldn't have it. It was his money and property he said, and he'd dispose of it how he wanted, and that was that. If I wouldn't do it his way, he said, he'd go elsewhere. Not that I thought anyone else in the town would want him – he'd worn out his welcome with every other law firm in the area long ago – and there was the part of me that thought it was pretty churlish to start picking a fight with him in his last days."

"So what did he want to do?" Tiff wondered, getting a top-up on her wine. "What was so difficult?"

Mike rolled his eyes. "Willetts has three daughters, and after what I've told you of him, you won't be surprised to know that none of them would have thrown water on him if he was on fire. He'd managed to estrange all of them – not that on subsequent meeting I found any of them to be particularly endearing or nice people, either. These apples didn't fall very far from his tree, I'm afraid. But in his last months, I think Willetts wanted to try and reunite them with one another, even if they wouldn't visit or speak to him.

"He'd built this glorious development out towards the border, you see. There's a large pool, big enough to have fish in it and for you to be able to take a rowing boat out on if you liked, and he had three houses built around the one side. I think the reason he got planning permission for that and other projects was because he specialised in wooden houses, and by that I mean the luxury Scandinavian sort. But I think some of the councils looked at the construction and thought that these weren't the kind of places that would be there for centuries, and if necessary they would be easy to remove if they became eyesores. So he got in where other kinds of plans wouldn't.

"So far so good. But I think his acumen must have been failing a bit by the time he got to this last project, because the location is just all wrong. Yes, it's in a stunning spot, but it's remote – or at least, too remote for people to commute to and from on a daily basis. Of course, he thought his daughters and their families would be using them as holiday homes, but they want none of that. They want the houses sold and the money from them."

"Oh dear," Tiff said sympathetically, "so already you're into breaking the clauses of the will with regard to the future sale of the properties. If he wanted them to stay within the family, but they want none of it, it does put you in a difficult position. I see what you mean about complicated."

Mike nodded. "And not helped by stipulations that none of the houses can be sold individually. I know why he did it. He didn't want one sister bailing out then leaving the other two living with a potentially disruptive neighbour – but to be honest, it would be the neighbour I'd feel sorry for."

He sighed and poured them some more coffee, taking Jenna's over to her as she was pinned under the two hounds, who were bookending her on the one sofa, a head resting on each knee.

"It didn't help that the houses weren't quite finished when Willetts died. So there was that delay. Then the sisters were finally persuaded to go and at least look at them, but I had to go out three separate times because they refused to all go on the same day. At that point they each categorically refused to have anything to do with the houses except the money from them. Well I've tried to sell them, but I'm still trying to get this damned clause lifted that insists that they can't be broken into three separate units for a sale, and of course I haven't had so much as a sniff for three houses all together. Each one on its own ought to fetch the thick end of six hundred thousand, but put together I'm trying to find someone with a cool one-

and-a-half million to spend – and anyone with that sort of money wants one super luxury house, not three. And as you can imagine, the daughters aren't inclined to drop the price!"

Tiff was starting to wear a pained expression. "Bloody hell, Mike, that's a nightmare. So where are you with this now?"

Mike mirrored her look of dismay. "Well I've tried all ends up to get tenants for the places. It took me no small effort to get the sisters to see sense on that one, but at least they're grasping enough to recognise that designer eco houses would demand a fairly steep rent, and some money is better than none. But as soon as I take someone around the places, and they see how far off the road they are, they're not interested. Most people with that kind of money are looking to work in Shrewsbury, you see, and it's just not viable.

"So I've tried a new tack with the sisters, which is to get the places let out for holiday homes for a while, or at least until I can break the terms of the will – which would be a whole lot easier if the three of them as the benefactors would stop bickering, and just let me do my job! But for that to work I think we need someone on-site all the time. You see, we're a bit late to get much for this season. Most places are already booked up, so it'll only be last minute bookings, and we need to be flexible enough to cope with that. And I'm deeply concerned about leaving those places all empty during the summer months. In the winter nobody would go out that way, but with the better weather coming, it's just tempting fate for some bunch of travellers to spot it and start squatting in the houses."

Tiff's groan of dismay all by itself told Jenna that that would be disastrous. "I'm guessing that once they were in, getting them out again would be horrendous?" she presumed, and got nods from both Tiff and Mike.

"And that's before you take into account the damage," Tiff added. "Our office has dealt with a few cases like this, and in every one you find that the sods have ripped out kitchens and sold the units, not to mention the bathrooms. You're lucky if there are even any light fittings left!"

"And that," Mike said firmly, "is why I'm looking for a house sitter. Not that I'd expect them to tackle any marauding travellers," he added hurriedly. "That'd be a case of locking the doors and calling the police. But it would be far easier to get the coppers out if I can say I've got a lone caretaker in the travellers' sights, rather than just an empty house. And getting them out within the day to get shot of trespassers is a whole different thing than me turning up and finding they've been encamped there for a fortnight already. Of course I don't expect that to happen, but I'd be foolish not to allow for it. And if we're to let these places for holidays, then at the very least I need someone to go in and clean the place between visitors and put clean sheets on the beds." And it was at that point when he turned to Jenna with a smile and said, "How would you fancy being our caretaker for the summer?"

As Jenna's jaw dropped, Tiff clapped her hands in delight. "Oh Mike! That's just perfect!"

"But my job," Jenna protested weakly. "It sounds lovely, really it does, but I need my permanent job. There's no way I have enough leave – let alone them allowing me to pick and choose when I have it at such notice."

"Good Heavens," Mike protested, "I didn't mean unpaid! And I wouldn't be much of a solicitor if I couldn't get you a car of some sorts out of the deal. Couldn't you ask for unpaid leave from your job?"

"Yes!" Tiff leapt in. "Christ, Jenna, you always say that your overtime vanishes just when you need it over the summer because of the students they take back. Well let them have the bloody students! They won't be going back until well into September, and if I haven't found you a better job to go to after that then I'd be utterly ashamed of myself. Come on!" she pushed, seeing Jenna begin to waiver. "You'd have no expenses here, just your food, and we'd more than cover what you pay in rent on the bloody flat of yours. How long have you been without any sort of a break? Too damned long, that's for sure! Well this would be a good three month break at a minimum, and it's one you jolly well deserve. Come on, Jenna, be kind to yourself for once!"

Seeing her still undecided, Mike added, "When I said they were in the wrong place, I don't mean they're out in the back of beyond. You're well within reach of Ludlow, and Knighton's even closer, but I suppose your nearest village would be Clun or Bishop's Castle. But they're down twisting lanes in the heart of Clun Forest, and that's what makes the commute to Shrewsbury so bad. Get stuck behind a farm tractor and you could add half-an-hour onto your journey, no trouble. There are plenty of farms around there, though. In fact, one of them is one of our clients. I'm sure if we explained the situation to him he'd be willing to be an emergency back-up for you – he and his wife are really nice people."

He put on his most pleading expression. "The big thing for me, Jenna, is that I know you'd be trustworthy. I could interview a dozen people and I'd still have to take a chance on what they put down in the way of references and stuff, and to be frank, I haven't had a single application. If it had been a house in Shrewsbury, for instance, or Ludlow, I'd have been inundated with applicants, but there aren't many people who enjoy that much peace and quiet who haven't already relocated out into the country."

Jenna's head was spinning. All her reserves – those survival instincts which told her not to take risks – were screaming at her not to take the offer, but the other part of her was practically weeping with joy just at the thought. A whole summer of not having to deal with ratty customers taking their frustrations out on her. A whole summer of actually being able to enjoy the nicer weather. Damn it, even if it turned out to be the wettest summer on record, just to be out in the countryside and able to go for walks in her wellies would be bliss.

And what she'd not told Tiff yet was about her awful new section manager – another lad barely into his twenties who thought he knew everything, and who only wanted the girls who gazed adoringly at his good looks. The fact that he was a spiteful brat to anyone else, seemed to be something the store management were either turning a blind eye to, or were too incompetent to see. And Jenna had been down this route before. There was always a brisk turnover of the junior management, as they got shunted around the store to expand their experience, and three managers previously they had inflicted another such monster on the counters' staff. That time it had been two of the older men who had been bullied out of their jobs, but Jenna knew that sooner or later she would come into the crosshairs and one of these types would decide that he didn't want her on his section. And despite Tiff's outrage at these practices, and her saying that it was illegal, Jenna knew that the reality was that amongst poorly paid retail workers these big companies got away with murder, because nobody had the clout to stand up to them, not even the unions.

"Come on, hon'," Tiff said gently, coming to crouch in front of her friend and taking one of her hands and chafing it. "You said yourself you won't get any teaching come the new uni year. And you could bring your exam marking out here and take it back in as needed – and the 'A' level marking! You don't *have* to do that in your crumby flat, do you? You could do it in a nice house looking out over a pond. Wouldn't that be so much nicer?"

"Yes it would," Jenna agreed weakly, feeling her resolve starting to weaken.

"And you being rested and more your old self after a proper break, will help you see a new job in a better light. I don't want to see you staggering into some new job already on your knees, so that it seems like you're trying to climb some impossible mountain. What I'm thinking of, you could practically do with your eyes closed when you're well. We just need to get you back there." Then she decided to drop the bomb if it would push Jenna the right way.

"Look, I didn't want to say anything about this before, because I didn't want to upset you. But after Christmas, I'm not going to be around for three months. We're opening a new office in Strasburg to take advantage of the EU headquarters there – I'm not sure how that will work out if we come out of Europe, mind you, but Richard says it would be better in that case for us to have a foot in the door before it closes. Well he wants me to go with him to set the place up. And I'm really excited about that.

"But after the way I found you the other week, I'm also worried sick about leaving you where you are. I really, really want you far away from Claire, for one thing. If she doesn't even know where you are, then she can't cause trouble, can she? And you could be upfront with the housing association. Tell them straight that you have the chance of a three month job you can't afford to turn down, and that you'll have accommodation provided. That way they'll know the flat is temporarily empty, just in case idiot Kyle causes trouble. …Come on, Jenna. You can leave all that behind you once and for all."

Jenna got up and put her coffee cup down, the dogs getting up with her as if tuned in to her distress. "Let me think for a moment, will you?"

She let herself out of the door and walked off down the garden, the two dogs shadowing her like bodyguards.

"Will she do it?" Mike asked worriedly. "We haven't scared her off, have we? I mean, you she'll take a certain amount from, but she hardly knows me. I must admit I hadn't realised what a rough life she's had until you told me today, and part of me wishes I'd waited until she got to know me better."

However Tiff was already shaking her head. "No, Mike, you did the right thing. You didn't know it, but you only had two more days to get to her, because by Wednesday she'll be fretting about getting back in time to go to work on Friday."

Mike rubbed his hands over his face, then sat staring off into space as he said, "Half of me wonders why on earth she put up with that job for so long, but I've met enough vulnerable people in my time to get that she needed an anchor in her life. …God, I've been so bloody lucky. My parents backed me at every turn, and my sisters too. I'll never really know how it must have felt to have no safety net from so young an age."

Tiff nodded. "My parents have been distant all my life, but at least I always had a home to go to, or rather, at least somewhere that was a roof over my head, and where I knew I'd be fed and warm. But I had enough lack of parental enthusiasm to at least be able to grasp some of what Jenna's been through.

"And another thing, Mike, is that she was just going home from work on that night she was attacked, you know. Another late shift, and her walking home alone.

Bloody awful though my parents can be at times, if nothing else, Dad would give me the money for a taxi ride home when I was that age, even if he couldn't be bothered to come and collect me himself. But I think another part of her stress is that she's still doing those dreadful late shifts, and she's *still* walking home alone. I know Malvern's a far cry from inner Birmingham, but it still must dredge up an awful lot of unwanted memories every time she does that. It's another reason why I want to get her into a nice stable nine-to-five job before I vanish off after Christmas – no more bloody late nights!"

Mike gave her a wan smile. "At the absolute worst I'll get her the job of clerk in our office. I can't imagine it will be more than a day or so before Delia hands in her notice. She was always very much old Hornby's secretary, even though her job description is as clerk, and she should help all of us. She's appalled at the way you two have swooped in on his territory, and she's been reduced to tears by Zachary so many times I can't think for a second that she'd ever work for him."

Tiff gave him a high-five, but added, "Now we've just got to get Zach the Twat out! He gives Jenna the creeps, and I'm not sure how she'd cope with one of his tantrums, even with all the rest of her stresses removed."

"Oh, I wouldn't worry too much about him," Mike said, leaning back to grab the bottle of wine and refill their glasses. "I'll get you a taxi back to the hotel by the way. No, Zach won't linger long without the buffer of old Hornby. And that's not just me being unduly optimistic, either. As soon as we knew this whole shake up was really happening, he's been dropping hints about him having something better on the horizon. My guess is that he's been putting feelers out for quite a while down in London and now he's pushing a bit harder. I think the only thing holding him back is waiting to see if he gets senior partner here, because he would have to wait longer to get that status in a new firm."

Tiff snorted. "Then I think I need to push my boss to have a frank phone call with him! …Oh, here she comes! …Well, hon', what's your answer?"

Jenna looked pale but determined. "I want to see the place first, okay? I have to know that I'm not going to feel scared to death out there on my own. But as long as it's okay, then yes, I'll take the house-sitter's job."

Chapter 7

Tiff happily paid for a second taxi to take them back to Mike's to retrieve her car on Monday morning, not least because she already had a plan in place. Mike had quietly offered Tiff the use of the twin spare room the previous night, rather than drive when he realised how much she had drunk, but equally feared that it might really freak Jenna out; and in turn Tiff had said that she needed to get back to make a phone call anyway, and so they had left with a local taxi. On Sunday evening she had therefore retreated into the bathroom and had a long conversation with her boss out of Jenna's hearing, and had emerged with a Cheshire cat grin but would say nothing more. Once at Mike's on Monday, though, she broke her news.

"Mike, you need to take Jenna to see the houses this morning."

"This morning? But ...but I can't! I'm duty solicitor again! And anyway, Monday's always nuts with calls when the drunks of the weekend have sobered up enough to realise how much trouble they're in and start screaming for a legal representative. "

Tiff shook her head. "No *you* aren't on duty – the *firm* is. And if Zach the Twat doesn't take those calls, even if it's only one, then he's in deep shit." That was said with a smirk of satisfaction. "Richard is also going to make a personal call to dearest Zachary, and I want you well out of the way when the explosion comes after it. He can scream himself hoarse at me and Suzy – we don't have to share an office with him beyond the next week or so – so let him blame us for telling tales to HQ. You don't need that additional grief.

"Anyway," she said with an even smugger grin, "you're genuinely out on client business, aren't you? Finding a sitter for this prestigious client is just as valid as sorting out the drunks. Go on, take Jenna out to see this place that's so hard to get anyone to buy, and leave the office to Suzy and me to deal with."

In something of a daze, Mike helped Jenna up into his Land Rover, and put Silas and Marni into the back. "She's quite the force of nature, isn't she?" he said in bemused tones, as he pulled away in the wake of Tiff zipping off in the Smart Sport.

"Tell me about it," Jenna laughed. "I've got used to it now, and in fairness she's got more like this from working in a bustling corporate office. When we were students she was always determined, but she wasn't quite so forceful – she'd have scared me to death if she had been."

It was one of those deceptive English spring mornings, beautifully and sunny with wisps of white fluffy clouds drifting high up in an otherwise clear sky, but with a definite crisp nip still in the air. It felt ripe with new beginnings, and it was impossible for Jenna not to feel that she was somehow embarking on a wonderful adventure. They drove back far enough into Ludlow to pick up the A49 as it bypassed the town, but only carried on northwards as far as Bromfield before turning off west. They passed though the pretty village of Leintwardine, making Jenna gasp in surprise, as she realised that they were following the course of the same River Teme which flowed into the River Severn near where she lived, but here much higher up its course. But then the countryside began to change again. In a very short time they were into the Shropshire Hills, where wooded slopes twisted and turned, forcing the roads to do the same.

"Oh this is so pretty," Jenna sighed wistfully. "I've never been this far west before, never knew it was so lovely. I always thought you had to get right into Wales before you got such beautiful scenery."

"Well it's not as grand as the Welsh mountains," Mike admitted, "but I've always had a soft spot for our own rugged bits. I've spent many a happy weekend out with the dogs round here." Then he grinned at her and added, "And for you as a medievalist, there are enough castles around here to keep even you satisfied. Clun for one. It wasn't just some scruffy border outpost, you know, it was very much the big, prestigious castle. You definitely want to have a look around that."

"Castles?" breathed Jenna. "You have castles? *Oooh*!"

"Yep," Mike chuckled, "and proper castles too – none of your pretend Victorian piles out here. Clun, Stokesay, and of course Wigmore, you can't ignore Wigmore, seat of the Mortimers."

Jenna's eyes had widened into saucers. "Oh my God! I can't believe I didn't remember that! Of course, the Mortimers – they were such key players for centuries, especially in the reigns of the King Edwards – one, two *and* three. I mean, I knew they had their power from being one of the royal watchdogs on the Welsh borders, it's just that I never envisaged them coming from such a wonderfully wild sort of place. I thought their side of the border was more typically English – you know, neat tended fields and hedgerows kind of thing, more like Worcestershire which I know."

Mike laughed. "Not much neat about these hills. No, it was this rough terrain that made them such formidable men to cross. You can see how someone could set themselves up as king of their own little domain here, can't you? Because it would be the very devil to winkle someone out of when most of the castles are up on high ground, and your own folk would send you warnings of any strangers in the area."

"Oh yes. And I've just thought of something else. It's not that much further north of here where we think the poem *Gawain and the Green Knight* was written, albeit just over the border into Cheshire. But looking at this land now, I can just imagine how you could believe that there would be some wild creature attached to the land, some knight who was more Green Man than human."

"Well it's not quite that wild nowadays, but I could well believe that seven or eight hundred years ago this might have seemed a very dangerous region to anyone used to the softer shires." He'd turned off again, and now they were heading northwards again on an even smaller road. "This is what I meant about it being terrible for commuting," he explained. "The other way here would have been to turn off in Leintwardine and go north and then turn west, at which point you'd eventually be coming down south on this road we're going north on, but it's a hell of a detour whichever way. You can't avoid doing a big loop either way you come at it, and if either the Teme or the River Clun is in flood – and if one is, you can bet the other one will be – then the roads can sometimes get closed off altogether. Outsiders often buy in to these little villages and only last a couple of years before the reality of living in the countryside bites."

They passed through another tiny village with a church lying back from the road.

"At least that one has a pub," Mike laughed. "The other one north of here only has a church!"

"Gosh, what a hotbed of vice and iniquity!" Jenna joked back. "What do the local kids do on a Saturday night?"

"Come into Ludlow and get pissed," Mike replied dryly, "hence me being busy on a Monday morning – usually. I have to say that this is far more fun!"

And looking at the way the worried frown had vanished from his forehead, Jenna realised what a weight Mike must be carrying for much of the time. Whatever else Tiff's scheming might be bringing about, it made Jenna glad that they were out here this morning, and it was only reinforcing her belief that Mike had shouldered most of the burden of keeping the Ludlow office open for too long. Tiff could well be being over-confident about her ability to sway her boss, but Jenna had no doubts that her friend had the measure of the ghastly Zachary, and that he would walk away from the job rather than deal with the dregs of Ludlow. As if reading her mind, Mike said,

"Not that we have any custody suites at Ludlow police station. Anyone who actually needs to be locked up has to be taken to Shrewsbury, so it's more likely that someone there will get the job of going into an interview with the real bad boys in that instance. But it doesn't mean that some of our locals don't wake up on Monday morning and suddenly realise what they did over the weekend is going to land them in seriously hot water. And heaven help us, even out here we do have our own small coterie of persistent offenders, who aren't much fun to be around when they're nursing a good hangover."

"Then I hope they puke on Zach's posh boots," Jenna said cheerfully. "I can't think of a better bloke for that to happen to."

Mike took his eyes off the twisting road long enough to shoot Jenna a surprised glance. "Wow, you really don't like him, do you?"

"No, I don't." Then she realised that she needed to explain a bit more if he wasn't to think that she was the sort of air-head who just took random dislikes to men who'd done her no harm. "I know his sort, Mike. God help me, I've suffered enough at their hands. And I'm not talking about my being attacked, either. When you work at the lower end of the employment market, as I do, you find yourself at the mercy of your managers, and supermarkets hardly attract the shining lights of this world. Let's face it, if you could get something better, you certainly wouldn't be working late nights and every weekend, and getting your ear bent by irate customers out of choice, especially when most of those complaints are more in the customer's head than anything you could hope to do something about."

She gave a bitter laugh. "We really do get the ones nobody else wants. Granted, many of them are in those positions because they're just not that bright. They don't have what it takes to do something more high-powered, even if they fancy that they do. And it's a shocking comment on our society that I'm far from being the only highly-qualified graduate working for such idiots, simply because *we* can't get anything else either.

"But in amongst the inept and confused, you get a small but significant number of managers who are so like Zachary. They come from families where they've been filled with a misguided sense of their own entitlement." She gave Mike a lopsided smile. "I mean, their mums and dads have had enough money to send them to some sort of minor private school, for a start off. So they've never really mixed with us ordinary mortals. They've never had school friends whose dads have been laid off from a job through no fault of their own, for instance, and who as a result can't go on the next school trip, or whatever, because mum and dad just can't afford it. The people who fall out of *their* social circles either just vanish from view – because once the fancy house has been repossessed and the money stops flowing, they can't join in the endless-bottles-of-champagne lunches, etc. – or they're such out and out crooks that they get locked up.

"Honestly, Mike, we've had two managers like Zach in the time I've had my current job. Both of them spoiled brats. Both of them products of minor public schools, but so utterly useless that there's nowhere else to go employment-wise that would even begin to satisfy their egos. Because people like that have to have power over somebody. They have to be able to mix with their fancy friends and say, "Oh, well I'm the *manager* at so-and-so's," knowing full well that their 'friends' haven't a clue what that really means – they've just heard the word 'manager' and equated that with power."

Her voice became filled with disgust as she added, "In both cases I had over a year of my life being made absolute hell by them. So I had plenty of time to get to know them and what they were. Over that kind of time you have plenty of opportunities to see them as they really are, and to recognise those traits when you see them again."

Mike threw her another worried glance. "It was that bad?"

"Oh yes! To the extent that I said that if ever one of them came back to our store, my notice would be written and on the manager's desk within the hour, and I'd be out the door – even if that meant I was reduced to camping in a tent on the Malverns in midwinter! And believe me, I don't make reckless promises like that without damned good reason."

"But what about the unions?"

Jenna laughed bitterly. "Unions? Mike, the unions that represent us shop workers don't have any clout. The best they could do would be to help represent you if you got unjustly accused of stealing something. And even then, you wouldn't get your job back. All they'd be doing is clearing your name so that you might have a vague hope of getting another job — and the way the various store managers within an area talk to one another, you'd pretty much guarantee that you'd have to move well away from where you were." She saw his growing look of horror. "Oh yes, it's that petty. Offend one and you offend them all — or rather, they won't take a chance on you. I've known stores that have absolutely haemorrhaged staff because of bullying, and yet still the other stores in the area are wary of taking one or two of those people on. Somehow it's never the manager in question's fault, nor his immediate underlings'.

"So I hope you understand now why I'm so wary of Zachary. It's not just because he's loathsome — and he is! It's that from where I'm coming from, I see him as downright dangerous." She huffed disgustedly. "In fact, I'd say to you to be very, very careful around him for the next few weeks. Because men like him get dangerously spiteful when they feel they're being cornered. He can't do much about Tiff and Suzy because *a)* they'll be gone soon anyway; and *b)* because he's not their boss, and they're too highly thought of by people who really know them for him to be able to tarnish their reputations much. But you be careful, Mike, because if I'm not mistaken, he'll soon start seeing this mess he's got himself into as your fault, and he'll do everything he can to either push the blame onto you; or if he can't do that, then to make you pay — as he sees it — for putting him in such a bad light. God forbid that he should take the blame himself! Because the Zachs of this world can't ever take criticism."

Then seeing the worried frown come back, Jenna wished she hadn't been quite so blunt. But on the other hand, she would have felt dreadful if a nice bloke like Mike had come to grief at Zach's hands and she had never tried to warn him. No, better to have had her say and know that she had done her best. If Mike chose to disregard her, then that was his choice, and there wasn't much she could do about that. And she did feel rather obliged to him, because if this house-sitting job did come off, then he would have done her an immense favour. She wasn't quite filled with Tiff's optimism just yet that some great job was just around the corner to fill the rest of this year, but she wasn't such a sad case that she couldn't relish the prospect of taking some time to just step away from her endless daily grind. Even if this only turned out to be a couple of months living out in the wilds, and not doing her groundhog-day life for a while, it would be a blessing she was ready to grab with both hands.

When Mike turned off the proper road, which itself was a lane only just about capable of allowing two cars to pass, Jenna got a real feeling of just how isolated the houses were likely to be. Having turned off in the first village Mike had described, he assured her that the minor road they had been on for some miles only continued beyond where they were heading for another three miles before connecting with the main A488 going down into Knighton, but to Jenna they could have been tens of miles from civilisation. Now they were climbing up a rough track of a road which wasn't even properly metalled, with steep valley walls on either side of it, a small stream trickling down to join the River Redlake back at the proper road, and not another vehicle in sight.

Yet the oddest thing was that Jenna realised that she wasn't the slightest bit intimidated by this landscape. The woods were mixed natives trees, not the forbidding ranks of Forestry Commission pine plantations, and the air smelled clean and fresh. Sheep were dotted across the distant hillsides, and there was something altogether wholesome about the place.

"So what do you think of the Shropshire Hills?" Mike asked, changing down a gear again as the incline got even steeper.

"Amazing!" Jenna gasped. Then she gave a squeak of amazement as Mike turned into a driveway, and almost immediately she saw two of the three houses in front of her, and the small lake they were on the edge of. "Oh, my God! This is idyllic!"

The three houses were very close to one another, and yet had been cleverly angled so that they didn't look at one another at all. A small tarmacked drive led across the back of all three houses, presumably to avoid spoiling the view at the front, and Jenna could see that three detached garages lay on the left side as the house sat on the drive's right. Ultra modern, the houses had nonetheless been faced using pale timber, or bleached wood, which softened their impact on this untamed spot.

The first one they could see had a balcony projecting out from what Jenna guessed would be the master bedroom, and by some architectural wizardry the balcony managed to be large enough to allow for a table and chairs, yet without there being any supporting pillars below. Instead, the balcony's overhang provided shelter for the room-wide patio doors of the lounge beneath it, and for the lovely seating area they gave out onto. A bay windowed room on the other side of another pair of glass doors then allowed further views out across the lake.

The second house was different altogether. This one had a sloped projecting roof which made it look like the prow of some Viking ship, with floor-to-ceiling windows which were angled, rising the full two floors and emphasising the point. On one side the roof was longer, coming down in a continuous slope to cover a single storey set of rooms, with the upper floor having inset roof-lights. On the other side it had the appearance of a more conventional roof, allowing for side windows in the first floor roofs. Despite being asymmetrical, it was a beautiful house, the jutting roof providing cover for a colonial style veranda facing the lake.

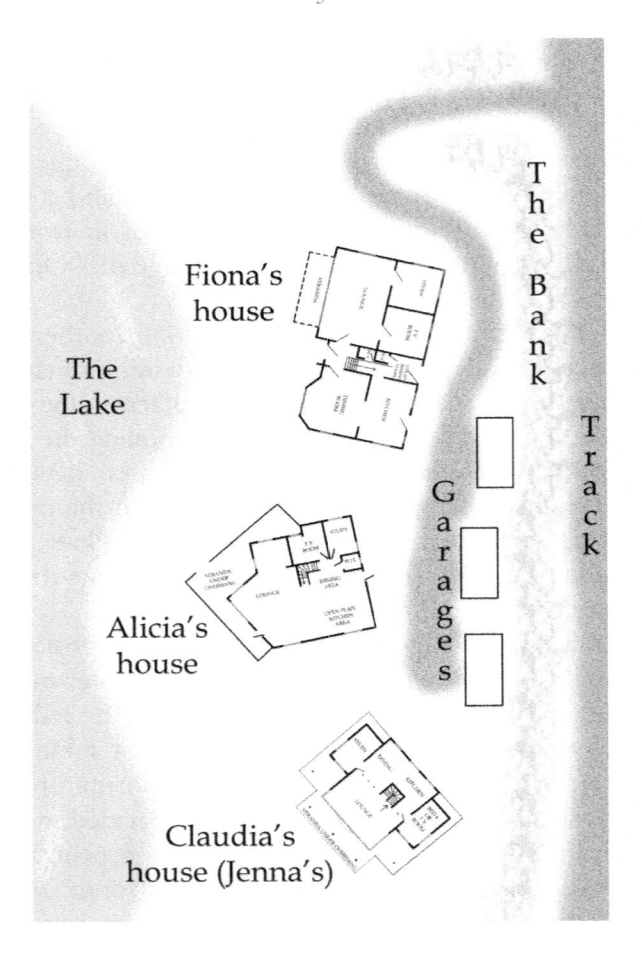

"Oh Mike, how on earth can somebody not want to live here?" she breathed.

He had come around to her side and now helped her down from the Land Rover, going to the back and letting

Silas and Marnie out. The two hounds promptly streaked off, tearing around the open grassed area with excited yips as they took it in turns to chase one another.

"Well I won't need to walk them tonight," Mike said with a laugh. "By the time we leave they'll be exhausted. ...But in answer to your question, just remember how long it's taken us to get here, and then imagine doing that every morning and evening – even in the winter."

Jenna sighed. "I suppose so. But in this day and age, a lot of professionals work from home. You wouldn't think it would be that hard to do here. After all, some folk do it out on the Scottish islands, and if the internet connections here aren't as good as the cities, they must be way better than out there. And if you were any sort of artist the quality of light would be an absolute gift; or to an author, or even a screen writer, surely the peace and quiet out here would be a boon?"

All Mike could do was shrug. "If that's the case, then all I can say is that they haven't been beating a track to my door. Come on, I'll show you around."

He took out a bunch of keys and made for the first house. "This is the largest of the three, but only by virtue of the master bedroom having a dressing room as well as an en-suite. The far house is the smallest, having only one en-suite." He gestured to where Jenna could now see that the third house was more of a bungalow, having only a small upper floor under the eaves, but still with a jutting roof which made the huge veranda almost another room.

"Tut!" Jenna giggled. "What a deal breaker! How have I ever coped without two en-suites?"

Mike laughed with her. "I know. How the other half live, eh?" He threw open the door from the hall into the lounge with a flourish. "And here, Lady Jenna, is where your butler will serve you afternoon tea."

Fiona's house

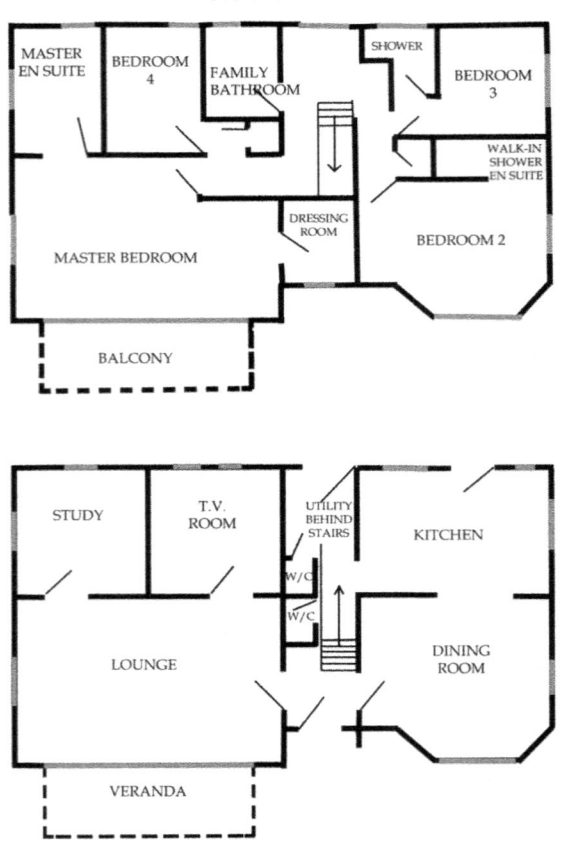

[Floor plan of upper floor showing: Master En Suite, Bedroom 4, Family Bathroom, Shower, Bedroom 3, Walk-in Shower En Suite, Dressing Room, Bedroom 2, Master Bedroom, and Balcony.]

[Floor plan of ground floor showing: Study, T.V. Room, Utility Behind Stairs, Kitchen, W/C, W/C, Lounge, Dining Room, and Veranda.]

Jenna put a dramatic hand to her forehead in Victorian melodrama style. "I don't know how Jeeves is going to cope," she joked. "We'll have to get the Earl Grey flown in by helicopter," and they both laughed. Then she looked down at the floor and her expression changed to one of horror. "White carpets? *Pure white?* You have got to be joking! What idiot thought they would be a good idea?"

"The interior designer the old boy employed, presumably."

"Well for God's sake keep Silas and Marni out of here! I'm not sure that I know enough tricks to get the marks of muddy paws out of shag-pile that pristine!"

Mike immediately shot back and firmly closed the front door before the two dogs could follow them in. Jenna slipped her trainers off before she dared step onto the deep and immaculate carpet, and then padded through to where a door looked as though it might lead to a dining room.

"Good grief! More white carpets! Did they never think of what one dropped lasagne would do to this?" she said as she peered round the door. "Oh, and guess what — white tiles on the floor of the kitchen! At least those would mop clean, though." She turned back to Mike. "I've got to say that if I was a prospective buyer, these carpets would be the final straw — especially if they're all through the house." She turned around in the lounge. "How big is this room? I'd guess at least eighteen feet either way, and probably closer to twenty-four, and that dining room isn't much smaller, so can you imagine what the carpeting bill would come to if you've got to replace the lot before you even move in?"

Mike looked stricken. "I never thought of it like that."

"Well you can bet that any wife who's been up here has! The kind of city woman who likes wall-to-wall white won't want to be living out here. And the horsey, county-set type, with their green wellies, will have the cleaning of this place sized up in a heartbeat. Are there decent floorboards under this? Because if so, I think you might do better to have these carpets taken up and the boards waxed or varnished. That'd be much more practical. A new owner could then move in and leave re-carpeting until they were ready. It'd be a far more attractive prospect."

Looking a little stunned, Mike waved a hand towards the stairs. "I think you'd better come and look upstairs, then." He turned and led the way upwards, turning to look back at her and say, "I'm so glad I brought you here. Even if you don't want the job, you've given me a whole new perspective on these houses."

"I haven't said 'no' yet," Jenna said with a smile. "But I think I can say that this wouldn't be the house I'd want to stop in if I did take it."

What she didn't want to say out loud to Mike, for fear of him thinking she really was cracked, was that she'd felt an awful atmosphere about this house the moment she'd walked in through the door. Quite what it could be she couldn't imagine. After all, it was hardly like an old house, where the chances were that somebody would have died there at some point in its history. These were brand new – there hadn't even been a disruptive teenager in the place as far as she knew. And that brought back memories of conversations with Mel, who had always maintained that children were very receptive to things which adults would dismiss as mere fancy.

"And teenagers can be far more potent than most people recognise," she remembered Mel saying. "It's all that bottled up emotion that they don't know what to do with." They had gone to the house some other friends shared, with the purpose of Mel doing a house cleansing after all of them had confessed to having terrible nightmares since moving in – nightmares which could only have had their root in the house, since the six students were all on very different courses. "Of course most teenagers just have the usual tantrums and get it all out of their systems," Mel had continued, as she proceeded to light incense in each of the rooms. "But just occasionally you find one who is particularly disruptive, either because they are overly sensitive to things going on around them, or are deeply unpleasant people themselves.

"I'm not asking you to believe in ghosts," she had added, seeing two of the lads who were scientists looking askance at her. "But is it so impossible for you to believe that someone like that could leave an imprint on a place? We don't know nearly enough about how electro-magnetic fields affect people, for instance. One of these days we may get to a point where you'll be able to bring some kind of meter in to a place like this, and say, 'ah yes, these readings are abnormal.' I know we aren't there yet, but can you discount the possibility that it might happen? And in that case, maybe this residue, or whatever it is, is strong enough to have an impact on other people who come into the room or house long after the original one has gone?"

Jenna had believed her alright, because the hairs on the backs of her arms and on the back of her neck had stood on end from the moment she had gone into that house, right up until Mel had finished doing her thing, and it was that same sensation she was having now. There was something very wrong with this house, and no amount of money would persuade her to spend a night in it.

Chapter 8

By the time they had done the tour of the four spacious double bedrooms, Jenna's impression hadn't got any better. She also had the beginnings of a worrying idea of a rather more worldly sort, and when they had locked up and gone back to the Land Rover for a coffee from the flask Mike had brought with them, she ventured to say,

"I'm sorry, Mike, but I just don't buy this ultra-white thing as being the concept of any interior designer. Heaven knows, I can barely afford a pot of paint for my flat, so I'm not pretending that I rub shoulders with the likes of them. But where I live we have several designers' studios, and if I go out for a walk, I go past one or other of them on a fairly regular basis. So I know what they put in their windows to showcase what they do, and that monstrosity in there isn't it. And what's more, I think I can tell you why.

"Designers aren't that different from any other person who sells their skills. And that means that they want satisfied customers who will recommend them. Nothing brings in new business like someone having their friends recommend that they go to whoever it is; or the friends have been so taken with the new lounge – or whatever – that they've actually asked who designed it. But that place," and she waved a despairing hand at the house, "that's a bloody disaster! You can tell that nobody has ever even spent the night in there, because I'd defy any normal human being to be able to spend more than an hour or two in the place and not leave a mark on it.

"So I'm wondering – given what you said about the acrimonious relationship between the builder and his daughters – whether whichever one of them was due to have this house didn't deliberately ask for this out of spite?" She saw Mike's eyes widen in dismay as she continued, "You know, knowing that she had no intention of ever setting foot in the place, she demanded all-white throughout. She probably thought that what would happen would be that her father would get hacked off with waiting for her to take the place, and then try to sell it. And so she wanted him to make a loss out of it, or at least not his usual healthy profit."

Mike was looking decidedly pale now. "Bloody Fiona Greaves!" he muttered bleakly, then gave Jenna a thin smile. "The oldest of the three Willetts witches. She's as spiteful as they come – *and* she's the one who's been giving me the most grief about not getting a buyer."

"Covering up to the others that she was the one who put a dirty great fly in the ointment…"

"…By complaining longest and loudest," Mike sighed, but nodding in agreement.

"Do you know if they've been in each other's assigned houses?"

Mike pulled a face. "God, no! It took me all I could do to have them each come out and see the one he'd left them! They had no intention of looking around the other two."

"So Fiona – that was the name, wasn't it? – probably knows that her sisters have never set foot inside 'her' house, anymore than she's been in theirs, and that they won't be the ones to throw the blame back at her – unless someone tells them," and she looked very pointedly at

Mike. "If they start getting unbearable, that might be a useful ace to have up your sleeve."

Mike flicked the dregs of coffee out of his mug and picked up the set of keys again. "I think you'd better come and give me your considered opinion of the other two places, then."

The second house turned out to be a different kind of nightmare. Here only the absolutely essential structural walls had been put in, making for a massive open-plan downstairs, and with two of the bedrooms opening onto a galleried space above part of it.

"Holy-moly!" Jenna breathed when they got up to the first bedroom. "Not a scrap of privacy! You couldn't even ask a guest couple to sleep in here. Everyone would hear them if they as much as rolled over and farted in their sleep – much less any sort of bedroom frolics. And you couldn't put kids to bed in here. They'd be constantly distracted by what was going on down below, not to mention hearing every word of inappropriate, post-watershed TV shows or films. ...I'm so sorry, Mike, but I think you need to tell them that they're going to have to put a bit of money into this place, and have these two rooms made more private if it's ever going to sell. Even if it's only glass panels, that'd be something."

And again she had this horrible creepy feeling about the place, but here it was almost as though the house was actively watching her. On the two turns of the staircase she could have sworn she half saw someone out of the corner of her eye. Yet as soon as she looked harder she knew there couldn't have been anyone there, because there was nowhere for them to have hidden from her. She wasn't even sure it was a 'someone' rather than a 'something', but it felt bitter and twisted whatever it was.

She went to the waist-high glass barrier which was the only thing stopping anyone from walking off the edge of the gallery, and looked down onto the lounge while keeping a tight grip on the balustrade above it – why did she feel like she was going to be pushed over it?

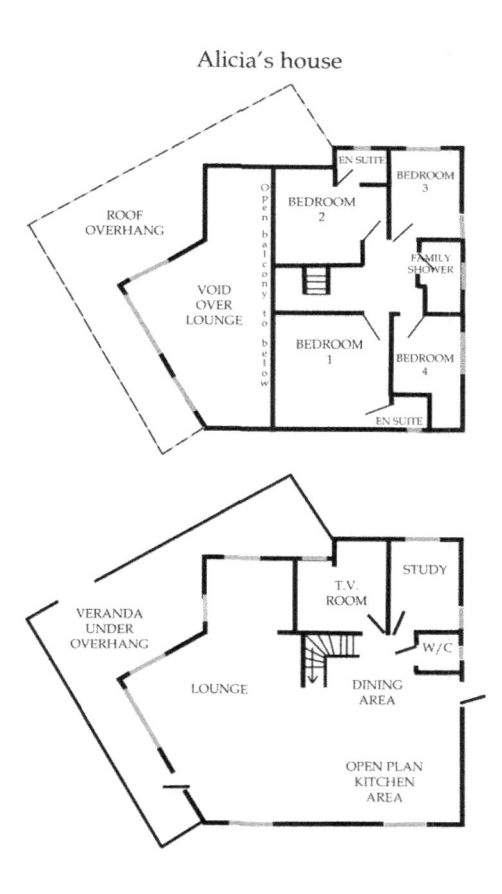

Alicia's house

"And what's with all that coir matting on the ground floor?" she asked, trying to keep her mind on the practical. "That's almost as bad as the white shag-pile in the other one, apart from the fact that it'll wear a bit better. It's a good tough flooring for something like a garden room, or a conservatory, but I reckon anyone paying the price of these houses would want something a bit more comfortable. So again you're back to the cost of re-carpeting the whole place. Tiff's mom put it in in some of their downstairs rooms, you know, back when it was all the latest fad. Horrible scratchy stuff to sit on, as I recall, and when their cat got fleas, well so did the house! Tiff would probably tell you how long that *didn't* stay down for, but I'm sure it wasn't long – and her mom's the kind of lady who'll grit her teeth and bear it if she thinks it looks the latest thing, so it must have been grim if she ripped it up fast."

Poor Mike could only groan, "This just keeps getting worse and worse." He wandered over and leaned on the balustrade beside her. "After all you've said, I can see that there's no point in even trying to let these out as holiday homes, is there?"

Jenna shook her head apologetically. "No. I'm so sorry, Mike. I think any of the major letting agencies would say exactly the sort of thing I have. This one has no privacy for half the people staying here – especially as this room and the other one along the gallery are the ones with the en-suites, so they're obviously the ones most people would normally want. And if you let the other house, you don't want to know what kind of state it would be in by the time three or four families had been through it. It would look the most frightful mess, because it would look positively filthy, and no family wants to pay top dollar to come on holiday to a place that looks downright grubby even if it is a new-build."

Then the main bathroom turned out to be a slightly strange state-of-the-art wet-room, with the kind of shower that you would need to leave a user manual in place for, and no bath. And yet Jenna's keen eyes spotted something

Mike hadn't noticed before, and that was that the grouting on the wet-room floor looked as though it was drying out and pulling away from the tiles.

"Run water down that and whoever is in the kitchen down below is going to be joining in having a shower," she pointed out. "God, I'm so sorry, Mike. I feel like I'm just going around picking holes in everything. But I tell you, those fancy homes and gardens magazines we sell at work regularly have articles in them about this sort of thing, and while I don't remember much, I do recall that they often say that wet-rooms are better on the ground floor precisely because it's easier to seal the floors, since you can concrete them and put the magic water-sealant stuff on more easily."

"I didn't have you down as the 'homes and gardens' kind of reader."

Jenna laughed. "Hey, a girl can dream, can't she? …Well okay, you've discovered my dirty little secret: when I'm feeling really fed up with my life, I can just about afford to treat myself to one of those magazines. And then I spend a couple of happy evenings designing the dream home I'll never have. It's all fairy stories, of course, but it's brightened some gloomy evenings over the years."

And why did she feel another of those shivers as she'd said 'fairy'? Damn it, this house was another one she couldn't wait to get out of.

Meanwhile, Mike didn't dare say what he was feeling, which was that he found it even more depressing that Jenna should have had nothing else to look forward to than staring at the pages of a magazine. Right now he was torn between wanting to go and drown himself in the lake outside, to avoid ever having to deal with these three white elephants he'd been saddled with, and wanting desperately to find a way to lift Jenna up to a better way of life. She deserved so much more, he believed, and was rather surprised at himself as he realised just how much this did matter to him. How had this young woman managed to impress herself upon him so much in such a short space of time? Why of all the women he'd met over the years was it Jenna who was really getting under his skin?

And what on earth was he going to do to make it possible for her to stay here for a while? Clearly using her as a manager/caretaker for holiday lets was right out of the picture – because he totally grasped what she had said, and was kicking himself for not having spotted the same things sooner – but there was still the security issue to consider. These places were still too vulnerable to squatters moving in, tucked away out here far out of sight, so there was still a chance he could wangle her the job of watching over them. However his feelings towards the three sisters had hardened even more in the light of Jenna's astute assessments of the first two houses, and he was now convinced that at least Fiona and Alicia, the oldest and youngest of Brian Willetts' daughters, had been actively spiting their father with their ridiculous demands over what was to be done with their houses. So ever serve them right if they were now finding those petty schemes backfiring on them as they deprived them of their inheritance.

"House number three?" he asked Jenna, praying that she wouldn't say she'd had enough by now.

"Hey, why not?" she replied with a good deal more cheer than he could muster. "Let's see what nightmare lies around that corner," and she gave him a cheerful grin.

He wouldn't have been quite so relieved, though, had he known that she was secretly worrying how she could tell him that she couldn't bring herself to stop here under any circumstances unless the other house was a very different kettle of fish.

Yet when he opened the door into the final house, he was completely unprepared for her to say,

"Oh, this is lovely!" in such a surprised voice. And Jenna herself was shocked at how different this house felt.

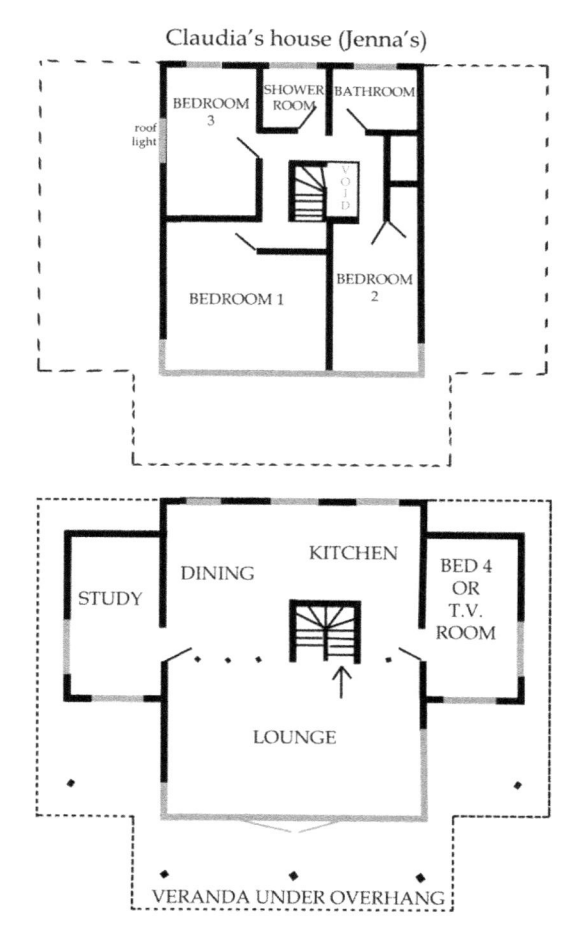

Claudia's house (Jenna's)

[Floor plan — Upper floor: Bedroom 3, Shower Room, Bathroom, roof light, Void (stairs), Bedroom 1, Bedroom 2]

[Floor plan — Ground floor: Study, Dining, Kitchen, Bed 4 or T.V. Room, Lounge, Veranda under overhang]

Here the wooden exterior had been allowed to show on the inside too, and although there was a lot of bleached wood on the walls and floors, they were only pale, not the glaring harsh white of the first house. The wooden ceilings had been painted white, but the overall effect was softened by the natural wood tones of things like the kitchen work surfaces and the bare wood staircase. And here the open-plan effect had been handled much more subtly. The main seating area in front of the ceiling-to-floor windows was subdivided from the kitchen by the stair supports having a kind of lattice-effect infill; and if the side rooms were not exactly separate, they at least had only wide archways through to them, rather than being wholly revealed. Even better, although the main front window ran up to the upper floor just like the others, here it had been made more into an expression of light, with ceiling-to-floor windows instead of conventional ones as in the first house; but with a proper floor all the way across, unlike the second, so that there was no gallery staring down on the dining room any more than there was one watching over the lounge.

"Now *this* is more like it!" Jenna declared, turning round and round to take it all in. "Nice exposed wooden floor, but easy to keep clean. Proper bedrooms." She wandered through the kitchen. "Oh yes, and a decent extractor for over the hob. Would I be right in thinking that this is the sister who actually cooks?"

"Good God! How could you know that?"

Jenna did a double-take. "I'm right?"

"Claudia has her own cookery school. Very nouvelle cuisine, mind you, but yes, she cooks. How on earth did you know?"

"The extractor," Jenna replied, still slight surprised that her guess had been that accurate. "Neither of the other kitchens had one that was wired up. The hoods were just for show. But if you were going to cook in an open-plan place like this, you'd have to have some way to get rid of the smells. It's different if you've got a separate kitchen like mine. If I cook fish, I can always open the window – even in winter, because I can close the door and keep my living room warm. But here? How could you open the windows with a gale coming in off the water? The whole house would be freezing in no time."

Mike was nodding now, seeing what she meant. "You're right! In my house I can open a window too, because my kitchen still has a window close to the cooker, and of course my garden is more sheltered." He was feeling a bit more cheerful now that Jenna had taken a liking to at least one of the houses. Clearly this would be the one she would choose to live in if she came to act as caretaker, and it was less of an issue her taking the most habitable one if there was no chance at all of letting them out. "Let's go upstairs," he said, hoping and praying that there wouldn't be anything up here which would put her off.

Mercifully Jenna was as taken with the bedrooms as the ground floor, and Mike privately conceded that if Claudia was at times the snootiest and most superior-acting of the three sisters, she had at least acted with a modicum of common sense where the house was concerned. Indeed he was already starting to think that she might be the one he could get on his side first with regard both to Jenna, and getting some work done on the other two houses. He had a feeling that she would be vitriolic in her response to hearing what her sisters had done with the other two places just to spite their father, especially since it was clearly not hers which was holding up finding a buyer.

As he made some notes on his i-pad, Jenna explored further, but was surprised when Mike had to tap her on the shoulder to bring her back to the here and now. What was that place she had been daydreaming about? Where had those images come from? And letting go of the beautiful wooden newel post felt almost like a physical wrench. Why was that?

"I think I owe you another decent meal out," Mike declared as they set off back down the road, Silas and Marnie lying crashed out in the back, fast asleep after chasing around for ages. "You've given me an awful lot of ammunition which I can use on the three Willetts sisters – not that that's any of their surnames now."

"What are their husbands like? Might it not be easier to get them around to the idea that they're going to have to pay out to get the larger return from the sale?"

Mike gave a small snort of mirth. "Alicia's been divorced twice and hasn't found another sucker yet, although she's quite vigorously on the hunt from the gossip Delia has picked up. Fiona's on her second marriage with the most hen-pecked husband I've ever met – poor sod! And Claudia's husband is out on an oil-rig somewhere in the Gulf of Mexico, I believe, and doing his damnedest not to come back! So no, not much help forthcoming in the husband department."

Trying to ignore the strange tugging feeling to go back, Jenna wondered, "Do you think it's that toxic relationship with their father that's caused all of them to have trouble with the men in their lives?"

Mike pulled a face. "Could be. But it's also probably because they're all a bit too much like him. They all want their own way over everything." He slowed and sounded the horn at a sheep which was standing in the middle of the track and was refusing to move out of the way. "Come on, you daft beast, shift! ...There, was that so hard? ...Dopey animal!"

He picked up speed again, returning to what he'd been saying with, "The woman who used to clean for the family told me that there used to be some almighty rows when all three girls were still living at home. Heaven knows what the mother was like – probably either some poor sheep of a woman, or another bloody nightmare like the rest of them. She certainly stuck it out with Willetts long enough, although there was some talk of her being out of her mind on prescriptions drugs when she had the car crash that killed her."

"Charming family!"

"Oh yes. I just wish it wasn't me who had to deal with them."

Jenna looked out of the window for a while, then asked Mike, "How often do the buses run around here?"

"Buses?" Mike laughed. "You've got to be joking! No busses around here." Then sensed that something was very wrong, and risked a glance Jenna's way. She was suddenly looking very miserable. "What's wrong? Why do you ask?"

"I don't think I can take the job, then," she told him.

"Eh? Why not? You liked the last house."

She sighed mournfully. "It's not that. I don't have a car. I can't drive."

The idea was so alien to Mike that it took him a moment for it to sink in. "What, 'don't drive' as in 'haven't had a car for years'? Because I'm sure we could sort you something out."

But Jenna was already shaking her head. "No, I mean I never even learned. Why would I? I've always lived in cities and towns where there were buses. And money's been so short that since the time I was old enough to learn how to drive, I could never afford the lessons."

Mike was just about to say, 'but they're not that expensive', when he remembered what Tiff had said on the quiet to him about how little Jenna earned. Mike had never thought of himself as well-off, but it now hammered in on him that in comparison to Jenna he was positively wealthy. *Don't be an idiot*, he told himself firmly. *Think before you speak! She was no more to know that there wouldn't be a bus she could catch, any more than you could have guessed that she wasn't a driver.*

"I'm sure we can find a way around that," he found himself saying, in the positive tones he used for his more fragile clients. But was it remotely practical to have Jenna out here if she had no transport of her own? She would need an awful lot of support if she did come. *And why would you complain about that?* His subconscious voice chided him. *You want to see more of her, well isn't this your ideal chance, and without it seeming like you're pouncing on her and scaring her away?*

However the first thing that Jenna said when they got back to the office and Tiff turned to greet them was,

"It isn't going to work. I can't get out there on my own."

"But it's not *that* far," Tiff protested, only to get Jenna riposte with tears in her eyes,

"It is when there aren't any buses!"

Tiff's stricken look at least made Mike feel a bit better, because it was clear that even Tiff had forgotten that Jenna couldn't drive.

"You could…" Tiff began to say and then ran aground as she struggled to come up with a solution, and it was clear to Mike that there weren't many occasions when Tiff had run into something so fundamental that she couldn't bend people or situations to make things happen, because she too was starting to look worried.

"I'm going back to the hotel," Jenna declared. "I'm glad I could help, Mike, but I wish I'd never seen that last lovely house. At least my magazines were only dreams. It's worse when you've been able to actually touch the dream for a while," and she left leaving Tiff making urgent, 'what the hell happened?' signals to Mike behind her back.

Chapter 9

When Tiff got back to the hotel that night it was clear that Jenna had been crying, but rather more worrying to Tiff, she had also been packing.

"What's this?" she demanded of her friend, really worried now.

"I'm going home tomorrow," Jenna declared huskily. "I'm grateful for the break, Tiff, really I am, but if I stay any longer I won't want to leave." She gave a sniff and cuffed her eyes. "It's all so lovely out here. The place is great, the people are so nice – well except for Zach – and having that promise of living out in the countryside dangling before me was like a dream come true. But it's never going to happen, is it? How can I go out there? I'd have to be dependent on someone all the time to even go and do basic shopping. I can't ask that of Mike. I'm supposed to be helping him, not making even more work – if he's going out to the houses two or three times a week, then there's no need for a caretaker, is there?"

"I thought you liked Mike?" Tiff said weakly, fearing that all of her hard work priming Suzy and her boss might be for nothing, and even worse, that Jenna would go back and just fall into the same old self-destructive routine.

"I do. I like him a lot."

"So what's the problem?"

Jenna blushed. "I like him too much. What's a man like him going to be doing hanging around with someone like me? He's an up-and-coming solicitor, he's a nice bloke, he loves his mum enough to be making sure she's well-cared for, and all in all he's a great catch. So if he can have his pick of the local wealthy farmers' daughters, and any other prime single ladies of the county, why on earth would he look twice at a disaster like me? ...And I don't want to make a fool of myself, Tiff. I couldn't bear it if he felt he had to tell me to back off because I was being too clingy."

Tiff groaned and threw herself backwards onto the bed. "Good God, Jenna! Can't you see that he really likes you too? If he wanted these imaginary women you're talking about, he could have dated them years ago! But he hasn't. And he's been here long enough to have had the chance. Please, if nothing else, don't put yourself down like that."

She sat up and put on her sternest expression. "If you don't want to come into the office with me for the next two days, that's fine, but I'm not having you waste your money on train or bus fares. I said I'd take you back on Thursday in time for your next shift, and I meant it."

"I've been and bought my tickets," Jenna said miserably. "I'm sorry, Tiff, but if I've got to go back, then I need to go now or I never will. And where will I be then?"

Biting back the waspish comment she half wanted to make, Tiff had to remind herself that Jenna wasn't some office intern who wasn't doing what she was told, this was her fragile friend who'd already done such a lot to try and improve her own life. To an outsider, Jenna might sound as though she was running away from the challenge of a new future, but Tiff knew that Jenna was incredibly brave, and that a substantial part of the problem here was that she was wholly unused to having anyone help her, especially men.

"Alright," she conceded, "Go back tomorrow if you want, but I shall be coming over to see you on Thursday. …No! No arguments about that! I'd already told Richard that I'll be taking Thursday off, but be coming back to work on Saturday and Sunday if necessary. So there'll be no issue there. But I want to see for myself that you're not sitting at home crying yourself sick, because I know you! You might think you're unworthy of all this good stuff, but I can see in your eyes just how much you'd love to be able to come and live out here. You want this, even if you won't admit it yet. And I wouldn't be being much of a friend to you if I wasn't determined to move heaven and earth to help make it happen. So no arguments – I'll see you on Thursday!" *And if I have my way I'll be bringing you back too*, Tiff resolved.

It took until midday for Jenna to make it back home to Malvern on the train, despite having got to the station early, and as she dragged her bag and herself along the all too familiar route from the main station to her flat, she thought she couldn't have felt more wretched if she'd tried. Compared to where she'd once lived, Malvern was idyllic. What was not to like about a pretty Victorian spa town perched on some oh-so-very-English hills? And it wasn't the town itself that was draining her spirit to rock bottom at the moment. It was the prospect of going back to her job and all that that implied. That horrible sensation of going nowhere fast, and with every choice she could make being limited by her fundamental lack of money.

Oh she'd known long ago that her opportunities were limited by her inability to drive, and it was something she'd tried so often to find a way around. But when even a single lesson cost more than she earned in two or three hours, and a block of them would have wiped out over half a month's wages in one go when she could barely survive on what she earned anyway, she had long since resigned herself to the impossibility. After all, one or two lessons a month wasn't going to get her very far when there was no chance of practising in between. And so to have this of all reasons be the one which had instantly crushed the house-sitting job left a more bitter than normal taste in her mouth.

She was so absorbed in wishing with all her might that she could find some way to have even that brief respite, that she never noticed the smartly dressed woman standing by her front door until she was nearly on top of her.

"Can I help you?" she asked worriedly. Who on earth was this? What had happened?

"I'm Claire Heath from the housing association," the woman said, coming and holding out her hand to be shaken. "You're a hard woman to get hold of Ms Cornwell."

"Am I? I'm sorry. I wasn't expecting you"

"Weren't you? We tried to contact you, but your phone seemed to be switched off, and we posted letters through your door."

Thoroughly worried now, Jenna could only gulp, "I'm sorry, I've been away. I didn't have much in the way of a signal for my phone."

"Been away?" Ms Heath sounded suspicious, and that woke Jenna up enough to be cautious. She'd had to fight enough officials in her time to have a good inbuilt radar for when things were about to go horribly wrong. So she was careful in her reply of,

"A friend of mine needed some help with basic office work over in Ludlow. I had a week off my normal job, so I've been over there helping. Her company paid for the hotel, so don't think I was living it up in Spain, or anything."

"Ludlow? Oh. " Whatever Ms Heath had been expecting it obviously wasn't that. "Can anyone corroborate that?"

"Corroborate? That sounds very formal – like I'm being accused of something. What's happened?"

It must have dawned on Ms Heath that either Jenna was an exceptional actress, or she genuinely didn't know, because she stepped back to the house and gestured to Jenna's front door. To Jenna's horror, she saw that where the pane of glass had once been, a piece of wood had been nailed across, and there were the kind of marks on the door that looked as though somebody had tried to kick their way in.

As she gulped, "Oh my God!" Ms Heath said primly,

"There have been complaints about the men you bring here."

"*What?* What men? I don't bring *men* back here! I haven't even got a boyfriend! Bloody hell, Miss whatever-your-name-is, haven't you read my case files? I was relocated here because of the aftermaths of the trial of a man who damned near beat me to death. A man who was a total stranger to me, by the way, but who went down after his sentencing swearing that his mates would come and get me. So under what possible circumstances do you think that I would be bringing men here – and you did mean men in the plural, and not just one, didn't you?"

At least Ms Heath had the grace to look somewhat abashed at Jenna's emotionally charged backlash, but she wasn't about to concede any ground just yet.

"Your neighbour, Mrs Wilson, is very worried, and so is her son. It was he who dialled 999 when he heard men shouting and swearing outside his mother's front door. It's a good job he was there, because Mrs Wilson was so frightened, she's refused to set foot back in her flat until she knows you've gone and taken your men friends with you."

Now that the initial shock had worn off, Jenna was starting to get angry. "They're not my bloody men friends!" she snapped. "So did the police come? They ought to have, because I'm on their list of vulnerable people in the area. Did they make any arrests?"

Pulling a piece of paper out of her smart leather document wallet, Ms Heath read the names out. "Liam Adebeyo, Haseem Shah, and Mohammed Faree, all of mixed decent and from Birmingham. You do keep some exotic company Ms Cornwell."

"Company? I've never even heard of those men!" Jenna protested. "Who are they? And what do they want with me?"

Ms Heath turned the paper around so that Jenna could see it and the photographs which were obviously police mug-shots. "So you really don't know these men?"

Jenna stared at the three unfamiliar faces. "I've never seen them in my life!"

"Then why were they hammering on your door demanding that you send 'him' out? Who is this person they think you had staying with you?"

And suddenly light dawned for Jenna. This was the very nightmare she had been dreading with Kyle. Worse, Ms Heath was face to face with her and spotted her reaction, demanding,

"So I'll ask you again, who is it that's been staying here who these men wanted?"

Sinking onto the low stone wall by the path, Jenna looked up at Ms Heath with eyes filled with despair. "He wasn't staying here. He's never *stayed* here, only visited for a few hours. And he's not my boyfriend, either. He's the spoilt rotten brother of someone I was friends with." She heaved a huge sigh, starting to feel sick. "A few weeks ago he and his sister turned up here. He tried to worm his way into my flat, but I kneed him in the balls and told him to piss off." She shook her head wearily. "I told Claire back then that I had my suspicions that he'd been up to no good for some time, and that he kept trying to have a relationship with me, not because he cared one way or another for me, but because it would give him somewhere else to creep away to when things got a bit too hot around their family home.

"But I swear to you, I had no idea what exactly he was into – and still don't have. I was just going on the fact that I'd been alert enough to spot that, although he always made out that he was going out to work to his mum and sisters, he never seemed to have any money coming in. There was always some improbable story as to why he needed to borrow money off them that they never saw through, but I did. His sister's name is Claire Adaruzzio, and she and her husband live in Edgbaston. Their mum is Caroline Sumner, and she also lives in Edgbaston, but whether Kyle – the idiot those men were after – is still living with her, I honestly don't know."

Ms Heath seemed to have un-bent a fraction. "So the man they were looking for is called Kyle…?"

"Kyle Sumner. I'll happily give the police a detailed description of him, if that'll help."

"And can somebody corroborate that you were in Ludlow at the time this attempted break-in happened?"

"God, yes! In fact it's a branch of one of the big Birmingham solicitors."

That really seemed to stop Ms Heath in her tracks. "Oh, a solicitors? Oh, I see." She paused for a moment then said in rather more apologetic tones, "But all the same, I'm afraid we're going to have to ask you to leave with immediate effect. You have to understand that we have a lot of vulnerable elderly people in this block of buildings. We cannot have them frightened to go out of their own front doors, and we don't have enough vacant properties to be able to move all of those who have expressed concerns. If you really are the innocent party in all of this, then we'll do our best to re-house you, but for the moment we'll have to put you into a room in one of our listed bed-and-breakfast properties."

"A B&B?" Jenna felt herself going cold all over. She still had nightmares about her previous months living in one of those after the trial and before she got her first bedsit. A time when she had never felt safe, and had barricaded herself into her bedroom every night, because the huge old house had accommodated a random mix of otherwise homeless people, which had included single men who were drug addicts. "But that's so unfair! I haven't done anything!"

"I'm sure it is, but we have to choose between moving one person who is young and fit, or five who are elderly, immobile, and have much greater restrictions on where we can place them. ...Now then, who were these people you were with? Do you have a phone number for them?"

Jenna just about had the presence of mind to not reel off Tiff's mobile, but to pull out Mike's business card which he had thrust into her hand just as she'd left that morning, with the words, "If ever you need help, just call me." How bloody prophetic had that been? Not even five hours later and she was in a situation that was taking her right back into the hellish world she'd worked so hard to get out of.

"Your key should still work," she heard Ms Heath saying, as if from far away. "Luckily the police got here just as those men were breaking the glass, having failed to kick the door in, so the property is still secure." 'The property' Jenna noticed, this was already no longer her home. "If you let us in, I'll make this call, and then we'll see about arranging how quickly we can get you into somewhere else."

"You need to ask for Tiffany Fairbourne," Jenna heard herself saying weakly as she wrestled the door open, the kicking having done nothing to help its existing tendency to stick at the bottom. But once in the living room, as she sank gratefully onto the battered old sofa, she heard Ms Heath saying,

"Oh hello Mr Campbell, my name is…"

Utterly depressed and distressed, Jenna tuned out to what Ms Heath said beyond that, until something in the other woman's voice brought her back to the present. Ms Heath was holding the phone a little away from her ear, and even from across the room she could hear Mike's voice, but it wasn't Mike in the way he spoke to her. There was no mistaking that it was one absolutely furious solicitor on the other end of the phone, and if he wasn't actually shouting, the way his words were being spat out like machine-gun bullets was severely rattling Ms Heath.

Whenever she could get a word in, she was hastily protesting, "No! No we wouldn't do anything presumptuous, Mr Campbell. …No, no, we have no wish for this to become a legal matter. …No, absolutely not! We're not victimising Miss Cornwell. …No, we are not blame-shifting the vandalism of our property onto an innocent party." And so it went on, until Ms Heath finally finished the call, now looking so shaken herself that Jenna felt obliged to say,

"Would you like a cup of tea? Haven't got any milk, I'm afraid. Or coffee if you prefer that black?"

"Err… No thank you. …Heavens! He's quite a force of nature isn't he, your Mr Campbell? I wouldn't want to be crossing him in a magistrate's court."

It gave Jenna a shiver of a much more pleasurable kind to hear Mike being referred to as 'her' Mr Campbell, even if the chances of that being true were next to none. If nothing else, it was a pleasant change to find a man who was prepared to stand up for her, when in the past she had only ever been able to count on her female friends. Maybe not every change was for the worst?

Ms Heath didn't linger long after the call to Mike, but had to admit that the chances of Jenna staying in this flat were still remote. And Jenna could appreciate why. Without her here there was no reason why whoever was hunting Kyle should come here, and that would make it a lot easier for the police to make a case against the three in custody and any others who showed up. But it was breaking her heart to think of leaving forever.

It was quite one thing to go over to Ludlow for a break, or to contemplate being away for a nice three or four month break. But whenever she had thought of leaving here permanently it had always been with the presumption that she would be taking her few treasured possessions with her, like her bookcases and the sofa. Well with a bit of luck she would be able to pack her precious textbooks into suitcases to take with her, but there was no way that the furniture could come with her to a B&B, because that would be already furnished. And no doubt once the dust settled, she would be given some financial help to get things like a bed for a new place, but she had carefully scoured the second-hand shops for these pieces to stretch her money out further, and the chances of finding more bargains like these were slim.

Beyond that there was also the emotional attachment. She had spent hours and hours with sandpaper taking the tatty varnish off the bookcases, and then carefully painting and stencilling the patterns onto them – mixing pots of remaindered coloured paint bought in the sales to get the right colours – so that they looked like they'd come out of somewhere a lot older and fancier than the junk yard. Her three dining chairs were all different shapes, collected on separate occasions, but again careful painting, and some time reupholstering the seats in matching, discounted remnants of a material which would normally have cost a fortune, had made them into a set she would be heartbroken to leave behind. Especially as she knew that when the workmen came in to repair and clear the flat ready for its next tenant, that these pieces would just get thrown into a skip – they probably wouldn't even get as far as another junk shop.

Going into the bedroom and lifting the loose floorboard where she had hidden her few precious treasures after she'd caught Kyle with them, she lifted them out, pulling her two suitcases from under the bed at the same time. But at that point her resolve melted away and she sat on the floor and unashamedly bawled her eyes out. When she was cried out, she dragged herself through to the kitchen and put the kettle on. Any appetite she ought to have had by this time had long gone, but she urgently needed the comfort of a hot drink before she could even think about starting to pack – and she was under no illusions as to how fast this move was going to happen.

She was so focused on standing in front of her books, and wondering how many the suitcases would take the weight of, that she didn't register that two cars had pulled up until there was a knock on the door.

"Jenna? Are you there, lovely?" Tiff's voice echoed up. "Please open the door!"

Tearing down the stairs, Jenna ripped open the battered door and threw herself into Tiff's arms, breaking down again, and not realising that there was someone with her until another hand touched her shoulder and Mike's voice said,

"This is outrageous! How dare they accuse you like that!"

"Come on," Tiff said gently. "Let's get you back inside before some other old busybody rings the police, and then you can tell us all about it."

Between sniffles and a terrible fit of hiccups, Jenna stumbled through her story again for Tiff and Mike, Tiff sitting on the sofa beside her, hugging her, and Mike on one of the dining chairs brought up to her other side.

"So how fast will they have you out of here?" Tiff asked in horror, as Jenna finally ran out of words.

"If I've got until the weekend I'd be surprised," Jenna hiccupped. "Like I said, they're weighing the safety of all the old folk around against me. It's not hard to see why they want me out of the way fast. There are twenty flats in this little enclave, and every one of the other tenants is at least over sixty – I got this flat because it's the one farthest from the main path and the entrance stairs are out of sight."

"Why would that matter?" Tiff asked, bemused.

"Because if someone falls by the door nobody can see them," Jenna explained. "With all the other flats, they'd be seen by at least one neighbour if not two or three. And most of the people here are at least a bit bad on their feet. Not exactly the sort of folk who could get out of the way if things started getting a bit rough."

"Dear God," Mike sighed, leaning back in the chair. "I get what you're saying about the housing association not having much choice, but if this was happening to me, I don't think I'd be half as understanding as you're being, Jenna." Then he heaved himself to his feet and went to look at the bookcases. "How tall are these?"

"A bit under six feet, I think. Why?"

Mike turned and grinned. "Good job I came in the Landie, then. We'll have to rope the back closed, I suspect, but with the back seats flattened down we should be able to get the bookcases, this little two-seater sofa and your bed inside. The table will have to go on the top roped down, and with a bit of luck we'll squeeze the dining chairs inside too. That'll leave room for the books in the front with me. Do you reckon you can get Jenna's personal stuff in the Smart car, Tiff?"

"I'll get it in if it kills me!" Tiff declared fiercely. "We're not leaving you here like this, Jen!

"Is there anywhere we can get some boxes from?" was Mike's next question, and somehow suddenly feeling like a light had come on at the end of a very long and dark tunnel, Jenna said,

"Work! We can go in now. Actually it'll be a good time to go and ask for boxes because the evening shelf-fillers come in in the late afternoon to start their shift, and they should have finished some of the day's load already."

"Right!" Mike said, rubbing his hands together with something like relish. "Tiff, can you start packing Jenna's clothes into suitcases? We'll go and get some boxes to load the books into, and then while Jenna does that, you and I will start getting things like the sofa into the Landie."

Feeling rather swept off her feet, Jenna directed Mike to the supermarket where she worked, and was then astonished when he demanded to speak to the duty manager. By the time Jenna had taken two lots of cardboard boxes out to the Land Rover, Mike had somehow convinced the evening's manager – whom Jenna had always found to be overbearing and bullying – that Jenna was being taken out of the area for her own safety, and that the store had better consider her as being on long-term leave with immediate effect.

"I shall be ringing the branch manager in the morning to iron out the details," Mike informed the startled looking night manager, and with that swept Jenna out to the Land Rover. It was certainly a whole new side to Mike that Jenna would never have guessed existed. For a man who looked as though he ought to be auditioning for the part of Bilbo Baggins, with his warm smile and friendly manner, Mike was also turning out to have far more steel in his soul than Jenna would ever have believed he possessed. And there was a fire in those twinkling eyes just now that said woe betides anyone who crossed him when he was in this mood.

Nor was he any less determined when they got back to the flat. He obviously knew his vehicle well, because Jenna was astonished at the way he knew exactly which piece of her furniture would fit best where. The sofa was tipped onto its side but then comfortably straddled the wheel-arch on the one side, then the bed went in on the other – Mike producing a toolkit which made short work of disassembling the pine bed into so many pieces of wood and the separate mattress. As she carried the boxes of books down to the front foot-well of the Land Rover, she was amazed to find Mike up on the roof of the four-by-four, competently strapping her table upside down onto it, its legs protruding up into the air like four horns. The dining chairs in the end didn't quite fit inside, and joined the table on the roof, carefully tied down between the tables' legs as extra anchorage, but by ten o'clock that night, there was nothing of her own left in Jenna's flat.

"Let the bloody association argue with that!" Mike said with relish. "Right, ladies, I'll take this lot back to my house. You two go and have a peaceful night at the hotel – it'll be a quick drive at this time of night – and in the morning we'll sort out where we go from here."

Chapter 10

It was a surreal drive back to Ludlow for Jenna. Utterly exhausted, but having gone past the stage where she could sleep as yet, she found herself mentally drifting as the countryside passed by her in the darkness. She knew that she ought to be worried sick at the prospect of being homeless and jobless, yet she hadn't the energy to fret over either right now. And instead there was a warm glow somewhere deep inside over Mike not only sticking up for her over the phone, but actually coming all the way to her flat with Tiff and working so hard to rescue her. In another time and place that would also have been a cause for a certain amount of worry, because Jenna had had more than her share of men breaking their promises to her, even as just colleagues or supposed friends, as Kyle had started out being. But not tonight. Tonight was for counting her blessings that she wasn't having to deal with this disaster on her own. And so she watched the countryside flickering past the car window, and found herself seeing strange creatures in the shadows of trees or in patches of half-light where the headlights didn't quite reach. Whether they were in her mind or really out there she was beyond telling.

By the time they reached the hotel, it was all she could do to put one foot in front of the other to get to their room. And once inside she fell onto the bed and went out like a light. When she finally woke up, it was to find Tiff's alarm clock by her side saying it was already ten o'clock in the morning, and a note from Tiff saying that she'd gone into work, but that Jenna was to come and join them as soon as possible.

The prospect of encountering the revolting Zach hardly filled her with joy, but then she reminded herself that previously, for most of the time she'd been with Tiff and Suzy they had been in the other office, and well out of Zach's way. Breakfast was long over and done with at the hotel by the time she'd had a long and refreshing shower, and dug her remaining clean clothes out of her bag. So she headed out and found a coffee shop where she demolished a sandwich and a large Danish, along with a whole pot of tea. It was a reckless expense for someone who barely had any money, but today it felt as though all the rules had been torn up and thrown to the wind. Her ravenous hunger satiated, and yet still feeling peculiarly light inside, she felt just about fortified enough to walk to the office.

As she walked and breathed in the clean air, it dawned on her that she was feeling very differently about life today. Pausing to sit on a bench and think, she realised that what had happened yesterday had been preying on her mind for an awful long time now, and not just about Kyle. The endless struggle to keep a roof over her head had been a millstone around her neck, forcing her to stay in a job she absolutely hated. And although she wouldn't have said that she fretted over her job on a daily basis, nonetheless there had been the niggling doubts about how much longer she could actually put up with it before it drove her to a breakdown. Or what would happen to her if she had a work-related injury, such as a badly torn muscle as had happened to a couple of other girls she knew, and had then found that she could no longer do such physically strenuous work, at which point the decision would have been made for her. None of those variations, she had often thought, could ever be thought a good thing, but equally a controlled escape route had never presented itself to her either – beyond getting more teaching, that was, and that had turned out to be a dead end.

But now the worst had happened, and there was something wonderfully liberating in that. All the 'what if's had been made redundant overnight. The hundred and one variants on what she might have to do, or try to resolve, had gone out of the window at a stroke – because this reality was so bizarre that she had never even dreamed of it. Yes, she had worried about Kyle doing something like this, but in her imaginings she had always expected to be there in person when he rolled up with some drunken mate, or being hotly pursued by some thug he owed money to. So prioritising her own safety had been something she had hitherto thought long and hard about, and also about how she would handle the police who came in response to any call for help. For all of this to have happened in her absence was not only unexpected, it was actually quite a relief in a strange sort of way. And so it was feeling oddly light in spirit that Jenna made her way up the lovely old staircase to the office once more.

To be greeted by a delighted Silas and Marnie as she got in through the door was a treat, but it was Mike's cheerful,

"There you are! Great! Come and sit down and we'll tell you where we've got to so far," that was if anything even better.

In something of a happy daze, Jenna listened as Mike and Tiff between them told her of their morning. Her manager had been informed first thing by Mike, and if not exactly ecstatic at the shortness of notice, at least recognised that as the innocent victim in this strange affair, Jenna would need some time to sort her life out.

What Mike didn't tell her was that he had hinted heavily to the manager that Jenna might not be coming back at all, covering his own intentions by saying that, of course, a lot depended on where the housing association could re-home her as to whether she would even be able to get to the store.

"And after that I had strong words with the three Willetts sisters," he declared with a satisfied smile. "I told them I had run out of patience with them, and that it was time they pinned their ears back and listened to what the remaining options were."

"Gosh!" Jenna gasped, rather amazed at this sudden surge of assertiveness from him. "And did they accept what you said?"

He grinned at her. "By the time I'd told Claudia about what I'm afraid I claimed as *my* suspicions as to what her sisters had been playing at with their father, she would have agreed to pretty much anything, I think. All she wanted to do was to go around to the other two and throttle them! So I got in quick with Alicia, because she lives closest to Claudia. She's far from happy with me, but she knows that if she pushes me too hard and I dump them, there's not another solicitor in the town who will touch them with a barge pole. So there was a lot of grumbling, but I also sensed a touch of being miffed at being caught out in what she'd done. She was definitely guilty about something, anyway, so here's to you, Jenna, because without your sharp observations I might never have suspected that," and he raised his mug of tea to her in salute.

"As for Fiona – oh my word, she's really not happy! Her response to being caught out was to fly into a right old temper. But I told her straight: it doesn't matter whether you want to sell the properties, or if you want to rent them out, you're going to have to spend some money on making them habitable for a normal person. I gave her the choice of paying up herself for her house now, or for me to take it out of the final settlement. Not surprisingly she chose the latter!"

He laughed. "Still had to put up with a lot of bluster about me making sure that the selling price reflected the additional expense, but then that was before her sisters turned up on her doorstep – and I'm thinking that they both will, because Alicia half hinted that it was Fiona's idea to make their father jump through hoops of their making. So now that it's all gone wrong, Alicia's none too pleased with their oldest sister, because heaven forbid that she should be grown up enough to shoulder her own share of the blame.

"So thank you again, Jenna, for giving me something to use against my most troublesome clients. And in reward…" and he paused for effect before waving the keys at her, "you get to be the caretaker who oversees the refurbishment! You have a home for at least as long as that takes!"

And now Tiff joined in, a huge grin on her face too. "And of course those places are unfurnished, so all we have to do is take your stuff up there. You don't have to worry about putting any of it in storage – you'll need it to use."

"I'll come up and see you regularly, and take you shopping," Mike added. "The firm will stand you anything else you need, but all it will take is for the electricity to be turned on and you already have a fridge, freezer and cooker, so I don't think there'll be much else. And remembering the size of that freezer, I think you'll have more trouble filling it than of running out of stuff."

"And," said Tiff, looking hugely smug, "Zach the Twat is on notice!"

"What? Dismissed?" gasped Jenna.

"Well not quite," Tiff admitted, "but I'm glad you didn't have to witness the scene he made here when he got in on Monday morning and found that he had to take the duty solicitor's role. My God, he's a spoiled brat! He slammed doors, he called all of us names – and he was really abusive to Suzy. That's why she's not in today. She went home early and rang head office to say that she absolutely refused to come and work under those conditions when she was actually helping the company out. Delia went home in tears as well and has handed her notice in. She says she'll stay until we can find someone to replace her, but only if Mike's still here, because she won't be alone in the office with Zach."

She leaned forward and with a wicked grin added, "I reckon Delia had a bit of a thing for old Hornby! She's acting quite the jilted girlfriend, you know. Not that I think anything actually happened. *Euw*! I wish I hadn't said that now, because I've got this mental image of him table-ending her, *euw*!" and she laughed as she pulled a face.

Then she grinned at Jenna again. "So that means *I'm* here at least until the audit is done. Isn't that great? I'll be able to come up and see you and make sure you're settled in before I have to go back home. And Zach's been told that he's got to toe the line, because I'll be reporting back directly to Richard, and one hint that he's been shouting his mouth off at me, or that he's been refusing to pull his weight in the office, and he'll be on a serious disciplinary and transferred compulsorily to Birmingham.

"Bloody hell, Jenna, you should have seen his face when he took *that* call off Richard at the end of work yesterday! I was half expecting him to throw the biggest fit ever and walk out, but he somehow held it together until he'd left. But we've already heard that he went and got massively pissed last night, and strangely enough, he hasn't shown his face here yet!"

"Are you going to report him for that?" Against all of her expectations, Jenna found herself feeling a teeny bit sorry for Zach. Not a lot, mind you, but more than Mike and Tiff could ever grasp, she knew how hard it would be to get a job once you had come out of one under dubious circumstances, even if in this case it was something of a self-inflicted wound.

Tiff shrugged. "It depends. If he turns up tomorrow, keeps his head down and gets on with the job, then I might be persuaded to be lenient and say nothing. But if he comes in as though nothing has happened, and with no good explanation, then I'm afraid he'll have forced my hand."

Jenna felt a modicum of relief at that. She would have been bothered if Tiff had become so hardened by her job that she couldn't have any understanding of how Zach might be feeling. Yet Tiff was already wafting her hand as if to brush the spirit of Zach away.

"Now listen," she said, wagging a finger at Jenna, "with Delia heading out of the door – while I'm saying nothing to her or Zach – Mike and I have agreed that you are just the person to take over her position."

"But I'm not a secretary!" Jenna protested.

"You can type pretty fast and accurately," Tiff came back at her with. "I know you can because I've seen you! And anyway, this office doesn't need a secretary who only works with one of the team, it needs someone who can take on a wide range of clerical duties…"

"And I'm confident I can teach you most of them within a few weeks," Mike added cheerily. "Someone with your academic background will cope, no problem. All it requires is a bit of brain and a hefty dose of common sense. I'll have you up to speed in no time, because if I'm being frank, while Delia is a nice enough lady, she's hardly bright, so compared to her you're pretty much guaranteed to do better."

Jenna's smile had become a little fixed, and Tiff knew that she was already doubting herself. So she came and put her hand on her friend's arm and said reassuringly, "You'll be fine, honestly, you will. And if that isn't enough to convince you, you'll be replacing Delia on the payroll, so we'll be paying you…" and the amount she said had Jenna's jaw dropping.

"Really? Isn't that bit…?"

"…The going rate! What have I kept telling you? You needed a proper job with a proper wage coming in – well here it is. It's yours for the taking."

"Don't you have to advertise the job?" Jenna asked weakly.

"If we were replacing a secretary with a secretary, yes we would," agreed Mike. "But we're covering this by calling it restructuring, and our needing to get the right person in to compensate for the fact that there'll only be two solicitors instead of three. The fact that you've got a higher degree means you're far better qualified than anybody else we're likely to get applying from around here, and since Tiff has already submitted your application, and I've been put in charge of hiring and firing for the office, welcome to the team! We won't expect you to start just yet, not least because the whole Zach situation needs to settle down first, and because we genuinely do need a caretaker out at the houses. But because you're doing *that* job for us, it puts you on our company books already, and it then means that we can legitimately slide you sideways into the office. After all, you must be trustworthy if we're letting you have the keys to three houses which together represent the thick end of two million quid's worth."

"'Nother cup of tea in celebration?" Tiff asked, and

that seemed to be it, in one stroke Jenna's friends had found her somewhere to live and a job.

For the rest of that day, Jenna hovered around the office, but was too stunned to take in much of what was going on. That evening Mike took them out to a pretty country pub for a meal, and Jenna fell into bed to a deep and dreamless sleep when they got back, in no small measure brought on by the complete lifting of stress from off her. For the first time in her life she was facing a future where she wouldn't have to scrimp and save for every penny, and while she was under no illusions that she would still be far from rich by the time she had found herself somewhere to rent within Ludlow, it was still a massive step up from where she'd been just forty-eight hours earlier.

On Saturday morning, Mike and Tiff drove her out to the houses, and they spent a pleasant morning getting her furniture into the house she had fallen in love with.

"I want you to have a serious think about what needs to be done to each of the other houses to make them marketable," Mike told her, as they sat around her dining table by the huge picture window looking out onto the lake, enjoying a coffee and Jaffa cakes. "I completely trust you to be sensible about this. Obviously we only want to spend what we absolutely have to, but I have the phone number of a reputable decorator, and I think a coat of paint isn't going to wreck the budget. So take next week to have a wander around the houses and decide which rooms need a spruce up. We can go and get some colour cards from one of the big DIY stores in Hereford if you like?"

"That would be great," Jenna agreed, actually starting to enjoy herself now that she was here.

"That'll be tomorrow sorted, then."

Tiff waved her hand in protest. "Not me, though! If I don't go home and get some more clothes to see me through, I'm going to start looking very crumpled and be a bit smelly! It's back to Birmingham for me tomorrow, so you two go and have fun."

With that in mind, Jenna came back to the hotel with Tiff for the night, and in the morning Mike picked her up and they headed off to Hereford and one of the big DIY chain stores. While she was there, Jenna picked up various essentials, like a mop and bucket and a washing-up brush, plus various cleaning products, and most importantly, several of the huge sheets of plastic which decorators used to cover floors with.

"I know I said that the awful wall-to-wall white carpet will have to go," she admitted to Mike, "but I think it can probably stay in a couple of the bedrooms at least, and so I want to make sure it's well covered if we have workmen in. And of course any underlay will still be usable as long as nothing's soaked into it – that'll cut costs a bit."

"What about the coir matting in the other place?" he asked.

"Well again, it's probably fine in the dining-kitchen area, so I'll just keep it well covered. It's in the lounge and on the stairs that it's going to need replacing. I talked to Tiff, and she said her mum complained that the damned stuff had a tendency to sag a bit on steps – you know, stretch a bit and go slightly loose so that it snags at your feet, especially if you don't get the right weave. If you do want to let the place for a while, it'd be sensible to have a safe stair carpet, wouldn't it?"

With potential litigation in mind, Mike readily agreed to that, but also to Jenna's suggestion that on the stairs at least, carpet tiles might well fit the bill and come in much cheaper than a full carpet.

Since Mike was insistent on footing the bill knowing that Jenna would have a hiccup in her cash-flow, Jenna also took the opportunity to do a major supermarket shop, and then having been back to Mike's for lunch and to let the dogs out for a while, they took her supplies up to the house.

"I don't want you to have to take time out of the office on my behalf," Jenna said firmly. "Whenever the electricity is going to go on is a good enough reason for you to bring me back out here and leave me, but let's not give Zach any ammunition to use against you."

"You really think he's that dangerous?" Mike wondered.

"Absolutely! Think about it. His job is being threatened by you and Tiff. Now we all know it's his own fault, but I'd bet good money – if I had any – that he won't see it like that. In his mind he's the put-upon one, and now that Tiff's told head office, his back is against the wall. That makes him very dangerous, Mike, because he's almost at the point where he's got nothing to lose by lashing back at you two.

"And one of the ways he might think of doing that is if he sees you fussing over me in working hours, because to him, you'll be wasting work time and nobody taking you to task for it. It's a warped view of the world, I know, but someone like him doesn't think the way the rest of us do. Which is why I'd also ask you not to say a word about me eventually coming to join you – I know you weren't going to, but it won't be me he comes after so much, but you. I'm not his enemy, in his eyes, you are.

"So let's get everything set up so that you can just drop me round here one evening after work. That's why I've bought so much canned stuff rather than frozen. I can always fill the freezer later, and it's easy enough to pick up some bread and milk from a late-night garage or somewhere. That's all I'll need at short notice. Please trust me on this, Mike, it'll be better all round if Zach forgets that I exist."

At the time Mike agreed with her to keep the peace, but after he had dropped her back at the hotel and had got home again, he found himself wondering what life had to have been like for Jenna for her to be so mistrusting. He'd represented several clients like her over the years, but he'd never got to really know them beyond the job, and now it was making him think about what their lives had been like later on. Should he have made more enquiries than he had? Probably not. But at least it was giving him a good deal of satisfaction being able to act as Jenna's benefactor for now. Just looking at how she relaxed out at the house was giving him hope that this move was the new start she clearly needed, just as Tiff had said.

And who knew, maybe it would be a new start for him too? How soon, he wondered, dare he take her to meet his mum? Given that he'd never given her anything beyond a friendly kiss on the cheek, he knew it was an odd way to be thinking, but something about her had his subconscious telling him, 'she's the one'. Something he had never remotely felt before.

Chapter 11

The grove in front of her was filled with dappled sunlight, trees shimmering in a dozen different shades of green as a soft breeze rustled them. As she walked through it, she was aware of the birdsong above her, and somewhere off to the one side there was the sound of gently running water. And the scent! The scent of fresh greenery had an intensity she had never experienced before, almost as though this was a new world untouched by mankind. It was pure, clean and untrammelled.

As she turned to look about her, she knew at an instinctive level that she wasn't alone. But there was nothing sinister in that. Nobody who wished her any harm was lurking in the fern, woodruff and bluebell carpeted shadows. Instead it was a sense of companionship. Of her own kind being there, and of some sort of collective consciousness binding them all. A wholly natural, spider-like web that interconnected many who were like her, and yet without in any way restricting or controlling them as individuals.

Reaching out she touched the bark of a young oak tree. And jerked it back in shock! It had sunk in. Her hand hadn't just rested on the bark, it had gone in as if through a spongy surface. Tentatively she did it again, watching in awe as her hand went in and then the bark wrapped itself around it like the softest of gloves. Daring to push just a little more, it was as though something was flowing past her hand inside the tree. Sap! It was the sap she could feel, the very life essence of the tree. And the tree was alive, alive in a way she had never thought of. It too was connected to the other trees around it, and she felt compelled to step forwards so that she became one with it.

In that instant she felt as though, if she could only dive deep enough into this amazing green flow of life, she would be able to reach out and touch every other tree in the land in the end. Cut one and they all felt it. Nor was this like some drug-induced New Age trip on hallucinogens, weird and disturbing. Instead it felt more as though she was touching something totally natural which was both ancient and yet timeless. Something primal, something that had existed since life began.

"Now you understand," a voice which seemed to be inside her head said. "We are one with the world. We belong here, in the green, not severed from…" and the sensation defied her ability to pin it to a single word. 'Life' might have come close, but this was more than just one person encased in a body of flesh and bone; it was life in the much greater sense of all living things, and again that sensation of being somehow totally interlinked.

There was a noise. A shattering of the tranquillity. Something mechanical. Something man-made. And then just as her mind flagged it as 'chainsaw', the most excruciating pain seared through her and the world went black.

Jenna sat bolt upright in bed, aware that she had screamed as she woke, sweat pouring off her.

"What the…?"

For a moment she couldn't even think where she was. Not her flat, not the hotel. Then her memory returned, and she remembered that it was Thursday night, and Mike and Tiff had brought her out to the house after work, the electricity having gone on that afternoon. She was upstairs in the spacious bedroom which looked out onto over the lake, her own single bed looking lost in the vast expanse of the room. As she had fallen asleep she had been so happy to look out onto the lake and see above it a glorious expanse of stars – something she had never seen before thanks to the light pollution from street lamps and other signs of human habitation that were missing here.

Now, though, her heart was pounding and she could still feel a residual aching in her legs, as though she herself had been attacked by that chainsaw. And what sort of dream had that been? Jenna had never known herself dream so vividly that she could actually remember the scent of something after waking, yet the fresh, pungent greenery was still lingering – so much so that, as with other intense smells that she had occasionally experienced, she could taste it too.

Knowing that she was too disturbed to be able to lie back down and sleep right away, Jenna swung her legs out of bed, and when she felt that she could stand up without her legs giving way, stood up. She was alright while she stood on her own brightly coloured rag-rug, but the moment her bare feet touched the wooden boards of the bedroom floor, she felt the strange surge of emotions coming back again.

"Oh my God, what's happening to me?" she gulped, now starting to get worried. Weren't olfactory hallucinations supposed to be warnings of something? Was it a stroke? She couldn't remember in her current bothered state.

She turned back to the bedside rug and pushed her feet into her flip-flops, and for some reason, having that layer of plastic between her and the wooden floor allowed her to focus on reality enough to make it safely down the stairs and through to the kitchen. Putting the kettle on, she made herself a camomile tea to soothe her, and when it was brewed, took it through to the dining table. The comforting familiarity of sitting on her one carver chair – the one she always used if she felt a bit light-headed or had a migraine – and with her elbows resting on the table, as she'd done on many a night, brought her heart rate down, and she was finally able to think a bit more clearly about the strange dream.

It had been as if she had inhabited someone else's body, and the more she thought about it, the more she was convinced that it wasn't someone human. Not exactly animal either. But rather something or someone who was the embodiment of Nature – and definitely nature with a capital N, not just in the general sense. She took another sip of the hot tea and stared out at the lake, beautifully illuminated by a first-quarter moon on a crystal-clear night. There was nothing out there which could have triggered her dream. Not even a fox prowled about out there, and Jenna knew how eerie a fox cry could be from hearing the urban ones who would come and raid the bins by her flat. Those cries really could sound as though someone was being tormented if you didn't know what they were, and yet even before she'd looked for one, she had known that this hadn't been any fox cry. Nor had it been the call of a tawny owl percolating into her sleep, because again, she knew what they sounded like from the occasional one which would come to the big tree across the way from her front door. *My old front door*, she mentally corrected herself. She would never be going back there again.

Yet what was it about that dream that was poking her subconscious into thinking that she knew something about it? As she leaned back in the chair and let her eyes drift across the darkened room, they caught her bookcases, already refilled with her text books. And that was when it came to her. That final undergrad' year course she'd done on Old Norse. Officially it hadn't been a module, not part of the degree itself, but her tutor had run a bit of a side course for those like her who had been studying Old English and wanted to at least get the basics of Old Norse.

Jenna had been so taken with it that she'd done some further reading on her own about Norse mythology, and now something was prodding her that at some point in that reading she had come across whatever it was that was bothering her now.

"Well that's one for the morning," she said aloud, feeling better now that she felt she had more of a grip on reality again. "I'm not burning the lights to sit up all night hunting for that now."

Putting her mug into the sink, she went back up to bed and fell into a mercifully quiet sleep for the rest of the night.

Come the morning, she pulled the relevant books off the shelf, and dug into the cardboard lever-arch files of photocopied journal articles to find the ones she'd half-remembered the night before. With some serious reading ahead of her, she made her breakfast, and then spent a pleasant morning diving back into the stuff she loved best. Soon she would be covering the old table with the familiar pile of exam papers to be marked, for she was determined to honour her contract to do the marking both for her university students, and for the schools exams which she'd signed up for. Indeed she found that she was relishing the prospect of doing those now that she would be able to tackle them without her 'day job' getting in the way, and exhausting her before she even started.

Looking up from the photocopy she was reading, she felt a smile spreading across her face as she took in the lovely view. This was what she had always dreamed of having: her academic work to dive into, but in a peaceful and beautiful setting. Even if only for today, life, she reflected, was good.

By the time her stomach's growling reminded her it was time to break for a sandwich, she felt as though she needed a bit of a break to digest all she'd read anyway.

And so after munching her way through a large cheese and pickle sandwich, and another mug of decaf, she decided to make the most of a lovely day and go for a walk. After all, this was her first full day here alone, and she wanted to go exploring.

Putting on her battered walking boots, and throwing an outdoor fleece over her shoulders in case it got chilly before she got back, Jenna set out. Her idea was to see if she could walk all the way around the small lake. It couldn't be far, maybe two miles at the most. So if it became a bit of an energetic scramble in places, at least it shouldn't take too long.

As she swished through the long grass close to the houses, it occurred to her that this had probably been laid as lawns, but had been left to its own devices.

"Must make a note to ask Mike if I can have a mower up here," she said resolutely. She'd never mowed a lawn in her life, but how hard could it be? And it wasn't as if she would have to do the whole frontage in one go. If it proved hard work with the grass this length, she could always do it in sections. Again she found herself grinning at the prospect. Jenna Cornwell mowing lawns, eh? Who'd have thought it? That was another step in the right direction.

However, once she got to where the bushes and undergrowth of the woodland came down to the water, she found it much harder going. Nobody had ever cut a path through here, or if they had, then it had become overgrown a long time ago. What had looked so picturesque from the veranda and windows, now turned out to be wild woods of a less welcoming sort. Last year's brambles still threw long thorny tentacles out at every angle, snagging at her clothes and hair, and the tangle of native clematis which the old folk she'd known had called 'old man's beard' for its fluffy white seed-heads, wasn't half so attractive when it entwined itself around her boots and nearly had her falling into the prickly hawthorns.

Determined not to be beaten by this first encounter with raw nature, Jenna battled onwards, but what stopped her and forced her to turn back in the end wasn't the woods. Coming to a point where she almost fell into the small stream draining out of the lake, she was shocked to see that on its far bank was a fence. And not one that she was prepared to climb over either. Somebody had gone to considerable trouble to cut the undergrowth back for a short stretch along the bank, and to put in a wire-mesh fence of the kind that farmers used to keep livestock in. But no farm fence Jenna had ever seen had had the loops of barbed wire scrolling across its top like this one did. It reminded her more of the photos she'd seen of World War One trenches. The posts stood higher than normal so that they anchored the spirals of barbed wire and stopped them from sagging, and at regular intervals it was attached to the top of the fence. Even in the places where the loops had drooped a bit, it was still a formidable barrier.

More to the point, whoever had put the fence up had also put notices up. Off to her left and deeper within the wood, Jenna could just see a large sign which said in bright red, 'Private Property. Keep Out!' And it was facing her way, so presumably this wasn't something that Willetts had put in to stop random ramblers trampling across his lawns. This looked more as though it was facing towards him and his development.

Curiosity piqued, Jenna wrestled her way to her right and the shore of the lake. Sure enough, as soon as the fence reached the waterline, one branch went straight out into the water a short way, while another snaked back and began following the water's edge. Another large noticeboard stood on tall metal legs just into the shallows, proclaiming in bold red letters, 'Private Property. No access to hills. No unauthorised entry. No landing on this shore permitted.'

"Blimey!" Jenna gasped, rather taken aback. "Whoever you are you really mean business, don't you! No landing permitted? That sounds as though you're worried that someone in the houses might have a boat and come out here for a spot of fun. You must be a right old kill-joy if you're that bothered by the thought of people sitting by the water for a picnic."

Clearly she was going to get no farther, though, and so she fought her way back the way she had come. Once she was standing on the lawn again, she realised that the reason why she hadn't seen the sign before was because it was hidden behind a small promontory of trees from where she was standing. However, once she had walked along the lake's edge to just beyond Fiona's house, the sign came into view.

"I bet old man Willetts wasn't any too pleased about that," she mused, and then thought to explore and see how far she could get going anti-clockwise around the lake. Sure enough, once past what she now recognised must be the perimeter of Willetts' land by the definition of the tatty former lawn, she didn't get far before coming up against another barbed-wire fence, this one following a deep ditch in the more open countryside, at the bottom of which ran the feeder stream for the lake. And again there was a very hostile-sounding notice-board. 'Trespassers will ALWAYS be prosecuted!' it declared in large lettering. 'No access under ANY circumstances.'

The steep-sided little valley she was in continued to rise away from the houses on this side, and seeing the fence snaking away into the distance, Jenna felt compelled to explore. Returning and going out through the bank which formed the gateway to the houses, she turned left onto the track which Mike had driven her up on. It wasn't too steep this close to the houses, but to her surprise she saw that there were two more patches of water glinting in the sunshine not that much farther uphill than the lake. However nobody was going to be building by their banks unless part of the house would be on stilts, because there was no flat space here.

Breathing heavily as she trekked up the steep path, Jenna was grateful for all the walking she'd had to do around Malvern, where there were plenty of roads as steep as this. Such rugged countryside she might not have been familiar with, but she could tackle a stiff incline with the best, and she felt a glow of satisfaction over not panting too hard as she forged onwards. After what was probably only a quarter of a mile, but felt farther, the track did a sudden left hairpin turn to work its way briefly across the slope, and at this point Jenna found that she could just about see the houses through the trees. This early in the spring, most of the trees had yet to put on much foliage, and that meant that she was looking through the twiggy tops, but come the summer, the houses would be completely obscured.

"Hmm, very private," she declared. "You wouldn't get any hikers nosing down on you, not even in the main school holidays." A buzzard wheeled sedately on the thermals just above her, scouring the land for prey. "What do you think, buzzard? Did old man Willetts genuinely want a lovely retreat? Or was he doing this to piss off some rival? Because somebody isn't happy about those houses being there, and from what I can see up here, it surely wasn't because they were going to wreck the view."

It still wasn't quite three o'clock, and Jenna knew that her trip back down would be faster, so she decided to press on, sure of getting back before the light failed. She was enjoying this immensely!

Rounding the shoulder of the valley, the track took the slightly gentler route above it to the top of the hill, and there Jenna stood and drank in the view. Not a soul moved in this open and untamed landscape, and maybe because of that she felt completely safe. The wind tugged her hair this way and that, turning its natural waves into unruly curls she had to hold off her face with her fingers, and she was glad she still had her fleece jacket to slip on, but she hadn't felt so unreservedly happy in a very long time.

"Oh this is bliss!" she sighed, throwing her arms wide and letting the breeze ruffle her. The only thing which could have made this any more perfect would have been to have the company of a dog.

Feeling almost drunk on the fresh air, she slowly turned around, looking at the view from other angles. Roughly to the north the land fell away sharply for a short way to a high valley in which there seemed to be a complex of farm buildings surrounded by trees. Off to the east there was more open hillside, and to the west there was a continuing vista of rolling hills. Then down towards what she thought must be the south-west, but not as far around to the south as her track back to the houses, she saw the roofs of what looked like it might be a smallholding. Did the track lead there too? She retraced her steps and picked up the track she'd come up on and began going back down.

She found no side track all the way down, aside from one which clearly went to the farm in the trees, until she came to where the track kinked back left to head for the hairpin. Now, though, she realised that this turn almost formed a T-junction, and that there was a continuation straight on. Drawn to investigate, she set off down the rough track, which now showed the signs of four-wheeled vehicles having been up and down it, just as the track from there downwards did.

Now why didn't I spot this earlier? Jenna wondered. *Probably because I was so intent on getting to the top of the hill, but I also thought the tyre tracks were possibly just some farmer coming up here to tend his sheep. I never thought I might have a neighbour.*

However, that neighbour was clearly not friendly. The track this way was straighter, and so Jenna soon saw ahead of her another of the red warning notices. Going only close enough to be able to read it, she saw that it said, "Pentre Derwen. Private Property. Keep Out!" And across the track was a substantial metal farm gate with a chain linking it to its stout post and a big padlock on it. Either side of it was more of the cattle fence and the barbed-wire, ensuring that nobody on foot would just slip around the side of the big gate.

Whoever this was, they were determined to have their privacy, and Jenna had no desire to ruin such a lovely day by confronting what she was sure would be some grumpy and aggressive old man. So she turned back and took a leisurely walk back down to her new home. That didn't mean that she wasn't curious, though, and she resolved to ask Mike about who owned Pentre Derwen.

Once back in the house, she pulled her battered second-hand copy of a Welsh dictionary off the shelves as she padded back to the table with her mug of decaf, and looked up the place name, sure that it would have some meaning. Sure enough, 'pentre' meant valley, and 'derwen' could be an oak or holm-oak.

Well that would make sense, she thought as she went back to retrieve the pasta she was cooking and stir through some sauce, the walk having given her a ravenous appetite. "I wonder if any of the oak for these houses came from there?"

She hadn't realised she'd said the last out loud until she felt the wisp of something answering, "Yes!"

Chapter 12

Almost dropping the bowl of pasta, Jenna spun around, looking for who might have spoken.

"Who's there?" she called out. "Who are you?"

But nobody answered, and the room remained reassuringly silent.

Convinced that she must have imagined it, Jenna took her bowl to the table and dug in. When she'd even hungrily wiped the remains of the sauce up with a piece of bread, she sat back and looked at the notes she had made that morning.

What had triggered the memory had been the recollection of reading an old book about the religion of ancient Scandinavia. It had long been out of print, and second-hand copies had fetched way beyond what Jenna could pay, and so she had photocopied the bits she was interested in from the university library copy. It seemed that there were nature spirits in Norse mythology collectively known as *vættir*, she had noted – a word the author had translated as wights – which seemed to encompass all sorts of beings including elves and dwarfs. Well Jenna was sure she wasn't sharing her house with either of those, and nor was she infested with *húsvættir*, which were a Norse kind of brownie, and which could be as easily angered as the brownies of English legends. But something in what she'd then found about *disir* sounded a bit more like it, not least because these had more of an association with place names; and in her old notes she had made in the margins, she had wondered if these were some kind of dryad?

Originally the word dryad had applied to creatures of Greek mythology, but she was gratified to find that her memory hadn't wholly let her down, and her further notes said that there were Celtic references to creatures which, for want of a better translation of their name, were also called dryads in English. These Celtic variations on wood nymphs were female, and unlike the Greek ones which were attached to a specific tree, could move between trees, although they might have a particular favourite. Even more appropriate, they were originally associated with oak trees, although in later mythology they seemed to be linked with all varieties of native trees.

Well it's no wonder you were dreaming about wood nymphs, she told herself firmly. *You're surrounded by oak in this house!* The outer planking might be some kind of pine, or so she guessed, but the main support beams in here were definitely oak. After all, Jenna had been around enough old houses to know what that grain looked like, and if these weren't as blackened with age, nonetheless she was sure they were the same.

And certainly there were times when the house almost felt as if it was 'breathing'. As evening came on, and the wood cooled after being warmed by the sun for most of the day, it gave little creaks and groans. Nothing worrying, and having spent her first year at uni in an old building which formed part of the halls of residence, Jenna was fully aware of how disconcerting such very minor contractions could sound. *There, you see? It was nothing but your imagination playing tricks on you,* she rebuked herself.

Whether it was because she was worn out from her walk and slept too deeply to notice, or the dreams never came, Jenna had an undisturbed night and woke feeling refreshed – something which only reinforced her belief that it had been her subconscious playing tricks on her the previous night. She spent the day going around her house first of all, double-checking all of the rooms, and coming to the gratifying conclusion that there was very little here which needed changing. The grouting in the bathroom would need redoing, having been something of a botched job in the first place, and ideally the huge windows in the two front-facing bedrooms upstairs would need something like blinds in them, because facing southwards, they would become unbearably hot when summer came if they couldn't be shaded. But other than that, 'her' house was absolutely fine.

Unwilling to face the other two houses just yet, she then went and explored the three detached garages. In one she found a brand new ride-on mower, which had clearly been used once or twice but then temporarily abandoned up here, and having found the instruction manual, she very cautiously drove it out and made a first attempt at cutting the knee-high meadow which the lawn had become. She was so engrossed in this and learning how to drive it, that she didn't hear Mike drive up until the Land Rover eased its way onto the drive and came to a stop.

As she switched off the mower's motor, Mike called across,

"Leave that! I come bearing gifts – fish and chips! Come and get them while they're hot!"

Brushing the coating of grass clippings off her jeans, Jenna gladly hurried over to Mike, her stomach growling in a most unladylike fashion at the appetising waft of salt and vinegar.

"God, I'm starving!" she confessed as they sat on the steps of the veranda and ate the fish and chips out of the paper wrapping. "I never knew the countryside could give you such an appetite!"

Mike laughed, but was greatly reassured by the improvement in Jenna. He'd been worried sick for the last two days, knowing that while she had said she would be fine out here on her own, equally knowing that many a city dweller he had come across had found the quiet of the countryside deeply unnerving once confronted with it. It gave him the courage to decide to ask the questions that had been brewing up inside.

"Would you mind if I asked you some things?" he began tentatively. "I'm not trying to be some busybody. It's just that I don't want to unknowingly put you in any situation that makes you really uncomfortable, or worse, brings up bad memories." He nibbled another mouthful of chip before adding, "And although Tiff is your friend, I've seen enough of her in action by now to know that she might have put her own spin on some of what she told me."

He was relieved at Jenna's giggle of, "Oh heavens, yes! Tiff sees the world very much in her own light, bless her. I love the way she's always so optimistic. Sometimes that's been the saving of me when I get to be too gloomy. It's been reassuring to have someone around to talk to who can make you see things in a very different way. But I do get what you mean about her having her own bias. How are things with her and Zack, by the way?"

Mike waved a chip at her, adding, "The very reason I'm out here with these! Zack came with his overnight bag already packed this morning, and when he went to leave at about two o'clock, Tiff actually stood in front of him and demanded to know where the hell he thought he was going. They were still fighting like a couple of pit-bulls an hour later, and I'd had enough. God, I hate rows, Jenna. I'm not cut out for that sort of work atmosphere. My mum and dad never had shouting matches, and it might sound a bit old fashioned or wimp-ish, but I truly don't like all that bawling and screaming. It's different when it's some client. I can switch off to that. But not when it's right in my face and personal.

"I'd been intending to come out and see you tonight, anyway, and then I remembered that the mobile fish and chip van would be out this way this evening. He does a roaring trade with there being no takeaways in any of the villages, so everything's always freshly cooked, and he's got a nice little circuit on Thursday, Friday and Saturday nights. So I left a note on Tiff's desk and slipped out while they were still screaming in one another's faces, grabbed the chips, and here I am."

Jenna had been nodding along with him as he'd spoken. "Oh I so agree, I can't stand it when people start yelling at one another, although from a different starting point. My dad died when I was too young to really remember him, and mum had a succession of dodgy men after that, who she always broke up with by having steaming rows. Things would get thrown, the police would get called, and …*urgh*, well I don't need to paint you of all people a picture of what that can get like. So I tend to get very stressed when the shouting starts, because I'm just waiting for it to get worse."

"So where's your mum now?" Mike ventured to ask. "Don't answer that if you don't want to, though."

"I have no idea," Jenna said, almost surprising herself at how little that meant to her by now. "I was put into foster care when I was fourteen, along with the new baby she'd had, because it turned out that her new bloke was a convicted rapist."

Mike nearly choked on his piece of cod. "Bloody hell!"

"She was given a choice: get rid of him and have your kids back, or stay with him and have them permanently removed. She chose him."

"Oh Jenna, I'm so sorry, that's harsh." He couldn't imagine what it must feel like to be rejected like that by your mum, of all people.

She sighed and gave a little shrug. "If she'd been an affectionate mum all along it would have been worse. But she'd always treated me as unwanted excess baggage. The worst part was after I'd got attacked. My last foster parents came to see me, but of course in the long time I was in hospital, they'd had new kids sent to them, so there was nowhere for me to go back to, even though they wanted to take me in just as themselves, not as part of their contract. And I'd passed the magic sixteenth birthday, when you're past the foster services being interested and get shoved out into the world on your own. That was the point when I so badly wanted somebody to come and take care of me.

"My friend Mel says that this is why I can be so detached at times. She says I pull away from people not because I won't give them a chance – which is sometimes what Tiff thinks, I'm sure – but because after all this time, I just don't expect anyone to be there when I need them, and so I act to make sure I'm going to be okay without anticipating what anyone else might do. I become defensive out of a lifetime of having to do it, not to piss others off."

"Mel sounds very perceptive," Mike said, summoning up a smile, and hoping he wasn't looking too appalled at how abandoned Jenna seemed to have been for so long.

"Oh she is! I hope she comes home from India soon. I'd love to tell her all about this!"

"And you're sure you're alright with this situation?" He gratefully took the clean sheet of paper towel off Jenna to wipe the grease off his fingers. "I mean, err...it struck me that Tiff and I were a bit high-handed, coming in and sweeping you up like that last weekend. You'd had such reservations about coming out here before, and then what do we do? We come and whisk you off to the very place you thought you'd be too isolated in. I was rather worried about that."

However Jenna's smile was reassuring, and she was quick to say, "Thank you for that consideration, Mike, and I really appreciate your concern, but actually I'm okay. ...I think it's because I had spent so much time dreading the moment, that once it had come it was almost a relief, if that doesn't sound too cockeyed."

"No, I get what you mean – especially in the light of what you just told me about never expecting any help. From what Tiff said, you must have been dreading the day when that awful bloke dragged his mess to your door, but even worse, about having to deal with it all by yourself."

"Exactly!" *Oh my God, he gets it!* Jenna mentally gasped in amazement. The only other person who had ever truly grasped that had been Mel.

And somewhat emboldened, in his turn Mike now dared to ask, "But how come you never changed jobs before, Jenna? You're not unqualified. Surely there must have been *something* else you could have done? Office jobs aren't that hard to come by."

Yet Jenna shook her head. "Two reasons. The first is that it's shockingly hard to get into office work if you've not started out that way after school or uni. And crap though supermarket pay is, it's still better than office junior work. You have to understand that I left school at sixteen and then got things like A levels at night school while I was working to try and keep myself. I got my final one while I was able to do nothing much but lie in bed for months, and that's what opened up the chance to go to uni. I wasn't always well qualified at all.

"But also, few companies see a high qualification in something as obscure as medieval history as an immediate entry into commercial work, and a lot of new graduates take very poorly paid intern work for a while to get experience. They depend on the bank of mum and dad to get them through. But I genuinely couldn't afford to do that, especially once the cheap student lodgings had gone. Whereas with my shop job being something I was established in, and with my past history on record with social services because they'd previously needed to house me for my own safety, at least I got – and still get – some help with things like my rent in my current job. Grim though it is, can you see that it became a bit of a trap it was hard to get out of?"

"Oh, absolutely."

"And then the other thing has been about the locations. When I was up at uni in Birmingham, the offices there tend mostly to be in the city centre – which is precisely where I was attacked. Honestly, Mike, I'd have a meltdown just having to stand on a city street on a late winter's afternoon in the dark, doing nothing more than waiting for the bus after I'd been in town shopping, at like four o'clock. It was horrible! I'm so much better out in the suburbs than in the concrete canyons, and even then it's taken me a long time to be able to walk home from work late on in sleepy little Malvern, and not get back a gibbering wreck.

"Even living in Malvern and working in the centre of Worcester would have been a horrible strain, because again, there I feel hemmed in between the traffic and the buildings. And what Tiff didn't get was that I would have been trying to pick up a totally unfamiliar job at the same time as I was trying to overcome a new set of triggers for my nightmares. I only ever tried that once, just before I got the supermarket job. I was in bits by the end of the second week. I just couldn't cope."

"And Ludlow would be different?"

"Oh, God, yes! There's just not the weight of people and traffic around for a start off, and in the centre by your offices, those dinky little lanes don't allow anyone to come running up behind you – the pavements aren't wide enough, and the cars pass too close and too slowly for drivers not to see what might be happening. It's not so anonymous. I get that people just thought it was a fight between a pair of thugs when I got attacked, because I was so short of cash I'd bought a man's hoodie from the charity shop, and that's what I was wearing. But nobody stepped in to help. That sort of thing happens in big cities. People become that bit more defensive, more protective of themselves. They don't want to risk getting involved because the threat of some idiot turning on you with, say, a knife is so much greater."

"That wouldn't happen in Ludlow," Mike said with conviction. "I don't mean the knife thing – we do have our own home-grown idiots, although blessedly few – but the indifference, I meant."

"And that's exactly why I feel different about being out here. Now that the decks have been cleared of Kyle, so to speak, I feel as though I can see the wood for the trees a bit." Now came the acid test. Would Mike help? "I may have to call on you in a week or two's time to run me to the train station, if you would? You see I'm determined to fulfil my exam marking contracts, and that will mean going up to Birmingham to collect and drop off papers. You can dump me at the station as early as you want in the morning, and I'll happily wait until you've finished at night to bring me back, but I will need that ride into Ludlow itself."

Relieved that it was something as simple as that, Mike cheerfully said, "That'll be no problem! Just let me know when and I'll gladly come and pick you up."

He was deeply reassured that she would also settle into life and work in the office, now. Understanding where her fears had come from, and not just Tiff's rather vague concerns, had given him a whole new perspective.

Deciding to change the subject to something a touch more cheerful, he now said, "I was surprised to see you with the mower. If you've got to grips with that so fast, I'm sure it won't take long to teach you how to drive."

"Well I was a bit worried that I might end up by tearing off into the lake!" Jenna admitted with a laugh. "I've never been so nervous of a machine as when I started it up and then got it going. The first few passes I did were at a snail's pace. I could probably have done them faster by hand with a scythe! I had visions of you having to tow me and the mower out with the Land Rover!" and they both laughed. "Would I be right in thinking that old man Willetts envisaged having a beautifully mown lawn reaching down to the water's edge?"

"Oh yes, very much the immaculate sward – although given that he wouldn't pay for new turf to be laid by that stage, given how his daughters were mucking him about already, I think he was overly optimistic to think that he'd get this hill grass quite that tamed."

"And how did he get this land? Because…" and Jenna told Mike of her explorations and the signs and barbed wire.

"Oh heck, I hadn't realised that Robin Harrison had taken that much offence," Mike groaned when she'd finished. "Yes, you are right, the animosity is over the land. You see this bit was part of some land owned by one of the wealthier families in the area, and they got hit for inheritance tax. Nothing odd about that. But of course, when they came to sell the land off, they needed to get as much for it as possible. Now Robin's dad and grandfather all farmed that small-holding up the road, but for them it was something of a hobby aside from their main jobs. I guess you'd say that they were playing at being farmers more than actually doing much. There was an old boy who lived up in the attached cottage all year and kept an eye on the sheep and stuff, but the Harrisons mostly only came out here at weekends.

"Well at that stage it was all very friendly, because the Harrisons had social aspirations, and so when the owners of this patch used to come up and have picnics and barbeques out here in the summer, they were always invited. But things had changed long before this land came on the market. For a start off, the older generation had died or moved. The days of the families socialising were a thing of the past. And then the younger son, Robin, came back from the second Gulf War a very changed man. I can't remember who he was with – the marines or the para's, I think – but that was the war when there were a lot of men who later developed horrible side effects from some of the chemicals they got exposed to, and Robin was one of them. Once upon a time he seemed set for a long and distinguished military career, something his mum and dad were so proud of. But he came back from Iraq, quit the army, and basically hid himself away out here on the farm."

"Oh, poor man!"

Mike grimaced. "I know. He's certainly paranoid. Sometimes it's not too bad and for a few weeks he'll come down into town, and you'll see him about the place getting his supplies. Then he'll just vanish for months. God knows what he lives on in those times, but you don't get any thanks for going up and trying to see if he's okay. I had to soothe some very ruffled feathers when he chased social services off with a rifle some years ago!"

"You got him off?"

"Let's just say that because he's obviously well in most respects, and he never comes into town to cause any trouble, it was hard for them to make a case for taking him in to get treatment, if there is any for what ails him. And because of his training, I was able to say that he knew the difference between threatening and actually shooting – in that sense he's way less of a threat than some of the crankier old farmers. I think what saved the day then was that there's such a backlog of people needing to go into care, that since he's clearly self-sufficient, the decision was made to leave him alone, although we did confiscate the rifle!

"And that was how things were left until the field here came up for sale. Now Robin lives the life of a monk, so his army pension has been building up nicely, and together with what he inherited alongside his three sisters from their parents, I think he was sure he'd be able to buy this land and keep himself even more private. But of course Willetts could out bid him at every step – and did!

"That was bad enough, but then Willetts decided to build these houses and Robin went absolutely nuts." Mike gave a sigh and shook his head. "I've stood up on that driveway you've described, trying to convince him that he wouldn't even know there were people down here, but he wouldn't have it. He was convinced that at the drop of a hat he was going to be surrounded with a bunch of noisy townies, who would frighten his sheep and ruin his life."

Mike paused and looked off into the distance. "Funny... I've only just remembered this, telling you about it all, but he got incredibly distressed about it all, saying that somebody had been killed." He shrugged. "I tried to take him seriously, but honestly, Jenna, there wasn't even anyone who'd gone missing, let alone killed. Yet to hear him, the place was strewn with bodies.

"In the end, all I could put it down to was the sound of the chainsaws cutting up the timbers, and the carpenters' nail-guns, all taking him back to a very bad place in his mind. But at the time he was adamant – somebody up here was being murdered, and the way it came out, it was as if it was happening over and over again. That's why I thought it was dredging up memories of Iraq, and seeing other soldiers getting wounded, because nobody gets to die more than once."

Then he suddenly thought to add. "I'm not trying to scare you, by the way! I haven't heard of Robin coming down here bawling and shouting since the frames of these houses went up. And I'm absolutely certain that he'd never harm a woman. You've got nothing to fear from him. But by the same token, please don't be tempted to go up and try and see him by yourself. If there are any issues, for heaven's sake come to me with them, and I'll deal with them. He knows me by now, even if I'm hardly his favourite person."

Jenna assured him that she wouldn't do anything so foolish, but at the same time she couldn't help wondering whether the times when she had thought she had heard voices might not be this poor soul wandering about outside. Sound carried differently out here, where there was so little background noise. And in an odd way it was reassuring to think that she might have been hearing him from over on the other side of the water, rather than imagining someone creeping around right outside.

Chapter 13

On Friday night Mike had driven back home, but had promised to come back up the next morning to go through the other houses with her. That was something Jenna was very grateful for when the time came, because in contrast to the week, when the weather had been glorious, the weekend came in wet and windy. Heavy dark skies threw strange shadows in the houses, and a gusting wind tearing in from the south-west made for some strange noises as it found tight spots to whistle through. Jenna swiftly found herself shutting the double-glazed windows tightly, because the eerie whistling of the wind when they were open just a crack for ventilation had her nearly jumping out of her skin on several occasions – and that was just in her house where she was already starting to feel at home.

So she was very glad to hear the Land Rover's engine, and then see Marnie and Silas streaking across the grass towards her. Rather more confident of her ability to remove mucky paw marks in this house, she gladly welcomed them inside, and was much amused that they promptly took over her sofa like a couple of furry bookends.

"Oh God, you two are an embarrassment," Mike declared as he followed them in and saw where they had landed.

"It's okay," Jenna laughed, "that cover's washable, and they're not dirty."

Mike shook his head. "I don't know what it is with the long dogs, but they're all absolute wimps. One drop of rain and that's it, they're inside and by the fire and determined not to move."

"Well at least they're not dragging you out across the hillside in this."

"True. Dad's old spaniel demanded a long walk come hell or high water. Many's the time Dad came in drenched to the skin, and Flossy all ready to go back out and do it all over again." Mike pulled a face. "Don't think I'm up to that! So I'm quite glad that these two are as they are. I just wish that they didn't think that every sofa they encounter is theirs by right."

Clearly there would be no problem leaving the two of them inside, and so Jenna and Mike dodged the downpours to go across to what she now knew was Alicia's house.

"I can think of no clearer sign of Brian Willetts' failing health than the number of issues there are with these houses," Mike said regretfully as they let themselves in. "Honestly Jenna, he may have been a crabby, unpleasant old goat, but by golly he knew his stuff when it came to building. That shoddy work in your bathroom would have been spotted the first time he went in there, and believe me, he used to personally inspect every house he built before it went on the market. He was a small-scale developer, doing prestige builds of never more than half a dozen houses at a time, and they sold because of the quality. I've never know there to be so many 'snagging' issues, as they're called, with one of his houses before."

"And what a shame that it should have been with stuff that his daughters were messing him about over," Jenna sympathised. "Shall we start upstairs?"

They began with the wet-room, and Mike was soon concluding, "I think the best thing we can do with this is just get a proper floor put in, take out that weird shower, and just put in a normal bath with a shower over it. With a bit of luck we can get a suite on offer at one of the builders' suppliers. It'll be a whole heap cheaper than trying to make this right."

"I was thinking that," Jenna admitted. "I don't have your experience of dealing with property, but it felt like the common sense thing to do."

Having then decided that an inoffensive magnolia might be a better colour for the walls of the two smaller bedrooms, given that they would be where most families would be expecting the children to sleep, they went through to the galleried bedrooms.

"Good grief, these don't get any better second time around," Jenna lamented, struggling to resist the urge to bolt out of the room and get downstairs as fast as possible. What on earth was it about these two bedrooms that gave her the creeps so much? They switched the lights on, for it had gone incredibly dark outside for the time of day, and it was now that it became apparent that the only natural light coming into these two rooms was from the huge picture window beyond the gallery. "How are you going to separate these from the lounge when they haven't got any other windows?"

"Velux," Mike said morosely, mentioning the brand leader in roof-lights. "Thank God these rooms are up under the eaves. It's not going to be cheap because of the disruption to the tiles, but it'll have to be done, and I reckon possibly two per bedroom, too. Hell's teeth, Alicia's going to have a meltdown over the cost."

"Ever serve her right," Jenna said with a sniff of disgust. "I'm just sorry that you're the one who has to deal with her."

Fishing into one of the pockets of his tweed jacket, Mike produced a professional-looking measuring tape and began working out where the new inserts would need to go, so that he could at least try and get a quote for the work. Leaving him to such technicalities unless he called her to hold the end of the tape, Jenna found herself wandering to the gallery. A belt of rain had come in, obscuring even the far side of the lake, and so she leaned on the wooden rail with no particular thoughts in mind.

You must die! The thought suddenly pounded in on her, making her gasp, but before she could do or say anything, she felt herself being shoved hard by something in the middle of her back. Pitching forwards from the force of the shove, she found herself tipping over the rail and screamed.

Somehow she registered Mike's equally panicked, "Jenna!" A clatter must have been the dropped tape-measure, and then his hand clamped over one of hers that was flailing to find something to grip.

With a sob she allowed him to yank her back to him, and as he pulled her tight into his arms, she realised that his heart was pounding almost as fast as hers.

"That's it! This bloody gallery goes!" she heard him saying in a choked voice, partly muffled by him having his face in her hair.

When they could both move without shaking, Mike held her back at arms' length, asking, "Are you alright?"

She managed to nod. What was she going to say if he asked what had happened? How could she say she felt as if she had been pushed without it sounding like an accusation against him? And yet she knew beyond a shadow of a doubt that it hadn't been him.

"I felt something," she said shakily, then saw how pale Mike looked even as he nodded.

"Errm, pleased don't think I'm some nutcase, Jenna, but just for a second I swear I saw someone behind you –

and no, I don't believe in ghosts and stuff, but I don't know how else to describe what I saw."

Relieved that at least he wouldn't think her a total freak, she confessed, "I heard someone. Or rather, I heard a voice inside my head. Oh Mike, it was horrible. It was so angry, and yet so terribly sad at the same time."

Mike pulled her to him again. "I'm not sure what he'll say, but I know a Catholic priest who reckons he deals with hauntings. I've a good mind to get in touch and see if he'll come out here and do his stuff on this house. He's about the only person I can think of who wouldn't think I'd totally lost the plot describing what happened just."

Feeling that now she herself could confess, Jenna tentatively told him about the house cleansing she had witnessed Mel doing. "I didn't want to say anything earlier for fear of you thinking it was because I was all stressed up about things," she concluded, "but that house was a whole lot better after Mel had done her thing. So if you know this priest well enough to ask him, I'd say get him up here."

"Promise me you won't come in here by yourself, though," Mike added urgently.

"Not a chance! Nothing on God's green earth would get me back in here alone, I assure you! *Urgh*! Have you got enough measurements to be getting that quote with? Because I'd really like to get downstairs right now."

She hung onto Mike for grim death going down the stairs, and was glad she did when at the turn of the stairs the shove came again. This time it was only Mike's quick reactions which saved them both from falling the rest of the way down, and Jenna was sure she wasn't imagining it that the handrail seemed to try to wrench itself out of his hand as his tug pulled them backwards, rather than forwards, and they both sat down hard on the steps.

"Okay, that does it," Mike declared, rubbing a sore spot on his hip when they had made it to the ground floor, "I've had enough of this house for today. Come on, let's go back to yours and have a coffee. I think we've earned it!"

Under any other circumstance Mike would have put the way the front door slammed shut from out of his hand down to a draft from somewhere. But today he was just glad that he'd not had his hand on the door jamb, given the force with which it shut them out.

At Jenna's door they were even more disconcerted to find Marnie and Silas whining and pawing at the doorglass in their efforts to get to them, and it certainly wasn't because either dog wanted to go out. As soon as they got in through the door, the dogs were all over them, as if checking them to make sure they were okay. But once convinced that their beloved master and his new friend were still in one piece, the pair resumed their positions on the sofa and went to sleep.

"If nothing else, the fact that those two have settled again makes me think that there's nothing weird about this house," Mike said with considerable relief. "I'd have been packing you up and taking you home with me if they hadn't. I'd never forgive myself if I thought we'd rescued you from one danger only to put you in the way of another."

They had a break which included some lunch, and then with the storm front having passed over for now leaving just a grey, drizzly day, they decided to go across to Fiona's house. More alert to the atmosphere now, Jenna again got the shudders as they went inside and closed the front door behind them. If the other house felt as though it was trying to expel them, this one felt more like a prison, and Jenna knew she would be glad to get out as fast as possible.

"Do you think you could get that priest to come and do his thing in here as well?" she asked Mike, and then wished she had waited until they were outside before having voiced her thoughts. It was as if the house had heard her and disapproved, for the temperature seemed to drop by several degrees in seconds, making them both shiver.

"Definitely!" Mike agreed, then nearly jumped out of his skin as Jenna gave a small scream right behind him. Spinning around, he saw her with her hand clamped over her mouth, and the other hand shakily pointing into the lounge. There, on the immaculate white shag-pile was a growing stain of what looked horribly like blood.

"Where's that coming from?" Jenna whimpered.

It looked for all the world as though it was bubbling up from the ground as if from some hellish spring – and it was spreading!

"Salt," Mike declared. "Isn't that what you're supposed to put on things like red wine stains?"

"I think there was some in the kitchen."

They went through to the pristine cupboards and work surfaces, but found only bleach.

"No point in using that," Jenna whispered, and they warily crept back to the lounge.

To their astonishment there was nothing there. Not so much as a drop had marked the carpet. In fact, having forgotten to take their shoes off since coming in from outside, it was they who were leaving faint marks on the expensive wool.

"Where did it go?" Jenna gasped. "Please tell me you saw that too, and I wasn't just imagining it?"

"No, I saw it, alright," Mike said, severely rattled. He looked around him, desperately hoping to spot something like the lens of a digital projector, for that would mean that Robin Harrison had been in here and was trying to frighten people off with projected images. Having set the scene with all that talk of murder, it would at least be a logical step up for him to be making, which was more than Mike felt about the alternative. In a bizarre twist, he found himself actively wishing that he could find some evidence of Robin interfering, since that would be something earthly and altogether human. Yet nothing presented itself to him.

"Do you want to carry on?" he asked Jenna.

"Yes, if only to get this over and done with," she said resolutely. "If we can make our decisions today, then we don't have to set foot in this horrible place until after any work has been done. I don't mind keeping an eye on the outside, but I think it would be a very strong-minded squatter who could take being in here for long."

"You have a point," Mike agreed with a shudder.

"Upstairs or down first?"

He looked around warily and decided, "Let's do downstairs to start with – if we get upstairs and feel like it's too much, then at least we'll have got something done."

They went and stood in the bay-windowed dining room.

"You know actually, there's not much wrong with this that a different carpet and maybe a slightly less brilliant white on the walls wouldn't cure," Mike said after a moment. "I can't see anything that I would describe as a major building job in here. And being a dry construction, we don't have to worry about the place drying out and cracks appearing in the plaster – that's always an issue with new bricks and mortar."

Jenna peered cautiously around the archway leading into the kitchen and then went in. "Same here, really. The cooker hood needs to be properly connected, and I reckon it wouldn't hurt to check that the other things – like that built in freezer, for instance – have been wired up properly, but however dazzling these snow-white tiles will be in the summer, given that this room faces west, there's nothing here that a decent rug wouldn't cure. I mean personally, I think pure white in a kitchen is asking for a disaster, but again, the splash-backs are tiled, so they'll always wipe clean."

Feeling a little more optimistic, they ventured through to the utility, part of which had a sloping ceiling formed by the stairs, and here they found the first evidence of Fiona playing up.

"Why have *both* your downstairs toilets out here where everyone has to come through the utility to get to them?" wondered Jenna in disbelief. "You'd think someone like this Fiona would be planning on entertaining folks, so why would you have them traipse through to the grottiest part of the house every time they needed a pee? Because that's what a utility ends up becoming, doesn't it? Even Tiff's mom uses the utility as a general dumping ground for waterproofs, wellies, and things. Would you really want your guests to see your knickers going round in the washing machine?"

Mike laughed, but agreed that the one thing they might change down here was the orientation of the toilet nearer to the front. He was leaning against the door jamb of the tiny space, saying to Jenna that it was a good job that neither of them was tall, since a six foot man would have been banging his head on the stairs, when suddenly he was propelled inside the cubicle, and the door slammed shut.

"Mike? Mike, are you okay?" Jenna called, desperately trying to turn the handle to open the door again.

"Yep, just a bit shaken," his voice came back. "Damn it, there isn't even a window in here that I could get out of. ...No, the handle won't budge."

"It won't turn for me either."

"Stand back. I'm just going to have to kick my way out," and Jenna saw and heard the door shudder as Mike's heavy boot connected with it.

Clearly the door hadn't been of the best quality, because a few hefty kicks and the bottom panel cracked. A bit more application of his boot to get the shards of wood out of the way, and Mike was able to crawl out.

"Thank God I didn't take these boots off!" he said with relief, as he stood up and dusted himself off. "I couldn't have done that in just my socks."

Then both of them backed away in dismay as the door gently swung open as if it had been off the latch all the time.

"Right! We don't go into any rooms that haven't got a window in them!" Mike declared emphatically. "We can't guarantee that the doors on the main rooms will break as easily, and I'm not getting trapped in this bloody place."

They walked back through to the lounge and made sure that the sliding patio doors were open before they went any farther.

"We can always lock those from the other side once we're out," Mike said, picking up a heavy stone and placing it in the track of the door. "That should at least stop this one from closing tight."

A quick scrutiny of the two rooms at the back of the house behind the lounge, which Mike said had been grandly described on the plans as the study and the T.V. room, soon had them agreeing that all three rooms should get the same basic makeover as the dining room. But then they had to face going upstairs. Both of them were deeply reluctant, and went up with extreme caution, yet they got to the landing without any mishaps.

Up here, however, they found further evidence of something very wrong having gone on. The door into the master bedroom had been ripped off its hinges and thrown across the room, lying broken in the far corner having narrowly missed both windows, but taking a chunk out of the plaster with it.

"This wasn't like… like *this* when we came before!" Jenna exclaimed in dismay.

"No it wasn't," Mike agreed, going to look in the en suite. "Bloody hell! The shower tray's been ripped up in here!"

"What?" Jenna shot to his side, and then stared in disbelief at the wreckage in the bathroom, and the shower tray which was now on its side with the torn off flexible drain pipe dangling from it like some broken limb. "Thank God it didn't rip the shower itself and the pipes out. The place could have been flooded."

Dreading what they might find next, they went to look at the back bedrooms and the family bathroom which lay in between them. Yet these rooms looked completely undisturbed.

"How bizarre," Jenna murmured. "But *euw*, what's that smell?"

They had come around the head of the stairs and were now facing the other front bedroom, from which a thoroughly unpleasant smell was wafting. Cautiously shoving the door open with his boot, Mike stepped forward, his exclamation of, "What?" making Jenna stand on tiptoes to see over his shoulder. There in the centre of the pristine white carpet was a huge pile of rotting vegetation, and not just leaves. There was something which looked as though it had been brought up from the bottom of the lake spreading a filthy brown stain across the carpet.

"I don't want to sound to nutty," Jenna said warily, "but remembering that stain downstairs, is that real?"

Mike edged forwards, while Jenna braced herself against the door to stop it shutting. Bending down he tentatively reached out and touched the carpet.

"Absolutely sodden," he reported.

He gingerly shuffled a little closer and reached out a hand to the heap.

As his finger tips touched the pile of leafy material he yelped, "Ouch!" jerking his hand back and standing up quickly.

"What? What happened, Mike?"

He turned to her, shaking his hand. "Nettle rash! Or something very like it anyway. Look…" and he held up his hand so that Jenna could see the familiar redness of a nettle sting.

"Okay, that's it. I've had enough of this place!" she said firmly. "There's absolutely no point in us making plans to change any of this if it's going to be wrecked again inside of a week. The Willetts women will never believe that they've been hit by vandals like that twice in a row. Come on, let's get out of here."

They hurried as much as they dared down the stairs and out of the front door. Yet Mike was just giving the extra turn of the key to deadlock the door, when the rock he had put in the patio doorway shot out past them and landed with a thump on the grass. The patio door then slammed shut before they had even got near it. The house had shut them out!

Chapter 14

"I think you should come home with me," Mike said firmly as they hurried back to Jenna's house, where once again they could hear Silas and Marnie whining. "At least for tonight anyway. Maybe it's this storm that's causing everything to be so much worse, but I'm really not happy at the thought of you being alone up here when the mobile network might go down." He pointed to one of the far hills where they could now see flashes of lightning. "The nearest comm's tower is over there. If that gets hit, any signal will be gone and you won't be able to call for help."

That decided Jenna, and she gratefully grabbed a few bits for overnight and joined Mike in the Land Rover. Back at his house it was easier to feel normality returning, but Mike was more determined than ever to try and make contact with the priest he knew.

"It'll mean going to church in the morning, because our local vicar is his cousin – that's how I met Charles. So I'm going to have to ask Dermot if he has a number for Charles, because I've never socialised with either of them enough to have such a thing." Mike looked apologetic. "I'm afraid you'll see the great and the good of the town turning up. Out here it tends to be the other social gathering place aside from the pubs, and with a very different clientele. It isn't the big church, St Laurence's, but one of the smaller parish churches, I'm afraid, so you won't get to look at the lovely old medieval stuff again."

He pulled another face. "It's rather expected that if you're one of the pillars of society that you should go to church, but I'm afraid I gave up on that after the attitude I encountered when Dad died. To say that they weren't particularly Christian when it came to helping Mum is a bit of an understatement, and yet they'd both been staunch supporters of St Leonard's all their lives. I hope you won't find it too daunting."

Fortified by a large cooked breakfast, Jenna set out for the morning service with Mike, not wanting to say that she had never even been to a Sunday morning service before. She just hoped she'd be able to pick up when to stand or sit in the right places. However the service itself passed without incident, and if the vicar waffled on a bit during the sermon, it at least gave her the chance to look around at the rather nice architecture. It was probably well after the medieval period, she decided, might even be Georgian, but it had a couple of elegant windows with what looked like original stained glass in them, and she felt she could at least compliment this vicar, Dermot Constantine, on them as a conversation starter.

What she wasn't prepared for was the length of time it took to get out of the church. She could just about see the gowned figures of the vicar and his curate in the doorway as they shuffled slowly towards it, but the pair seemed determined to have a full conversation with every parishioner who went out past them. Then she heard Mike softly groan and looked at him in consternation.

With a sickly smile he nodded ahead of them, saying, "The smart black overcoat with the red silk scarf. That's Mr Hornby."

"What? As in your old boss, Mr Hornby?"

"The very one." Mike tugged her back a few paces, allowing the people behind them to go past. "Bugger!" he swore softly. "I forgot he comes here. Of all the people to run into it had to be him."

"Why?"

"Well he knows why I don't come any more – God know we had enough... *hmmm*, vigorous discussions, let's call them, because you don't get to have an actual row with him. He considers himself far too refined for that. But that means he's going to know that something's amiss if I've set foot in this place again, and you can bet your boots he'll come over and ask why, too! Heaven forbid that he should mind his own business."

Jenna gave a sudden giggle.

"What?" Mike asked warily.

"Well you could always say you've come to ask about getting banns read. Say I'm your cousin or something, who wants to get married in a pretty church. He's never going to know the difference, is he?"

Mike's snort of amusement made the couple in front of them turn around and glare at such frivolity. "Miss Jenna Cornwall," he whispered with a chuckle, "are you proposing that I should lie in front of a man of God?" He didn't want to give voice to the ideas that her words had had skittering through his head about her in white!

She leaned in and whispered back. "Given that I wouldn't give a monkey's about any God who would want this lot of stuffed shirts as followers, what the heck, why not? Is this vicar here likely to come and do his hoo-doo stuff on the houses."

Mike had to smother another chuckle. "I think dear Vicar Constantine would have kittens at the very thought. So no, I had no intention of telling him precisely why I needed his cousin's help. It's just that it would've been a lot easier to fob him off with a story without old Hornby breathing down my neck."

They shuffled up to the door, finding themselves now the last ones out, and Mike dared to think that they might yet be able to have a word with the vicar alone when the man brayed loudly,

"Good heavens! Young Mike Campbell! What a delight to see you here!"

Jenna felt Mike's wince, not least because Dermot Constantine couldn't have been more than ten or fifteen years older than Mike, so it was patronising for him to call Mike 'young'.

"Hello Dermot," Mike said with strangled politeness. "Don't get too excited, this isn't going to be habit forming, I just came because I need to contact Charles on someone else's behalf. Do you have a number for him?"

"And who would that be?" Dermot asked in such unctuous tones that Jenna wanted to gag. The man was all falsehood, of that she was sure, and he certainly didn't really mean his follow-up of, "Is it one of my flock that's in trouble? Can I help?"

Yet as Mike gave an airy wave of his hand and said, "Oh no, it's nobody you would know, Dermot. A regular rogue out Shrewsbury way. A client…" a cut-glass upper-class English voice sliced across with,

"Client? What client? What have you been up to since I've been gone?"

"Mr Hornby," Mike wrung out. "How nice to see you. How's retirement suiting you?"

Jenna thought Mike had been remarkably polite given how rude the old man had been in butting in, but that was nothing compared to the explosion when Hornby saw her.

"And how dare you bring this woman here! Truly, Michael, I do not know what's got into you! I've heard all about her, you know. Dear Zachary has kept me informed of all the goings on, and I have to say that I think you've both behaved disgracefully. It wouldn't have happened in my time, no indeed it wouldn't! Screaming and shouting in the office? It's a disgrace! You're dragging my practice into the dirt, young man, and after I was the one to give you a chance, too. Ungrateful that's what it is.

"And you!" he turned on Jenna. "You're nothing but a jumped up clerk! How dare you take it upon yourself to reprimand a man of Zachary's calibre? You're a disgrace!"

"She's not..." Mike tried to get in, but got cut off with,

"...No she's not! She's not a member of the practice. She's not legally trained, and she's damned well not going to get rid of *my* successor to *my* business. So you can pack your bags young woman and go back to wherever it was you crawled out of, because I am going for a meeting with Richard Mann tomorrow and I shall be demanding that he fires you!"

For a moment Jenna had felt herself going cold and her stomach churning in the familiar response to aggression, but then as the realisation set in that he thought she was Tiff, she found herself becoming more angry than upset. Who was this old goat to bawl her out her in the church porch for something she hadn't even done?

"Well bloody good luck with that, sunshine!" she snapped back, amazing even herself that she had the nerve to step forward and poke him in the chest with her finger. "For a start off, you've got the wrong girl. I don't even work for your crumby company, so bloody good luck with getting me fired!" She saw her words hit home and Mr Hornby took a step backwards in dismay.

Pressing home the advantage she stepped forwards, making him take another step backwards to fetch up against an imposing old gravestone.

"And as for you giving Mike a chance, my understanding is that the company who owns your office had to bring him in to sort out the right old mess that Mister I'm-so-up-my-own-arse Zachary has created. You wouldn't even have a practice left to brag about if it wasn't for Mike, and Richard Mann knows that. So good luck with that meeting tomorrow – you're going to fucking need it!"

"But…but…but why are you here, then?" Hornby protested irately, spluttering like an old engine whose timing was shot to pieces.

"Exactly for what I said I was," Mike snapped. "Don't worry, I won't be here next week or any week after that, so you can carry on playing the great man without me stepping on your toes. I just need Charles' phone number. And yes, it is for a client, but it's nobody you would ever deign to notice, so to be frank, it's now none of your business."

Hornby's jowly face reset in belligerence. "You're a severe disappointment, young Michael. What your dear mother and father would have said to all this I shudder to think," and Jenna saw how Mike flinched at that. Hornby had found the one thing which would really upset Mike, and that made her angry.

It was the first time in a very long while that her sense of self-preservation got overrode by anger, and it was enough that she snapped back, "Well at least his father won't be turning in his grave in embarrassment like yours!"

Hornby's face set into a sneer. "Dear me, Michael, you really are associating with the low-lifes now. Is that a Birmingham accent I hear? Is she another of Mann's scummy little helpers?"

"She told you," Mike riposted icily, "she doesn't work for our company," just about stopping himself from adding 'yet'. "And I have to say Mr Hornby, that it's probably a very good thing you've retired if you think it's appropriate to abuse young women who've done you no harm in this way. I always wondered why Delia was so easily upset. Is this the way you've been talking to her for the past few years? I do hope not, because she didn't deserve that. And if I were you, I'd keep your bigoted comments about Birmingham and its inhabitants to yourself tomorrow when you're there – they're not likely to take kindly to them.

"As for Zach, whatever hot water he's in now, it's been none of my doing. You should have kept him on a tighter leash, or set him up on his own, if you didn't want the wrath of the parent company falling on him after you went. He's paying for your mistakes now, not mine." And with that parting shot, Mike grasped Jenna's arm and marched her out of the graveyard and down the road, leaving Hornby spluttering again, and Constantine's horsey neighing of,

"Parent company? What parent company's that, Mr Hornby?" ensuring that Hornby would be even more furious with Mike for exploding that myth of his ownership he'd kept going for the twenty years since the take-over.

"Bloody hell, I need a pint!" was the next thing Mike said when they had crossed the bridge back into the main part of town. "I don't normally start drinking this early on a Sunday, but today I can make an exception."

He led the way into a cosy old pub on Lower Broad Street, and leaving Jenna to grab a seat at a small table, he eased his way through the jovial Sunday lunchtime crowd, and returned shortly with a pint for himself and a large red wine for Jenna.

"Cheers." He clinked glasses with her and took another restorative gulp.

"This is much more like my idea of what to do on a

Sunday," Jenna confessed. "As my first every Sunday service, I have to say it didn't do much for me."

"Your first?" Then Mike grimaced. "Oh hell, that sounded just like bloody Hornby. Sorry, Jenna, that wasn't how I meant it."

"I know."

"It's just that having grown up with church on Sunday as part of the routine, it never occurred to me that you wouldn't have had that kind of childhood."

She laughed. "More mosques down Sparkbrook than churches these days. And the Christian churches over there are very much of the evangelical sort. I don't see Mr snooty Hornby 'gettin' on down' to a gospel choir surrounded by fervent West Indian ladies of a certain age."

Mike almost choked on his beer at the thought. "Good grief, no! You went to a church like that?"

"I went to the local Congregational church a few times with a school pal. Carmen's mum was almost a caricature – you know, the very large Jamaican lady with the extraordinarily flowery hat – but you could never have ridiculed her because she was too warm and generous. She swept up waifs and strays like me without a second thought, fed us to bursting point on her glorious cooking, and dispensed hefty doses of good common sense advice. I loved her to bits. She was way kinder to me than my own mum ever was. It was such a shame that she died young of breast cancer while we were still at school. When I was recovering I would have given anything for one of her big hugs. But it's left me with an abiding respect for people who devoutly believe in the way she did, not like that bunch of old hypocrites up the road. They wouldn't know a Christian act if it came up and bit them on the arse."

Mike chuckled. "It's so good to know that you'll mingle well with the county set," he teased. "But then again, I can see Hornby's personal clients buggering off in short order anyway. They won't want to deal with me. But then they were never the ones bringing in the real money either, so they're no loss. Mrs Willoughby wanting to discuss changing her will yet again – and she does that every six months or so, but never actually does it – takes up a lot of time but gets us nothing back." He laughed again. "I think you'll be much more comfortable with Henry Palmer, who's got a thriving pig business and regularly asks us to check over new contracts for him. Salt of the earth is Henry."

"I'm afraid I'm a proper townie. I love eating sausages and bacon, but I can't bear the thought of cute little piglets getting slaughtered."

"Oh you'll be okay with Henry. He deals with rare breeds, so his beasts all get to live to a proper age, and live outside as they were meant to. I gather he's even gone as far as to plant more woodland for them to rootle in, although I don't think it's fully established yet. The last work I did for him was commissioning someone to build bespoke wooden hut for them for the winter."

Jenna raised her glass again. "Then here's to more of Henry and his pigs, and less of Mrs Willoughby."

Having returned home rather merry, and then consuming a large Sunday lunch, it was only as the evening set in that Jenna thought to ask,

"What are we going to do about getting a priest, though? I can't imagine you're going to get much out of Vicar Constantine after our run in with his favourite parishioner. I presume Mr Hornby is always generous where the collection is concerned? Wouldn't do to seem tight-fisted if you think you can grease God's palm via his vicar."

"Blimey, you've got him taped, alright! ...Hmm, I'll just have to go out to the Catholic church and see if they can track Charles down. How hard can it be? He must be on somebody's books somewhere."

"Could I go and ask? You're not going to be driving me back out to the houses after the amount you've had to drink today, so I guess I'm here for the night in your spare room again – which is lovely, by the way. I love that cottage furniture! Why don't I go out there tomorrow and see if I can find anything out?"

Mike looked slightly surprised. "Are you sure?" He was still trying to work out what would faze Jenna and what she would be comfortable with.

"Mike, I spend every weekend talking to strangers across the counter. It's not that that I find daunting. It's when something comes up that's really personal that it gets worse for me. Something that trips one of my trigger mechanisms – that's when I start getting a bit wobbly. Asking some random priest about where another one is isn't going to rattle me."

In fact she had a feeling that she might do better than Mike at this. If nothing else, having been around Mel for so long she knew the right terminology to be using. Mike might think he needed to ask for an exorcism, but Jenna knew that what they really wanted was a cleansing. It would have to be much more extreme for an exorcism to be needed, and anyway, that tended to be more for people than for houses. So she was quietly confident that she would be able to couch her request in terms that wouldn't alienate a very Christian priest, and she guessed that even out here with a higher percentage of church-goers, they must get some rather uninformed requests.

A quick internet search told them that mass on weekdays was at nine thirty, with morning prayers coming fifteen minutes before then.

"Drop me off just before nine and I'll hang around until I can find someone," Jenna decided. "It's not the longest hike back into town from there, and I'm hardly on a schedule at the moment."

Therefore nine o'clock on Monday morning found her sheltering from a sudden shower in the neo-Byzantine porch of St Peter's and waiting for the priest, who turned out to be a substitute covering for the resident priest, who was on holiday. After she had carefully explained what they needed, being tactful in describing what she and Mike had witnessed, she paused and looked expectantly at the priest. His slightly fixed smile told her that he hadn't taken her seriously even before his response of,

"I'll give you some holy water. That should do the trick."

Evidently he had no intention of coming out himself, and he was even more reticent to hand on Charles' details. All Jenna could get on that score was that Charles was off in some charitable mission somewhere, but then that meant that he wouldn't be near enough to come and help anyway. Making herself thank the priest politely, Jenna took the time walking back into town with the small phial of holy water to think hard about what she had seen Mel do. Could she reproduce it by herself? She wasn't quite sure. One thing she would need would be incense, and preferably the proper stuff, not just the sticks most gift places would sell. She also had a feeling that she would need white sage – hardly something she could pop into the local green grocers for – and frankincense, with possibly a bit of myrrh for good measure. *It's going to have to be Amazon*, she sighed to herself, *but whether they can get it to me fast enough is another matter. I can't imagine there are enough people wanting Prime delivery of that stuff to make it worthwhile.*

Feeling that she had already let Mike pay for far too much already, and with the knowledge that she would get paid soon for her caretaking role, she went in search of somewhere where she could sit and place an order. Tiff had handed on to her her old i-phone a year or so back, and it was more to do with Jenna's fear of running up a bill she couldn't pay, rather than her inability to use it, which had stopped her from going online with it until now. Sitting in the coffee shop she was getting to know rather well, she had to have a couple of goes before she got her Amazon account up, but once on there she soon found what she wanted. What was rather more of a decision was where to have it delivered to? Obviously she would be deleting her old home address, but would anyone find their way up to the houses? Probably not. Better, then, to have it sent to the office – however odd that might seem – because at least there would always be somebody there to receive it.

With the order for charcoal discs and four different lots of incense placed, she walked on to the office, only stopping to buy a small water mister of the kind people used for exotic houseplants. If she was going to make the best use of the holy water, then she would need to spray it in small quantities, not splash it around.

"How did you get on?" Mike asked as she eased her way in through the door balancing a cardboard box in her hand, having been unable to resist the cakes on display at a nearby bakery.

"Ooh! Are those doughnuts?" Tiff exclaimed almost at the same time. "Oh you darling! I'm starving!"

Jenna shook her head. "Tiff, you're always starving, and it's really irritating that you never put a pound on either."

Tiff gave a smug grin. "Sorry, can't help it. I'm a lean burn engine."

"Well I'm not," Jenna laughed ruefully, "and after Mike's breakfast and lunch yesterday, I feel like I've piled on about half a stone already. Not that I didn't enjoy every sinful mouthful," she added with a smile for Mike, "but I hope the local shops carry super-sized clothing, because I'm going to need them if I'm not careful!"

"But you're still eating the cinnamon bun," Tiff teased.

"Of course I'm still eating the cinnamon bun …so keep your sticky mitts off it and eat your own doughnut! What would you like, Mike? Danish or doughnut?"

"Ooh, Danish please! There's coffee on the go over there. Help yourself to a mug."

"When did the coffee machine arrive?" Jenna wondered as she strolled across to the sleek black machine now perched on the wide windowsill.

"It came with me from Birmingham," Tiff declared. "I have no objection to working hard, but I'm damned if I'm going to do it without decent coffee! Ooh, yummy, second doughnut left – marvellous! …There's a tin with some proper coffee in it in Delia's old desk if you want to use the cafetière I brought with me, but I stocked up on those nifty little pod things that you just pop in the machine – so much easier. Try the cappuccino, Jenna, it's delish'!"

"Did you find Father Charles?" Mike tried again.

Jenna grimaced. "Unfortunately no, and the regular guy is off on some missionary holiday in Uganda, or somewhere like that, so his fill-in wasn't willing to go hunting for a phone number for some random woman who'd walked in off the street. All he'd say is that Charles is in Bolivia, I think it was. Sorry, Mike, but I don't think it would have been any better if you'd been there. Bless him, he was a nice chap, but a bit clueless about the nastier things that can lurk in this world."

"It's all that unnatural celibacy," Tiff said with studied innocence. "They'd be so much better if they had a good shag every now and then."

"Tiff!" Jenna protested, laughing, while Mike went a strange puce colour, clearly not used to such frankness. "Anyway, I think I've got more chance of success having a go myself."

"Are you going all Melanie Clarke on me?" Tiff demanded with mock sternness, referring to Mel.

"Might be… I hope you aren't going to be too prudish about it, because there are 'essential supplies' coming from Amazon to this office, hopefully by the end of the week, since I don't have a home address to use."

"Prudish? *Moi*? Perish the thought!"Tiff said with a toss of her immaculate chestnut bob. "I'm a die-hard liberal me, positively bohemian. I'll even join in with the dancing naked around the bonfire as long as it's not too chilly. I can't stand it when I start getting frostbite on my nipples," at which point they had to rescue Mike with some vigorous back-slapping after he inhaled a currant from his Danish.

Chapter 15

It took until Tuesday for Jenna to convince Mike to let her go back to the houses, but at that point Tiff joined them, curious to see what all the fuss was about. As Tiff's Smart sports car eased its way into the drive beside Mike's Land Rover, she unfurled herself from it declaring,

"You didn't tell me it was up a wild track. Jeez, Mike, I've nearly had the exhaust off this thing three times!"

"I did offer you a lift," Mike protested, "but you wouldn't have it."

"*Hmph!*" Tiff sniffed, coming to link arms with Jenna and swinging her around so that they marched off together leaving Mike in their wake. "So come on, then, what's all the fuss about?"

Luckily Mike was getting the hang of Tiff's sarcastic sense of humour by now, and didn't take offence.

"This, Miss Tiffany Fairbourne, is the house that first tried to lock us in, and then practically threw us out," Mike said, gesturing to Fiona's house and playing along with Tiff's mock haughtiness.

"Looks pretty harmless."

"Tiff, you have no idea," Jenna sighed. "Honestly… Look at this stone out here. That was *thrown* from the patio door – and not by either of us! And we'd literally just come out of the front door. There is no way that there could have been anyone else in the house with us."

Looking at the sizable rock now embedded in the

roughly mowed lawn, Tiff had to admit that it was puzzling.

"Okay, so what do we do now?"

Jenna put her bag down on the small patio and dug into it for the few incense sticks she had been able to rustle up in Ludlow. "Well this is a far cry from what Mel did, but it's the best I can do at short notice. I'm going to light the incense sticks and put them by the door and the patio door. If you'll then open both lots of doors, Mike, but without going in, then we should recite the Lord's Prayer while I spray the door jambs with the holy water."

Tiff looked sceptical. "Is that really going to work?"

"Honestly? I have no idea," Jenna replied. "But it's the best I can come up with, so I guess we have to try?"

"We definitely have to try," Mike said with conviction, making Tiff look sideways at him. Jenna she could forgive such flaky thinking, knowing her background and how much Mel had helped her, but Mike? He'd been all sensible suggestions and down to earth applications at work. So if he thought it was necessary, then maybe there really was something odd going on up here?

Jenna had got the incense sticks going in their little wooden holders, and positioned with one by the front door and one either side of the big patio doors, with a final one around at the back door, although they left that one closed.

"Right, here we go then folks. Mike, would you open the doors please? …Great, now all together: Our Father…"

They began chanting the familiar prayer, Tiff without any expectation of anything, but when Jenna sprayed the holy water onto the front door jamb, Tiff nearly leapt out of her skin when an unearthly scream of pain reverberated about the place.

"What the hell was that?" she gasped.

"No! Keep going!" Jenna insisted. "Hallowed be thy name…"

She sprayed again, and another agonised shriek echoed out across the water. With the front door frame duly doused, Jenna made to move to the patio door and then stopped.

"What's the matter?" Mike asked.

"Well it just occurred to me that if I do this door too, then there's nowhere for the spirit – or whatever it is – to get out, is there? So maybe I should leave this and just do the ground floor windows instead?"

"I'm in your hands," Mike declared, holding his own hands up in a defensive gesture. "You're the nearest thing we have to an expert here, you decide."

When Jenna had eked out the holy water to a spray on each ground floor sill, Tiff asked,

"Well? Are we going in?"

"You and I are," Mike replied, "but that's because I want someone who's known within the company to witness the destruction we found. I want Jenna kept out of this as much as possible." And for that he had Tiff's whole-hearted approval. "But I also want Jenna on the outside, just in case we get locked in and really can't get out this time. Somebody needs to be able to go and call for help."

"Good grief, Mike," Tiff protested, "you're taking this a bit seriously, aren't you?"

"Wait until you see what's inside," was all he would say in response, but when he had taken Tiff up to the master bedroom, and she saw how far the door had been thrown, she began to revise her opinions.

"And you're sure this happened in between you and Jenna coming in here when you brought her up her the first time, and this last time?" Tiff asked, but knowing in her heart that of course Mike would have reported it sooner if it had.

"Come and have a look at this," was all Mike would say, and led her through to the other front bedroom.

The stench from the rotting vegetation hadn't improved over the weekend, and Tiff gagged on it. "Bloody hell, Mike! Who would do such a thing?"

"Precisely. This is from the lake, Tiff – the *lake*! Jenna couldn't have done this, even if I was prepared to think that she was having some sort of mental breakdown and causing this damage. Jenna couldn't have got far enough out to get this tangle up from the bottom – and that's where I think it's come from. She told me she can't even swim! And there sure isn't a boat anywhere on the lake. But I needed to prove to you that it isn't anything to do with her, can you see?"

Sighing heavily, Tiff nodded. Of course there would be questions if they told head office that this damage had happened after Jenna had arrived. "We'll have to say it happened before she got here, won't we?"

"Yes, I'm afraid we will. The only good thing about it is that it more than justifies having a caretaker up here now, if we paint it as simple vandalism."

"Hmm. I don't suppose Silas and Marie would stay up here with her? I'd feel a bit better about this if she had two big dogs with her."

However Mike was shaking his head before she'd even finished. "I'm sorry, Tiff. They love her already, but I don't think they'd stay here without me. They don't know her well enough for that yet. And to be frank, neither of my two are exactly guard-dog material. They'd be more likely to take to their heels and not stop running until they were in Wales – and I love them too much to risk that happening."

"Could you stay? I'd cover you coming in late to the office."

However Jenna put her foot down over that when they told her. "Don't be daft," she insisted. "There's been nothing here in my house to threaten me. But bloody Zach has been laying down the poison already with old Hornby. I know nothing kicked off today, but Hornby probably didn't get back from Birmingham until late on on Monday, and he probably spent today licking his wounds. I'd really be expecting for all hell to break loose tomorrow if Hornby and Zach have had chance to confer tonight. So you two need to be in presenting a united front tomorrow. Be the consummate professionals in case head office rings up. I don't think we've heard the last of those two yet."

"So what about the other house?" Tiff asked. "Have you any more of that holy water, left?"

Jenna shook her head. "Not a drop. Like I said, I don't think the priest was that convinced. He was just trying to offer me a placebo. I thought to do Fiona's house first, because that's the one where actual damage has been done to it. Please don't think I'm cracking up, Tiff, but that house feels angry."

Tiff gave Jenna her usual sardonic smile, but found herself more disconcerted than she would let on because 'angry' was exactly the word she would have used to describe what she had felt in there. Totally unused to such experiences, it was doing nothing for her normal confidence to find herself wondering whether there might have been something in all that stuff Mel spouted after all.

They went into Alicia's house, and once again Tiff found herself shivering for no apparent reason. Nor was that helped by Jenna saying,

"This house feels like its watching you."

"Well that balcony won't help that much," Tiff declared with a sarcastic sniff, as she looked up at it. "It's like those old minstrels' galleries. Half the time the lords were watching their tenants from up above, and the rest of the time the servants were spying on their lord. It must have been like the bloody Cold War centuries before that was even thought of."

Jenna was shaking her head, though. "I get the reference, Tiff, but I don't recall any medieval or Tudor gallery looming over a room like this. They're normally tucked up one end of a hall, not spreading right across it like this. And come here… See? When you get to the staircase, someone upstairs can see right into the kitchen and almost all of the back of the ground floor."

However Tiff was determined to disregard such flights of fancy, although she would never have admitted that it was as much to stop her own jitters. Damn it, Jenna was making her nervous too. So she strolled around the ground floor and then said,

"What about this weird shower room, then?"

Before Jenna or Mike could stop her, Tiff had bounded off upstairs.

"Oh God, Tiff, wait!" Jenna called, but then gave Mike palpitations by haring off in her wake.

"Bloody hell, wait for me, both of you!" he called and tore up after them, much relieved at finding them staring into the shower room, but unharmed, when he got to the top.

"Shit!" Tiff declared. "This is a mess, and no mistake."

Looking over Jenna's shoulder, Mike found himself gasping in dismay. What had just been crumbled grouting only days before was now looking more like crazy paving. There wasn't a floor tile that wasn't cracked into pieces and lifting in places.

"Tiff, this wasn't like this on Saturday," gulped Jenna,

pulling out the i-phone. "Look… I took photos! See? The floor needed work, but it wasn't wrecked."

Tiff looked at the photos, and the date and time stamp on them as Jenna swiped them for her to see.

"Oh this is ridiculous!" she snapped. "Someone must have come in here to do that much damage! You two left here over two days ago. That's plenty of time for someone to come in and vandalise the place." She stormed off, flinging the door open on the smaller bedroom to the left. "Where are you, you little shits? Come on! Time's up! Joke's over!"

She spun on her heels and turned from the room, but consequently didn't see how fast the door slammed shut after her. Jenna and Mike, still having a worried conversation about the wet-room, heard the door slam and looked Tiff's way. Behind Tiff there seemed to be a pale something. If you could have such a thing as a pale shadow, then that was it. Ethereal and intangible, it looked vaguely human and yet not at the same time. For the briefest of instants there almost seemed to be a face. A very female face, and one who was as angry as Tiff.

As Tiff stomped into the second bedroom it was behind her, and deeply worried, Jenna and Mike followed too. Tiff had got as far as the en-suite and was looking around with a scowl on her face, when suddenly the en-suite door was slammed onto her fingers. With a screech of pain, Tiff let go, but then believing that someone inside the room had to have done it, she kicked hard at the door while swearing foully.

"You little bastard!" she snarled. "I'll have you up in front of the magistrates for criminal damage!" and putting her shoulder to the door, she almost fell into the room when she encountered no resistance. As she toppled and stumbled, ending up draped over the toilet, Mike reached the door and put his weight against it to prevent it from shutting again. Jenna shot past him and went to help a bruise and distressed Tiff up.

"Where the hell did they go?" Tiff demanded. "The person who was in here? Where did they go? Did they go past you?"

"Nobody went past us," Jenna said gently. "It's what we've been trying to tell you, Tiff – there's something very wrong with this house."

"Bollocks!" Nursing her bruised and painful fingers, Tiff was in no mood to be placated. "Doors don't just bounce back at you like that of their own accord."

"I didn't say it wasn't push…" Jenna tried to say, but already Tiff was going past Mike and into the main bedroom.

"No Tiff, please!" Mike pleaded. "Don't go so near the rai…! Oh Jesus!"

Again for the briefest of flashes a figure had appeared behind Tiff and was shoving her, but whereas Jenna had been stationary when it had struck her, Tiff's own momentum drove her forward and over the rail. With a scream as she realised what was happening, Tiff just had the presence of mind to grab at the wooden balustrade. It stopped her from falling, but it also swung her hard into the glass panel beneath the wooden rail as she virtually somersaulted over, driving some of the breath out of her. With the '*oofff*' of her exhaled breath misting the glass, Jenna and Mike saw her terrified expression as her already bruised hand started to slip.

"Tiff!" Jenna screamed, and ran forwards, but having the presence of mind to dive onto the floor to reach under the glass panel to try and catch her friend's flailing hand. There was only about six inches between the floor and the bottom of the panel, and it scraped Jenna's arm painfully, but she managed to get a bracing hold on Tiff's arm, which allowed her good hand to slither down to the support post for the panel and get a better grip. Wriggling sideways an inch or two, Jenna was then able to catch the wrist of Tiff's bruised hand, but it was wrenching her own arm badly, and she knew she couldn't hold on for more than a minute or so.

Mike went the other way, taking the stairs downwards two at a time, and dashing to get underneath Tiff. She was a much bigger woman than Jenna, and he knew already he hadn't the strength to pull her back up to the balcony. Nor was he sure that it would be safe to even try to. At some point in that manoeuvre, one or both of him and Jenna would have to lean out over that damned balustrade again, and Mike was scared stiff that at that point they might all end up by falling if the apparition struck again.

"Tiff!" he called. "Tiff! Stop kicking! I'm going to reach up to your legs, okay? It's only eight or nine feet to the floor, and you're tall. You've only a couple of feet to drop now that you're hanging down below the balcony. Jenna, can you keep a hold of her hand enough to just slow her fall a bit?"

"Yes! I've got her!"

"Okay, when I say 'now', Tiff you let go, and Jenna, let her slide out of your grip." He saw Tiff's white face turn to him. "I can't fully break your fall, Tiff, but I'll try to make sure you don't smack your head or anything. Okay? Are you ready? ...Now!"

In a tangle of limbs, Tiff tumbled down onto Mike, who found himself hitting the floor hard with her on top of him, but without her cracking her head on the coir matting.

"Fuck! Fuck! Fuck! My ankle!" Tiff howled, but Mike was more relieved to hear Jenna's boots clattering down the stairs, and to see her emerging unscathed.

"Let me have a look," Jenna demanded, gently moving Tiff's hands away from the ankle. "It's okay. I think you've just got a nasty sprain. Come on, let's get you back to my place."

With Tiff draped between them, Jenna and Mike got her into the lounge and onto Jenna's sofa. Mike then went and got his first aid kit out of the Land Rover while Jenna made Tiff a hot, sweet drink for the shock. By the time Jenna had strapped the ankle up, Tiff's colour was returning to something more like normal, and she was even able to laugh shakily when Jenna teased her about it being the first time she'd been grateful that Tiff was so tall, meaning she hadn't had quite so far to fall.

"I still think it wouldn't hurt to get that ankle properly looked at, though," Mike said firmly. "The community hospital's minor injuries unit will be still be open. I think we should get you down there."

Jenna nodded. "I agree. You take her down in the Land Rover, Mike."

"And you!"

"No. Look, both of you. I haven't been threatened in any way in here. I'll be fine. But if you're going to convince the company that you haven't bolted the stable door after the horse has gone, so to speak, then I need to stay up here and continue playing the care-taker, don't I?"

"I'm not happy about that at all," Mike confessed, looking hopefully at Tiff, but she was too busy rubbing at her increasingly swelling leg to back him up.

"Please, Mike, take Tiff to the hospital. Before you go, we'll go around and switch on whatever outside lights there are. That at least gives the illusion that someone's on watch, because it's only us three who are in any way aware that what we've encountered is abnormal …spooky …weird …whatever. We have to keep up the appearance of normality while we try to figure out how on earth to deal with this."

It took much more convincing to get Tiff and Mike to leave her alone at the house, but by just after seven o'clock Jenna had waved them farewell with promises that she wouldn't enter the other two houses alone.

Sinking into her familiar sofa with a mug of camomile tea, Jenna felt almost a sense of relief at being on her own again. It wasn't that she didn't want Tiff around, and certainly she loved being with Mike. Rather it was that she was just so unused to having any kind of company that after a while she found it all a bit exhausting. Having been used to spending every evening alone in the years since she had last shared student accommodation, aside from the odd night out at a friend's house, she had become used to the silence of single living, and it was going to take a while to adapt to having regular company once more.

Switching on her floor lamp, which was positioned right behind the sofa, she picked up the novel she had been reading, acquired in one of her trawls of the charity bookshops. *I'll be able to buy them new soon*, she thought with a small squirm of delight. Obviously she would need to invest some of her first pay cheques in decent clothes for the office, but having had to make do on so little for so long, Jenna was the mistress of bargain hunting for clothes, and she had no doubt that she would find what she wanted without paying a fortune for them. Books, on the other hand, were something that she would willingly pay a good price for, and with that happy thought in mind, she lost herself in Jim Butcher's wizard's world.

The forest was back again and once more Jenna was swept up in the sense of interconnectedness.

'Please don't do that again' were words she felt as much as heard. There was a sense of someone in terrible pain followed by the thought, 'She hurts. She hurts badly.'

'Who hurts?' Jenna tried to ask, aware that her attempts to communicate were clumsy and blunt. Words lacked the wonderful subtlety of conceptual thoughts, and she tried to broadcast the thought, 'I don't understand. I'm so sorry. I'm doing my best, but I don't know what you're trying to tell me.'

'We are...' and the response seemed to convey personas who were so intertwined with nature that they were inextricable from it.

In the dream Jenna struggled to formulate her thoughts, part of her subconscious trying to reach back to the daytime and what she had read, while another part of her was curiously questing forward in the dream-world.

A flash of an image. A woman who seemed to be a tree. Was she actually the tree? Was she all tree? Was she only part of it? Or was she just communicating with it? Jenna's dream-mind fluttered from question to question.

Another image came, slightly more stable. A woman's figure seemed to be melded with a tree, her upper torso separate from the tree truck, as if she was some branch growing out of it, but with one arm still attached to it and in branch form. Then slowly the woman appeared to rise from out of the tree, like some green goddess, until she was a totally separate being. She walked out along a branch and then seemed to float across into the branches of another tree, where she proceeded to then slowly dissolve into the trunk of it until there was nothing to see once more but tree.

Jenna's dream-mind reeled, still too connected to her own reality to be able to process what she had just been shown. And she felt at some gut-instinct level that she had been deliberately shown that. What had she just seen? More to the point who had she just seen? Was there only one of them or more?

'Many of us,' surged into her mind. 'We are many, we are one.'

That staggered Jenna. How many of these might there be?

'Not as many as we once were,' came the answer before she could properly ask. 'Once we were...' and the impression Jenna got was of legions of these creatures. 'That was before you,' and here 'you' didn't mean Jenna personally but humanity. 'Until then we knew no...' and again there was a concept of an ending that had been wholly alien to them until then.

With a shock she realised that they meant death, they had never known death until mankind came, and that death was associated with the cutting down of huge primordial forests, also seeped through into her mind.

'That was millennia ago!' Jenna's dream-mind protested, her hazy thoughts trying to project the concept of the Stone Age, or at least the Iron Age. 'That wasn't us!'

'But it was us,' the thought came back, and in a sweeping flow of consciousness, Jenna received images that implied that while a natural cycle of retreating into dormancy was followed by new growth over and over again, there had never been anything as final as death as she understood it.

'You remember?'

'We do. I do. She does.' And the 'she' linked across to something trapped like a fox by its leg in a gin-trap within the wood of the houses next door, possibly more than one something.

Jenna's mind did another double-take. To have memories which spanned centuries defied her ability to take in, but then her head truly began to spin as she realised that the dream creature was now showing her the longevity of their connection with one another, and even worse, the terrible wrench of separation when they were parted after so long together. They were close beyond anything any human could share because they shared a collective consciousness, and yet at the same time they had the capability to be individuals too. And yet like the humans they so dreaded contact with, each *one would respond differently to the process of a total separation beyond that of the dormancy they regarded as normal. Some, she was shown, had gone into a dreamlike state never to waken, unable to contemplate a world where their soul-mates – and it was soul-mates at a vastly deeper level than Jenna had ever thought possible – were no longer there to be linked to. Others coped better and had lingered with a closer touch to the modern world, though their concept of modern was of something sudden, unexpected, and catastrophic, landing on them out of the blue very recently. And others became enraged, changing into something dark and warped from their original nature.*

'They want you gone,' the mind-link told her. 'They see you as an infestation, a sickness upon the world. To them you are worse than any fungus or lichen. They only take what they need to survive. You and yours destroy for the sake of it,' and Jenna couldn't argue with that. You couldn't hear the news and the worries about climate change, and not be aware of man's disastrous impact upon the planet.

'And now you begin to understand,' the dream-voice said with something sounding close to relief. 'If you understand, you may yet help.'

Chapter 16

When she woke Jenna found that she could remember almost all of the strange dream, and it disconcerted her badly. Why did she have the feeling that it related somehow to what was going on right here with the three houses? And who was responsible for that pain and suffering? She certainly wasn't. She'd not been part of any decisions regarding the houses, and it was more than a little ridiculous if some ethereal being, who was half in this world and half not, was looking to her to make things right. What power did she have over anyone or anything? She was just the hired help, not a decision maker. For that they needed to look to the Willetts sisters, not her.

For a brief moment she found herself longing to just be able to go back to her old little flat and have nothing more to do with all of this strangeness. But then her common sense kicked in. She was not stuck here forever. This, whatever it was, was just temporary, and if it got too much then she'd just have to ask Mike to find her a cheap bedsit in town until she could afford better. As long as the promised job came through – and she had no reason to think that Mike and Tiff would let her down that badly – then she'd be in a better position than she'd ever been before when it came to looking for a new permanent place to live.

And there was nothing bad in her thinking back to her flat, she reassured herself – after all, those four tiny rooms had been her sanctuary for longer than anywhere else she'd lived. It would be pretty odd if she didn't miss it at times, especially as she'd not remotely been planning to leave it. Her ejection from it was all down to Kyle and his shenanigans, and the speed with which it had all happened was bound to leave her feeling as though her world had been ripped apart. There'd be more to worry about, she told herself firmly, if she didn't have some very mixed feelings about the whole affair, because that would mean she was keeping all her emotions bottled up, and she knew how toxic that could become from bitter past experience.

So she forced herself to get up and get showered and dressed, and then eat a proper breakfast. However, in her current state of mind, she couldn't stand the thought of just hanging about the house for the day. Mike and Tiff would be dealing with enough problems down at the office, so it would be pretty selfish of her to ring them up to come and get her – if, indeed, Tiff had even made it in today. At that point she felt terribly guilty for not having thought to call and find out how Tiff was already, and went to find her mobile phone to ring Tiff.

"How's the ankle?" she asked when a drowsy sounding Tiff answered the phone.

"Painful!" was the reply. "You were right, it's not broken, but it's badly sprained. I've been told to rest it completely for today, so I'm hiding away here for the day."

"Have you had breakfast?" Now Jenna felt awful for feeling so self-pitying when Tiff was injured. "Oh God, I'm so sorry, I've just realised that the hotel doesn't do room service, does it? Damn! I should have come down with you last night after all. I wish I was there with you to fetch you stuff."

"It's okay," Tiff declared, starting to sound a bit brighter. "Actually I'm at Mike's not the hotel. He's set me up downstairs, so I've plenty of tea and coffee to hand,

and he's promised me a proper meal tonight when he gets in."

Oh, thought Jenna, suddenly feeling rather deflated. *So Mike's now playing* your *knight in shining armour, is he?* She didn't want to feel jealous, but she knew how Tiff could wind men around her little finger, having seen it played out before her eyes on so many occasions. And suddenly she had an extra dose of sympathy with the women Tiff worked with, especially Gail who had so wanted her chance with the useless Carl, but who had been shoved aside by the Tiffany juggernaut. And that was the trouble with Tiff. She was never the one to lose out to another woman, so she had no idea how it felt to suddenly see the prospect of a relationship you really want to have a shot at, vanishing over the horizon before you'd even had chance to open your mouth.

Nor would it be Mike's fault. Tiff could be exactly what he'd said she was – a force of nature it was almost impossible to resist. He'd be swept along by her, and then be left wondering what the hell had happened when she gaily swept off to pastures new, leaving him behind without ever thinking to ask him if he wanted to come too. And that was something else that Jenna had seen her do in the past, but for the first time she truly understood why Mel had disliked Tiff so much.

"She's careless of people," Mel had told her. "Oh, you're right, she doesn't deliberately set out to do them harm, Jenna. But there're other ways of trashing someone's life than actively setting out to do it. The thing is, most of us grow up enough to wake up to that fact at some point. But until the day when someone truly breaks Tiff's heart, she's got no incentive to try and see the train wrecks she leaves in her wake, because it's like she's Teflon coated. Nothing touches her. She has no deep desire for a lasting relationship, so it's no skin off her nose if she suddenly thinks, '*Naah*, I don't like his choice of shirts,' or whatever – the stuff someone more committed would choose to overlook.

"She's no incentive to work at a relationship, and with her not wanting kids that's another element out of the way. What's almost worse, she's having too much *fun* jumping from one man to another, dumping them before they leave her, and she's earning enough that she has no need of a man to help support her. Be careful, Jenna! Don't introduce her to any man you care for until you're really settled in that relationship – or at least not unless you want to pick him back up again after Tiff's dazzled him and then dumped him."

At the time Jenna had thought Mel harsh, and since she loved both of her friends equally, had thought that Tiff was Mel's weak spot, her Achilles heel. After all, everyone had somebody they just didn't like, regardless of circumstances. But now, as her imagination played out the scene of Tiff reclining smouldering and elegant on Mike's sofa, and saying in that sexy, dark-chocolate voice of hers, "Oh you are a darling, thank you!" she could easily envisage Mike being 'dazzled'.

It was enough to make her want to sit down on the sofa and sob, but she forced herself to go and pull on a warm sweater, put on her boots, grab her outdoor fleece, and go out. If she couldn't get away from the houses by car, she still had her own two feet, and if nothing else, a walk back up to the hilltop would blow a few miseries away. Sitting in the house would only bring her down further, and she wasn't going to allow herself that.

Mike had left her his large scale Ordnance Survey map of the area, and so she now knew that if she carried on from where she'd got to the previous time, that eventually she would come to a T-junction of paths, and a left turn would take her to another track which would bring her back around the hilltop in a loop.

Don't mope, she told herself sternly as she started walking. *You always knew that the chances of him sticking with you would be slim. Pound to a penny he has aspirations to have half a dozen kids, so once he found out that you couldn't, that would have been the end of it anyway. You've just saved yourself the heartache by waking up to reality before you got in too deep. Smile and be nice to him, but don't build up your hopes. When Tiff said he wanted you, she was seeing it through her rose-tinted glasses where it's inconceivable that any man* wouldn't *want her. You know the reality, though. It's nice to dream for a while, but the only person who'd want you is someone as damaged as you are.*

And this time, walking up on the hills on a grey day with low clouds threatening a shower or two, Jenna found herself thinking that the previous day in the sunshine was how she should see that rosy version of the future, lovely for a day or so but no more likely to last than a British sunny day, and that what she was seeing now was more how ninety-five percent of her life would be.

Forget the car, her doubting mind told her. *Get yourself a little moped or motorbike. Cheaper to both buy and run. You can always come up here then on your own for a walk, just like you went for walks up on the Malvern Hills and looked out towards the Black Mountains. You used to have lovely afternoons out with just a packed sandwich and a flask of coffee. That was real, that's what you can have again. All you need is a place with a lounge and kitchenette, a shower room, and a bedroom big enough to get your stuff into. You're only just hitting thirty, there's time for you to do a year at work to get the payslips to prove you're there permanently, and then you might even manage a little mortgage on somewhere. Somewhere where you could have your own versions of Silas and Marnie.*

In a bleak kind of way, that cheered her up. She had found something within her ability to achieve without relying on anyone else, something she could aim for that only depended on her ability to get up and get herself in to work each day. God knew, she had been forcing herself to keep putting one foot in front of the other for long enough until now to know that she could do that, especially if the rewards were greater and she actually liked the person she was working with. *He can still be your friend*, she told herself, *so don't go making it uncomfortable to be around him for both of your sakes.*

Tramping onwards with that determined mindset, she soon found herself up on the open hillside again. And if the view wasn't quite so spectacular today, it was still lovely, and that also calmed Jenna's fretting mind. So at a more leisurely pace, she now set off over ground she hadn't covered before, and was quite surprised to find that she reached the picnic spot marked on the map far quicker than she had anticipated.

Pausing for a drink of water, and to munch the chocolate wafer bar she'd brought with her, she was pleased to see a couple of young men on mountain bikes go sailing past her, having come up another way from a different small road. Clearly this countryside wasn't that isolated, so she could walk up here alone on the paths and hope to be found if she was the one who then twisted an ankle, or otherwise fell and hurt herself. This kind of forward thinking was second nature to her by now, and to be able to tick her mental security boxes settled her anxious mind even further.

So she was feeling quite her old self by the time she began walking back down. The dream – both the one last night and her aspirations – had been relegated to being just that, a dream, and she felt as though her life was sinking back into a more familiar pattern. She easily found the mountain bike track she'd been looking for, and followed it to where the footpath met it. But as she swung along the path heading back towards her track, she suddenly realised that she was coming up on Pentre Derwen from the far side.

"Oh sod!" she exclaimed out loud as the realisation set in. Was she really going to have to go all the way back up the hill to cut across and pick up the other path? A soft drizzle had just set in, and her enthusiasm for a whole day out on the hillside was waning rapidly. More in hope than any expectation of it happening, she decided to still try and walk the track, hoping that maybe Robin Harrison had got so fed up with hopeful hikers trying to get past his house, that he had fenced off a detour around it. Even if it was a bit of a scramble it would still be faster than retracing her steps.

Yet as the track began to sweep the smallholding's way, she saw a good-looking man coming the other way towards her. Stopping, she waited until he came level with her and then asked,

"So the way's closed, is it?"

"Yes."

"Oh damn. Looks like I'm going to get wet after all," she sighed, and then looked up at her fellow hiker. In contrast to Mike, who was only a couple of inches taller than her at around five feet six or seven, this man had to be easily six feet tall, and was well-muscled with it, going by the way that the olive-brown sweater clung around his biceps. She guessed he was probably in his early forties by the fine lines around his eyes, but he was otherwise wearing well. There was no grey in the cropped mid-brown hair, and he was clean-shaven and wearing what looked like very good quality clothes, if a little well-worn.

"What brings you out on the hillside alone?" he asked, and by his accent he was probably local, but not with the Welsh lilt of the farmers and ordinary folk. There was the touch of a posh private school in there, if Jenna wasn't mistaken, recognising it from her more well-off customers of the past. "It's not really a good idea to go walking out here if nobody knows where you are. How far away is your car?"

"Oh, I haven't come by car," Jenna said, trying to sound confident. "I'm living just down the track. I've just come out for a walk."

The man's face suddenly froze.

"You aren't one of *them*," the man said, and in that moment Jenna realised that he must be Robin, and that he was referring to the women he had probably seen with Mike inspecting the houses. Why on earth had she been expecting some old curmudgeon in his sixties after what Mike had told her? Of course he wouldn't be that old, but even allowing for that, she hadn't expected him to be quite so easy on the eye.

"No, I'm not," she said with a gulp. "Just the caretaker."

He quirked an eyebrow. "Caretaker?"

"The houses can't be… be sold… not just yet," Jenna found herself stammering out. Oh crap! Just the man Mike had warned her not to try and meet! "Problem. …With the will …and stuff. …Work's got to be done …on the houses."

"Oh really?" Oddly, her jitteriness seemed to be doing more to melt the ice between them than if she'd been all confidence and bluster.

"I'm there to stop squatters moving in," she added faintly, suddenly realising how bloody ridiculous that sounded. How was she, all of five feet four and a hundred and thirty pounds tops – and that when dripping wet – likely to fend off a bunch of hard-nosed travellers?

As if hearing her thoughts, Robin, looked slightly askance. "That's pretty irresponsible of the Willetts' – putting a lass like you in all by herself. I presume you don't have some tame rugby player lounging on the sofa back down there?"

Jenna mutely shook her head, then mentally kicked herself. Bloody fool! That had just told him that she really was up here defenceless.

Yet to her surprise, all that Robin did was turn back saying, "Come on, I'd better get you safely back down there, then. Don't want the emergency services combing the hills for you when you get stranded." And yet that sounded neither like a threat nor as if he was pissed off about it, but rather as though he was very gently teasing her.

She found herself trotting along in his wake, carefully not saying anything, and soon they came to another of the steel five-bar gates. Robin twirled the combination on the padlock and undid the chain.

"Come on, then," he said, standing back and holding the gate open for her a way, "I don't bite."

"Your signs make it sound like you do," Jenna dared to respond.

"Good! Then they're doing their job."

"Oh." There wasn't much she could say to that, and so she concentrated on keeping right behind him as they walked through the main yard of the smallholding. To her surprise the place was spick and span, the yard broomed clean, and the low farm buildings all looking as though they had had regular coats of fresh paint. No wonder Mike had said that social services had found it hard to make a case for taking him in for treatment. This wasn't the home of a man who seemed to be losing the plot.

"Why you?" he asked her unexpectedly, as he opened the far gate and came through with her.

"Sorry?" The fact that he seemed set to walk her right to her door had her off balance as much as the question.

"Why you? Who on earth chose you to be the caretaker? You don't seem like the kind of callous, hard-nosed bitch who'd be friends with one of the three witches. They'd eat you alive in no time. So where did you come from? I can't imagine they forked out for a job advert in the local paper – not that they'd have got any takers with their reputations around here."

"Oh …erm, my friend works for the company who own the solicitors' where Mike Campbell works. She was over here helping them for an audit. Mr Hornby …well he left under something of a cloud."

"Did he, by God? Bloody good! About time the old bastard got his comeuppance."

"You didn't like him much?"

"Couldn't bloody stand him! Two-faced, sanctimonious old fart."

For some reason his unguarded response tickled Jenna, perhaps because it was so close to her own, and she couldn't help but laugh.

"He had a hissy fit at me outside of St Leonard's," she confessed. "Tried to make out he could fire me. I had a lot of fun pointing out that he'd got the wrong girl and I wasn't my friend."

"Sounds like she must have made some waves."

With her recent thoughts on Tiff surging to the surface again, she said dryly, "Oh she's good at that."

His head cocked to one side but he didn't actually question her further on that. Instead he suddenly peered through the still-bare trees tops and said, "I thought you said you didn't have a car? Whose is that, then?"

Jenna saw the Smart car was forming a bright red dot on the driveway.

"Ah, that's my friend's car – did I tell you she sprained her ankle? Well she'd come up in her car yesterday but couldn't drive it back. I can't drive, so I haven't been able to take it back for her."

Robin looked at her intently, and she could practically see the thought bubble above his head that was asking what the hell a woman who couldn't even drive was doing out here in the wilds. She expected him to escort her to the turn in the track and then leave her to it, so she was completely taken aback when instead he said,

"There's clearly a lot more going on here than you've been able to tell me so far. I think you'd better come back to my place. Don't worry, I won't put arsenic in your tea, and I make a very respectable fruit cake."

Like an expert sheepdog, he positioned himself so that she found herself going back along the track without him ever actually touching her.

What the hell am I doing? She thought worriedly. *This is going into the lion's den. Am I going to come out again? And if I don't make it back down to the house, will anyone think to come looking for me up here when I said it's somewhere I'd never come?*

Chapter 17

When they got to the cottage door, Robin unlocked it but held it open for Jenna to go in first, very much the gentleman. Inside Jenna was surprised to find a warm and cosy space, very much the dream cottage she would love to have one day. A couple of well-used squashy armchairs were either side of a big old inglenook fireplace, and a wood-burning stove within its depths had embers gently glowing in it, just taking the chill off the room on this cool spring day. Like many old cottages, the windows were small, and so it was dimly lit until Robin turned on the standard lamp by the chairs.

"Make yourself comfortable. I'll just go and put the kettle on. Which would you prefer, tea or coffee?"

"Errm, if you have decaf' I'd love a coffee, but otherwise a weak tea would be nice."

To her amazement he just gave that half smile again and said, "It's all decaf' up here. I can't cope with caffeine anymore."

He vanished into the kitchen, returning a couple of minutes later with two steaming mugs, and a plate with several slices of a dark and scrumptious-looking fruit cake on them.

"Dig in," he invited her, picking up a slice for himself after he'd put her mug and the plate on the stone shelf of the inglenook beside her. Given that he was biting into his own slice, Jenna thought it would be a bit rude not to take a slice. He was hardly likely to be doping his own cake, unless he was far more unstable than even Mike had allowed for.

He let her eat the cake and take a drink of her coffee before asking her anything, but then said,

"So what's the story, then? Why would the Willetts witches think that anyone's going to come and squat in their precious houses?"

For a moment Jenna wondered just how much she should tell him, but then reasoned that he possibly knew half of it already, and that she should consider her own safety too. Pissing off this very capable, and rather damaged, former soldier was probably not the best of ideas. And so she gave him the outline of why Tiff had been sent to the office, and of Mike's troubles with finding buyers for the houses.

"The three daughters must have truly had it in for their father," she concluded, "because you can only think that they made some of these decisions out of spite. Nobody would actually want the finishes on the houses that they demanded."

"Doesn't surprise me," Robin said laconically.

"I heard you wanted the land yourself," Jenna dared to venture. "It's not surprising that you don't have a good impression of them."

"Oh it's more than an impression! I went to school with Fiona, and in a brief moment of teenage madness, went out with Claudia."

"Jeez!"

Her surprise must have made Robin realise that in her turn, she didn't know a whole chunk of the story either, and he took a deep breath before beginning to elaborate, "Oh yes, I knew that whole family. At first, when we were small kids, I used to feel sorry for the girls. When you're small you just see someone else's dad as nasty or nice, and to me he was plain nasty. They used to tell the rest of us kids about the punishments he used to dole out, and they were always worse than anything we used to get, so of course we were all sympathy.

"But then when I went out with Claudia for those few crazy months, I got more of an insider's view of them, and some of Brian's actions began to look a bit less extreme. I'm not saying he was a pleasant man, by any means. Very much the hard-nosed, self-made man who didn't much care who he stepped on in the process. But at home, good grief, if I'd come home to the endless screaming fits and fights like he had for years, I think I'd have employed some extreme measures to try and establish some kind of order, too. The trouble was, their mum didn't know how to handle three such strong-willed girls, and so her tactic became bribery to get them to do what she wanted. But ultimately all that taught them was that pester-power worked.

"I quickly moved on from Claudia, because she tried the same games with me, going on and on about where she wanted me to take her, or to buy here. Well I was just a kid with some pocket money and the earnings from my paper round. I didn't have the kind of money to do what she wanted. It just wasn't possible."

He stopped and gave a wry laugh. "I don't think she's ever fully forgiven me for being the first boy who ever dumped her. But I sure as hell wasn't the last."

"I've never met them, but that seems to be the impression everyone has of them."

"Haven't you? Ah well, I'd better give you a description so that you can avoid them if you see them coming your way. You'll spot Fiona a mile away. She strides around like she owns the place. Like her dad she's tall, certainly for a woman, and she's dark-haired like him too, and more than a bit horse-faced – hardly the feminine sort. Usually she'll be in a tweed jacket and boots. Likes to think she's fitting in with the horsey set except she can't ride, which is probably a good thing for the horses around here.

"Claudia's actually a natural blonde, like her mum, and I reckon she's got the middle kid thing by the bucket load. Always trying to out-shine her sisters, and to be fair, trying to compete with an aggressive older sister like Fiona, and a younger out-and-out brat like Alicia, would warp any sister. And Alicia, *pfffh*! Very large, very loud, and always overdressed for the occasion! Tons of make-up and always under the mistaken apprehension that flashing her boobs will bring a man to heel. At least Claudia always knew how to behave in public."

"Mike says she has a successful cookery school."

"Yes, in that respect, because she's worked at it rather than wanting her successive husbands to buy her into things like the others, she's got farther than her sisters."

"I'm told that the house that I'm in, which is the one at the far end of the drive, is hers, and that's the one that is actually sellable – aside from the slightly odd atmosphere. But that's nothing compared to the other two. *Urgh*, they really give me the creeps!"

Robin sat upright. "Do they? In what way?"

Jenna blushed. "Oh heck, you'll think me really mad if I tell you."

He snorted. "People have been saying I'm mad ever since I came out of the army. I wouldn't let that worry you."

"Why?" Jenna asked, hoping that this would deflect the questions away from her.

For a moment she thought that Robin would take offence and not answer. However he seemed to be weighing her up for a moment and then said,

"Gulf War Syndrome, basically. Do you know what that is?"

"Not really."

"The other name for it is organophosphate poisoning. The big issue back then was that the government wouldn't fund any medical research into it for fear of being landed with a huge compensation bill. So I wasn't fit to stay in the army, but when I came out, our local GPs in the area hadn't a clue what was wrong with me. There weren't any tests that they could do for it, and the ones they did do came back negative. So it was easiest to just put it down to psychological shock.

"But for me it was hideous. The shakes were the worst. They'd come in phases, but for several years never fully went away. And I used to ache. Oh my God, I used to ache. Every joint. Some days I felt like I'd shake myself apart. Some of my teeth started falling out – and that's dreadful when you haven't got out of your thirties yet! I've got a plate in both top and bottom now, and what remains of my own teeth aren't in good shape anymore. And then there was the insomnia. That could be chronic at times, and if you know anything about it, you'll know that nobody does well going without sleep for long periods. That's when I first started to see them – but that's another part of the story."

He leaned forwards, arms resting on his knees, to look her in the face. "That's when the rumours started about me, I know it was. The trouble was, in the absence of any medication, the only thing which got me any relief was beer. The hops helped me sleep, and the alcohol dulled the aching. It got so bad I had to start brewing my own, because when I was in one of my bad phases, I didn't trust myself to be able to drive down into town and get back in one piece. I never dared start on the spirits. I feared if I did, I'd be on a bottle of whisky a day before I knew it. At least with beer you reach a point where the sheer volume of it slows you down.

"It took a long time. A good ten years, in fact. But then the symptoms gradually faded. The toxins must simply have worked their way out of my system, I reckon, but of course the reputation of a drunken madman stuck."

"That's awful!" Jenna sympathised. "And nobody helped you?"

Robin shrugged. "There wasn't really anyone *to* help me. My mum and dad had gone into a care home, and genuinely didn't grasp what had happened to me out there. My sisters had small kids and couldn't cope with me around as well – and in fairness, I couldn't cope with the noise of the kids either, when every sound grated on my nerves. And the doctors couldn't treat what they didn't understand. If I'm angry at anyone, it's at the government for letting down all of us who fought for our country. In later years there's been more research into the effects of organophosphates as ordinary members of the public, who work with things like fertilisers, have become affected.

"I'm out the other side now. But it's left me feeling pretty sour towards the people who treated me like I was a pariah. And the Willetts women didn't help with that. Lots of comments to the effect of, 'I always knew he'd go bad,' were the last thing I needed when I was staggering around town, not drunk but wobbly on my feet. They laid down a lot of the poisonous gossip about me, and because they'd known me for years, they were believed."

Jenna was sitting open-mouthed, appalled that Robin had been so badly treated. "Good heavens, I can see why the last person you would have wanted to become your new neighbour was those three!"

Robin reached over and took another slice of cake, taking a bite before answering, "I don't know whether you'll believe me – given that you've seen through them enough to spot the way they were behaving towards their own father – but I think they deliberately went for this spot because of me. They thought I'd be an easy push-over."

"I think I'd believe almost anything of them right now."

"Well they always wanted this place, you see."

"Did they? Isn't it a bit remote for them?"

"Come and have a look," was all Robin said, but got up and led her through to where she now discovered that a lovely cedar-wood conservatory had been put onto the back of the house, already aging to an elegant silver finish. What took her breath away, though, was the view. Even on a dank day like this it was beautiful, for Robin's house looked out across an unspoilt valley to the hills beyond. There wasn't even a road in sight, and although over to the right there might have been the hint of the roofs of something like a farm or small hamlet, come the summer when the trees were in full leaf, you wouldn't even see that.

"Oh my word, this is beautiful!" Jenna breathed in awe. "How absolutely lovely!"

"Brian Willetts wanted to demolish my house, and build a hotel here for Fiona to run, with Claudia making it a gourmet destination."

"You what?" Jenna spun to stare at him, horrified. "*Noooo*! You'd ruin it!"

Robin smiled. "Glad you can see it. Nobody else could."

"Would they have got planning permission? Please tell me not."

"I wasn't going to risk it, and anyway, why would I sell? This was just the place I needed to recuperate, and now it's my home. I'm not selling!"

"I should think not!" Then another thought came to Jenna. "Is that why you were so worried when Willetts bought the land by the lake? Did you think that if he didn't get the view, then he'd settle for the lakeside? …Oh God, I can just imagine some ghastly faux alpine-chalet-style hotel fitting onto that site!"

"Christ! You're the first person I've met who gets it!" and remembering her own feelings over finally being understood, Jenna knew just how much of a relief that was for him. "Yes, that was exactly it. I had visions of four, or even five storeys if you counted 'quaint' attic rooms, of bright orange pine going up. I've been to hotels like that in Austria, and you can easily have twenty bedrooms, maybe even thirty, in a place with a footprint of what's down there. And the sort of customers they'd have been attracting would have been the spa and cuisine crowd, not folks who wanted walks in the peace and quiet."

"Thank God they didn't get it! I presume that they put in an application for it?"

"I'm not sure. It got as far as a proposal, I know that, but what knocked it on the head from the start was the problem of access for the big timbers coming in. You can bring bricks in in smaller loads, but not huge beams, and the council weren't about to allow something as permanent as a brick- or stone-built hotel. So the whole track would have needed shoring up, and some of the bends straightening out. When the council told Brian that he'd have to foot the whole bill for that, he soon realised that he'd be doubling his costs and then some.

"But that's when I think the three witches got going on him, or at least I think Fiona and Alicia did. And it's why I was so against the houses being built. You see the trouble is, once you've got buildings on a site, it's so much harder to refuse a change of purpose."

"What? You mean take the house down and buil…! Holy shit! The conniving baggages! That's why they demanded all the weird stuff! …God! …Mike told me that Brian Willetts only got the planning permission on the basis that he was building homes for his own family, not a commercial development."

Robin had come to lean against the wooden post beside her, and looked sadly out across the untouched rolling hills. "You see now why I was so upset. He just didn't see it – Campbell, that is. He's a nice enough bloke, but that's actually his problem. He's good at representing the underdogs and victims of crimes because he's genuinely sympathetic. But it means that he's just not prepared for the level of conniving malice that dreadful family brings with them. He couldn't see how Willetts was just going around the regulations."

Jenna nodded sympathetically. "He didn't see what they'd done with the houses until I pointed it out to him. I was the one who said, 'who the heck would want wall-to-wall brilliant white carpets?' And, 'why are the downstairs loos only accessible by going through the kitchen?' You're right, he is nice, maybe a bit too nice for his own good."

For a moment there was silence, and then Robin said, "And there's something else."

"Oh?"

"Well knowing now what I said about the problems of huge timbers being brought into the site, can you see the big question hanging over the houses that are there now?"

It took a moment of thinking, and then Jenna suddenly recalled the lovely thick oak posts around her staircase. "Oh God, the posts in the houses! Where did they come from?"

"Illegal felling on my land."

"Noooo! ...What? ...You mean he just came along and cut down the trees he wanted?"

Robin's face was full of pain at the memory. "Beautiful big old oaks in their prime. His men just came in and took them down. Didn't even bother with the branches. They just took the trunks."

With her dream coming back to her, Jenna could feel her eyes filling with tears. That chainsaw bite …it had been real. Not for her, but for something living on this land.

"Was that why you made the accusations of murder? Of killing?" It hadn't been the best reasoned accusation for what had gone on, but Jenna was full of compassion for another damaged soul like herself, who might not have been feeling well at the time when all this had started. If Robin had been having one of his last bad turns, maybe even brought on by what was happening, then she could see how it all came together. He'd have been making impassioned pleas, and getting more and more frustrated when nobody was taking him seriously.

Yet Robin seemed to be struggling to find the words to reply.

"I do understand," Jenna said gently. "It must have felt as though they were raping your home. Awful, just awful."

Instead Robin said cautiously, "Can I ask you something? I hope you won't think I've completely lost it."

"Yes." Jenna was a bit wary now.

"Have you had weird dreams since you've been here?"

"How on earth did you know that?"

He winced. "Okay. I'm not a menace to you or anything, please believe that. But when I was ill was when the dreams first started. I thought initially that they were just some kind of hallucination, because to be frank, I wasn't sleeping that deeply most of the time, and there's that weird state you get to when you're not quite asleep, but not quite awake either, and later you're not too sure what was real and what not. But I started to hear and see some kind of folk. That was bad enough, but then they started talking to me, and it was about stuff I knew I'd never have come up with on my own."

"Not women in trees?" Jenna suggested, half hoping he'd say no, but knowing she'd be relieved if he said yes. "Actually part of the trees, not just climbing them?"

She saw her relief mirrored on Robin's face. "I knew there was something special about you. Yes. It's taken me a while, but I think they might be dryads…"

"…Celtic nature spirits who live in trees, and oak trees in particular," Jenna finished, and saw his eyes widen in surprise.

"Wow! You got there a lot faster than I did."

She laughed. "A degree in all things medieval – including origin myths from the Anglo-Saxon period – and then some digging into Norse mythology as well, kind of gave me a head start. All I had to do was to go to the books I brought with me."

"Medieval? Nice! …So you'll understand that having made some connection to whoever they are, it was their screams of pain and distress which warned me of what was going on. Willetts was crafty enough to send his men to the woods just around the shoulder of the hill, so I didn't hear the chainsaws straight away from in here. But they started calling out to me. And then the first one of them died."

Robin's voice became choked with the emotion of the memory as he continued, "I think she was trying to save the tree. I sort of saw things through her eyes. She didn't understand what the men were laughing over, but I think they just thought it funny that there was some kind of face in the tree. But Jesus, that scream of pain when the chainsaw went straight through her tree, and possibly part of her too." He shivered, and Jenna automatically reached out and put a consoling hand on his arm. "It was even worse than seeing one of my mates getting wounded in Iraq. All the same emotions, but feeling the wound for myself at the same time. ...It flattened me. I couldn't get out of bed for a couple of days. Took me straight back to the worst of what I'd seen.

"When I could get up I went looking. ...Carnage, that's the only word for it. I'd take you down and show you, but if they've been in your head too, you'd get the same vibes off it that I do. ...Rips you apart, it does. ...First time I went into the grove where they cut three down, I passed out – and after the things I've seen, I don't do that over nothing. The place reeks like a slaughterhouse if you're tuned in to the destruction of plants, as well as flesh and blood. It's horrible."

"How many?" Jenna was almost afraid to hear the answer.

"Easily a dozen. I know that sounds vague, but by the time they'd got past about eight I was just reeling. I was so knocked about by it, I didn't dare drive down into the town to report it. I could hardly walk straight, let alone steer the car, and I'd never have forgiven myself if I'd ploughed into some poor kid and added their death to the list."

"Sensible of you, but I'm guessing that it was at this point you tackled Mike about the 'murders'?"

"Yes, how did you guess?"

"He said you weren't making a lot of sense, and were staggering about. The trouble was, he totally misunderstood you. He did try and take you seriously, for what it's worth. He went back and made a lot of enquiries about missing people, he just didn't grasp what you meant."

Robin gave a wry smile. "Maybe he's not that bad after all if he did that. At least he tried. Willetts just got a restraining order put on me. Well two can play at that game. That's when the fences went up! And believe me, the first ones went up across the tracks his men wanted to use. The cheeky bastard had the nerve to ring me up and demand to know what I was playing at!"

"What? The bare-faced cheek of it!"

"Exactly. I put him straight, I can tell you. Told him that in every case those fences were a foot inside of my perimeter, my land, and if his men set as much as one foot over it, or took those fences down, I'd sue them for trespass. I had to pay for someone to come and do the fencing for me, and that wasn't cheap. Normally I could have managed it myself, but not at that point. But the good thing was, it meant that I had to hand over the surveyor's measurements for the whole of this land.

"I'd had it done years ago when mum and dad were still here, and they wanted to make their wills. At the time we only thought about the value of the land that would be divided between me and my sisters, but I've never been so glad that I kept a copy of that survey up here. It meant that there was a third party who could back me up on where my boundaries were, because the company who did it are used to putting farm fences in over remote land, and could do their own GPS measurements to make sure the fence was in the right place. *And* they noticed that someone had been felling on my land, and that there were tyre tracks going away from my place.

"But the worst of it is, Jenna, I asked Willets in that phone-call why he was using green oak. Nobody does that. You have to wait for the wood to dry out before you use it to build with, and with oak, that takes a long time. He just fluffed around the question. Wouldn't give me an answer. But afterwards I realised why. As the oak dries out, those houses will start to warp…"

"...So that will give him every excuse to say he needs to pull them down!"

"It will, but what's worse, he'll then have his oak beams already dried and ready to use..."

"...For the hotel! Oh my God! I wondered why on earth you would use such huge beams in a house the size of the one I'm in. There are seven massive ones which go from ceiling to floor! Three have the staircase sort of hanging on them, and the others support the upper floor, but it doesn't sit on them. It's like the upstairs joists – which you can see – are kind of pegged into them. I noticed them because I've been in a lot of old buildings, as you can imagine, and although I'm far from a DIY expert, much less a builder, there was something about them which didn't look 'right' to me. Does that make sense? When you've been in as many medieval and Tudor timber-frames as me, you get an eye for the way they interlock the beams. Those old craftsmen really knew their stuff, and so it stuck out like a sore thumb that the house I'm in was built in a strange way."

"Seven just in your house?" Robin looked a little sick. "If there are that many in there, then my estimation might be very much on the low side."

Jenna went and hugged his arm. "If it's any consolation, I don't think there are as many in Fiona's house – that's the one that looks more like a conventional house," and she told him about the destruction they had found in there, but how it was focused on the front of the house. "I think one of your dryads might be trapped in there, and is going rapidly insane," she concluded, "because the images they showed me were of beings totally interconnected. I can't imagine how one of them would react if they felt they had become severed from the others of their kind.

"Not knowing what I was dealing with, I tried to do a cleansing – something my friend Mel showed me how to do when a bad spirit gets trapped in a place. But in my dreams last night, the dryad who seems to come to me most was begging me not to do it again. I was already having second thoughts when I heard this terrible scream of pain as I started spraying the holy water around, but not knowing what I was dealing with, there was a part of me that wondered whether it was just the evil spirit railing against being ejected. I know better now, but I wish Mel was here. I think she'd know what to do to help release that poor dryad."

"If she's as good as you say she is, then I wish she was here too."

At that point Jenna's mobile suddenly began making noises in her fleece pocket. Pulling it out she answered it and heard Mike's voice asking,

"Where are you Jenna? Are you alright? I'm at the house but I can't see you. Where are you?"

"I'm with Robin Harrison at his house," and she heard the sharp intake of breath at the other end. Mike was not taking that news well.

Chapter 18

"Are you okay?" Mike's voice asked worriedly.

"I'm absolutely fine," Jenna said firmly" In fact we'll walk down to meet you. There's a lot more going on than you realised. You really need to hear more of Robin's side of things because it'll make a lot of sense of what's been going on."

"Sense? From Robin?"

Jenna was glad she had moved a couple of paces away from Robin so that he wouldn't hear the doubt in Mike's voice leaking out from the phone.

"Yes! Very much so! Just give us time to walk down and we'll explain," and she ended the call. Part of her wanted so much to just run down to Mike, but the wary part of her was warning her to be cautious and not make assumptions about a relationship that might not be there. And there was a different part of her which was pulling her towards Robin. Here was someone who was as messed up as she was, and if it was ridiculous to start reading potential relationships in after just one afternoon tea together, nonetheless she did find it very easy to be around him. They seemed to read one another's reactions so well, and reacted to things in the same way. *And it's not like you'd have to worry about bringing kids into a world with two damaged parents,* her inner voice reminded her. *If you and Robin got together and it was a jumbled mess, as long as you two were happy with it, it would hardly affect anyone else.*

She felt even more of a connection with Robin when he didn't argue with her about going down to meet Mike, but saw it in the same light as her, as an opportunity to set the record straight. No grudge-holding, no ego and 'I have to be right' attitude. It was enough that he was going to be listened to.

As they swung down the track and turned into the driveway, Jenna half expected to see Tiff there leaning on Mike's arm proprietarily. That she wasn't was something of a relief. This was going to be a tricky enough meeting without all of her emotions being yanked about by her friend playing the prima donna – and Tiff could do that, she admitted to herself. Wonderful friend though she could be, Tiff also loved to dominate a scene, and this ought to be Robin's moment to get some validation.

"I was worried about you!" were Mike's first words, and his face made that seem like an understatement.

"It's okay," Robin said, coming to her rescue. "She'd been for a walk and we met on the track. It was raining, so I invited her in for a cuppa."

"And seriously, Mike," Jenna said, coming to take his arm and steering him towards her house, "you need to come inside and have one, and hear all about this. It's an eye opener, and no mistake!"

If at first Mike was wary of Robin, by the time Jenna had finished explaining how Robin had been affected by the dryads, Mike was starting to unbend. And when they got to the part about the illegal felling on Robin's land, he finally began to grasp what they were trying to get him to see. At the end he sat back in the carver chair looking faintly shell-shocked.

"The miserable, conniving, devious, old shit-bag," were his first words. "And you're right, Robin! It would be so much harder to get a planning application thrown out for a low-rise hotel now that the land has already been built on." He stared blankly out of the huge windows for a moment, obviously thinking hard. "You know the one piece of the puzzle you hadn't put in is what happens now that Brian is dead. I think that's what's thrown all this up in the air.

"While he was alive, the daughters were pressing on with the plan, the difference being that Brian knew that his case would be so much stronger if the three of them had actually come and lived up here. He'd have had a much harder time persuading the council if it was known that the houses had stood empty for the whole time. But of course, a petty-minded trio like those three wouldn't have bothered to think ahead like that. They'd have just seen it as their father trying to force them to do something they didn't want. With the possible exception of Claudia, they've never been prepared to play the long game over anything.

"And then Brian went and did the unthinkable – he up and died on them! And I suspect that at that point Fiona, if none of the others, went and spoke to Brian's foreman, and he most probably told her how long she would have to wait to see any return on their cunning plan. And I have to tell you, it would've had to be a year or two at least. The council don't get hoodwinked quite that easily.

"Fiona wouldn't want to wait," said Robin wryly. "Never been known for her patience, that one."

"No she hasn't," Mike agreed. "And the timing fits, too. All of a sudden, there were her and Alicia beating a path to my door, demanding that I sell the houses and give them the money they were owed. At the time I was puzzled as to why they'd hung on this long. Why, I wondered, could they have not just said to Brian, 'thanks, Dad, but there's no way I'm going to live up a track in the middle of nowhere'. That never made sense to me."

Jenna nodded. "But now it does."

"Oh yes, now it does! Because that was the turning point, the moment when there was nothing left to hang on for."

"And now you're left with them badgering you to try and sell these places," Robin sympathised. He looked around him. "Aside from the fact that I can definitely feel a presence in here, which I think is me being so tuned in to the dryads, it's quite a nice place. I'm surprised you've found it so hard to get rid of?"

"I can't sign off on one without there being buyer in places for the other two," Mike explained. "And that makes sense now, as well. Brian knew what his daughters were like, and that there'd be a strong chance of them falling out at some point. So he had it written into the development that it could only be sold with a completion on all three houses, because you see, regardless of which house got the most money, the proceeds get split equally three ways."

"Good God, isn't that a bit odd?" Robin asked.

"It is, but I think Brian was wise to a couple of things. Firstly he knew, had he lived long enough to see the hotel built, that Claudia would have been the only one to work at it. Now she could have bought her sisters out of it eventually, but I think what Brian was thinking more of, was Alicia – who always wants instant gratification – losing interest and wanting out before the first year had passed. Well with the terms as they stand, the place couldn't be put on the market unless all three of them agreed to it. But I think he was also wise to the fact that Claudia and Fiona have a bit more about them, and that there was always the chance that they would band together and short-change Alicia over a sale – for instance if some company had come in with a takeover offer. It's very carefully wrapped up all ways.

"But now they've truly come unstuck, because the only way any of them will get any money, is if we can sell the houses all at the same time. A job lot would be nice, but that would take little short of a miracle, especially now that you've told me about the green oak being used, Robin. That would bugger up a mortgage surveyor's report in a heartbeat." He huffed and shook his head. "What the heck I'm going to do with these places now, I do not know," and he stared around him at the house forlornly.

"I know this is a big ask," Jenna said tentatively, "but, Robin, would you just come and have a look at the other houses? I'm not saying go in. I wouldn't ask that of you. But would you go as close as you feel comfortable and tell us what you pick up on?"

"Why?" he asked warily.

Producing her phone and showing him the photos she'd taken of the damage, Jenna explained, "This is going to take some serious work whatever happens, so I'm wondering if you've given us the excuse Mike needs to have some structural work done? And that made me wonder whether, if we removed the affected beams, that we might be able to free the dryads too? And in that case, it might be an idea to know whether we can communicate with them and let them know that we're coming in to help. But also, how many of them there are? Is it only one per house, or are there more than one? At the moment we have no idea."

"Fair enough," Robin agreed, but Mike looked gloomy.

"Sorry, Jenna, but I can't see me getting that kind of agreement out of the sisters."

"What choice do they have? I mean, seriously, Mike. What options do they have left? These houses could sit here for decades until they rot if they keep getting trashed by these spirits. Now you can't tell three women who've probably never had an empathic moment in their lives about the dryads. But couldn't you tell a bit of a fib about the green oak warping the houses, and that that's why doors have come off their hinges, and floors have buckled breaking tiles?"

"Genius!" Mike gasped. "However did you think of that?"

"Well I have got a higher degree," Jenna protested. "I'm not thick! I may get a bit wobbly around the edges at times, but my brain still works."

She heard Robin's snort of amusement from beside her on the sofa, and guessed that he must have had similar comments in his time as well. Mike looked embarrassed,

"Sorry," he mumbled, clearly feeling a bit put out at having shown himself up in front of Robin.

"Right!" Robin declared decisively. "What's the plan of battle, then? I'll go and get as close to the houses as I can stomach. Then what? Are you going to tackle the terrible trio, Mike? Tell them that Daddy's get rich quick scheme has come back to bite them on the arse? And what about you, Jenna?"

She sat up that bit straighter. "I'm going to stay right here. For a start off, we need to have proof that random vandals haven't been getting in if Mike's to convince the sisters that it's the houses warping that's doing the damage…"

"…And just hope that they didn't listen too closely to what he said over the dinner table all those years," Mike added morosely.

"Oh, buck up," was Robin's cheerful rejoinder. "Those three wouldn't know a rivet from a nail, or a joist from a lintel! Holy crap, Mike, have a bit of faith in Jenna's scheme. If you go in like that, they definitely won't believe you – you have guilt written all over your face. You're not trying to embezzle them out of their inheritance. You're *trying* to find a way to fulfil their father's will. And to be frank, there can't be many solicitors who would have put as much effort into this as you have. Others would probably have given up by now in the face of so much interference from their clients, and just be saying, 'yes, we're still trying to find a buyer,' and then carrying on with the rest of their work. I wish old Hornby had acted with half as much integrity when I was buying my sisters out of the farm to raise money for mum and dad's nursing home fees."

Mike blinked. "I thought your mum and dad died?"

"No, still going strong in their late eighties. They don't know much of what's going on around them anymore, and we had to move them to a nursing home nearer to my oldest sister in Manchester, which came in a lot cheaper than the first one round here. But then again, thanks to bloody Hornby, we paid over the odds for them in the time that they were there. And we had to pay new solicitor's fees later on to make sure that the deeds were properly in my name. I swear that old goat was in cahoots with the owner of the nursing home to fleece us of everything we had. It wouldn't surprise me if he'd known about Willetts wanting to buy our place to put a hotel on it, and had convinced the nursing home that if they pushed the price up, I would have no choice but to sell up.

"And of course at that point, I'd have had to ask a premium price of Willetts – or so Hornby must have thought – and that would have meant that his commission would have been a very nice lump sum, thank you very much. The idea that I just wouldn't sell had never crossed his mind. And nor, it seems, had it that we might simply move mum and dad to somewhere cheaper. They need proper care, and if that happens in a modern low-rise block, instead of a converted Georgian manor house, there's very little difference now that they don't really remember that they used to live out in the country. The new place is wonderful, run by a former mental health matron, and she was great about giving us time to sort the finances out – not like those rogues Hornby put my sisters onto, while I was too sick to be of much help."

Somehow the knowledge that Hornby had acted so deviously pulled Mike together faster than anything else. "Time for another of the team to put things right, then," he declared with more assertiveness, and got up to lead the way along the path to Alicia's house.

Standing outside it, Robin admitted that he might not get much further than the front door. "She's really angry ...no wait! There are two of them in here. The one I felt first is trapped at the front of the house."

"Would that be in the beam of the balcony?" Jenna suggested.

"Very possibly. The other one is at the back of the house."

"That's where all the destruction of the wet-room has taken place," Mike confirmed. "Without wishing to sound too much like a weirdo, can you tell them that we're going to try and get them out, and that Jenna and I aren't the ones who trapped them?"

"I'll have a go, but to be honest, Jenna might have as much success reaching the one in her house. By the feel of it, because this house is all wood, those three can just about contact one another, even if they are all trapped where they are."

He moved on to Fiona's house but froze several feet away from the front door.

"God! Sorry folks, I can't go any nearer than this. Oh shit! She's gone, lost it, crazy. It's like a wild animal that's been sent mad by pain. She been tipped over the edge, and now she's a savage kind of feral. I really wouldn't go in there until you've been able to free the ones in the other houses. They might just be able to get through to her, but I can't."

Jenna put a consoling hand on Robin's arm, not seeing Mike's look of anguish as she did so. "Never mind. At least you tried. And thanks to you we're a lot closer to finding a solution."

Robin took a deep breath and seemed to shake off the house's atmosphere. "There is one thing. I think I should have both of your mobile numbers. For Jenna's sake, Mike, I'm a lot closer than you if she gets into trouble, and if I see anything untoward, then I can get in touch with you even if she can't. I promise you I'll keep an eye on her."

Unfortunately that wasn't quite the consolation to Mike that it was meant to be. He was finding himself feeling horribly conflicted over the sudden reappearance of a considerably more stable and charismatic Robin, and who Jenna seemed to have taken a deep liking to. Why did he always have to lose out to the charmers?

"I'd better get back to my patient," he said with a sigh. "I don't suppose you would consider driving the Landie back down, Robin, while I take that stupid sports car back? I'll bring you back up straight away."

The way he had said 'patient' had had Jenna's heart giving a little leap, for it sounded very much as though Tiff was overplaying the wounded heroine. And 'stupid sports car'? That really sounded like he'd had enough of her even after one night.

"Oh dear, is Tiff being a handful?" she asked him innocently and got a bleak look in return. "Why don't I travel down with you? We could then take her back to the hotel, and then you can bring me back here with Robin?"

"Hotel! Marvellous idea," Mike declared with relief, and so they all piled into the cars and headed for Ludlow.

At Mike's house both Jenna and Mike were quietly amused at the way that Tiff flirted outrageously with Robin, and at the way he was clearly completely unimpressed with her. By the time they had stuck her into the Land Rover – being easier on her bandaged leg – and Mike had driven her car to the hotel, you could almost see the worry setting in with Tiff that the usual magic wasn't working on Robin. A man immune to her charms was a rarity in her world. She was so woebegone that Jenna offered to stay the night with her, which Mike backed up smartly since it gave him a chance to take Robin back without Jenna, and therefore not leave her within walking distance of this new friend.

"Oh Tiff, you do look sorry for yourself," Jenna said, returning to the room with the bottle of gin and two of tonic that she'd nipped out to get after Mike had left. "Here you go, get that down you."

"I can't wait to get back to Birmingham and my nice bar on Colmore Row that knows just how to make a proper Martini," Tiff declared with the air of one who had had much to put up with of late.

"And all those nice young men who buy them for you," Jenna teased, but then was even more tickled at the way Tiff brightened at the prospect.

Yes, you go back to where you truly belong, my friend, Jenna thought affectionately. *You did me the most enormous favour in bringing me out here, and one I suspect I'll be forever grateful to you for, but strangely, I think I belong here far more than you do.*

In the morning she helped Tiff get ready, persuading her that trousers as tight as her pairs were wouldn't be the easiest thing to pull on over her bandaged ankle, and instead opting for the nearest thing Tiff possessed to a long, floaty skirt. Then with a borrowed walking stick from Mike in one hand, and Jenna lending an arm on the other, they got out to the taxi which Tiff had ordered to take them the short ride into the office. Feeling that she had to make sure Tiff got up the stairs alright, Jenna went with her, and then nearly screamed with delight, for there, waiting in the office, was Mel.

"Mel!" she squeaked, letting go of Tiff and throwing her arms around her other best friend. "Oh God, it's so *good* to see you!"

"Jenna! Blessed be! I was worried sick. I went to your old flat and found it all boarded up. And then Mrs Wilson told me what had gone on and I was even more worried. Thank the goddess her eyesight is better than her hearing, and she must have been watching you get all packed up, because she described someone who could only have been you, Tiff. But then I got hold of your office – nice website photo, by the way, because it was that which tipped me off that I'd found the right person after I'd Googled you – and they said you weren't working out of that office for the time being. It still took me going in and explaining why I needed to find you before they'd even tell me which branch office you'd gone to. A nice chap by the name of Carl, who seems to be pining for you, actually came after me to tell me, and he said he can't wait for you to get back. Something to do with the office being very quiet without you, and him being haunted by a co-worker called Gail?"

As Tiff looked smug at the compliments, Jenna whispered, "Gail got hit by the Tiffany effect, poor woman. Tiff doesn't want Carl, but he can't see past her," and got Mel's silent 'oh' of understanding.

"And who'd this luscious beauty," Zack's nasal drawl came from behind them, at which Mel lurched forward from the rather vigorous slap on her bottom from Zack.

What he wasn't expecting was for Mel to spin on her

toes and give him an almighty face-slap, with the riposte of, "Not yours, so keep your grubby paws to yourself!"

"Morning ladies," Mike's voice said, peering around the stunned Zack.

"Mike!" Jenna gasped. "Look who's here! This is Mel!"

"Lovely to meet you," Mike managed to wring out, having squeezed past the frozen Zach and holding out his hand. Quite what he'd been expecting he wasn't sure, but it wasn't the exotic creature he was facing.

Bright red hennaed dreadlocks were only the start of it. Mel was an inch or two shorter than Jenna, yet seemed to be filled with a force that radiated out beyond the confines of her skin, and that skin at the moment was liberally covered with henna tattoos. Not to mention the piercings, which allowed a wild assortment of studs and hoops to dangle from both ears; plus one in each eyebrow, and one in her lip. A riot of brilliantly coloured Indian-inspired clothing topped knee-high printed Dr Marten boots, completing the picture of an exotic bird having just flown in.

"Namaste, Mike," Mel responded with a small bow, both hands together. "I see the divine in you."

"Thanks," said Mike weakly, wondering how much stranger his world could get with Jenna in it.

"You've arrived like Gandalf, precisely when you were needed," Jenna was saying with so much enthusiasm that it made Mike pray that Mel wouldn't turn out to have a dark side like Tiff. For Tiff was great as a colleague, but the twenty-four hours Mike had spent with her in his house had swiftly convinced him that he would be glad to finally wave her off, and leave his office to settle down again. Demanding wasn't the half of it, and he now realised where her resolution to deal with Zack had sprung from, for Tiff lived with the expectation that what she wanted she would get. *Please don't let Mel be another one like her,* he found himself devoutly wishing. *I want to like at least one of Jenna's close friends. I couldn't bear it if I thought that all these years she's been the one dancing in attendance on them and never getting any limelight of her own.* And he was convinced now that in any night out with Tiff, that Jenna would have been left in the shadows while Tiff grabbed the spotlight, which probably had something to do with why Jenna hadn't been snapped up by some right-thinking man. *But at least it's given me the chance to meet her,* he thought, *and Robin bloody Harrison can bugger off if he thinks he's going to butt in!*

Chapter 19

"Are you back for good?" Jenna was asking Mel excitedly, "Oh please say that you are."

"For the time being, at least," Mel said, and seeing how much that meant to Jenna, gave her another hug. That at least put Mel in Mike's good books. Here was someone who truly seemed to see Jenna.

"There's a lovely coffee shop down the road," said Jenna enthusiastically, "come on, we can go and catch up." She turned to Mike and mouthed 'houses' and then flicked a grimace towards Zack's back as he retreated into his office.

Catching on to what Jenna was thinking, Mike didn't have to force the return smile. "Great idea. I think I'll call that expert we were talking about," because on the way down last night, Mike had said that the obvious person to call in to advise on the removal of the oak beams was Brian Willett's foreman, Garry White. Since Garry was still holding the fort at the site office of the last houses Brian had signed a contract to build, and was overseeing their completion, he had access to the men with the right skills for the job.

"Could someone please get me a coffee first?" a pathetic voice came from Tiff's desk, and Jenna turned around to see Tiff looking very woebegone at being sidelined by Mel. But Jenna also thought she looked very pale.

"Are you sure you're okay to be in?" she asked. "I can't imagine that Richard would think it so very awful if you went back to the hotel to rest. If you keep your ankle elevated for another day or so it's bound to heal better. Come back in after the weekend."

A snort came from Zack's doorway. "Oh really? And who put you in charge?"

Mike groaned. "For the love of God, Zack, pack it in! It's a sensible suggestion, and the hospital did say for her to keep off her leg for at least a couple of days. If I have to go out on a call, are you going to help her by making her coffees? Don't forget the loo is down four steps."

Zack's expression turned to one of horror. The very thought of having to help Tiff down the steps to the office toilet was too much for him. "Get out!" he snapped and turned back into his room.

"Christ! I wasn't asking him to wipe my bum!" Tiff said, and Jenna was surprised to see her on the verge of tears. Tiff must really be feeling crap if she was letting Zack get to her like that.

At that point Jenna's mobile rang, startling her with the unexpectedness of a call.

"Hi, it's Marilyn at the History Office," a friendly voice on the other end said. "Your exam papers are in — come and get 'em!"

"Oh! Oh, right! How long have I got to get them back in?"

"You've got a hundred, and we need them back by Friday morning next week." Jenna heard Marilyn sigh. "Sorry to have dumped so many onto you, but having said he'd do it, Tony seems to have gone incommunicado on us, and if we can't contact him, we can't tell him the papers are here. Sorry, lovely, you've got a fun week ahead!"

"I'll be in later today," Jenna promised, forcing herself to sound bright and cheerful. But when she'd ended the call she groaned. "Bloody uni marking's just come in," she explained to the others, who were all looking at her. "Sod it, I'm going to have to go and catch the train. If I'm going to get through that many papers, I'm going to need all the time I can get."

"Train be damned," Mel said breezily, "I've got *Peggy Sue* parked around the corner, I'll drive you! It's not like I don't know the way."

Mike looked confused. "Peggy Sue?"

Jenna laughed and explained, "It's Mel's classic 2CV. Her cousins are mechanics, and it's rather their pride and joy. Just wait 'til you see the psychedelic paint-job!"

"God, you've not still got that old thing?" Tiff asked in dismay. The thought of having a car which had gone out of production so long ago, and had none of the modern accoutrements, was appalling to her.

"Designed to carry French farmers across ploughed fields without breaking the basket of eggs they had on board," Mel riposted with good humour. "It'll still be going when your car's computer has thrown a fit and it won't work. Come on, let's get you back to the hotel, and then I'll take Jenna up to uni."

It took a bit longer than that to get Tiff out by virtue of her needing to use the loo first, and so as they came back into to the main office, Mike was just putting the phone down and grabbing his briefcase. "I've got hold of Garry," he said softly to Jenna. "He says it would be better if I can go to him." He flicked a glance towards Zack's door. "Something about not wanting to be overheard and having the plans over there." Raising his voice he called, "Zack, I've got to go out. Had a call. You're 'it' in the office for now. Won't be too long." And with that he grinned at the women and then fled before Zack could protest.

That meant that he didn't hear Zack's snapped, "Well shut the main door, then! I'm not watching the outer office!"

So Mel and Jenna helped Tiff down the stairs, but as Mel went to get *Peggy Sue*, Tiff suddenly declared, "Oh damn! I've left my phone on the desk."

"Give me the keys, I'll go and get it," Jenna volunteered.

Hurrying up the stairs, it never occurred to her that in her soft-soled trainers Zack wouldn't hear her come into the office, and one of the first things Tiff had had done was have the hinges and lock on the outer door oiled so that they stopped their dreadful creaking. Leaving the door open, she had just got to the desk and grabbed the phone, when she heard Zack on the phone saying,

"No it's fine, Fiona, come into the office. The rest of the traitors are out now, and it'll be easier to talk without your sister barging in on us. I can't imagine the company spy will be in today, and Michael has gone to deal with some scummy case, as usual. Mr Hornby was right, we should never have got involved in that sort of work, it's most unbecoming. We should have been focusing on clients of your standing – something which you're quite right to say that Michael doesn't understand. ...Okay. See you in about fifteen minutes then. I'll have the prosecco on chill."

Fearing he was about to head to the tiny kitchenette beyond the main office, Jenna hurried out and used the key to close the door without a sound. Bloody hell! Was Zack going behind Mike's back to strike some kind of deal with Fiona? That was something she was going to have to relay back to him by this evening at the latest, but she wouldn't disturb him just now, not while he was dealing with the foreman.

They piled Tiff into the front seat of the 2CV, looking as if she might die from embarrassment alone at being seen in such a thing, and then hurtled around to the hotel. Leaving Tiff with a coffee in the foyer, and suddenly looking brighter for having a nice young rep' paying her attention, Jenna and Mel got on the road for Birmingham.

By the time they pulled in through the university's imposing North Gate, Mel was wholly on board, yet her first question to Jenna was,

"And how do you feel about Mike? I saw the way you looked at him, and he at you. You clearly like one another."

Jenna sighed. "I like Mike a lot, and to be frank with you, Mel, I've never been so glad as to find that he found Tiff a bit too much after twenty-four hours of her in his house. But realistically, is he ever going to want me when he finds out about you-know-what?"

"Oh, Jen, not every guy you meet wants tribes of kids, you know. And for some it's more important to be with the woman they love for the rest of their lives, than to have maybe less than half of that time with kids about the place. Mike seems like the kind of man who's capable of recognising that children grow up and leave home, whereas a good marriage can last a lifetime."

"Do you think so? I really wish that would be the case."

"Well you aren't going to know unless you give him the chance, are you?" Mel reached out and hugged Jenna to her as they were walking across the car park towards the Humanities building. "Please, please don't cut yourself off from chances of happiness. If you don't let anyone near you, you really won't find the man who can accept you for all that you are."

"You haven't found anyone."

"Yet! ...It's 'yet', Jen! I'm still a very long way from giving up on dating. Granted I've found out that I've been kissing a fair few frogs, but I haven't given up hope on the prince just yet. ...So when was the last date you went on?"

"*Hmph*! With Kyle! And what a disaster that was."

Mel snorted in exasperation. "That's because *Kyle* is a disaster – not you! He couldn't hold down a relationship with anyone who wasn't prepared to step straight into his mum's shoes and run his life for him. And I seem to remember the last time I talked to you about this on the phone, you said that that was never going to be you. Come on, Jen, that wasn't anything like what a proper date should be like, not ever. In that respect I'm with Tiff all the way in wanting to strangle Claire for ever putting you in that situation – especially if it's made you so wary that you pass by the chance of something with a thoroughly nice bloke like Mike."

The conversation had to be suspended while Jenna picked up the pile of exam papers, but once they were on the way back out of the building again, she said,

"Oh Mel, it's so good to have you back again. I can't believe you turned up just now when I need your kind of common sense advice so much."

"Ah ...about that..."

"Mel?"

"Not so much the coincidence actually. ...You see, after Tiff found you – this was after Kyle had turned up and she discovered you in such a state – she made a real effort to track my mum and dad down, and ask them to forward an email to me. I know I haven't always got on with Tiff – we're too different for that – but when it comes to you, we're singing from the same hymn sheet, I've discovered. You see she told me all of what had gone on up to that point, and said that she would be working abroad for six months after Christmas. She begged me to consider coming home for a while, because she didn't want to leave you without the support of any friends, and in that she was most vocal in her condemnation of Claire.

"Well I'd come to the end of the one contract, and was back in the UK to see Mum and Dad, so I asked the agency if I could delay picking up the next one. I hadn't been intending to. I'd been thinking of moving on to the next project, which would have been in Africa, and then taking some longer leave once I was in place. But after I'd heard from Tiff, I thought I'd better take that leave now and come and see for myself. …Mind you, I wasn't expecting you to need my help in quite the way you've explained!"

"Oh, now I feel so guilty," Jenna gulped. "Truly, Mel, I'll find my way, you don't have to give up doing what you love just for me."

Mel opened the boot for Jenna to put the heavy bag of papers in, then said firmly, "You're not making me do anything I don't want, so don't you dare feel guilty. If I'm being truthful, Jen, I wasn't too keen on this next project anyway, and I was half looking for a reason to back out of it even before Tiff's email arrived. Being a lone western woman in India has its challenges, but they're nothing to the parts of Africa the charity works in. I'm all for helping, but I draw the line at putting myself deliberately in harm's way. So I'm only too glad to be taking some time out to help you with your problem. And that's something my mum and dad are very grateful to you for, as well. I don't think either of them were remotely happy about me heading into one of the less stable parts of Ghana. So you may find yourself getting quite the hero's welcome when we go back to visit them together."

That quelled some of Jenna's qualms about her friend's return, and so they had a more relaxed drive back, discussing what would be the best thing to do, with Mel saying that she would very much like to visit the grove where the trees had been cut down. It was an easy matter to go via her parents' house in Wolverhampton to pick up extra clothes, and as Mel had suggested, Jenna was given an especially warm welcome.

"You try and keep her with you for as long as possible!" her mum told Jenna at one point when Mel had nipped out of the room, followed by her dad saying,

"We'll send money if needs be. Anything to keep her a bit closer to home for a while! We were worried stiff all the time she was in India. We'll both be grey-haired and nervous wrecks if she goes to Africa."

With great reluctance Jenna left with Mel, thinking that it was actually harder for her to leave this loving home than for Mel. Mel knew beyond a doubt that there would always be a place for her here, but for Jenna it was like briefly being able to relax in a warm and all-embracing bath of kindness, which was something she'd never had the chance to take for granted.

"You're so lucky to have your mum and dad," she said as they headed west once more.

"Oh I know," Mel agreed with a reassuring smile. "I don't make a lot of it, but I do appreciate how lucky I am, and I do try to make it up to mum and dad every so often. So count this as one of those times."

With Mel being able to drive straight up to the house, there was no need to go via Mike's, but Jenna did call him on the way, explaining that they had picked up a couple of suitcases of clothing for Mel so that she would be able to stay for a while. And there was obvious relief in Mike's voice when he said,

"I'm so glad you won't be alone up there."

"How did you get on with Garry what's-his-name?"

"Garry White? Very interesting! Apparently he objected all the way through to Brian putting the unseasoned oak timbers in. In fact he pretty much did the three houses under protest."

"Did he, indeed!"

"Oh yes! So he wasn't the slightest bit shocked at me turning up and saying that the oak would have to come out. In fact he said he was surprised that nobody had come to ask for that to be done sooner. So high-five to you, Jenna, for thinking of that as a plausible excuse."

With Jenna's phone being on speaker, Mel had heard what he said and interjected with,

"She always was the brightest of us all. Clever girl, our Jen!"

"She is," Mike agreed. "And the next bit of good news is that Garry said that Alicia's house would be the easiest one to take the oak beams out of. He said that basically they can put acrow-props in to hold the balcony up. He says that if they place the props at about one metre intervals, there should be no danger of the balcony collapsing, and then it'll just be a case of undoing the bolts holding the oak beam in place and sliding it out. Then they can just slip an RSJ in in its place.

"Even better, they can do much the same with the beam at the back! You see, he was always expecting to have to come and take them out, so when he and his lads were putting them in, they did it in a way that would make it easy for themselves later on. So you two will be able to stay in the end house while that work is going on. What I've suggested to Garry is that if they can make what was Alicia's house safe – although I didn't elaborate on the extra kind of 'safe' we've been thinking of – then when the work on that is done, you two can move across into there to keep an eye on the site, and the lads will start taking the beams out of your current house. That's going to be more disruptive to the house, because they're effectively in the middle of the upstairs floor. But again, Garry says that as long as they do it half of the house at a time, it should be relatively straight forward, because the roof doesn't wholly rest on those beams. He's again talking about using steel supports if necessary, because he can weld them, but thinks that Brian always over-engineered the houses as an excuse to put the oak in, and that smaller wooden beams could well do the job just as well. Luckily he knows where he can get his hands on some."

"Oh that is good news."

"It is. In fact Garry sort of knew that Brian was going to try and fiddle the planning applications, because he repeatedly questioned why he was so insistent on those huge beams. He's told me today that the three houses would have had to be up for a fair old while for beams of that thickness to season, and he'd had a stand-up argument with Brian about what that would do to the houses in the process."

"Good grief! Well done Garry! It sounds as though at least he had a conscience over what was going on. What about Fiona's house?"

They heard Mike's deep sigh. "Not such good news, I'm afraid. That really is going to make a right old mess of the house. But Fiona only has herself to blame for that. If she'd been willing to leave exposed beams, as in the other two houses, then it wouldn't be so bad now. It was her insistence that everything be plastered over that's going to cause the mess. So if the other two end up getting less money than expected, they'll have to blame her."

Suddenly Jenna remembered what she'd over heard that morning and relayed it on to Mike, ending with the apology, "I'm so sorry, Mike, what with everything going on, I forgot that I needed to tell you that."

"It's not you who needs to apologise," Mike said firmly, but with anger audible in his voice. "Bloody hell, I've just about had enough of Zack's arsing around!"

Mel leaned a little towards the phone to ask, "Are you going to challenge him over it?"

There was a moment's silence as Mike considered, but then he said, "No, actually I'm not. I'm going to wait and see what Fiona's next move is. At the moment we've only got your word for it, Jenna, and while I believe you implicitly, I can hardly go to Richard Mann with it. I need those two to do something that can't be wriggled out of, that shows them up for the devious little shits they are. At that point I can then ring Richard and tell him what Zack's been up to, and this time I'm sure it will get him fired."

Again Mel leaned nearer to the phone to say, "Given what you've had to put up with, I think that's remarkably restrained of you. Jenna's told me of the awful atmosphere you've had to work in. I don't think many people would be as charitable."

"It's not being charitable," Mike's disembodied voice answered wearily. "It's rather that I know from cases in the past how things go when it just comes down to one person's word against another's. Given that I've been given a step up in the company, it could be misconstrued as power going to my head, while Zack can be very good at playing the hard done by one. Tiff might back me up, but Richard would have to tread very carefully if he wasn't to get accusations of taking his girlfriend's word for it over an experienced member of the team, i.e. Zack's."

When Mike had rung off, Mel asked Jenna, "Is it that well-known in the company that Tiff is Richard's lover? She's walking a delicate line if it is."

However Jenna shook her head. "No, I think in the normal way of things they play it very cool when they encounter one another professionally. I just felt I had to tell Mike so that he understood just how much power Tiff has. He was starting to get very suspicious over why she was so sure that Richard would see things her way, and how a mere office manager could, to all intents and purposes, pull rank on one of the actual legal team. I think Suzy from Hereford knew already, and is keeping the secret, but I didn't want Mike to ask Tiff outright in the office where Zack might hear. Mike's so honest he wouldn't think that Zack would listen at keyholes – or at least he didn't until what I've just told him sank in."

Mel smiled. "Like I said – nice bloke. Just what you need!"

Chapter 20

On Friday Jenna got stuck into the marking while Mel unpacked. However, that night they were invited up to Robin's for dinner, and once again Jenna found herself feeling like a wallflower. While Robin had been nice to her, it was now very apparent how different it would have been if he had fancied her. One look at Mel, as she sprang out of the 2CV like some kind of alien fairy, and Robin was smitten, that was very clear. Then she saw that Mike had beaten them here, and the way he was looking almost relieved at the proprietorial way that Robin ushered Mel inside, then smiled at her, made Jenna stop and think that maybe, just maybe, he was glad that Robin wasn't focusing on her. Did that mean that he really was interested?

He leaned closer to whisper to her as they followed the other two in, "I came early bearing veggie burgers! You did say that Mel doesn't eat meat, didn't you?"

"Errr, yes."

"Only I think Robin's idea of a feast is a bit meat heavy!" and Mike gave her a conspiratorial wink. "I didn't want your friend to be offended when she's only just got here. Honestly, Jenna, I can't tell you how relieved I am that you're not in that house alone now."

Feeling a strange relief that Mike's concern had been focused on herself, Jenna was able to join in the cheerful conversation over some very rare beef, and heaps of Yorkshire pudding and roast potatoes, but with limited vegetables. In fact she was rather amused at the way that

Mel whispered to her, "This man's a heart attack waiting to happen!" during one of Robin's forays into the kitchen for more custard for the chocolate pudding.

"And are you planning on rescuing him?" she teased.

Mel rocked a hand in indecision, but smiling. "He might yet be the frog who transforms!"

All of which made for a very relaxed meal until Robin asked in all innocence, "So have you two and Tiff always been a threesome? Only I have to say that you seem an unlikely combination."

"Oh no," Mel replied airily, "there were more of us than that at uni. All told there were eight of us on the medieval course, two lads and six girls – which might not sound many, but we shared lectures with both the main history and English courses. Ben and Adrian soon found being in a girl-heavy group a bit much, so they became friends with more of the guys doing straight history."

"And they were never as heavily into the medieval stuff as we were," Jenna admitted. "In fact Adrian transferred across to the ordinary history degree in our second year. But the first of us girls we lost contact with was Rachel, and through no falling out, either. Her poor mum had a couple of bad strokes – and she was only in her late forties, too. So from the Christmas of our final year, Rachel was regularly dashing back up to Newcastle to help her dad. We all felt so sorry for her, because her older brother didn't seem to be pulling his weight, even though he still lived at home."

"Yes, it was grim for her," Mel agreed. "After only a year or so, we even stopped getting Christmas cards from her. I often wonder if she couldn't bear to hear how everyone else was getting on with their lives, while she was stuck back where she started from. ...Terribly sad."

Jenna nodded. "Then there was Olivia, who did post-grad getting a librarian and archivist qualification, and she's now up working for the Museum of Scotland in Edinburgh. She married one of her colleagues whose family are out on Harris in the Outer Hebrides. So even before they had a family, any leave they got was heading out that way, and in between at weekends they were visiting her mum and dad in Lancaster. There wasn't really time for her to come down to me, and I couldn't afford to go to her."

"And in fairness," Mel added, "even though I could afford to go up there, their flat was so tiny I always felt bad for asking to crash there. And of course with Edinburgh being so on the tourist trail, at certain times of the year the hotel prices shoot through the roof, and I wasn't *that* well off."

"We still keep in touch through Christmas and birthday cards," said Jenna, "and as soon as I get a new address of my own, I must let her have it. She'll be worried sick if her cards get sent back with 'gone away' or 'not known at this address' on them, as will Kate. Olivia and Kate were almost as close to me as Tiff and Mel, although Kate was probably more Tiff's friend. And then Kate got married to her boyfriend she'd had all the way through uni, and so when his job took them down to London, she followed. She's got two little boys and is expecting her third, and Olivia has a little girl and the last I heard was hoping that she was going to have another."

And that was when the bomb dropped.

"So don't either of you want kids?" Robin asked tactlessly, making Mike wince.

"Robin! You can't ask…!" he began protesting, but Mel answered without reservation,

"Oh I do! It's just the man that's been lacking. But it's different for Jenna."

At this point Mike noticed that Jenna's head had dropped so that none of them could see her face, but he knew instinctively that something was very wrong, even before Mel continued,

"Jenna can't have kids, but it's not by choice. When that bastard attacked her, he left her so damaged that her surgeons ended up having to give her a radical hysterectomy. That was before she came to university. I can't tell you how brave she's been to pick up her life like this. That's why Tiff and I might disagree over everything else, but we both keep an eye on our Jen."

For a moment there was a stunned silence, then a choked up Mike said, "Tiff never told me that."

While Jenna's heart sank even further into her boots as she feared what was to come, Mel replied firmly, "Tiff knows everything *except* about the fact that Jenna can't have kids – she thinks that it's from choice. That's because she doesn't truly get what it means to Jenna. We sort of discovered that in general conversations before we got to the details, you see.

"My Aunty Lin chose not to have kids, but she's really sympathetic to Jenna and women like her, because she says that she can no more turn on the desire to have kids than they can turn it off. But unlike my Aunty Lin, Tiff was, and is, all over Olivia and Kate's kids; and of course, having always had a good job ever since she graduated, she could afford to travel to see them. That's made me think that she's going to get into her forties and then suddenly wish she'd taken the time out to have a family of her own, but being Tiff, she thinks she can have her cake and eat it, and at the time of her own choosing, too."

"Mel, please…" Jenna said faintly.

"No, lovely. These are friends. They need to know why you sometimes get so low, and it's because you had so many choices snatched out of your hands before you knew you even wanted to make them."

Robin was looking dumbstruck, but Mike's solicitor's brain was in overdrive.

"When Tiff said you'd been assaulted, I somehow thought that guy had attacked you to try and snatch your bag, or something, and then realising you were a girl, then tried to rape you. Some muggings are pretty violent. But I had no idea your injuries were that bad. ...I mean ...I know Tiff said you were hospitalised, but the severity of your..." he seemed to run out of words to ask any more, instead saying, "I do hope your legal team got the maximum sentence for him?"

"He got sent down for attempted murder," Mel announced, "and I hope the bastard rots inside!"

"Attempted murder?" The severity of the crime ramped up another notch in Mike's mind. "Of a total stranger? With no motive? ...Jeez!" Mike knew only too well that in most cases there was at least some sort of personal connection, and more often than not it was someone close to the victim. No wonder Jenna had struggled to move on! And Mike's respect for her went up even further as he finally grasped what she had meant about being alone on a city street being traumatic.

Then he recalled the circumstances of her coming back to Ludlow, and his hand clasped over hers. "Dear God! That explains why you were in such shock at the whole thing about Kyle. If he ever comes this way looking for you, I'll have a restraining order on him so fast he'll be lucky to get over the county border, much less near you!"

"Damned right!" Robin agreed. "And if the little shit makes it up here, I'll break both of his legs for him and chuck him in the river! What an absolute turd! Fancy dragging his shit to your door. You don't need wankers like that in your life."

"See!" Mel said to Jenna with a smile of satisfaction.

"I told you they'd understand," and Jenna found herself looking in amazement at her two new guardian angels.

Not a word had been said about her being less than a woman for not being able to have kids, and that was such a novelty to her that it made her wonder if Mel wasn't right. Maybe the time had come when she would find someone who wanted her just the way she was? And feeling Mike giving her hand another squeeze of reassurance, she dared to hope that it might be him.

Jenna and Mel returned to their house that night in an almost festive mood, and with the promise of going back up to Robin's in the morning to visit the groves where the oaks had been felled. Another batch of marking would have to be done in the morning, Jenna insisted, or she'd never get it done. But there was only so much she could do of that in one sitting without going cross-eyed over some of the appalling handwriting. So by lunchtime, she assured the others, she would be only too glad to get up and go for a walk.

Therefore as Saturday afternoon arrived dry and with some watery sunshine occasionally peering through the clouds, Mel drove them once more up to Robin's, and they set out for the first grove. The three of them began by going down a steep incline from Robin's home, but at the same time working their way sideways around the hillside, at which point Jenna realised that they were coming into the woods she could see across the lake from the far side.

"My God, Willetts really had this sussed, didn't he?" she panted as she followed Robin. "He got his timber from as close as it was possible to get."

However Robin waved a hand slightly backwards towards their right. "The first grove is that way, just around the shoulder of the hill. There's a rough track coming down this way from the little road which crests the hill opposite us here, and then the track climbs up again on this side, which was part of what Willetts used. He brought in a caterpillar-tracked vehicle of some kind from that way, to drag each oak up to the path we're about to meet, and then across to the lake. Wait until you see the damage they did. It's hideous."

They came out from the woodland abruptly, to see a scar across the hillside immediately in front of them. It wasn't that wide, and Jenna guessed that another reason for Brian Willetts getting the oaks brought in one at a time was that it kept the destructive trail narrow, and invisible from the proper roads. Already they knew that whoever had done this hadn't been Garry White and his men. Of this crime they, at least, were innocent. Some unknown contractor had done this, and Robin and Mike had agreed the night before that it was probably a couple of men doing the work on the quiet, for no reputable lumberjack or tree surgeon would have touched this job.

The crushed undergrowth led back the way Robin had said as well as heading to the house site, but they only walked a few yards in the lake's direction before a spur went downhill again, which Robin led them on. Again, only a few yards farther on they came to the grove, and Mel and Jenna gasped in horror to see the devastation. It was bad enough that they could see the seven stumps of what had clearly been magnificent and mature trees, but the multitude of huge branches left scattered about the place was heartbreakingly wasteful.

"How old must those trees have been?" Mel said with a catch in her voice. "Just think of all that must have happened in their lifetimes. They must have been centuries old. What stories they could have told."

Robin pointed south-west. "Over there is the ancient hill-fort of Caer Caradoc, and the legend is that the native

Briton chieftain, Caractacus, fought his last battle with the Romans there in 50AD. It's not the only contender for the battle site, mind you, Hereford Beacon and the other Caer Caradoc nearer to Church Stretton being the main ones. But I've always had a fancy that if Caractacus – or Caradoc – knew a thing or two about warfare, then this remote valley, where the Romans couldn't put their straight roads through to get reinforcements to the front at speed, would have been just the sort of place he would have made his stand."

"Is that as one soldier speaking of another?" Mel asked, and Jenna could see that she was much taken with the idea.

Robin gave his wry smile. "Yeah, you could say that." Then he shivered and looked around the clearing. "There's times when I think that those old chieftains of what we'd now call the Welsh, were deeply in tune with the land they lived in, and they must have been appalled by the Romans and their war machines. When the dreams of the dryads came, there were also ones where I felt like I was one of those old Britons, fighting another battle from two thousand years before the ones I was actually in. And then it would shift again, and I'd feel that there was another fight for not such different principles going on between me and Brian Willetts."

He stopped and looked embarrassed. "You'll think me daft, eh?"

"Oh no!" Mel said, and Jenna could see her eyes shining in the way only Mel's could when she was inspired by something or someone. "I think you're far from daft. I've learned so much on my travels, and I think that sometimes a serious illness or injury seems to shake something free in a person's mind. Not loose in the sense of losing your mind, but more as though it shakes off all the accumulated rubbish we pick up along the way, and leaves those people free to see once more what they used to see as children. Kids are so unencumbered by expectations and baggage, they view the world more openly and honestly. Here in the west we try too hard to put every last thing into a nice neat pigeonhole that we can stick a label on, and rationalise to the nth degree. It's as if folk are terrified of things which are unknowable, and rather than marvelling at the wonder and mystery of them, they close their eyes and whistle loudly as they walk past that particular 'graveyard'."

Robin looked surprised but said, "In that case, I wish Brian Willetts had been a bit more scared of the 'graveyard ghosts' he might provoke in this instance. A hefty dose of the heebie-jeebies might have saved us all a lot of misery." He took Mel's arm, guiding her towards the centre of the clearing, a growing expression of pain and grief on his own face. "This is where it's worst."

Following them, Jenna was surprised to come up to Mel's other side and see the tears streaming down her friend's face.

"Mel?"

"Oh, Jen, the pain that's here!"

Mel moved unsteadily to the one stump and sat down on it, but rather than finding some relief, she instead let out a howl of anguish.

"Mel?"

Jenna was fine until she dashed to Mel's side and put her hand on her friend's shoulder. It was as if a whole extra level of connection had been made, and Jenna felt the surge of sensations slam into her, both physically and emotionally.

She felt pain – gut-wrenching, searing pain.

She felt devastating loss.

Loss of ones so close they defied any human

comparison, but also of self. Of a piece of herself having being shorn away, and with it a part of her very identity.

And she felt grief of the most profound kind for those losses in all of their forms.

The way they were washing over Mel and into Jenna brought with them Mel's sensations of being utterly overwhelmed, and Jenna saw what she had always known, which was the depths of Mel's compassion for others, and her empathy which she couldn't switch off.

But for Jenna herself it was different again. Yes, she felt everything that Mel did, but in her case those sensations and emotions were nothing new. All they did was hit her old scars, and if she reeled as if having taken a body blow, at the same time they didn't crush her world. She rode the incoming waves the way she always did, accepting the torrent of emotions and sensations, and the fact that she couldn't change them. She had survived before, she would survive again. It might knock her to the ground, but she would get back up again, even if metaphorically it was like first getting her hands underneath her, and then pushing herself up onto her hands and knees, and then slowly rising to her feet again. It could take a while before she would even be able to take a step, much less walk, when such crushing damage struck she knew, but all of Jenna's old survival instincts rose to the surface in response to the influx of suffering from the dryads.

Stranger still, something of Jenna's responses must have begun washing back through Mel to the dryads. The first she knew of that was Mel suddenly looking up at her and sobbing, "Jen?" and then fainting, utterly overwhelmed by receiving her friend's trauma on top of what she was already getting from the dryads. Yet Jenna found herself rooted to the spot. She was vaguely aware of Robin beside them frantically calling Mel's name, and then picking her up to carry her out of the clearing. But Jenna stayed put, the connection now coming directly to her.

"You know this?" was a question more felt than spoken, but there was no mistaking the surprise of the collective dryad consciousness as they felt her responses.

"Oh yes," Jenna managed to say back. "I've felt what you feel."

There was a tumble of emotions in response to that. In some instances — and Jenna thought that maybe these were the individual dryads she was now sensing — they were astonished that one of these dreaded humans should have felt something so deeply. Others were wondering how anyone survived this torment. And in others there was a strange and growing sense of kinship. From those she felt the question, "How?"

"Do you mean how did I survive? How did I recover?"

"Yes."

Jenna allowed her remembered emotions to flow as she tried to explain, "At the time I thought I wouldn't. I thought I would die there. And then when I found out just how much I had been damaged," and here she let her feelings over never having the chance to a family to flow, "I wasn't even sure that I wanted to go on living. ...It was all too much. Too much taken from me, and at the same time too much to carry with me and yet still be able to go on." And here she felt something akin to relief coming back to her for that understanding.

"But if you don't die yourself," Jenna tried to explain, "then at some point you're faced with a choice. Do you just wither away? Because at that point you may be alive, but you aren't *living*. Or do you try to find a new way of being yourself? You can't go back, and you'll never be the same — not after something like you and I have been through. I'm not the girl I was before. I'm nothing like her anymore. And it's taken a long time, I won't pretend it hasn't. But all I could think of was that if I didn't try and live some kind of life, some new life I'd never even had to consider before, then the person who did this to me would still have some kind of power over me. And I didn't want that. He'd left me powerless and wounded once, I wasn't going to let him cripple the whole of the rest of my life."

She felt the ripple of what might best be called astonishment radiate out through the dryad network. And it wasn't just for the words she had managed to formulate, but because Jenna was having to do it through gritted teeth as she braced herself against the ongoing waves of pain and misery. They were astonished at the way she was determinedly pushing those sensations aside, not suppressing them, but just refusing to let them crush her.

"You are a rare creature," one of the dryads spoke in her mind. "We have never met your like before."

Jenna managed to send back, "Well in one way I'm glad about that. Mercifully there aren't that many people who've gone through what I have. No every human is brutal and uncaring." And then she realised she could do something more than just pass on advice here.

"Your loved ones you lost ...at least four of them are trapped in the buildings down there," and she tried to visualise the houses by the lake.

A surge of new horror flooded in, making Jenna gasp at the emotional weight of it, but at least one of the dryads was now alert to the fact that she was trying to tell them something, and that voice began calling to the others to try and stop overwhelming Jenna. When she could draw her breath again, Jenna went on,

"We are trying to set them free. Please understand that. Our kind has lost the memories of yours, so at first we simply didn't understand what had happened. And please believe me when I tell you that the man who had the oaks cut down is *not* the kind of human we…" and she tried to send the concepts of respect, admiration and acceptance.

"But once we realised that there are some of your folk trapped in the houses, we began trying to work out how to set them free." She pictured in her mind Alicia's house, and then men coming and putting the acrow-props in, and the beams coming out. It was all a bit fuzzy, because Jenna herself wasn't entirely sure how Garry and his men were going to do it, but she hoped that she had conveyed the idea to them. "When that's done, we'll do the same on…" and she imagined the house where she was staying. "It won't be fast, but it's probably no slower than if they take the houses down altogether.

"If we take the beams the dryads are trapped in out onto the grass, will they be able to then get free?" she asked, and although there was some doubts in the responses she got back, on the whole it seemed that the other dryads thought that they would be able to help their friends once they were back out in the open air again. If nothing else, they seemed to think they would be able to regain contact with them.

Now, though, she had to break the bad news. "I'm afraid we think the dryad in the last house isn't at all well," and she tried to send some sort of image of madness that the dryads might relate to. Being so connected to the earth and to the permanence of nature, Jenna wondered whether they had any point of reference for losing your mind. Was there any point with them when the world around you stopped making any sort of sense? "We'll get her out," she carried on, "But she might never be 'right' ever again. We don't know your kind, but amongst us, there are some who never recover from such wounds to the mind."

There was some anger coming back at her for the state of the final dryad, but it wasn't directed at Jenna personally. And then there was suddenly another sensation. With a jolt, Jenna realised that Robin had come back and had his hand on her shoulder, and was calling her name.

"Jenna! Wake up, Jenna! Jen! Can you hear me? Jen!"

The connection with Robin now put her in the middle, and she felt his huff of breath as the waves which had hit her winded him. But she also felt his pain, and so did the dryads.

"We have felt this one before," one of them said kindly. "He too is hurt," but in Robin's case they were perplexed by the images of modern warfare which came through the link. Jenna's personal harm they could understand, but the sweep of modern war, with its machines and weapons, was so alien to them as to be incomprehensible. And now Jenna saw the only fighting they had ever seen back in Caradoc's time – that was where that had come from in Robin's dreams! They felt pity towards him, but not the connection they had made with her, yet at the same time they picked up on Robin's worry that this was doing Jenna more harm, and his desperate desire to get her and Mel away from this place.

Like the tide going out, the images and sensations gradually receded from Jenna's mind, until she was able to see the real world around her. As soon as she could, she managed to gulp,

"Give me a sec'! Just need to get my breath!"

Feeling herself shaking like a leaf at the way the whole experience had drained her of energy, Jenna finally managed to rouse herself enough to walk, and like pair of drunks, she and Robin staggered out of the grove.

The farther away they got the more they recovered, and up on the track they found Mel, still lying in the recovery position Robin had left her in.

"Oh God, she's still out cold," Robin said despairingly.

Kneeling beside her friend, Jenna found a pulse and replied, "Yes, but she's breathing normally, and her pulse is actually a lot steadier than mine is at the moment. I don't think she's taken any permanent harm from this."

"I'll have to carry her," and Robin managed to get her up and draped over his shoulders with Jenna's help. Then slowly, they began crabbing their way up and across the hillside again. Twice Robin had to stop to rest, and Jenna found herself having to help him up some of the rougher patches as exhaustion set in with him as well.

When they finally got back to his cottage, all they could do was put Mel onto a bed and then collapse into the armchairs themselves. The next thing Jenna knew, she woke up and it was getting dark. Robin was still out for the count, but snoring gently, and when she went through to where Mel was, it was to find her friend drowsy but once more in the land of the living. Brewing up a strong pot of tea, Jenna took one through to Mel, along with a chunk of Robin's fruitcake, and they sat in companionable silence, eating and drinking, but neither of them able to speak of what they had been through just yet. Coughing and swearing from the living room told them that Robin had woken up, and so Jenna took him through more of the tea and cake, but it wasn't long before he and Mel were back asleep again.

And that left Jenna with a quandary. What if the dryads tried to contact their lost ones through her? Would they think her faithless if they reached out and then couldn't find her down at the houses? She had reached some sort of understanding with them, but their respective concepts of reality and the world were so different there were bound to be discrepancies. And would those differences lead to misunderstandings if she didn't make the attempt to keep the link going?

Making herself a sandwich to give her a bit more energy, Jenna decided that she must walk back down to the house. Luckily it was downhill, for she had no illusions that she would have managed another scramble uphill. But a steady walk down she felt she could manage. And she also wanted to talk to Mike, but on her own. She wasn't sure how jumbled Robin and Mel's understandings of what had happened might be. Mel in particular had felt as though she was being tugged all over the place while they had been connected. And so Jenna wanted to be able to sit on her own sofa and try to explain this to Mike without any interruptions.

Finding some paper, and using one of Mel's pens from her bag, which was still on the living room table, Jenna wrote them a note to explain where she'd gone, concluding with, 'don't worry, I've got my mobile with me. I'll be in contact at all times. If you don't wake up until the morning, I'll come up and see you first thing.' And then borrowing one of Robin's walking poles for extra stability, Jenna set off into the evening light.

Chapter 21

The reason why Mike had not come up later in the afternoon to join the others, as promised, was because he had troubles of his own. For no good reason that he could put his finger on, he had got up on Saturday morning with the strong urge to go into the office. Maybe it was what Jenna had overheard that was preying on his mind, but he felt compelled to go in and have a look around while nobody else was there. And then it hit him – Zack hadn't brought his overnight bag in with him yesterday, and that all by itself was abnormal. So was Zack staying in Ludlow for the weekend? And if so, why? He had no friends here, or at least not as far as Mike knew. Zack had gone to school on the far side of Shrewsbury, so there were no old school chums around here to visit. Was he conspiring with old Hornby in some way?

The more he thought of it, the more Mike knew he was going to have to go and have a dig around. It went against his nature to go prying into someone else's desk and papers, but by now the nagging questions were too strong to ignore, and he knew that if only to protect Jenna, he had to know what Zack and Hornby were up to. Tiff had the backing of a powerful male friend in the company, but if he was to get Jenna into the position of office manager, he couldn't afford to have his former colleagues blackening her name before she'd even started.

He drove in to town, and then thought to park somewhere other than his designated parking slot.

Nothing would be a clearer signal that he was inside than if Zack happened to walk past and noticed the Land Rover, and being discovered red-handed in a search by Zack would do his cause no good either. So he pulled in at one of the car parks a bit farther away from the office, and then had the shock of seeing Zack's top-of-the-range BMW there. *Bloody hell, are you trying to stay unnoticed, too?* he wondered, and rapidly pulled back out of the bay he was in, and over to the far side of the car park into the shadow of a big old chestnut tree. There were enough farmers' Land Rovers in the area for his to not be recognisable unless Zack was right on top of it.

Blessing the fact that he'd seen the BMW before he'd gone blundering into the office unawares, Mike approached the building far more cautiously. Instead of taking the direct route, he looped around by the side streets, so that he came to the main door on the same side of the street, and therefore out of sight of the office windows. Easing the key into the lock, he held his breath for a moment as he gently opened the door, just waiting for the burglar alarm to go off, for in Zack's shoes he would have reset the alarm once inside in order to give him advanced warning of someone else coming in. The fact that Zack hadn't reset it made him wonder whether someone else was meeting Zack up there?

So he went up the old staircase on the sides of the treads to minimise any creaks, and saw that the main office door was just pushed to, but not latched. Feeling a bit daft at playing the spy game, nonetheless Mike didn't walk straight up to the door, but paused by the hinged edge to look through the frosted glass and gilt-lettered panel as best he could. He knew he wouldn't get a clear view of the office, but he would still see the outline of people moving about in there by their shadows, since the door faced the window.

He saw no movement, and listening carefully, he was sure he could hear voices but that they weren't in the main office. So he eased the door open, gently pushing it back to its former position, and stepping quickly away from the glass panel towards his desk on the left-hand side of the large room. Zack's office was beyond his on the same side, with its door at the far end by the window. Opposite it on the right side was Hornby's former office, and Mike was wondering which one Zack was in. If Hornby was in with him, then they would be in the senior partner's room, but would Zack be so confident to step into Hornby's shoes on his own?

As he was listening to work out which room they were in, he suddenly heard the downstairs door slam shut, and then heavy treads coming up the stairs. The only thing to do was to duck down under his own desk, which fortunately was of the old fashioned kind, with drawers on either side and a panel across the back. In the winter Mike had cursed that panel, because it cut his feet and legs off from the extra heaters they had to use to supplement the ancient radiators, but for the first time he was now grateful for it. Unless somebody actually came around to his side of the desk he was invisible.

The office door opened and was allowed to slam shut, and as a pair of high heels clicked across the floor, Zack's voice came from his own office calling,

"In here, Alicia!"

Risking the briefest of glances out from his hiding place as she passed the end of the office to head into Zack and whoever else was in there, Mike caught a glimpse of her peroxide blonde hair, the flame red dress stretched over her ample bust, and the way she tottered along on a ridiculously high pair of equally bright red heels. That the heels actually carried her substantial weight was quite a tribute to their maker, Mike thought, because they looked spindly enough to have snapped. As it was, one snagged in the gap in the old floorboards, nearly pitching her through the doorway on her nose, and he heard her swear,

"Fucking death trap of an office! I do hope you'll move to somewhere more modern, Zack. This was fine for an old fart like Hornby, but you won't get the right sort of clients in a dump like this."

"Oh shut up and sit down, Alicia!" an impatient woman's voice snapped, earning the response,

"Don't you tell *me* what to do, Fiona! If I hadn't listened to you we wouldn't be in this mess!"

"Now, now, ladies," Zack's oily voice said. "Is Claudia joining us?"

"No she's not," Alicia's voice replied. "Bloody fool said that we'd caused her enough trouble as it was. Can you believe that she said that I'd be better off listening to what fucking Campbell says? Some rubbish about him having a grip on reality, and if we want to get anything at all out of that miserable old miser dying, then we'd be best letting him deal with things. I told her straight, I'm not being cheated out of what I know our father had squirreled away. And I want the proper price for those houses! I'm not scratching a living if he sells them for next to nothing!"

"My dear lady, you won't be scratching for anything by the time I've done," Zack consoled her. "Now then, have either of you been up to the houses of late to see this supposed damage Campbell was talking about? Personally I find the whole thing ridiculous. Those houses were fine when I went up there with Mr Hornby at your father's invitation."

That was a bit rich, Mike thought, remembering back to the way Brian Willetts had been far from pleased to find that Hornby and Zack had tagged along with him when it had been he whom Brian had invited, not them. Whatever

Brian's many other faults were, he'd certainly been shrewd enough to not want either of those two dealing with his affairs, and it worried Mike that now Zack was talking to the two women as though he was in full possession of all the facts.

"I'm sure we can get this ridiculous clause about all three houses having to have their sales completed at the same time changed," he was going on. And under the desk Mike found himself shaking his head. Oh no he wouldn't! Mike had already looked thoroughly into that, knowing the clauses inside and out because he'd been the one who'd had to draft them for Brian; and having consulted the head-office partners who dealt with this sort of thing all the time, the conclusion had been, given that Brian had been definitely of sound mind when he drew up the clauses and his will, that they were binding. But Zack was still ploughing on, making promises to swing things the sisters' way which Mike knew would be impossible to keep.

It didn't take long before Alicia was saying impatiently,

"Well as long as you don't take too long over all of this, you have my permission to go ahead. I don't want the details, I just want the money!"

"Then you'll meet us up at the houses on Monday morning?" Zack said as he came to the office door to see Alicia leave.

"Oh don't you worry, I'll be there! I want to make sure that that itinerant slut Campbell has put in on the pretext of being a caretaker isn't doing the damage on the sly! I bet she comes cheap for a spot of vandalism."

It was all Mike could do to stay silent. Of all the slurs to cast at Jenna, 'itinerant slut' seemed the most unfair and cruel, and he ground his teeth as he heard Zack laughing and saying,

"Well she'll be out on her ear by Monday night."

"Good!" and Alicia clattered her way back down the stairs, her curses at the way her heels nearly made her overbalance echoing back up the stairwell.

However Zack didn't show any signs of leaving.

"Coffee, Fiona?" he offered, and went into the kitchenette, coming back with two cups.

Guessing that they would be there for a little while, Mike risked coming out from under the desk, both to hear what they were saying better, and to ease the cramp in his legs.

"They're both fools," he heard Fiona say bitterly. "I wish she'd break her bloody neck on those stupid heels. Then at least I'd only have to split things two ways."

"Oh, my dear, you really don't have to worry about that," Zack said, making Mike's hair on the back of his neck stand on end. Christ Almighty, was he planning murder? But no, "I can prepare one set of accounts for you, and quite another for your sisters," he was continuing. "Do you really see Alicia bothering to inspect every step of the process?"

"She doesn't have the brains! The first time she gets to a word with more than two syllables, she'll switch off."

"And if Claudia is willing to accept the pittance Campbell is going to get for the properties, as long as we show her an improvement on that, I don't think we need to worry about her making waves, do we?"

"Oh, Zack, it's so refreshing to be dealing with a partner who knows where to place his priorities. What do you say that we go and do a little inspecting of our own before Monday? It'll be a miracle if Alicia turns up anyway. It takes her two hours just to do her make-up and hair, and she's hardly an early riser after the bottle of wine she has every night. And I don't think we need to include Claudia. She's more bothered about that stupid local cheese tasting event she's putting on this weekend. Let's keep things between ourselves, eh?"

The conversation turned to more general chitchat and Mike wondered whether he should get up and go now, while they were distracted. But then he really wanted to have a look through whatever papers Zack had drawn up. If he was being treacherous enough to falsify accusations against Jenna which would end up in Richard Mann's hands, then Mike wanted to know about them before they got sent. So he lurked by his desk until there were sounds of the pair in the next room about to leave, then crept back under again.

Fiona went first, but Zack was only a short way behind her. As he closed the office door, Mike let him get just down the first two quarter-turns of the staircase before sliding silently out of the main office. He followed Zack down cautiously, and then as the outer door slammed shut and the alarm did its succession of beeps as warning for people to exit before it fully set, he careered down the stairs and positioned himself right by the alarm panel. Allowing the alarm to set, for he guessed that Zack wouldn't move on until he was sure it had, Mike then gave him time to move away, staying very still. Then he took the main alarm off, so that he would be able to walk around in the offices without triggering the motion sensors, but put the bottom door's alarm back on so that he would have advance warning if Zack returned.

Going back up at a steadier pace, Mike went straight through into Zack's office, and then stopped in amazement. He'd not been in here in a long time, any meetings usually taking place in Hornby's office, and so he was quite unprepared for the chaos he saw inside. How on earth Zack ever found anything was beyond him, and it dawned on him that this was another reason why Zack so resented Tiff and Suzy's efforts to bring some order to the place. Zack must have been worried to death that they would come in here and go through it all like a pair of whirlwinds, unearthing past misdemeanours and howling mistakes that Zack had forgotten he'd left around.

Where the hell to start, though? It wasn't as though he needed to be careful to put anything back where it had been, because most of the piles of files and papers were balanced precariously as it was. There must have been many times already when Zack came in to discover that a slammed door had caused an avalanche. But which heap to start on first?

Reasoning that since he'd only just met with the two sisters, Mike started on the desk, and was rewarded with finding drafts of letters concerning both the will, and the clauses regarding the houses. All of these Mike took through to the photocopier and made his own copies of. Then he went back, and within the hour had amassed a fair pile of his own copies, most of which implicated Zack most horribly in trying to both undermine the firm and Mike himself, not to mention being catastrophically misleading to the clients he was purportedly representing – and given that Brian Willetts' will had said quite categorically that the whole thing was to be handled by Mike, there was some serious doubt as to whether Zack could be said to be representing them in any form at all.

Feeling positively filthy from the whole process, Mike bagged up the copies and left for home, making sure that he left no trace of his weekend visit. And once back there, he showered and then took Silas and Marnie out for a long walk to clear his head. He was so engrossed in his own discoveries that he forgot altogether that he'd been supposed to be going up to Robin's later on to see the groves. Instead he spent some time on his computer sending a long and detailed email to Richard Mann, including scanned copies of the relevant documents he'd copied at the office, and then rang Tiff's mobile. She had departed for Birmingham on the train yesterday, saying that she would spend the weekend resting in her own flat, but Mike felt that the least he could do was warn her of the impending storm, and by the time he had finished bringing her up to speed, she was as furious as he was.

"I'll ring Richard right away," she announced, although Mike could have sworn he'd heard a man's voice in the background, and had his suspicions that Richard was all of a few feet away from Tiff. "I'll get him to pick up your email right away. This is something that shouldn't wait until Monday!"

Jenna was so engrossed in watching where her feet went that it was only the flash of light catching the corner of her eye that made her look up. She had made it around the hairpin in the track without slithering on the loose pebbles, blessing the fact that she had worn her walking boots in expectation of the walk to the grove, and had just come into line with the view back down to the houses. Not sure quite what she had seen, she looked about her, registering that the long shadows of evening highlighted where the oaks had been dragged around the lake. Alert to what she was looking for now, she could tell that last autumn's spurt of growth in the brambles and bracken had already begun to disguise the traces of Willetts' crime, but that hadn't been what had caught her attention.

Then she saw it again. Two lights on the driveway. It must have been a car coming up the track whose headlights she had seen just moments ago, and which had temporarily disappeared as the car had turned in through the bank of the gateway. She peered hard, wondering if Mike had tried to get in touch with them, and having reached nobody, was now panicking. But it occurred to her that these headlights weren't the Land Rover's, not least because they were the new trendy ones which shone with a bluer light. Nor was that Tiff, for the Smart Sport's headlights were also the more normal yellow.

Suddenly alert to the fact that this must be a stranger, Jenna dug into her fleece pocket and pulled out her phone, then swore as she realised that just here she had no signal. Damn it, she would have to wait until she was right down by the houses again before it might return, and even then, she knew that by Fiona's house the signal was masked until you got out onto the rough lawn. She was going to have to creep in unseen and try to find a safe place to call Mike from. And for the first time she regretted that her fleece was a bright pink. She'd bought it precisely because it was visible, and very definitely a girly colour – she had no wish to ever be mistaken for a lad in a dark hoodie ever again. But tonight she knew it would stand out even in the twilight.

Then she remembered that the lining material was just a standard grey, and shrugging out of the fleece, she turned it inside out before putting it back on again. It was hardly camouflage, and Robin would probably laugh at her for doing it, but then Robin wasn't capable of so much as swatting a fly at the moment, so she could hardly call on him for help. *Come on, girl, you've got this*, she told herself firmly. *You don't have to rugby tackle whoever is there. Just get down to where you've got a signal and call Mike. He can do the 999 call if it's needed. And you'll look less of a twit if you can tell him what that car is and the registration.*

Down at the bank, she began creeping very carefully along it, making sure that she was on the downhill side so that she wasn't exposed if this unknown somebody was on the drive. The car's lights were out now, and Jenna could hear the metallic clicks as the engine cooled down. There was the faint petrol smell of a car engine that had been worked hard, and she could now see that it was some kind of sleek saloon car – not exactly a low-slung sports car, but something equally incompatible with the steep, rough climb it had made.

Making a couple of darting glances around the bank, she satisfied herself that there was nobody out on the drive. And so in a fast scuttle, she shot across to the far side of the car. Peeping up over its bonnet, she scanned the houses and then jumped as a light came on in the middle one, the yellow beam spilling out across the gravel even though the huge picture windows weren't visible from here. However, that was reassuring because it meant that she had nothing to fear from someone watching her from Fiona's house.

Easing herself cautiously to her feet, she moved to the back of the car, which also put the bulk of Fiona's house in between her and whoever was in Alicia's, and then pulled out her mobile. To her great relief the signal showed at full strength and she also had a nearly full battery. Pulling up Mike's number she rang it, and was much relieved when he answered on only the second ring.

"Where have you been? I've been trying to get you?" his worried voice demanded.

"I'm so sorry, Mike. A lot's happened, but I can't tell you all of it right now because I need your help."

"Help? Why? What's happened? Are you okay?"

"Don't panic, yes I am."

"Why are you whispering?"

"Well that's just it. Mike, I've just walked back down from Robin's and he and Mel are a bit knocked out, so I can't ask for their help. But the thing is, there's someone in Alicia's house."

"What? Who?"

"I don't know, that's why I'm calling. There's a car on the drive that just pulled up as I was walking down. It's a…" and she squatted down to peer at the badge, "…Audi TT …looks like it's a convertible …silver or pale grey."

"Bloody hell! That's Alicia's. What's she doing up there? Jenna, be very careful, she's convinced that you and I are acting against her," and he briefly told her of his discoveries earlier on. "Whatever you do, don't confront Alicia," he concluded. "Nothing you say will change what she thinks of us, and she's prone to lashing out. We've had to defend her twice for hitting other women when she's been a bit the worse for drink, and I don't imagine any thoughts of drinking and driving will have stopped her from going up there with a few inside her already. Go inside your house, lock the doors, and don't put any lights on. Don't give her any clue that you're in there. I'm on my way, just stay safe."

Chapter 22

Deciding that the safest way to get to her house was around the back by the garages, Jenna took that route, keeping to the grass rather than the gravel, and safely made it to her back door. It took a moment for her to realise that the reason why the door wouldn't open for her was because it was bolted on the inside. She'd never expected to have to come in this way, and so had instead made sure that it was securely locked up. Kicking herself for her own paranoia now working against her, she had to work her way around the far side of the house, for the gap between her house and where Alicia was wouldn't have hidden a cat, much less her, after she'd conscientiously mown the grass there too.

The far side of her house was in pitch blackness and she found herself stumbling over the huge ruts in the longer grass, belatedly realising that this must have got churned up when the oak beams got dragged in. At least she made it to her veranda steps without mimicking Tiff's accident, and paused to look across to Alicia's house. The place was fully lit now, and Jenna could hear someone stamping about and talking to themselves. Going on Mike's comments, she suspected that Alicia was at least a little drunk and probably cursing her roundly, assuming that the wreckage she was seeing was all Jenna's fault. Mike was right, this wasn't a woman she wanted to cross when she was in such a temper.

Therefore she waited until she heard Alicia's voice receding, as if on the far side of the house, and then scurried up her own veranda steps and in through the glass door. Hurrying into the kitchen, where she would be hidden from sight, she only put on one of the low lights under the upper units rather than the main light, and then put the kettle on and made herself a mint tea. Blessing her foresight for having picked up a couple of pots of Pot Noodles for emergencies, she poured the hot water onto one of those as well. They were far from her favourite meal, but she had learned long ago that they were useful for getting something warm into you when other options weren't available, and right now she didn't want to start cooking only for the smell to waft across to Alicia.

With some hot food inside her, Jenna began to feel much better, and she also had the dubious benefit of having been in a job where she'd become used to keeping working even when exhausted. So although she was dog-tired after the draining day she'd had, there was part of her that wanted to keep going, and to make sure that Alicia didn't deliberately cause more damage which she could then blame on herself. It also dawned on her that she had the best part of half an hour to wait before Mike could hope to get here, and in that time Alicia might well leave.

So she began by going upstairs to the third bedroom in this house, which was the only one of the upstairs rooms with a window facing the right way. It was a roof light, and Jenna had to stand on tiptoes to look through it, but then realised she'd totally miscalculated. If Alicia was upstairs in her own house, then of course Jenna wasn't going to see her, because the only window on her side of that house upstairs was the frosted one of the en-suite.

Mentally kicking herself for not having remembered her own complaints to Mike about the lack of windows in the main bedroom on this side of Alicia's house, Jenna knew that she was going to have to go through to her own bedroom, and look out through the larger windows to have any hope of seeing anything. It was risky, because if she could see Alicia, then the chances were that Alicia might see her. But at least she'd done as Mike said, and had locked her door behind her, so if Alicia came rampaging around here, that should slow her up for a while.

However, even in her main bedroom Jenna could see nothing, and reluctantly she was about to go downstairs when she felt the sensation she now equated with the dryads.

"Hello. Are you there?" she called out cautiously. "I've been speaking to your friends today. I've explained to them that we're going to try to get you out. It won't be quick, but it will happen. Do you understand me? Can you hear me?"

I hear you, a voice came inside her head. *Thank you, and I sense my kin's touch in you. You must have allowed them a lot of contact to leave such a strong impression.*

"Well it was a bit of a rough ride for me," Jenna admitted, "and I'm still very tired from it, but I'm so glad we managed to talk. Don't worry, I won't try anything like the cleansing I did before."

It's not you or I who I'm worried about just now, the dryad confessed. *Please, you must go to the house next door and get that woman out.*

"I'm so sorry. I don't think she'd listen to me. She's someone who sees me as her enemy. She might even attack me if I go."

If you don't, then I fear for what my sisters are going to do, and there was something in the way the dryad said that which made Jenna shiver.

"They'd harm her?" Even as she said it she knew that these were the dryads who had pushed her and tried to kill

Tiff. "Oh, God. Okay, I'll go and try, but I'm not hopeful she'll listen."

Leaving her front door open so that she could always make a run for it if Alicia came out full of rage and tried to attack her, Jenna went outside and around to where she could look in through the huge windows of the all-glass frontage. Standing well clear of the house, she called,

"Alicia? ...Alicia? ...Can you hear me? Please come out of the house." What could she say to persuade this bloody woman to leave? "They've started loosening the bolts on the beams." A total lie, but it might just work. "Alicia, please come out, it's not safe. ...Alicia? The house isn't safe. Please come out!"

Moments later she saw an overweight woman in a tight red dress come stamping towards her from the back of the house on the upper floor. A bottle of some sort of fizzy wine, going by its shape, dangled from one hand, and Jenna guessed that she was already seriously tipsy. Then she saw a second and empty bottle lying on its side on the lounge floor and amended that to steaming drunk.

"No! Don't come to the balcony!" Jenna called urgently. "Come downstairs! Please ...come downstairs! It's not safe up there!"

And then she saw them. Two white, shifting shapes of women, converging on Alicia. But what truly shook Jenna was that they seemed to have grown in stature since she and Mike had seen the one behind Tiff.

Alicia came to stand at the balcony, dumping the bottle on the floor and hands almost wringing the wooden balustrade in her anger, her face a mask of fury, and screamed at Jenna, "I'll have you for this you thieving bitch! You fucking vandal! I'll have your job! I'll bloody *crush* you! I'll have you through the fucking courts for this! You're dog meat ...*scum*! You'll be living rough on the streets by the time I've done with you! You can't cross me

…I'll have your fucking guts for this! Campbell won't save you this ti…"

She never got the last words out. As her temper rose to a crescendo it seemed to feed the fury in the dryads, and when they struck it was with incredible force. Alicia had to weigh the best part of two hundred and eighty pounds, but the dryads tossed her off the balcony as if she weighed a fraction of that. And worse, they were fast. Fast enough to reach out their spirit hands and swirl the long scarf matching the dress around Alicia's throat, and then flick it around the balustrade. How they ever made the knot, Jenna never could work out, but Alicia's flight out from the balcony was halted, and her considerable weight fell, only to be stopped by the scarf.

The scarf wasn't in the right place for the fall to break her neck. Instead it just tightened around her throat, and Jenna could see her hands clawing at her neck as her feet kicked wildly to try and find something to rest on. Dashing to the door, Jenna tried to get in to her, but the door was firmly locked. About to run back to her house for her own set of keys, Jenna suddenly found herself frozen to the spot as she saw one of the dryads float out into the air beside Alicia, and whatever face she was presenting to the hanging woman it was enough to incite even more terror in her own face. For a second Jenna even thought she saw the dryad's head thrown back in laughter, and she stumbled away from the scene.

On shaky legs she ran into the house and grabbed her keys from off the table, ignoring the voice in her head which pleaded with her,

No! Don't go in there! Please, don't go!

Stumbling back towards the other house, she was barely off her own veranda when she heard the massive thump which signalled Alicia's body hitting the floor. Frantic by now, Jenna fumbled with the keys, but no matter what she did, nothing would open the door. She was still trying every key on the ring in the hope that she'd missed the right one when Mike pulled in to the drive.

She heard rather than saw him running to her side, and then he was taking the keys off her and trying the door.

"Bloody hell, what's she done to the lock?" she heard him saying in frustration as he too failed to get the door open.

"The dryads pushed her," Jenna sobbed. "I saw them do it."

"Oh Jen," and Mike dropped the keys to pull her to him. Moments later she heard him starting to use his mobile, but with only three keys pressed she knew he had dialled 999. "...All three," he replied in response to the question of which service he needed. "A woman had fallen from the balcony of a house, but we've no idea if she's alive or not, because we can't get into the house to help her. ...No, actually I'm her solicitor. ...No, I don't believe she was suicidal, that's why I'm asking the police to come out. I don't know if there's someone locked inside the house with her."

When he'd rung off, Jenna asked, "Why did you say that about someone in the house?"

"Because I want the police here when we break in! I want it crystal clear that you couldn't possibly have done this and then locked the door after you." He didn't want to upset Jenna further by saying that he feared there'd be a lot of accusations thrown her way from Fiona if nobody else. Then Jenna felt him stiffen and turned to see what he had seen in the house to do that. There, standing over the body of Alicia were the two dryads, and it seemed as though they were stabbing her with something. Whatever it was, it was as ghostly as they were, and while there was no sign of any blood running from Alicia, her body still jolted with every stab.

"Oye! Stop it! Enough!" Mike yelled, banging on the glass to get their attention.

Two faces which once upon a time must have been beautiful turned to him with bared teeth, lips pulled back over them in a feral snarl.

"Enough! Go on! Get away from her!" Mike continued, using the voice he would have done to get the dogs to behave. Something in his tone certainly seemed to get through to the dryads, and they melted away upstairs, leaving Alicia unmoving on the floor.

It took far too long to Jenna for the sound of the sirens to reach them, and even longer for the fire engine and the paramedic's four-wheeled drive response vehicle to make it up the hill. Mike hurried to meet them, and swiftly explained what had happened in terms they would accept. Two burly firemen came over and began attacking the door with axes, but it still took them all their time to get in.

"Why the hell would you want toughened glass that strong on a house out here?" the one asked Mike as the paramedic hurried in. "With the normal double-glazing we'd have been in ages ago, but that wood's tough, and the glass was deep set into it."

"She's gone," the paramedic said, coming back out. "No point in me hanging around. This is one for the police and the pathologist now, although going by the empty bottle, she was as drunk as a skunk when it happened." Then he took in Jenna standing and shaking to the side. "I'll have a look at you, though," he said, and got her to go into her house with him. When he returned he told Mike that he'd given Jenna a mild sedative, but suggested that he go and sit with her. "There's nothing more that you can do until the police get here," he said sympathetically. "Go and keep her company."

At some point in that long night, Jenna was aware of a big bear of a detective coming to talk to her, but the fact that she couldn't seem to stop herself from saying over and over,

"I couldn't get in to her, I couldn't save her," swiftly convinced him that if there was foul play involved, then Jenna wasn't the one.

"Just bring her to the station to give a statement when she's calmer," one of the local DSs who Mike knew told him. "Let's be realistic, the victim had to be twice Jenna's weight. It's hardly likely that Jenna would have been able to heave her over that balcony."

It also helped that Mike had just dashed down to the local convenience store, having run out of milk, when Jenna had phoned him, and at the time he'd been idly chatting to one of the uniformed officers who'd called in in his patrol car for a take-away coffee to keep him going through the usual Saturday night mayhem. Having a police witness to prove that Mike hadn't had time to get up there and do the job before he'd made the 999 call saved him a lot of questions. So once the pathologist had confirmed the time of death, nobody seriously doubted that things had happened just as Mike said, and that he had arrived to find a traumatised Jenna, and Alicia already on the floor.

Refusing to leave Jenna at the house this time, Mike bundled her into the Land Rover and drove her back to his house. He half expected to be woken by her having nightmares, but she was so exhausted that she slept soundly through until ten o'clock the next morning. By that time he'd received a panic-stricken phone call from Robin and Mel, who having finally surfaced earlier, had found Jenna's note, and then had been horrified to drive down to the houses and find the police incident tape across the front of the middle house. Indeed Jenna had only just emerged from the shower when Robin's Subaru screeched to a halt outside Mike's, and their two friends hurried in looking distraught.

It took the rest of Sunday morning for Jenna, Mel and Robin to fill Mike in on what had happened to them earlier on Saturday, for Mike to reveal what he had found out at the office, and then for Jenna and Mike to tell the others of their grim evening.

"Please tell me that there's somewhere that does food all day on a Sunday," Mel pleaded at the end. "I feel a desperate need to go out and just be amongst normal people."

Mike, however, looked less enthusiastic. "I'm so sorry, Mel, but looking at the time now we wouldn't get to the pubs in Clun in time for Sunday lunch, and I really don't think it's wise to go out in Ludlow. The bush telegraph will get word to Fiona in a heartbeat that her callous solicitor was out wining and dining only hours after discovering the body of her sister. I completely understand what you want and why, but if we do, it could end up back-firing on us badly."

"What about Hereford?" Robin suggested. "I don't mind driving – I wasn't up until after midnight like you, Mike. We could be there in no time, and you can't tell me that Fiona's reach runs that far."

Seizing on his offer with relief, the four of them piled into the Subaru, and headed southwards. In one of the old pubs tucked away down a side street close to the cathedral, they found that they were still in time for its extended Sunday lunch serving, and spent a pleasant couple of hours just enjoying the food. By the time they'd had a gentle wander around the cathedral so that Jenna and Mel could feed their medieval addiction, everyone was feeling considerably more normal.

"Please tell me that you're not even considering going to the house tonight," Mel said to Jenna as they sat together in the back of the car.

"No she is not!" Mike answered emphatically from the front. "She's staying at my house!"

"Good. I'd be worried sick if you were."

"There's just one thing, though," Jenna said with no enthusiasm. "I really feel that if I'm not going to be there tonight, that I really should go and pick up those exam papers."

"Oh, Jen, nobody's going to hold you to ransom if you're late handing them back given the circumstances," Mel protested, but Jenna waved a hand to signal that wasn't what she had meant.

"Lord, no, I'm not going to start on them tonight or anything daft like that. No, it's just that it would be terrible if Fiona and Zack still went up there this evening, and out of spite decided to go into Claudia's house. We don't know if Zack has any spare keys, do we? Those papers are my responsibility. I'd feel even worse if my students' chances to do well got ruined because that spiteful pair decided to take the papers out and burn them."

"Shit, I'd forgotten about that," Mike groaned. "You're right. Not that I think even Fiona's so callous as to brush off her sister's death quite that easily, but it would be foolish not to think that Zack might."

And so going via Mike's to get the Land Rover, they drove in convoy up to the houses, Jenna quietly amused at the way nothing was said, but that Mel was going back with Robin. If nothing else came out of this horrendous weekend than her friend finally finding the man she could live with, it wouldn't be all bad. At the driveway to the houses, Mike turned in and Robin gave a cheerful beep of the horn in farewell as he and Mel carried on up the track. What neither of them were expecting was to find two cars on the drive already, and as Mike slammed the brakes on, the bulk of the Land Rover hid the other cars from Robin and Mel's view.

There on the drive was Zack's huge BMW, but keeping it company was one of the new style Jaguar SUVs.

"Oh crap, Zack *and* Fiona," Mike groaned.

"Mike, I can't! I just can't face them. Not today. Not after everything," Jenna pleaded. "Can we just go and get the exam papers and leave?"

Mike quite understood how she felt, because he wasn't far behind that point himself.

"Of course we can. Come on, we'll do what you did and go around the back. At least once we're by Alicia's house we can get to the front of yours without them seeing us." And oddly he did think of that third house as Jenna's now. She'd made more of the place than Claudia ever had.

And so Mike reversed the Land Rover back out onto the track before he switched off, pointing it downhill ready for a swift getaway, and they got out being very careful to close the doors silently. At least knowing that Robin and Mel had gone ahead, there was no danger of anyone else coming down the track and crashing into the Land Rover, but Mike left the side lights on for their own benefit when they came back. It was pitch black up here away from any other habitation, and the sky was covered with heavy low clouds promising rain later. Not even a solitary star twinkled above, much less the moon. Yet Mike was reluctant to switch his torch on while they were alongside Fiona's house.

They were fine while they passed behind the study and TV room, since there were no windows to the rear in those rooms, and even the back door from the utility area was in darkness. But as they came up to where they could see the kitchen windows and doors, the lights in there suddenly snapped on and the back of the house was flooded with light. There was the thump of something being slammed down on one of the kitchen work surfaces and then a harsh woman's voice cut the silence. Of all the times for it to happen, Fiona and Zack were starting a flaming row in the kitchen.

Chapter 23

"I don't care!" Fiona screeched at Zack. "She was still my little sister! Don't you get that you supercilious moron? We might have had nothing in common. I may have loathed the sight of her. But she was mine!"

"Well that's a change of tune," Zack responded snidely. "You were quick enough to agree to fleecing her blind yesterday. That wasn't very sisterly, was it? So you've a bit of a cheek coming the grieving sibling now."

There was the sound of a very hard slap as Jenna and Mike stood rooted to the spot by the utility door. Please God they wouldn't take this row outside, because if either of them came out of the kitchen back door there was no way that they wouldn't be seen.

"You shouldn't have done that," they heard Zack respond coldly. "You lot may have got away with slapping the shit out of one another, but you don't do it to me!"

"And who do you think you are? If you're going to take over the firm like you keep saying you are, then you need to keep on my right side. I've ruined better men than you! That fool up the hill for a start off. Don't you cross me, Zachary, or you'll find your clientele walking away from you faster than you can open bottles of that cheap prosecco you think you're fooling your clients into thinking is champagne."

"Really?" Zack's snide drawl sent shivers down Jenna' spine, and for the first time Mike understood what Jenna had seen and he had not – Zack really was dangerous when crossed. "I don't think you quite realise who you're dealing with here. I'm not some empty-headed squaddie with a dose of PTSD. I've got connections of my own."

They saw Zack's shadow coming closer to the second window, and then realised that he must be leaning against the sink unit with his back to them. Unfortunately, that meant that Fiona was now facing them, and Mike pulled Jenna down so that they could creep under the first window. As soon as the chance came, they were going to get past that damned glass back door, because once beyond it they could make a run for it.

Now, though, they heard Zack saying, "You've got quite a load on board, if I may say so. Wouldn't do your reputation any good if I made a call to the local constabulary when you leave, now would it? Pillar of the community, Mrs Fiona Greaves, done and up in front of the magistrates for being way over the limit. And you don't exactly stick to the speed limit in that Jag', do you? Been done a couple of times already. So your record isn't exactly pristine."

"You watch it!" Fiona snarled, and they saw her shadow joining with Zack's as she came to do her usual trick of poking him in the chest. Mike had seen her do it before, and knew that she would be right in Zack's face.

"Quick!" he whispered to Jenna. "Now!" and they scurried across the doorway like two field mice avoiding the cat, continuing in a crouched run beneath the second window sill too.

Leaving Fiona to make whatever threats she had in mind, they now hurried to Jenna's house and went inside.

"Bloody hell, what lousy luck," Mike sighed, as Jenna scooped up the marking, and put it in the tough canvas bag she used for carrying such things around in.

"How on earth are we going to get back to the car?" Jenna fretted.

"Pretty bloody quick!" was Mike's response. "While they're at each other's throats, they're not looking for us. Come on, we're going!"

They got as far as the corner of Alicia's house, and then found that they could see into the kitchen of Fiona's from its side window. The other two were still shouting in one another's faces, and with no sign of running out of steam.

"Do you know, I reckon we might be better going across the front," Mike said. "If we get down by the lake, we're already a bit lower than here, and if they're still in the kitchen, then they won't see much out of the dining room window on a night like this."

"Let's do it. I can't wait to get away from them and all that anger."

It turned out that Mike was right, and from down on the lawn they must have been nearly invisible. As they hurried past the house, they could see that the fight was getting physical, and if Jenna wasn't much mistaken, Zack was going to be sporting some spectacular scratches down his face after Fiona clawed at him. However she and Mike were more concerned with their safety than Zack's destroyed looks, and both of them heaved a huge sigh of relief as they got back to the Land Rover and closed the doors.

"Thank God for that," Mike sighed. "Come on, let's get home to the dogs. I don't know about you, but I'm ready for a bit of peace and quiet."

They sat in companionable silence until they were almost at the junction with the main road to Leintwardine and Ludlow, at which point Jenna mused,

"All that anger. Where does it come from in some people? You know I'm sure that it was Alicia's fury which was fuelling the dryads. I think the reason they didn't respond quite so violently towards us was because we weren't bringing our own rage into the mix. ...That poor dryad up there, she's mad as a coot already without th…"

Jenna stopped in mid word, the same thought hitting Mike as he slammed on the brakes.

"Oh shit!" he gasped. "How could we have forgotten the dryad? Oh bloody hell! What if the same happens as with Alicia, and this one turns on them and traps them in the house like she did with us?"

He flung the Land Rover into a three-point turn and put his foot down to go back.

"Not on our own, though!" Jenna warned. "They're both bigger people than us. If they turn on us instead, we'll be the ones who come off worst. I'm calling Robin and Mel. They can meet us on the track."

"Then warn them to park just a bit up hill. The Jag' and the BMW are right in the entrance to the driveway. I only just missed them because I was going slowly. Having seen how fast Robin drives, he'll crash into them if he takes that turn at speed."

As Mike tore along the lanes as fast as he dared, Jenna called Robin and told him and Mel what they'd witnessed.

"They're neither of them pleasant people," she admitted, "and we probably won't get a word of thanks for saving their necks, not least because they won't believe a word we say about the dryads, even if they've had her right in front of them. But I don't think that poor dryad deserves to be swamped with their mucky thoughts either, and you both know how the dryads picked up on all of our feelings when we were in the glade. We promised we'd try and save all of them, and our intentions showed them that we included the mad one too, so we can't not try. If we have to communicate with them again, they have to feel the truth that we did our best."

"We'll start down there now," Robin said decisively. "It might even go down slightly better if Fiona and Zack see two relative strangers rather than you two. We may succeed where you can't."

"Don't take any chances, Robin," Mike called across from the driver's seat. "Zack may look like the archetypal upper class twit, but he's done some martial arts at that posh school he went to, and he's always bragging that he was good at it."

"Mike, have a little faith," Robin replied dryly. "It's one thing chucking your opponent onto the mat in a school contest. I was a lieutenant in the Marines, and we play for keeps!"

By the time they got back to the houses, the Land Rover's headlights reflected off the Subaru's just a bit farther up the track, alerting them to Robin and Mel already being there. Knowing about the other two cars, this time Mike just swung far enough into the drive to be able to turn and reverse up to the Subaru, but what neither of them was expecting was to see Mel come running out to meet them.

"We've called the fire brigade," she gasped. "The house is on fire!"

"What? How did that happen?" a flabbergasted Mike demanded. "There's nothing in there to catch alight. The electrics are all brand new and certified. It's not like they were going to have a frying pan catch fire or anything."

"Robin's trying to get in through the side window of the lounge with an axe," Mel added, as they ran with her into the driveway, but then they saw Robin standing back, the axe dangling in his hand in defeat.

"It's no good. I'm having the same trouble as the fire brigade did with Alicia's," he explained when they were closer. "Those downstairs windows are of some kind of toughened glass, and this is just a piddling little hand axe I carry in the car to clear away the odd dead branch that falls on the track. It's got none of the weight of the firemen's axes."

"Can you see anyone?" Jenna asked worriedly. "They can't have gone if the cars are still here."

Then there was a *whoosh*, and the flames spread into the lounge, at which point it occurred to Mike and Jenna that the whole reason they'd been able to see Mel and Robin's faces was because of the red light blazing out of the far side of the house.

"Dear God!" Mike intoned, Robin nodding and adding,

"The far side was already too hot for me to try and get in when we arrived. The kitchen with the back door was an inferno, and whether the heat has warped the front door, or the dryad has locked them in, but it won't budge an inch. I think the only thing that's slowing this fire down is that there's nothing like curtains and sofas to burn. Mind you, that wool carpet is going up pretty fast now."

They backed away as the heat rose another notch, Jenna saying regretfully, "How bloody tragic that the very carpet she was using to play her father with might be what kills her."

Then Robin, ever the practical one, decided, "We should try and move these cars. The fire engine won't get in past them."

However, even with the four of them heaving at it, Zack's BMW wouldn't move an inch. Fiona's Jaguar was easier, and they could only speculate that she hadn't bothered to put the handbrake on on the level drive. The hardest part with that one was stopping it from picking up speed and ending up in the lake, and it was only Robin running and grabbing the heavy rock off the lawn, and shoving under the one front wheels, that held it.

"Another weird twist," Jenna observed regretfully. "We put that rock in to stop the dryad from shutting us in the house, and her throwing it out onto the lawn is enough for us to save the damned car, but not its owner. ...Don't suppose chucking that at the patio door would do any good? It'd be worth losing the Jag' if it saved a life, even one as miserable as Fiona's or Zack's."

"Already tried it," Robin said, giving her shoulder a squeeze of consolation. "That's why it was that bit farther down the lawn. I heaved it at the glass and it bounced back. All it did was leave a scratch mark and nearly flatten me, 'cause I wasn't expecting it to do that."

Then a hideous scream came from inside the building.

"Oh no! The dryad!" Jenna wept. "She's burning too!"

As the reds and oranges of the flames lit up the upstairs windows, they briefly saw the now-familiar ghost-like figure of a dryad, backlit by the fire as it writhed in its agony, unable to escape.

"Oh the poor thing!" sobbed Mel, burying her face in Robin's shoulder, and Mike, seeing Jenna standing transfixed, turned her away and pulled her to him, hugging her tight so that she could only look out into the red-shot blackness of the lake.

By the time the fire brigade got to them, it was clear that nothing was going to save Fiona's house.

"They've had to come from Clun down the lanes," Robin explained, "and they're all local lads who have to come in from their homes to a call. It's not like a city brigade already on call clearing the streets with their blues and twos, and getting to a fire in minutes. These days there's nobody around here on permanent fire-station watch. One of the hazards of living out in the countryside, I'm afraid."

The greater weight of the fire engine was used to shove the BMW out of the way, and at least the lake provided an ample source of water, but it was soon clear that the best the firemen could do was to douse Alicia's house and the garages to prevent them from catching alight.

"Second time in two days?" the watch officer said, taking off his helmet to wipe his soot-blackened face. "Blimey, Mike, what are you playing at?"

"The bloody Willetts women, not me," Mike said morosely.

"And you're sure that somebody was inside there?"

"Terry, those two cars belong to the oldest sister, Fiona, and my colleague Zachary Carlton Smith. Neither of them are the rugged outdoors type, so I very much doubt that they've gone for a midnight ramble. And I can assure you that they would never have been up here for some lovers tryst in the woods. Both are more the silk sheets types than the tumble in the moonlight kind. If the cars are here, then they were inside, God help them. And to be frank, if one of them didn't start it, I don't know how else this house would have caught fire in the first place. As Robin said to me earlier, there was nothing in there to burn."

"Bugger." The fire officer grimaced. "That's going to mean a full investigation, then."

"Unfortunately, I think you're right."

And once again it wasn't long before the police arrived.

"DI Bill Scathlock, temporarily in charge once again," the big detective said, reintroducing himself. "Mr Campbell, you do seem to have the most accident prone clients. Now what's all this about arson?"

Yet again Mike found himself doing most of the talking, but with one slight change to their story. He and the others had already agreed that it would sound daft if they tried to explain their fears over the dryad locking

Fiona and Zack into the house, and so they told the absolute truth about how they had all felt terrible over Alicia's death, and had gone out for the meal in Hereford. Where they altered the tale very slightly was to say that Robin and Mel had picked up Jenna's uni marking for her on their way down to Mike's, but that it had lain forgotten about in the boot of his car until they had gone their separate ways.

"Robin and Mel were coming down to meet us at the house with the exam papers to save us going all the way up the track," Mike explained. "That's how they got here first. None of us expected to see any other cars here. In fact I damned near ran into them when I arrived, because I wasn't expecting them to be blocking the way," not saying that that had actually been the first time he'd come here, not the last. "Robin had already called the fire service by then."

At that point Robin took over, telling nothing but the truth of how he had tried to get inside but had failed.

"And you say this is the older sister of the woman who died on Saturday?" DI Scathlock questioned.

"That's right," Mike said with a sigh. "Christ, poor Claudia. How the hell do I tell her she's lost another sister so soon after Alicia and their father? None of them were likeable people, but they didn't deserve this."

"So Mrs Greaves had enemies?" Scathlock picked up perceptively.

Mike rolled his eyes wearily. "I'll give you a list, but there are so many, I may well miss a few she's pissed off without me knowing. I only know the ones where there was litigation involved."

The local DS who had driven up with Scathlock was nodding, "That's right, gov'. Bloody notorious the Willetts sisters were. God knows what was wrong with that family, but we'll be far from having a lack of suspects with this one."

As the big DI wandered off to talk to the fire chief, Mike asked DS Houseman, "Who is this guy? Where are your regular governors?" In one way the last thing he wanted was some razor-sharp DI questioning things too hard.

"Lucinda is off on maternity leave. Wally's on a long holiday celebrating his thirtieth wedding anniversary – been planned for nearly a year, has that, even before Lucinda got up the duff – and then of all the rotten luck, poor Si' got whipped into hospital with a strangulated hernia. We'd got a seconded DS who's up for promotion in to cover Lucinda, but everyone expected Si' to be there to hold his hand if necessary, and of course Wally's due back in a bit over a fortnight. But when the shit hit the fan with Si' and we had another case turn up, the Super' screamed for help, and they sent him. Mr Scathlock's from over on the South Worcester patch, but to be fair he's bloody good. We'd have really been in the shit without him. Don't worry, Mike, he's not one to jump to conclusions like Wally tends to do. And you've got the advantage of him not being local enough to have any preconceived ideas. Si's missus being the leading light in the local WI sometimes gives him a skewed view of the local petty politics. Mr Scathlock won't take any notice of stuff like that."

'Mr Scathlock', Mike noticed. That was a lot of respect coming from Charlie Houseman who wasn't far from retirement and had seen his share DIs come and go, both the good and the bad. Please God this Scathlock wasn't too keen and questioned too hard, because in their current states, Jenna and Mel might crumble and tell the whole truth, at which point they'd all look like a bunch of total flakes. Then he remembered the email he'd sent to

Richard Mann. Damn it, he would have to come clean over that, because if Zack was dead – and Mike hadn't wanted to say it to Jenna and Mel, but there was no way that anyone had survived that fire – then it was likely that Richard Mann himself might come down here and start asking difficult questions. Better to tell Scathlock this now, rather than look like he'd been covering something up later.

And so with great reluctance, Mike waited until Scathlock had finished with the fire watch officer and then went to speak with him.

"Look, there's something else you'd better know," he began regretfully. "Come on down to the far house and I'll tell you what else has been going on."

Inside Jenna's house, while she and Mel made tea in relays for the firemen and then themselves, scraping together Jenna's assortment of random mugs to serve as many as possible in one go, Mike explained the office goings on to Scathlock and Houseman.

"There was no point in concealing the fact that Zack and I were at loggerheads," Mike finished regretfully. "You would have found out sooner than later, not least because the big boss is going to do his nut when I have to tell him about this. He'll see it as the firm being brought into disrepute, I'm sure. If Zack wanted his revenge on me, then in a bizarre way he might just get it now if Mr Mann wants to make a clean sweep of things, or close the office altogether."

However DI Scathlock sat back in Jenna's carver chair and gave Mike an assessing look. "By the sounds of it, though, if you've presented all this evidence to your boss of Carlton Smith going behind people's backs, and dragging the company's reputation through the dirt, you've come out if it as the man with their best interests at heart."

"Well I hope he sees it like that. God knows, Zack and I were too different to ever be close colleagues, much less friends, but once upon a time we used to rub along. It's only been since Mr Hornby's retirement that things have got so acrimonious. And I never understood why until I went looking in his office. All I was worried about was the way he was leading the Willetts sisters up the garden path with his wild promises about breaking the will, which he could never have kept. But having seen the mess his case files are in, it now makes me wonder whether all this aggression he started showing was out of fear of exposure for being hopelessly incompetent."

He heaved a regretful sigh. "Given the way he so smoothly manipulated Fiona, I'm almost at the stage of suspecting that he and Hornby were stuck with one another, because they each knew where the other's skeletons were buried. ...Shit! I didn't mean that literally!"

Scathlock chuckled. "I know you didn't. I wasn't expecting to find myself investigating a pair of murderous solicitors as well. I think what you're trying to say is that Hornby couldn't sack Carlton Smith because that one knew just how hopeless his boss was, too. And yet at the same time, Carlton Smith was struggling to get out of Hornby's grip, because Hornby knew a lot more of the cock-ups that Smith had made than he let on to your overall boss?"

"Exactly."

"Then since you've effectively prepared the ground for us by alerting your bosses to what Smith has been up to, I think after I've had a word with this Mr Mann, I'll be asking your Mr Hornby some very searching questions. Because it seems to me that Smith was very sure of the fact that you were on your way out of the company, and the only person who could have given him those assurances would have been Hornby. It certainly wouldn't have been Mr Mann, in my opinion. That might shed some light on Carlton Smith's motives.

"And it'll be interesting to see what Mr Mann's version of that meeting between him and Hornby comes out like, because the only way that Hornby could have got rid of you would have been either with Mann's blessing – and I can't imagine that that was forthcoming from what you've said – or somehow Hornby's got the money to buy his firm back from the parent company. And if that's the case, where's that money come from when he had to sell it in the first place?"

"Christ! I never thought of that!" was Mike's unguarded response, confirming Scathlock's impression that it would be very unlikely that Mike had had anything to do with the two deaths. He just wasn't devious enough to have lured a rogue like Carlton Smith up here, besides which, Houseman had confirmed that Carlton Smith had been a big man, and Scathlock couldn't imagine that Mike could have overwhelmed him unless he'd whacked him from behind with something heavy. Well the autopsy's would confirm that or not, with a bit of luck. Such heavily charred remains would challenge the senior pathologist for the region, but Scathlock knew her well, and had confidence that she would be able to give him at least her best assessment of cause of death.

As a result, everyone cleared off until the morning, when the first examinations of the fire would take place.

Standing out on the dark lawn, Robin offered, "Come and stay up at my place, please. You don't need to drive all the way back to yours, Mike."

But Mike shook his head. "Poor Silas and Marnie have been cooped up for hours. I'll be lucky if I don't walk in to puddles if not worse."

"Oh no, the poor dogs!" Jenna gasped. "Yes, we must go back and see to them."

And so for the second time that evening the friends said their goodbyes, hoping like mad that there wouldn't be another reason for them to meet up until tomorrow.

Chapter 24

With the start of the new week, Jenna accompanied Mike into the office, feeling too fuzzy-headed to be able to even think about doing any more of the marking. As they climbed the stairs to the office they heard voices up above, and when they got to the main office door it was to find an imposing, silver-haired man standing in the middle of the office with several people doing things under his direction. Tiff was there beside him, dressed in one of her smart suits, though in a pair of flat shoes for once, and she beamed encouragingly at Jenna and Mike.

"This is Jenna Cornwell," she said with a flourish of her hand towards her friend. "Jenna, this is Richard Mann."

"Pleased to meet you," was all Jenna could think to say, although she was already feeling a little sick as she realised that these other people were packing up files into cardboard boxes. Was Richard about to close the office after all?

"Michael," Richard said, coming to shake hands with Mike. "What a mess all this is, eh? Who'd have thought Zachary would have been such an idiot?" Mike could only smile worriedly. "Now then, I want you to go home …right now."

Then Richard must have registered the way Mike's face fell. "Don't look so worried. This isn't about you. I want you out of the way because I'm launching a full investigation into what's been going on in this office, and I want you absent while it's going on. So you'll be on paid leave for the foreseeable future until we get it sorted out. Don't worry, you've always been the one who sent his reports back to the head office on time and in full, and from everything Tiff and Suzy have told me, you've been trying to keep this office on track almost single-handedly.

"But because I'm now going to go through Hornby's dealings with a fine tooth-comb as well, I don't want to give that old weasel the chance to wriggle out of anything by saying that we've been swayed by anything you've said or done. From his viewpoint he has to think that we're looking as hard at you as we are at him and Zachary. That's why I want you out of the way. Don't worry, your job is secure. But if we have to throw the book at Hornby, we have to be seen to have been impartial."

Feeling more than a little stunned, Mike and Jenna went back downstairs and out into the street.

"When he said your job was secure, do you think he meant here. Or is he thinking of somewhere like Hereford?" Jenna asked worriedly. She didn't want to sound selfish, but she'd burned an awful lot of bridges of her own on the promise of the job in Mike's office. It was going to be a tough year if she turned out to be unemployed.

"I wish I knew," Mike answered, equally as concerned. "Come on, let's go and pick up the mutts and go and see Robin and Mel. Just at the moment they're about the only people I feel I can cope with being around."

As they drove up the track, their way was blocked by a queue of vehicles, including a fire incident investigation truck, and the forensic team's vehicles. Pulling the Land Rover back out of the way into a bit of a cutting a short way down the hill, they left it there and started walking up the hill with Silas and Marnie this time secured on their leads.

When they came level with the entrance to the houses, they were spotted by DI Scathlock, who was standing on the drive talking to a woman swathed in a white forensic coverall. "Mr Campbell? What are you doing here?" and the detective strode over to them, clearly wondering why they were being so nosy about the crime scene.

While Marnie shoved her muzzle into Scathlock's hand to be fussed, Jenna hurriedly explained, "We weren't coming here at all. We're actually going up to Robin's farm, but we couldn't get the Land Rover past all these vehicles, so we're walking up."

"Ah. So no work today, Mr Campbell?"

Feeling far from happy at having to explain himself all over again, Mike gave Scathlock the abbreviated form of what Richard Mann had said, but was then shocked when Scathlock added,

"I see. Seems he took my early morning conversation to heart, then, although I believe he was already somewhere in the area by last night, going by the way your head office put me through to his mobile."

"Your conversation?" Mike was stunned.

"Yes, well your boss is many things, but he's not used to investigating his own team in quite such forensic detail. So I told him that if he wanted you to come back to this office and with a clear reputation, it might be wise to keep you completely out of any dirt-digging that has to be done."

He looked around him, looking for all the world as though he was scenting the country air as much as Silas and Marnie were, both of whom were now leaning affectionately against Scathlock's legs having their ears silked. "Small communities like this can be bloody funny when the blame starts getting thrown around. Sometimes folk can be very quick to forget the truth of the matter, and only see what's more convenient for themselves. If your Mr Hornby has fooled a fair few of the local worthies, they won't be best pleased at having been made to look like idiots – by their lights – even if it's only in respect of them having wined and dined someone whom they thought of as one of the pillars of their community in their own homes, and who's now turned out to be an absolute old rogue.

"Not much into forgiving and forgetting are your aspiring classes. I've run into them before. It doesn't happen in big cities, because people aren't so on top of one another, but out in places like this, it's not unknown for a right old witch-hunt to take place – and sadly, it's not always the guiltiest who suffer the worst damage to their reputations. So I told Mr Mann that my advice would to very publicly make it clear that you aren't remotely involved."

"Thank you," Mike said shakily. Hell's teeth, Houseman was right, this DI was sharp! Giving the two leads a tug, he said, "Come on, then you two, stop covering the detective in hairs, we'd better carry on up to Robin's."

"Lovely dogs," Scathlock said with a last ruffle of their ears, "go and enjoy taking them for a walk. The bad news – whatever it turns out to be – will arrive fast enough by itself."

The rest of the week passed in something of a blur for Mike and Jenna. She continued to stay at his house, even after the investigating teams had left, in no small part because she was frightened of what the reaction of the trapped dryads would be to the death of their sister. They had to have had some awareness of her death, and until

Jenna could tell them more of what had truly happened, she felt safer away from the place. The upside was that she got the rest of the marking done by Wednesday, thanks to Mike supplying endless mugs of decaf and cake, and then he took her up to Birmingham to hand the papers in on Thursday. Just getting rid of them felt like a weight off Jenna's shoulders. It was no small responsibility to have the fate of so many students in her hands when so much could have gone wrong.

On the Friday, Garry White arrived on site with the first of his workmen, and with Alicia's house still being considered a potential crime scene, Jenna had to move her things out of the way so that they could start work on her house. Luckily, by shifting everything to the back of the house, she could leave her limited furniture there safely, but her precious books once again got boxed up and this time brought down to Mike's. And with him looking for things to do with his time, she soon found him making a work space for her in the downstairs bedroom. What he hadn't said out loud to her was that he was hoping she wouldn't ever have to move out again.

With the turn of the week into Monday, they got a visit from DI Scathlock again, but this time bearing news.

"I thought you ought to know," he said as he gratefully accepted the offer of a coffee, and found himself book-ended on the sofa by the hounds, "that we've established cause of death for all three victims."

"I know there's no 'good' in any of this," Jenna said worriedly, "but just how bad is it?"

"For you? Not bad at all," Scathlock reassured her. "But for the Willetts family it's more than a bit harrowing, and that's why I thought I'd better tell you, Mr Campbell."

"Mike, please, call me Mike, everyone else does."

"Well then, Mike. Tragically it seems that Alicia Hopton – and I presume she was still known by her married name – died from the fall from the balcony. God knows how much she'd had to drink that night. I'm amazed that she got that Audi up to the house without killing herself earlier, because her blood alcohol levels were through the roof. And of course there was the empty bottle of prosecco downstairs, and the nearly empty one up on the balcony she fell from. The pathologist says that the strangulation marks of the scarf are a bit anomalous, but since that wasn't the cause of death, she's saying that the scarf must have snagged on something briefly. With the weight of the victim taken into consideration, even hanging for a short time would have done damage. And the force with which she hit the floor, combined with the alcohol thinning her blood, is what did for her. She bled to death internally."

Jenna found herself shivering at that, for in her mind she was convinced that that bleeding had been caused by the frantic dryads' stabs with whatever they had summoned.

Mistaking Jenna's reaction, Scathlock said, "Don't distress yourself any further. Even if you could have got in to her, with the time it takes for an ambulance to get out there, you couldn't have saved her. She'd have been lucky to make it if it had happened in a city, and she'd been in a hospital in half the time. Carol – that's the pathologist, who's a friend of mine – says that Alicia Hopton was an alcoholic who would have been lucky to live more than another five years at the rate she was drinking. It seems her liver was already shot to hell. Someone who'd lived a healthier lifestyle would have easily survived that fall, albeit with broken bones, but her blood vessels were already wrecked. Sadly Alicia contributed greatly to her own death."

"And what about the others?" Mike asked warily. If

Alicia's death was being labelled as accidental, it was still too soon to start being relieved.

Scathlock huffed. "This is where it gets nasty. I'm afraid I've had to break the news to Mr Greaves that had his wife survived, we would have been charging her with the murder of Zachary Carlton Smith."

"Murder?" Jenna squeaked as Mike gasped,

"Bloody hell!"

"I'm afraid so. I hope I'm not going to distress you too much by telling you this, Jenna, but you're better knowing, because it will soon be in the news. Carol found that the back of his head had been smashed in. Now that could have been due to falling timbers in the fire, although where his remains were found was under the staircase, where some of the big beams actually protected him from the worst of the cave-in. But the melted remains of a bloody great carving knife in his ribs rather makes us think that she whacked him first and then stabbed him with a knife she'd taken there for the purpose. I presume you two can confirm that there wasn't a handy block of knives just waiting for her in the kitchen already?"

"God, no!" Mike answered, as Jenna also shook her head. "There was nothing there but what the kitchen fitters had had to put in. The stuff that's in the house that Jenna was using is hers that she brought with her. There was nothing like that in any of the houses otherwise."

"Thank you, I thought as much, and there's a suspicious gap in the block at the Greaves' house, but with another knife being missing from it too, that wasn't conclusive had there been the possibility that the knife came from elsewhere. Carlton Smith doesn't seem to have ever used the fancy kitchen in his flat. His kitchen barely had normal knives and forks, and his bins were full of takeaways, so we've discounted the idea that he took the knife with the intention of killing her. On top of that, the fire investigators found traces of petrol, and the melted remnants of a couple of plastic containers of the sort you find being sold on filling station forecourts, which they're convinced was the start of the fire, and that it was set deliberately."

"I did think that there had to have been something like that," Mike admitted. "I just couldn't see how else the house would have burned so fast and so hot."

"That was the point the fire investigators made," Scathlock agreed. "So the scenario we're working on is that Mrs Greaves went out to the house with Carlton Smith, just as you'd told us they'd arranged, Mike. But rather than searching for signs of damages as they'd previously agreed, Mrs Greaves had already planned to murder Carlton Smith, blaming him for her sister's death.

"Although we'll never know for sure, I suspect that at that point, Mrs Greaves had somehow become aware that Carlton Smith's promises were just so much hot air. Mr Greaves is obviously very distressed, but he has managed to tell us that his wife was in a terrible temper that evening, swearing that she would make sure that Carlton Smith took his share of the blame, both for her sister's death and for defrauding herself. And having looked at her records after you prompted me, Mike, with her threats against a neighbour, and also a case of road rage, it's clear that she was more than capable of violence – it's just that this was the first time that she'd gone anything like this far.

"A supposedly anonymous letter has turned up, sent to Mr Hornby and forwarded onto us by the fraud officers investigating him, which tries to implicate Carlton Smith as the vengeful employee. It's all a bit disjointed, but it was clearly sent by Mrs Greaves – silly woman left her prints on the paper – and it seems she was trying to make everyone think that Carlton Smith went to the house and set the fire to spite her family, 'unfortunately' then getting trapped in the flames, and rather conveniently dying there. The truly grim thing is that it turned out to be Mrs Greaves who got trapped in her own fire."

"Dear God, what a terrible end to come to," said Mike, thoroughly shaken. He'd known that Fiona was vindictive, but not to that extent.

"Yes, isn't it just," Scathlock agreed. "Carlton Smith's family are apparently muttering about bringing a civil suit against the Willetts family, but I can't see that coming to anything."

The next news came via Tiff, who had returned to work in the Ludlow office to at least keep a presence there. It seemed that Richard was determined to keep it open, and much to Suzy's disgust, Darius Rouhani was being transferred from Hereford to provide the much needed legal side of the team. However, Tiff told them gleefully at a meal at Mike's, it turned out that at the time of the takeover, Mr Hornby had by some sleight of hand retained the deeds to the Ludlow office, despite Richard's company having paid him for it and the signatures for their handover having been processed. Consequently, that was why Richard Mann had now set the fraud squad onto Hornby, and the outlook for him wasn't good.

"The miserable old goat is going to get his comeuppance, mark my words," Tiff said. "And once that's got going, I can't see any reason why you shouldn't be able to come back to work, Mike, and you can come and start training with me, Jenna."

Nor was that the only news she brought. It seemed that Nicholas Greaves had only played the grieving widower up to the point when it transpired that the insurance company wouldn't be paying out on Fiona's share of the houses. Insurance companies took a grim view of clients who set fire to their own property, and then tried to fraudulently wring the compensation out of them. So when he'd been told that he wouldn't be getting a penny from that source, he promptly signed off on the offer of a take-over for his tiny market-garden business, and vanished off to Majorca with the woman who'd been the family cleaner.

"It seems he'd been knocking her off for years behind Fiona's back," Tiff chortled, "and this is the woman who Brian Willets left a sizable amount to, quite aside from the rest of his estate which was to be divided between the girls. Dear Mrs Murphy obviously has what it takes to have both Brian and Nicholas enthralled by her, although I have to say she must have a stronger stomach than me to have done what she must have done with those two – neither of them were charmers or much in the looks department. So good luck to her! At the rate this is all progressing, she'll be the one who's better off than Claudia!"

That made Mike feel very sorry for Claudia, who seemed to be the one person who had come out worst, yet who had done the least to deserve it. And so once he was back in the office, to Tiff's disgust he made a point of going to see her to discuss how the inheritance would now be sorted. Yet he came back with sobering news. Apparently Claudia wanted nothing to do with the houses or the site anymore, and Mike was charged with finding a buyer for it as fast as possible, regardless of price.

"She's selling up here, getting a divorce, and moving to the Dordogne," he told Jenna when they got home that night. "Poor woman, she's totally devastated by it all. She says she's found a canal barge to live on, and is going to run cookery schools down there, with no intention of ever returning. As long as she has enough to live on, that's all she wants. She's a pale shadow of the spoilt brat who ran Robin ragged all those years ago."

"Then maybe there's a chance she'll turn her life around?" Jenna said hopefully.

"More than a chance, actually. After I'd pointed out to her that Garry White hadn't had to stay on after her father's death, and that she owed him a debt of thanks if nothing else for the fact that she'll now be the sole beneficiary when that development they've just finished get sold, she truly astonished me. She said that in that case, Garry ought to have the business, and that she would accept the profits on the new builds as his payment for the business to her. I've got to draw up the formal sale documents, but she was the one who suggested he pay her a nominal pound for the yard where they have the offices, and all of the supplies in there.

"Clearly I'll have to make sure that any outlays that Garry has had to make to complete those other houses have been covered – it would be pretty unfair if he suddenly got landed with bills for things like double-glazed windows which he'll never see the profit from – but all in all she's been incredibly fair to him. And perhaps less surprising in the light of that, she doesn't want a penny from the sale of the dryads' houses I've been dealing with. She wants to make a donation of it to charities that care for battered women and children – and I don't think we want to go into why that might be, although she did say that it wasn't her father who had caused her so much pain."

"Her mother, do you think?" Tiff wondered.

"It certainly sounded like it, but also Fiona's first boyfriend was hinted at. Something about them sharing a perverse enjoyment of pain which they'd tried to share. *Urgh!* Anyway, we agreed that however much they get sold for, it will have to be enough to cover the cost of Garry and his lads doing this extra work. But Claudia herself agreed that getting anyone to buy two houses on the site of a triple violent death would be a tall order, and she's not wrong about that."

"It's all over the local weekly newspaper," Jenna admitted.

"Which is probably why Garry and his lads have had to fend off the ghouls who've come to gloat at the site. Good grief, what is it about people that they want to come and see such a place?"

"Morbid fascination, I suspect you'd find, if you ever bothered to talk to any of them," Jenna sighed. "It's like the idiots who slow down to gawp at an accident on the other side of a motorway, and end up causing an accident themselves. Unbelievable, but people do it. We had a poor old soul have a heart attack in the frozen isle at work some years ago, and you wouldn't have believed the number of so-called respectable people who just stopped to watch our first aiders trying to save her life, and got in the way of the paramedics when they came. That, or complained that they couldn't get past her to get their frozen chicken for Sunday lunch."

"That's awful!"

"And now you know why I'm so glad to be getting away from the front line of dealing with the public. Did Garry have to call the police?"

"No, but then Garry's a resourceful sort of chap, and he just parked the JCB in the way down the track. Faced with some serious walking to get to do their morbid sightseeing, the ghouls gave up."

"Well done, Garry!"

"Absolutely, and he had some good news for me when I went up to give him his. He says that by tomorrow all of the beams will be out of the house you've lived in, and he wants to know what we want to do with the green oak beams? He says that even if they're stored properly, it could take five years before they dry out enough to be usable in a building. And then you come back to the problem Brian had in the first place, only this time it will be how to get them down the track instead of up it. I'm told that the two at the centre of the house that went right up to the apex of the roof, are the best part of twenty-five feet long, and will almost certainly have to be sawn in two if they're to be moved."

Jenna thought carefully and then said, "I'm reluctant to tell him to cut them. Not least in case we can't fully disentangle the dryads from them. It would be most cruel to inflict another chainsaw on them."

"That was what I thought, but I wanted to see if you were of the same mind."

"What about using them to make an edging for the lake? When I was driving that mower, it was awfully hard to tell where the soggy grass began down by the lake."

"I think that's because Brian had all the rushes and water-edge plants pulled up in the mistaken belief that he could have an immaculate sward running to the water's edge. But this isn't some Capability Brown manicured landscape. The lake's level rises and falls depending on the season, and those rushes and marshy plants were what were anchoring the water's edge."

"Then why don't you tell Garry to find where the stable edge of the grass is, and then lay the beams end to end to form a new edge to the water? That gives him a plausible reason to leave them on site, and for us it gives us time to figure out whether we can free the dryads once they're out in the open?"

Chapter 25

As Garry and his team set to work on Alicia's house, both removing the beams and then creating some privacy in the exposed bedrooms, Mike began making tentative inquiries with the local estate agents he was on good terms with.

"It's not looking good," he told Jenna, as she emerged bleary-eyed from her second batch of exam marking, that having now arrived. "Tim over at Congreaves & Purvis says that ordinarily the houses would've fetched upwards of seven hundred grand now that we've put things right. He totally agreed with everything you said right at the start, by the way, about what would have driven the prices down, especially the bedrooms in Alicia's house."

Jenna smiled wanly. "I'd happily pass on being right for it not to have cost her her life."

Mike came and pulled her into a hug. "She made her own decisions, Jen. Nobody forced her to go up to the house when she was as drunk as a lord. All she had to do was stay away and let me handle this and she'd still be here today."

He guided her to the sofa and sat her down, pouring them both a glass of wine and then coming to sit by her.

"Mike? What's up?"

He gave her a conspiratorial grin. "Well I had been wondering how Robin would feel about potentially having two new lots of neighbours. Granted, he's come out of his shell in leaps and bounds since Mel's been up there with him, but it could still be his nightmare coming true.

"Now as I was saying, Tim said that under normal circumstances he might hope to get three-quarters of a million for each of the remaining houses. *But...* firstly, houses up at that price range don't sell fast, and by that he means possibly over a year and maybe even two, because your potential buyers are very limited up at those kinds of prices – or at least outside of a big city they are. And that comes back to what I said to you, as well. The inaccessibility of the houses chops the price down, because you either need to be someone like Robin, living off an early pension, or in the kind of job where you can work from home.

"Tim has a couple of other houses like those on his books, but was telling me that in the one case not one but two agents are still trying to find buyers, and that in both cases they are much, much closer to the main roads in terms of locations. When he came up and saw the houses, and how remote they are, but also the signs of work they've had done, he dropped the price even further. Unfortunately, although Garry was as careful as possible, there are still things like some scratches on the doorways where they got the beams through to take outside. And of course all the rooms now need redecorating because there are big stretches of bare plaster and wood where the new stuff has gone in, and I can't see it being worth paying a decorator to come in.

"That's because Tim said that the hardest sell would be because of the deaths. Let's face it, they made the Midlands TV news. So you could be sure that any prospective buyer will find out what happened up there sooner rather than later. All of which means that Tim says that he thinks the price would have to come down to about four hundred thousand to even get any interest."

Jenna blinked. "Good grief! That's half the original price!"

"Exactly, and in all fairness, I don't think it's fair to keep Claudia dangling for another couple of years before she can get some closure on all of this. Especially not since she's been so fair to Garry. I feel she should have the reward of a huge thank you from the charities, even if she won't take some of what's left for herself – which I will ask her about again in case she's changed her mind now that some of the shock has worn off." He leaned back and gave Jenna a smile again. "So… I was wondering… how would you feel if I bought them?"

"You? Mike, that's a huge amount of money! You'd be in debt up to your eyes, surely?" The sums of money he was blithely talking about were eye-wateringly high to her.

"Well yes and no. Don't forget that when Mum's time comes, I'll inherit the family home. And that got me thinking about something Tim said."

"Oh yes?"

"He said, 'Now if it was your house, I could sell that ten times over, what with the work you've had done.' So I asked him how much this would fetch, and he says that because it's in a good area and the right size for a normal family home, I could be looking at easily three hundred and fifty. Given that I bought this in a right old state, and because I always knew that I'd want to go back to mum and dad's house eventually, I took on my mortgage over half the normal time. I'll clear a very good profit on this, Jenna, and at that point I'd be able to pay a huge chunk off on the other houses."

Jenna was stunned, but not half so much as when Mike added, "I'm going up to inspect Mum and Dad's tonight – just the regular check to make sure the tenants haven't wrecked the place, although since they're a professional couple who are hardly ever there, that's never been an issue. I want you to come with me."

"Really?" Then she saw the sudden flicker of doubt in Mike's eyes as he stumbled over,

"I was hoping …I thought …well maybe you'd like to carry on living with me? I mean if you don't… If you'd rather… Oh hell, I'm making a right mess of this! Jenna, I've never met anyone else I care for as much as you, and I don't want to let you go. I'm not trying to rush you into decisions you don't feel you can make just yet, but I'd like to know that there's some hope for us as a couple?"

Jenna didn't say a word, but given that she launched herself at Mike and had her arms around his neck hugging him so tightly that he could barely breathe, he took it as a good sign. When she finally let him go, and he'd recovered enough breath to speak, he said,

"So I take it that you're coming with me tonight?"

"Oh yes! Oh absolutely yes!"

They went via his mother's hospice, and Jenna was saddened to see that she was barely conscious and so doped up on morphine that she hardly knew who Mike was, much less the good news he was telling her. It brought it home to her that it might only be days or weeks before Mike inherited his old home, and that was why he wasn't worried about a long period of paying a huge mortgage. Then when they pulled up outside Mike's parent's house, Jenna immediately understood why he would want to return here. Actually within the picture-perfect village of Leintwardine and just off the High Street, it was an adorable thatched, half-timbered cottage of some considerable age.

"Seventeenth century, Grade II listed," Mike said, wearing a huge grin as he added, "which I hope is close enough to medieval for your approval?"

"Oh Mike, it's adorable!"

He led her in through the five-barred farm gate, at which point she realised that what had once been a barn was now also converted into a house.

"Who lives there?"

"Nobody actually lives there. Dad did the conversion himself, and for years he and Mum topped up their pensions by running it as a holiday cottage. After Dad died I thought it was too much for Mum to have to do the weekly change-overs, so I got a cleaning company involved, and then a bit later handed the bookings over to one of the specialist companies, and that's how it's still running. It's still providing extra income, so between that and the rent from the house, Mum's well covered and there's still a bit extra going into the bank. But I wanted you to see it so that you understand that I wasn't just making grand plans based on nothing. I have something to back up any additional mortgage with, Jen, I'm not going out on a wing and a prayer."

He took her around the main cottage first, the tenants having introduced themselves and then headed for the pub while Mike did his inspection. Ancient timber beams were everywhere, with the lounge having a glorious inglenook fireplace which put Robin's in the pale. When they went through into the open kitchen-diner and found another backing onto the lounge's Jenna was ecstatic, and by the time they had been upstairs to the three lovely bedrooms up under the eaves, she was nearly dying from happiness.

The barn turned out to be everything Brian Willetts had clearly been hoping the two timber houses would be – open and filled with light – and now Jenna understood why Mike hadn't spotted so much in Alicia's house. For here was a gallery with bedrooms leading off it too, but with windows looking down onto the entrance hall below rather than being fully open, and as if reading her mind, Mike himself said,

"I just didn't see the difference, you know. Never having actually stayed in here, it never occurred to me that the bedrooms up at Alicia's had no privacy. I'd just been thinking of people looking down into the lounge."

Jenna wasn't about to nit-pick and point out that this house also had a quite separate sitting room from the lovely open hall, especially when Mike was making all of her dreams come true in one go. "So would you carry on letting this out?" she asked instead.

"I think so. It's better than having permanent neighbours who'd have to share the drive – fine if you get lucky and they're nice people, but potentially horrendous if they aren't. It means that if we wanted to have someone like Tiff come to stay, or your uni friends with their kids, we'd have somewhere they could come to for the whole week without worrying about being on top of us for the entire time."

His consideration for what she might want gave her another squirm of pleasure, but then it suddenly dawned on her what he'd been thinking of for the two other houses.

"Oh! And you have the right contacts already to let the Willetts house out for holidays!" she gasped, and Mike's beaming smile told her that she'd picked up on the right clues he'd given.

"We'll have to spend a lot of weekends up there getting them up to this standard, but once that's done, I'm sure you and I could manage the cleaning bit for the first year or so until we see how many takers we get. And the thing is, Jen, it would keep it quiet for Robin and the dryads. They'd have no more interference than they do from walkers on the hills already."

"Oh I like that idea! Yes, it would be good to take away the threat of further developments up there for everyone's sake. In fact, I think it's pretty clear that Mel is moving in with Robin, so she might quite like the chance to play housekeeper up there. She's much better with people than I am when it comes to the meet-and-greet kind of stuff."

"Excellent. Then we should broach the subject the next time we meet up. All we need to do then is hope that Mel had come up with something that will release the dryads – if they're still trapped, that is."

A couple of days later on the Saturday, Jenna and Mike met Robin and Mel at the house site once more. Garry and his men had done a neat job of laying the big oak beams out on the grass end to end, so that they formed a kind of kerb to the lawn.

"Okay, you three," Mike said. "You're the ones who formed the connections with the dryads. Can you feel if there's anyone still in there?"

"I think it would be best if we tried to meditate," Mel suggested. "We brought picnic rugs for us to sit on. Let's just try sitting out here in silence and see if anything comes to us."

Jenna and Mel sat side by side, bracketed by Mike and Robin, and with the two dogs sprawled by Mike's side. That Mel dropped straight into a meditative state, quickly followed by Jenna, didn't surprise Mike knowing as he did that they'd done this together before. He was rather more surprised to find that Robin could do it, and could only assume that he'd been getting some very personal coaching from Mel. For himself, all he could do was sit like some garden gnome, knees drawn up to his chest, and his hands and head resting on them, staring out over the water and hoping that by trying to empty his mind that it would be enough. But being the one with his eyes still open, he was the one who was first aware of the approaching dryads, as Silas and Marnie both suddenly stiffened and sat up, ears pricked, but not growling in warning.

Although the other three opened their eyes, the best Jenna could describe to Mike afterwards was that it was like being in a half-dream state, as if she was seeing both with her eyes and in her mind.

Greetings, the leading dryad spoke in their heads. *We are very glad to see you once more.*

"Did your friends get out?" Jenna tried to ask.

I am free, another voice spoke, *and I am very grateful to you for helping.*

"Ah, you were the one in my house," Jenna realised, feeling something familiar about the presence.

Yes, I was. And I am very thankful that I had you to deal with. My sisters were deeply scarred by the others they encountered.

"And are the two who were in the house behind us free as well?" Mel asked worriedly. "Or are they still trapped in these beams?"

Not exactly trapped, Jenna's dryad tried to explain. *Much of what they are is with us. But there is a part that still lingers with the bodies of the trees they loved so much.* And alongside her words was an image of something like a cloud which had left part of itself as moisture within the oak beams.

"Can we do anything to help them get that part of themselves back?" Again it was Mel who was asking as the one with some experience of what she'd described to the others as soul retrieval. "I'm familiar with the concept of someone suffering a great trauma that's so bad that the person effectively leaves something of themselves behind at the site of the experience, or at least loses contact with it. In those cases we ask the person to meditate and to go back in their minds to the time when the damage was done, but I don't suppose we can do that with your sisters?"

The dryads seemed to be considering her suggestion amongst themselves for a moment, then one floated back towards them.

We believe that if you wash these oaks in the water of the lake, then it will take some of the taint away from them, she said.

"I can see how that would work," Mel agreed. "They've had an awful lot of manhandling by humans, and that's bound to leave a residue. I'm thinking that it would be better if we got buckets of water and washed them with it, though. We can't move the beams any closer to the lake without submerging them, and I don't imagine that drowning the oaks would be helpful?"

No, please don't do that, the dryads agreed hurriedly, *we are not creatures of the lakes and streams – those are others of our kind.*

"Right, then if you'd hang around, we'll give this our best go," Mel declared. "Come on, everyone, it's a good job you got those buckets, Jenna."

Mel had half expected that some sort of immersion might be needed, and had brought several buckets down from Robin's, so with the ordinary bucket and the mop bucket from Jenna's, they had seven they could fill. Rather harder was getting to the lake to get the water, and soon Robin was in up to beyond his knees filling the buckets which he handed on to Mike, who always had wellingtons in the back of his car, and who was in up to his mid-calves. Jenna was then carrying them over to Mel, who began at the far end of the line of wood.

With incense burning in little dishes alongside the row of beams, Mel began to chant and sway, very gently pouring the water over the oaks so that each section was fully drenched before she moved onwards. As she got to the end of her chant and began again, Jenna picked it up and joined in with her, even if she hadn't a clue as to what the words meant. However, they had got one log fully soaked without anything happening, and Mike and Robin were giving one another worried looks, even if Jenna and Mel seemed undaunted.

They were so engrossed they didn't even register that someone else had arrived until the voice of DI Scathlock said, "I'll give you a hand with that," making them all nearly jump out of their skins.

As Mike and Robin froze where they stood in the water, and Mel and Jenna looked panic-stricken, they were amazed to see Scathlock taking off his jacket and dumping it on the ground, before coming closer to them.

"What are they?" he asked, giving a nod of his head towards the dryads floating at the edge of the wood by the waterline.

"You can see them?" Jenna gasped.

"Oh yes. I've had an experience or two with what you might call the strange and wonderful. Call me Bill, by the way. I'm off duty and I had this strange urge to come up here today of the kind that I've learned to listen to."

"Erm, they're dryads," Jenna told him.

"Ah, wood sprites, if I'm not mistaken? That would explain it."

The others looked even more bemused.

"It would?" Mike said for all of them.

"Yes, I had a bit of a run in with what you might call a force of nature who was being hunted by some very nasty …hmmm …well I don't need to go into that now. Suffice it to say that I have a bit of a connection with the Finnish version of these, however odd that might sound. A previous case involving a house surrounded by oaks, back on my home patch. I wondered why my hair was standing on end whenever I came to these houses."

"The dryads were trapped in the wood when these oaks were illegally felled," Jenna managed to pull herself together enough to explain. "That's why we had them taken out of the houses again, but the dryads say that there's still something of two of them caught in the wood. They say soaking the wood will help."

"Hold that thought," Bill Scathlock said, and going back up to the drive, he pulled his own Subaru past Robin's and closer to them. What surprised them even more was him opening the doors and then putting something on on the car's stereo. "I think this might prove more effective than your Hindu chants," he said to Mel with a smile. "I was left these recordings of Finnish folk music, and that connection I told you about used to have them playing in the house he inhabited for a while."

Whether it was the music or the presence of Bill himself, when they came to the second huge beam something was immediately different. The first buckets of water didn't just drain off as they had with the first, but seemed to steam although the log was far from warm, much less hot. And with Bill helping, the dousing could be done faster, although he agreed that the actual pouring should be done by Jenna and Mel.

"They're female spirits, so they may well react better to women helping them," he said practically, and certainly by the time they were halfway along the beam there was a definite sensation of something building.

Then suddenly there was an eldritch scream from deeper within the woods, and then a tendril of something cloud-like and white rose from the oak, pulling as though trying to get free. As if something then snapped, it suddenly catapulted into the air, then streaked for the woods and vanished.

"Was that one of them?" Mel called to the dryads, and one floated closer to answer,

Yes! Thank you, she is now free. Please don't stop. We can feel our other sister crying to be let out.

The next beam proved speedy work for it was clear that a simple cleansing was all that was needed here, but as they got on to the fourth of the oaks, even Mike and Bill could hear the agonised cries of what was caught inside it. Even so, nothing happened until they were halfway along the great beam, and when the ethereal 'body' of the dryad came free, this time it didn't shoot off to the woods, but instead was flipped to the next-but-two beam in line, which it thrashed about above except for one tendril which seemed anchored in the wood.

"On no, it's half in the other beam as well!" Jenna cried, and they all frantically filled and emptied the buckets, working as fast as they could to try and free it.

No! Start at this end! Jenna's dryad called, pointing to the farther end as Mel upended the first bucket beside the writhing form. *That way you're working her free. Doing it your way is like it's tightening a trap around her.*

Since nobody could question that, they hurriedly rearranged themselves and carried on pouring. With a final pain-filled yowl which had Mike glad he'd followed Bill's suggestion and put Silas and Marnie in Jenna's house, the dryad came free. It rose into the air, flinging itself around as if not quite able to believe that it wasn't still anchored down, still more of a blur of white than an actual form like the others. Several of the other dryads rose to surround it, and in a tumbling cloud of half-humanlike forms, they vanished across the lake and into the wood. Three separate forms remained behind, however, and they now came to join the humans at the lake edge.

We will be forever grateful to you, Jenna's dryad said, and knowing how long these creatures lived for, Jenna thought that 'forever' in their case might be a very long time indeed.

"I'm just glad we could help," she said. "And we can give you some more good news too. Mike, here, is going to buy this land. So you won't be persecuted again, either. People will come and stay here for a few days at a time, we hope, but nobody will be actually living here. So your only neighbour will be Robin who you already know."

"And me," Mel added. "I'll be living there too."

"Too right she will," Robin said with a grin, "and we'll finish washing the other oaks, but right now we're all a bit too tired to carry on. That'll be for another day now that there's not the urgency to do it. ...We have got everyone out, haven't we?"

Oh yes, we're are all free now. But there was the sense of a lingering sadness and of looking to the blackened remains of Fiona's house where the final dryad had perished.

As they too vanished into the woods, it was Bill who now said, "Please tell me somebody has beer up here, because I could really do with one!"

"Not here, but if you come up to my house, you're welcome to sample my homebrew," Robin declared, and so they all decamped up the hill.

With a pleasant late afternoon sunshine warming the patio outside of Robin's conservatory, making it comfortable for them to all sit out there while they dried off, they were finally able to tell Bill Scathlock more of the truth of what had gone on.

"I can see why you felt you couldn't tell me all of it," he admitted, "and rest assured I won't be attempting to set any of our records straight. I don't know quite how I'd explain dryads to my more sceptical colleagues. If I hadn't already had my share of strange cases, I'm not sure that I would have believed what I was seeing today. So you can breathe easy, nobody's going to be asking you any awkward questions."

He only stayed for the one drink and then left, but the others stayed sitting enjoying the view.

"How would you feel about me running meditation workshops from one of the houses?" Mel said suddenly, looking to Mike. "It's the ideal spot, and it's what I'd always been planning to do once I came back home for good. You can earn a passable living helping people to deal with the stresses of modern life."

"In which case," Robin added, "I'd like to come in with you on that purchase. Like you, Mike, I've got collateral in the form of the farm. I'd only held back because I knew I couldn't afford both houses. If you two are prepared to spend your weekends helping us, we could do most of the decorating and finishing of the houses ourselves."

Mel was nodding enthusiastically. "I guess you'd like to keep the house that Jen's been in, and I have to say that what was Alicia's house would be the better one for group therapies because of that huge galleried space in the lounge. Nothing's going to get rid of the taint of her death faster than giving it a good cleansing and using it for something positive."

"What about the ruins of Fiona's house?" Jenna wondered. "Presumably we can get someone into clear all the debris away, but won't there still be the concrete foundations left? It'll be a bit obvious to visitors that there must once have been another house there."

"You could put a Dutch barn type of construction on it," Mike mused thoughtfully, then seeing Jenna and Mel looking blank explained, "Just wood beams supporting a roof. With some tables and chairs under it, you could then do open-air sessions if you wanted to, Mel."

"Barbecue!" Robin said enthusiastically. "We could use what's left of the lounge chimney breast for a barbecue – okay, maybe a veggie one, Mel, but even vegetarians skewer things like peppers and tomatoes, don't they? And it would be nice if you could offer the chance of outside eating for your clients, even if the Welsh rain doesn't hold off very often."

"We could even get it licensed for other things," Mike said, giving Jenna a quick glance. "You know, like weddings. Somewhere where you could have your canine companions of honour included. Some people are bound to want small, more spiritual celebrations, eh, Robin?" and Robin gave him a grin back, realising that Mike was hinting that they might be the first couples to use it.

"Absolutely," he agreed swiftly before Jenna or Mel could do anything more than look surprised. "Potentially six bedrooms in our house, if we used the downstairs, and five in yours. Plenty of room to accommodate a small family gathering or two."

"And a self-catering cottage just down the road at my Mum and Dad's if anyone wanted to be a bit more separate."

"Err, do we get to have any say in this?" Mel asked with mock innocence, although going by the huge smile she was wearing, she had no intention of protesting.

"No, I don't think we do," Jenna said happily.

THE END

However, if you want to read more of Bill Scathlock, his first full-length appearance is in *Time's Bloodied Gold*, and his encounter with the Finnish nature spirit is in the second book, *Green Lord's Guardian*.

Thank you for taking the time to read this book.

I hope you would like to read other books like this, and the fastest way to do that is to sign up to my mailing list. I promise I won't bombard you with endless emails, but I would like to be able to let you know when any new books come out, or of any special offers I have on the existing ones.

Go to ljhutton.com to find the link or find me on Facebook

If you sign up, I will send you free goodies, some of which you won't get anywhere else!

Also, if you've enjoyed this book you personally (yes, *you*) can make a big difference to what happens next.

Reviews are one of the best ways to get other people to discover my books. I'm an independent author, so I don't have a publisher paying big bucks to spread the word or arrange huge promos in bookstore chains, there's just me and my computer.

But I have something that's actually better than all that corporate money – it's you, enthusiastic readers. Honest reviews help bring them to the attention of other readers (although if you think something needs fixing I would really like you to tell me first!). So if you've enjoyed this book, it would mean a great deal to me if you would spend a couple of minutes posting a review on the site where you purchased it.

About the Author

L. J. Hutton lives in Worcestershire and writes history, mystery and fantasy novels. If you would like to know more about any of these books you are very welcome to come and visit my online home at www.ljhutton.com

Alternatively, you can connect with me at Facebook

Also by L. J. Hutton

Time's Bloodied Gold

Standing stones built into an ancient church, a lost undercover detective and a dangerous gang trading treasures from the past. Can Bill Scathlock save his friend's life before his cover gets blown?

DI Bill Scathlock thought he'd seen the last of his troubled DS, Danny Sawaski, but he wasn't expecting him to disappear altogether! The Polish gang Danny was infiltrating are trafficking people to bring ancient artefacts to them, but those people aren't the usual victims, and neither is where they're coming from. With archaeologist friend Nick Robbins helping, Bill investigates, but why do people only appear at the old church, and who is the mad priest seen with the gang? With Danny's predicament getting ever more dangerous, the clock is ticking if Bill is to save him before he gets killed by the gang ...or arrested by his old colleagues!

The Room Within the Wall

A Roman shrine with a curse, a man accused of a murder he did not commit, and an archaeologist who holds the key to saving his life.

When archaeologist Pip comes across Cold Hunger Farm and the ancient Roman shrine to Attis embedded in its wall, it rakes up demons from her own past. Yet as she digs deeper into its records, shocking revelations come to light of heroic Georgian-era captain, Harry Green, accused of a vile and brutal murder – but who is the sinister woman manipulating his fiancée into making those claims? She sounds frighteningly like someone Pip knew, so how did she get into the past, and can Pip follow her to put things right again and save Harry's life before he's hanged?

Printed in Great Britain
by Amazon